THREE GIRLS
AND THEIR BROTHER

TERESA REBECK

Three Girls and Their Brother

HarperCollins*Publishers*

HarperCollins*Publishers*
77–85 Fulham Palace Road,
Hammersmith, London W6 8JB

www.harpercollins.co.uk

Published by HarperCollins*Publishers* 2008
1

A catalogue record for this book
is available from the British Library

ISBN 978 0 00 725632 7

This novel is entirely a work of fiction.
The names, characters and incidents portrayed in it
are the work of the author's imagination. Any resemblance
to actual persons, living or dead, events or localities
is entirely coincidental.

Set in Bembo by Palimpsest Book Production Limited,
Grangemouth, Stirlingshire

Printed and bound in Great Britain by
Clays Ltd, St Ives plc

Mixed Sources
Product group from well-managed
forests and other controlled sources
www.fsc.org Cert no. SW-COC-1806
© 1996 Forest Stewardship Council

FSC is a non-profit international organisation established to promote the
responsible management of the world's forests. Products carrying the FSC
label are independently certified to assure consumers that they come
from forests that are managed to meet the social, economic and
ecological needs of present and future generations.

Find out more about HarperCollins and the environment at
www.harpercollins.co.uk/green

For Cooper and Cleo,
my own little beauties

Acknowledgements

Many thanks to my agent Loretta Barrett whose conviction in this book and me turned a playwright into a novelist. Thanks also to my editors Susan Watt and Shaye Areheart for their relentless and good-natured brilliance, and to Laura Heberton whose consistent support through all steps of the process was as strong and necessary as the tea she sends from England. Misha Angrist, Kate Snodgrass, Melissa Silverstein, Scott Burkhardt and Ruth Cohen also have my heartfelt thanks for the myriad ways their friendship and intelligence sustained me in this journey.

Finally, thanks to my husband, Jess Lynn, my first and best reader, for believing in my work as much as he believes in me, for cheerfully christening me 'La Novelista' and for not caring what I wear to opening nights.

CONTENTS

PHILIP

CHAPTER ONE

Now that it's all over, everybody is saying it was the picture, that stupid picture was the primal cause of every disaster that would eventually befall my redheaded sisters. Not that it's anybody's fault; not that anybody *blames* anybody. It's more like fate; the picture had to happen, and then everything else had to happen because the picture happened. Everybody sitting around, shaking their heads and saying, How could they know? Like total doom is just the mystery du jour.

But you know, I'm like—the *New Yorker* calls you up and says we want to do this thing, take a picture of those girls, it's all set up, Herb Lang doing color for once because of all that red hair—to me, the question isn't, How could they know? The question is, Why go for it? Why would you go for it? Why not hurl yourself in the opposite direction, run for cover to Ohio or Iowa or Idaho, any one of those places where the most famous anybody ever gets is for like raising an especially gorgeous cow or something. I'm not saying it would have solved everything. But overall I don't know anyone who could now argue that moving to Ohio would not have been a better choice than announcing in the *New Yorker* that my sisters were the It Girls of the Twenty-First Century.

"Herb Lang is going to do us," Polly smirked. This is in the kitchen, all three of them are sort of lounging around, Daria's got her head in the refrigerator, and Polly is posing, like some glamour girl from the forties, her hip up against the counter and her cheekbones up against the light. On the one hand it's ridiculous when she tries that stuff, but on the other hand she seriously knows how to pull it off. She wears fishnet stockings half the time. So she's doing this thing with her hips and her cheekbones, and what she just said sounds just crazy enough to be possibly true, so I don't immediately call her a liar. I look over at Daria, who has closed the refrigerator door and is now leaning against the counter, opening an Evian. She's actually too cool to even glance my way, to see how I'm taking this earth-shattering piece of information, but you can tell from the way she's holding her head that she too is also smirking. Seriously, you should have seen those two. They looked like they'd already been *in* the goddamned *New Yorker*, and that thing that the Indians talk about, how pictures steal part of your soul, like that had happened already.

And yet, they also looked insanely beautiful. They always looked insanely beautiful. This is a sad truth of my life: Since the moment of my birth, I have always been surrounded by female beauty. It's a bit of a distraction. I mean, it is not something you ever get used to, even when you're related to it. Sometimes all three of them, it gets hard to concentrate. All that creamy skin and hair, shoulders and legs, lips—they're my sisters, don't get me wrong—but it's definitely overwhelming.

"Herb Lang? How'd you pull that off?" I say. I'm playing this very cool, which makes them doubly sure that I am impressed.

"It's for the *New Yorker*," Daria repeats.

Okay, our grandfather, just for the record, was Leo Heller. I never knew the guy, he was dead before I was even born, but, the point is, he was a really famous literary critic in the fifties, who wrote a lot of books about the history of American literature. Even though hardly anybody understands them, they are considered a big deal and, in addition, old Granddad at some point wrote an essay called "The Terror of the New," which apparently blew a lot of people's minds, if your mind actually gets blown by that stuff. So now "The Terror of the New" is one of those lines about literature and thought and America that people actually quote. People ask questions, like in graduate seminars, at universities, about how this or that idea fits into Heller's notion of "The Terror of the New." Literary critics write whole chapters of books about how Heller's theory of "The Terror of the New" explains the collapse of the Harlem Renaissance. Your average person of course doesn't know about any of this, unless they do. So if I say "I'm Leo Heller's grandson" to a specific subset of human beings, they'll act like that's the coolest thing possible. Everyone else will stare at me like I'm a moron.

But everyone at the *New Yorker*, trust me, knows all about "The Terror of the New." Which is why Daria actually didn't need to say anything else in explanation as to why Herb Lang might be taking their picture. Red hair, plus Leo Heller? Definitely *New Yorker* material.

"It Girls," I shrug, deliberately unimpressed. "Wow."

5

"All *three* of us," Amelia hisses, from the corner.

Okay now, the thing about Amelia is, she is nowhere near as big an idiot as Polly and Daria. She has that thing that happens to youngest children, sometimes, where she just sits and *watches* the disasters all the rest of us are cooking up, which makes it much easier for her not to participate in them. She's, like, a genius at this. Seriously, she basically figures out how everything's going to go hours or years ahead of everyone else, and then she tries to explain it to the rest of us morons, in an attempt to give us half a clue. None of us ever listens and then it all happens, just the way she said. It's quite spooky, to tell the truth, almost like she's a character out of a comic book, with super powers, that's how accurate it sometimes is. I'm not kidding.

"It's not going to go anywhere good," she notified us.

Nevertheless, three days later we found ourselves in the middle of a decrepit loft on the Lower East Side, surrounded by lights and photographers and droolers galore. It really just happened, like that fast: One day they call and say we're going to do this stupid thing that's going to change your lives forever, and then, like, suddenly there you are in some sort of deserted garment district kind of place where a lot of young women were chained to sewing machines in the nineteenth century, and now there are stylists everywhere. I got to see the whole thing because I faked a cold to get out of school, and then faked getting better when the car showed up. Mom was too out of her mind to notice, or care. The *New Yorker*! It Girls! It was enough to drive everyone bonkers.

Polly was in heaven, it was exactly the sort of thing she's been looking for her whole life, being the center of attention in a roomful of people who think being the center of attention is the only reason to live. Mom likewise was practically purring with delight. This is the thing you need to know about my mother: She was Miss Tennessee in 1977 and then the first runner up in the Miss America contest that same year. This is a dead fact, it's no joke. It's not the kind of information Mom ever actually spread around New York because the circles my dad traveled in would frown on that sort of thing, so she couldn't tell anybody and neither could we. When things were falling apart between them it would come up in fights, like the biggest skeleton we had in the old family closet, as if he didn't marry her in the first place because she's hot. At the same time, allow me to add that he did have a point. You look at the pictures of her in her swimsuits and evening gowns, they're fairly nerve-wracking. The big-hair thing was still going on in the seventies and so you truly have to flinch. Nevertheless, that is obviously not the way she looks at it, and in fact it's fairly clear that she has not actually ever recovered from the experience of being a beauty queen, and this played no small part in the collapse of her marriage to my dad, who is mostly sort of brainy and above it all, when he's not falling for stupid but gorgeous women.

So Polly's delirious, Mom is purring, Queen Daria is too cool to react, which is her way of pursuing her bliss, and Amelia just keeps looking at the floor, wishing it were over. All the hair and makeup people have to ask her about twelve zillion times to hold her head up. Then they start telling her how gorgeous she is—well, everyone's telling each other that, and it's hardly news, it's more like white noise in this place—and then they start telling her to smile. It was really kind of frightening, to tell the truth, and in addition you could see it was more or less making her head split. I finally slid over sort of to one side of her, she's drowning in gay men who are picking at everything, her hair of course, face, toenails; she was really just surrounded. So I sort of stood there like a fool and yelled, "Hey, Amelia, you look gooorrrrrgeouuuuus!" She looked around, just like suddenly mad as hell, and I thought, oh shit, she doesn't get it, and then she did, and she grinned and rolled her eyes at me. She really does hate all that stuff.

I of course am totally not supposed to be there. I'm just the idiot brother, only nobody of course knows even that much, because nobody introduces anybody around here. I swear, I don't know why anybody bothers teaching their kids manners; you go out into the world and expect people to say things like, "Hello, my name is Stu, what's yours?" Or even, "Hi, I'm the makeup guy, who are you?" But not one of these people does anything remotely like this; they are all too hip to introduce themselves to anyone, or take notice of some pathetic teenager hanging out in the corner because his sister has been abducted by the *New Yorker*. So everyone just keeps flicking their eyes over me like I'm just some total loser who snuck in without a hall pass and as soon as security shows up I'll get tossed. I'm standing around doing nothing, so obviously the only reason I would be there is because I'm desperate to be a part of this devastating scene, which means that my loserdom can provide everyone with an opportunity to be even more hip, because then they can strut around and prove to themselves that they're above saying hello to losers like me.

For all the frenzy, nothing really happens for the longest time.

I swear, hours they're working on the girls and running around and yelling at each other about lip gloss. The head stylist, who is bossing everybody around and making all the decisions, is some guy named Stu. Stu apparently has been hired by Herb, who doesn't want to have to be bothered with all the decisions about what the models are going to wear and how to do their hair up, so he brings in Stu, who arranges everything and then Herb can just show up and take the pictures. Actually, it might be the *New Yorker* that hires Stu to do all this. I can't remember. The point is, Stu is flying around like the queen bee he is, surrounded by flocks of minions who wait breathlessly while he decides who's going to wear what, what color toenail polish goes on which girl, and what to do with all that red hair. And then everybody tells him why that won't work, he screams, then changes his mind anyway, and it goes on like that for hours.

Which obviously takes a lot of concentration. There are maybe six thousand decisions to change your mind about. Do they all wear the same basic outfit, maybe three micro-minis in different colors, playing up the sister act? Micro-minis are so five minutes ago, maybe we should accentuate the classical allure of their beauty and just put them in evening gowns. Or do you put all three of them in get-ups which are all stylistically different, accentuating their separate personalities? Stu ends up going with a version of this last plan. There is great general relief at this point, and no one bothers to point out that Stu actually doesn't know what the differences in my sisters' personalities are, as he has just met them that morning. This is clearly going to be considered entirely irrelevant to the concept.

But Stu has moved on from evening gowns, and he's living

in a fantasy of three gorgeous girls with gorgeous red hair, all of them different, completely "about" different things, awakening male desires in three completely different ways. Daria is going to be the picture of elegance, the princess every boy yearns to marry, Audrey Hepburn at the ball; I swear the words "Audrey Hepburn" actually came out of Stu's mouth and Daria got a real glint in her eye. I thought Polly was going to strangle her. But then Stu starts in on Polly and her raw sexuality, compares her to Christina Aguilera, which, let's face it, isn't as good as Audrey Hepburn, but Polly knows enough to play it cool and sure enough it gets better. Stu starts going on about Naomi Campbell and how she supposedly has the best body in the business but Polly's is better, plus she exudes sex like all the supermodel greats—I swear, the words "supermodel greats" also came out of his mouth—and then he runs off a whole string of names which I had never heard of but she sure had. And then old Stu starts in on Amelia, and how she's this androgynous girl-boy figure, a wood nymph, the mysteries of nature and earth and mind, Shakespearean heroines, I kid you not, Stu was an impressive bullshit artist. Anyway, it all amounts to the fact that Amelia gets to wear blue jeans. Which is such a relief for her that she actually gives herself permission to enjoy the whole mess for five or ten minutes, and for that brief period of time no one has to tell her to smile.

The announcement that Amelia will be wearing blue jeans turns the tension down a point in general, as Polly and Daria seemed to dig the fact as well. Polly even had a sort of vague, sisterly moment where she told Amelia that that would look cool, blue jeans are so sexy. It was so warm and gooey it was not hard to figure out what was going on. The fact is, you put three sisters in a room and say, well, now everyone is going to see how pretty we can make you all look? And then keep at it for hours, with everyone screaming about how beautiful one thing or another is, eyes lips hair, hair hair hair; well, sooner or later the question of who is the *most* beautiful is going to rear its ugly head. As you may know, there's a whole Greek myth about this kind of situation; it supposedly started the Trojan War. Anyway, the point is, all three of my sisters are very beautiful; my mother's genes were ruthlessly efficient in this area. But Amelia got one thing from my dad the Jew that nobody else got: Her hair curls. In big, red-gold ringlets.

Which, as you can imagine, got their share of attention from the attention hounds. You should have heard them, in the middle of all that bullshit, there was this endless sort of dumb repetition, over and over, "And god, look at this one, it *curls*. Not only did she get the color, it *curls*. Fucking amazing . . . Did you see the curls? Christ. And there's a fucking lot of it. What a head of hair. And it *curls* . . ." So you can't blame Daria and Polly for getting a little worried; *I* was worried and what do I know? I'll tell you what I know: Amelia's only fourteen, Polly and Daria are seventeen and eighteen; it would be horrible beyond words for her to walk away with the shot. She's fourteen—put her in blue jeans, don't tempt fate.

So that's why we were all so relieved, for the moment. And once the blue-jeans decision was made, we moved onto the shades-of-green discussion. Different girls, different styles, red hair: The unifying element would naturally be shades of green. In which, as you might expect, my sisters all tend to look rather devastating. Any shade of green pretty much works. In spite of which Stu whips himself into a frenzy; none of the greens go together and some of them are olive and dowdy and these are beautiful girls: What idiot would put girls who look like this in olive? Which got the clothes stylist kind of defensive and she started to argue about what's in this season and Donna Karan's fall line and Stu sneers about camouflage chic, and drops several pieces on the floor, which makes her even madder, and that goes on for another couple of hours.

There was one person in the middle of all this nonsense who resembled a human being. This is the hair stylist, who actually is so concentrated on what she's doing that she doesn't yell at anyone, ever, which made me think for the longest time that she was just somebody's assistant. Then at one point I slid over to see what she was cooking up for Amelia and all those damn curls and she looked at me and said, "Hey, who are you?" Which just about knocked me over; it was the most interest anyone expressed in me all day.

I was so surprised that anyone had spoken to me that it took me a minute to respond, so Amelia said, "This is my brother, Philip," and the hair stylist grinned and said, "This exciting for you, to see your sisters doing a big photo shoot like this?" And again I was so stunned by anyone expressing interest in what I thought that I sort of mumbled and said, "I don't know." But this hair stylist didn't even seem to notice, or, if she did, she didn't particularly care or—here's a stunning possibility—she was too well mannered to act like I was a jerk. This person was almost like the opposite of everyone else in the room: Nothing rattled her, and she actually seemed to be enjoying herself, while everybody else was running around screaming and miserable. She kept telling Amelia her hair was gorgeous, so in that regard she was part of the general trend, but somehow, when she said it, it didn't sound like such a bad thing.

"God, look at that, that's something," she'd say, holding up a wad of curls. She had a funny accent, sort of British but with kind of a turn in it, it's hard to describe, you have to hear it. "You hit the jackpot, didn't you? Course what am I supposed to do with all this here? Can I cut some of this, around the face, you think, you mind? Just shape it a little, not much, get it too short you got a bit of a wedge going on, that's no good. What do you think, just a little round the face, yea? Wow, this color really is something. That's why they're doing this, right? The *New Yorker*? 'Cause of the color? Funny if you think about it, getting into a big magazine like that 'cause you got red hair. I mean it's pretty, but still. Kind of thing that makes you wonder."

"Our grandfather . . ." I offered, not even bothering to finish the thought. The hair stylist didn't care, she picked up the thread for me, and kept on rocking.

"Right, he was some famous writer, like a critic or something, somebody told me that and I said, *please*! Like everybody's really interested in the granddaughters of some big-deal intellectual shithead! That's just a riot! If those girls didn't have hair like that, there's no way the *New Yorker* would be interested, that's what I say. The fucking *New Yorker*. Supposed to be some big culture magazine, and you get your picture in it cause you got red hair! How cultural is that?" She just kept talking, not expecting anyone really to answer. It was soothing, frankly, because her voice was nice and she wasn't mean or stupid, and

13

she was also kind of saying stuff that you were thinking anyway so you felt less crazy when you listened to her.

She was a very unusual person. While she was just rattling on like that, it came out that after they blew up the World Trade Center she got so upset she decided to walk her dogs down there and hug people. This is a true story. I mean, obviously everybody got wigged out when that happened, that was a very strange time, but we were out in Brooklyn where, other than the smell in the air, and what happened to the firemen, things seemed pretty normal. Aside from the loss of telephones and not being able to go into the city and people crying on the street. But anyway, this La Aura—that was her name, La Aura, not just plain Laura, I thought that was so sweet, La Aura—she took her dogs, the second day after it happened, and just walked all the way down there, and no one stopped her.

"I think they thought the dogs were rescue dogs or some-thing, which I didn't say anything, I just kept walking and then they had those little stations, yea? Where people are handing out soup and donuts, you wouldn't believe the tray of donuts that was down there, it was huge." She held her hands out to show us, they must have had eight-dozen donuts in this box, that's how wide her arms went, to show us. "Anyway there's these two firemen there, in those black coats with the yellow bands, you know, that you just saw the whole time that happened, and they looked so tired, just really wiped, and I just said, 'How's it going?' And this one guy started to cry, so I put my arm around him and he just cried like that, it was wild. And I talked to a lot of people, I asked them how they do it and one of them said, you know, he put it all in a place where he just

14

couldn't deal with it right then, and he knew he'd deal with it later. And then someone else said, you know, the first two days, there were a lot of women, not a lot, but some, with the rescue teams, and it just got to be too much for them. That women take it in too much, what happens at a big disaster, they feel it too much, and that after two days there were only men down there, taking the bodies out. And god you know, hey! I'm a lesbian! I don't usually want to go along with all that gender shit, who does? But these guys were amazing. And I could see it was true, they were doing things no one else could even face, I couldn't of done it."

She's snipping away at Amelia's hair while she's telling us all this. And we're just listening, I swear, this woman was riveting. It turns out she hugged people for five hours, hugging and listening and telling them they were fine was like her thing she did to help; she went down and hugged people who needed hugs. She was really lively and very interesting and I did think, if I was in a catastrophe, I would want a hug from this person, I really would.

Anyway, she's telling us this stuff and clipping away a little bit at a time, really, it didn't look like anything, what La Aura was doing to Amelia's hair, it just looked like she was picking up a strand here or there and then cutting a tiny piece of it off then tossing the whole thing around again. But all of a sudden I look at Amelia, and she's just listening, and I just felt my chest do something—it squeezed and hurt for a second, because that's how beautiful she looked. And then a second later I wanted to cry, I swear, because part of what made her so pretty was her good heart and how much she cared about this haircutting

15

person being nice to sad firemen. A lot of fourteen-year-old girls, really what they care about is who's going to some idiot's party this weekend, or what movie star they saw in front of Lincoln Center last week. I guess in that way fourteen-year-old girls are not that different from most people out there. But Amelia still had that thing that really little kids have, where they want to throw their arms around total strangers on the street. You don't always see it because she's also kind of annoying a lot of the time, but when it does show up it's quite staggering, and there it was, in the middle of what turned out to be a really great haircut. No huge surprise there, that La Aura could really cut hair. Amelia looked unbelievable.

This is when another minion in black showed up and announced, "We need her, Laura." None of the minions seemed to understand that the woman's name wasn't Laura, it was La *Aura*. But La Aura didn't seem to mind, "Yea, okay, I'm about done, just let me see . . ." And then she scrunched all those curls around a little, just scrunching in her hand here and there, and Amelia's hair looked even better, and so La Aura signed off and they took Amelia across the room so she could try on different kinds of blue jeans and snaky little green tops. Daria and Polly were already over there, being transformed, respectively, into Audrey Hepburn and the supermodel of the century.

So then La Aura looks at me, and shrugs. "Those are great-looking girls," she informs me, as if it's news.

"Yea," I say.

"This is exciting, huh?" She doesn't seem to really think so. It's not that she thinks it's unexciting, it's just that she's seen it all before and everyone else thinks it's exciting.

16

"I guess," I say. Sometimes I really do sound like an idiot teenager. I can't seem to help it; my brain freezes up.

"You could use a haircut. How 'bout I do you, while we're waiting for Herb?" She says this so friendly there's no sense of boy, this kid with the glamorous sisters could really use some help. I mean, she's just kind of studying me, looking over the top of those glasses, businesslike, but, as I said, friendly too. I have to confess it took me by surprise. You live with a lot of beautiful women, you get used to the fact that no one is actually looking at you very much. So it's startling when it happens.

So La Aura starts in on my hair, and at first it was pretty nice. As I said, when she's cutting hair, La Aura sort of chatters on, about all sorts of things. Once she got off the World Trade Center she started yakking about movie stars and did I know any?, and then she kind of segued into numerology and astrology, and her dogs—she had somebody do a couple of charts on her dogs, which was surprisingly interesting to hear about—so I was more or less losing track of time when, all of a sudden, Herb arrives. Such a surprise, he's dressed completely in black, but he's old, he's considerably older than I would have thought. Even so, everyone immediately acts like he's god. They're all too cool to get excited, so no one flutters or gushes or anything like that, but they all start to circle in a very unimpressed but attentive way.

Herb basically seems all right, but honestly, it's hard to tell. He's real distant and doesn't seem to care about much. Stu waves Polly and Daria and Amelia into the front of the crowd, and introduces them, or actually it's more like he displays them, waving his arms around like a bad magician, showing off today's most impressive trick. Everyone fans out behind them, waiting, like

17

frightened and expectant little kids. I don't know what they thought Herb was going to do, but he didn't really do much. He sort of nodded and seemed to mumble something to Stu, I'm not even sure he said hello to Polly or Daria, not to mention Amelia, who had been elbowed to the back fairly quickly in this crucial moment. Mostly it seemed like what Herb wanted to do was talk to some guy who had been running around screwing enormous klieg lights into place with umbrellas bouncing the light back into the room and then out the windows again. So Herb found the lighting fanatic and they settled into a corner and mumbled to each other. And then they started laughing their heads off at some private joke; they couldn't give a shit about anybody else in the room. Stu put on a brave front, but you could see that he was all for killing Herb. Herb is an ungrateful asshole. This picture isn't about the light; it's about three pretty girls with pretty hair. What the hell is Herb's problem? Stu carries his disappointment and his rage around the room like a big fur coat. So everybody sees it, but they're all still too cool to comment on it. So Stu stews, Herb mutters, Daria and Polly are subtly posing around, La Aura's cutting my hair, and the next thing I know, Herb is looking at me and saying, "Who is this?"

Obviously, no one knows how to answer this question, as not one of them has bothered to ask me who I am, other than La Aura. So everyone sort of stares, stupefied for a moment, and then Mom takes the opportunity to insert herself into the spot-light.

"This is my son, Philip," she coos. She steps forward and poses and coos, I kid you not. The slightest bit of stress, and all the beauty queen training pops out of her subconscious like a bad dream. "The girls' brother. I'm their mother, Julia. We're so pleased to be here, really, this is such a thrill for all of us." And she holds out her hand gracefully and smiles that beauty queen smile.

Anyway, Herb glances at Mom, and to my wild relief he actually does shake her hand; Herb seems to have had some sort of marginal training in niceties at some point in his life. And then he glances at the girls—really, he's barely interested in any of this—and then he looks back at me, and says, "So, all of them? I'm doing all of them?"

Stu just about has a heart attack. "No no no no no, no no," he says, casually desperate at the thought. "Just the girls. Philip's just here for moral support, aren't you, Philip?" I was staggered that he actually knew my name. Which just goes to show you, you should never underestimate a screaming queen who is completely self-absorbed: They pay attention more than you think.

La Aura shoves me a little bit, reminding me that I'm supposed to actually say something when someone asks me a question. "Sure," I mumble. Really, I'm useless in a crunch, I completely even forget how to talk. So I'm sort of nodding like a fool, and mumbling, and Herb is just descending on me and La Aura, looking at the two of us.

"No, this is good," he announces, studying me. "Three sisters and their brother, you see them, the unit, the inherent contradictions, yes? Yes, Philip?" He's staring at me, with his photographer's eyes, I have no idea what he's seeing, but it does not seem to be me. La Aura shoves me again. "Sure," I say.

Okay. I'm just doing the best I can here. I didn't ask this guy to look at me, and if you want my opinion, the only reason he noticed me at all was because La Aura had done a pretty good job cutting my hair and suddenly there was something to look at—mainly, a decent haircut. I didn't go asking to be in that picture.

But the next thing I know, Herb has his arm around me—really, in a kindly way, Herb is one of those people who gets you to do things because he makes you feel important and charming, so you're lost in this haze of warm fuzzy feelings and not really paying attention to what you're doing, you're just going along. His arm is around me, he's chatting to me in this low voice and I'm just walking with him, across the room and toward the drapes and the windows and the klieg lights. I can't really hear much. He turns me, stands me by a window. There's a kind of rustling and hum going on now, but I can't see anything, as all those lights are on me, and everything behind them disappears. You really can see the dust motes in these moments, that's one thing I remember. And then the next thing I remember is Amelia, and Polly and Daria, moving around me like angels. Really, they all looked so pretty and I'm just a mess—the only thing any of those style dudes did to me was ignore me and let La Aura cut my hair, so I'm kind of standing there in blue jeans and a T-shirt and this big old sloppy other shirt on top of that. Daria meanwhile is glowing, practically, she's in this shimmery sea-green snakeskin-like evening gown, and her hair is piled on her head—really she didn't look like Audrey Hepburn, she looked more like Lady Macbeth, but a very glamorous version of Lady Macbeth, there was no question about that. And then Polly is in this incredible little number, the smallest dress

I think I have ever seen in my life, pale green, strapless, with black beads all over the joint, Stu apparently having decided that green was the theme but there was no point being ruthless about it. Her hair is spiky, a look I don't tend to respond to, but now that I know that the nice hairdresser La Aura is behind all this I decide it's sheer genius. I mean, Polly looked great, no doubt about it. Sort of like a very tasteful punk rocker. Then there's Amelia, hopping around like a little bird. Blue jeans, no shoes or socks, green toenails, which looked strangely beguiling, and some sort of tie-dyed green T-shirt. She really looked so simple, and so great, and so herself. So as it turns out, Stu isn't so stupid after all.

Except there *I* am, in the middle of this meticulously designed land of green dresses and red hair and great-looking girls. There I am, a big boring teenage boy, nothing matches, poor Stu hasn't had half a second to figure out how to fit me into his picture, when Herb starts snapping away, I mean that Herb got right to the point. Stu is dodging around behind him, trying to get a word in edgewise, you can hear him saying, "Herb, maybe if I had just a minute . . . Herb, listen, we had no idea you'd be interested in the brother . . . Herb, really . . . Herb . . ." But Herb is just clicking wildly, one camera then another, he had like six draped around his neck, he looked like some mythical beast with too many eyes growing out of his chest. I swear, after all that picking and changing minds, and nothing seeming to happen for hours, all of a sudden everything was happening at lightning speed and no one was thinking about anything at all. I don't remember much of this part, to be frank, maybe that's why it seems that way in retrospect. I was so surprised to be

21

suddenly tossed into the middle of the action, I think I may have been in a bit of a daze. So that's really what I remember. Stu, Herb, me feeling like a dweeb, Amelia laughing; she thought it was funny that I was suddenly part of the whole mess. Somebody put some music on, I guess, I don't remember if it was on before and they just turned it up, but all of a sudden Elvis Presley was blasting, loud. Mom kept yelling something from the sidelines, who knows what. Daria and Polly sort of kept turning around, following Herb, I think, like flowers turning toward the sun anytime he moved. That's really all I remember.

And then it was over. Not completely over, just over for me. Herb ran out of memory in half his cameras at the exact same moment he ran out of film in the other half, so he had to take a break and have some underling reload them. The music snaps off, people start to suck on water bottles, hair and makeup rush in to do a dust-up on the girls. So while this is going on, Stu takes Herb aside and whispers to him, respectful, but urgent and firm, and while Herb doesn't really seem to say anything in response, he does turn and look at me, with those photographer eyes again, and then he turns back to listen, while Stu keeps talking. Stu is talking and talking and talking. And then, after a minute, Herb shrugs, nods, he doesn't care, he sort of looks over, casual, and says, "Okay, the brother, we don't need you, let's do some with just the girls." Just like that, like I was just a stupid prop all along anyway. Which in fact I was.

I didn't care. Mostly I was relieved that it was over. The whole time it was going on—which was longer than I thought; afterwards I found out my part of the shoot went on for half an hour—I felt so self-conscious I just wanted to crawl into a hole and I couldn't, obviously, as everybody was staring at me. Well, they weren't looking at me, really; they were looking at Polly and Daria and Amelia, when they weren't looking at Stu and wondering if he was going to have heart failure. So I mostly spent the whole time looking at the ground and stuff. It was just, near the end, I more or less got in the swing of things. Amelia had decided it was just a big joke anyway, and so she's kind of doing this little dance with me, and I decide what the hell, and I start to dance back, so we're starting to have some fun finally. We were doing these old corny dances from the fifties, not that we know what they even look like. But we're just pretending to be big old hipsters. And then Polly I think was getting bored, or at least she got tired of competing with Daria for the front and center spot, so she started to dance with us, too. So the three of us were doing these ridiculous dances, and Daria was staring at us like we were just a bunch of juvenile delinquents, but also like some part of her actually finds us secretly amusing. So for maybe two minutes or something all of a sudden we were just ourselves again, not the selves we are when we're torturing each other, but the ones who know how to have fun.

So of course that would be when old Herb has to stop and reload. That's just the way of the universe, it seems like, sometimes. You take so long to figure things out and, just when you get there, when you really figure something out that's maybe kind of good, they tell you you're out of time. I don't know why that is, but it does seem that way. Like most of your life, you sit around all tense, going, I know life is supposed to feel better than this, how do I figure out how to feel better? And everybody's got opinions about how to feel better—get drunk,

23

go to the movies, read a comic book or a porno magazine, watch TV, whatever. And so you do all that, and it doesn't work, but you're trying, you know, everybody gets points for trying. And then something happens and it just clicks; one day you're lying under a tree or something and it suddenly feels like you almost know it, how to be yourself, and then you do know it, for a second, and then something else happens, a catastrophe, they blow up the World Trade Center or something. Someone dies. You lose everything. And then you think, why didn't I know how to feel happy and content and at home in my life when I had everything I ever needed? How come as soon as I knew it, it all went away?

Look, I'm not trying to say that getting kicked out of the picture was the equivalent of a big catastrophe for me. I just mean, I wish I had figured out how to enjoy the whole thing a little sooner. Because when me and Amelia and Polly started dancing, at the end? That was fun, it really was.

CHAPTER TWO

In between the picture-taking event and the picture coming out in seven zillion magazines and ruining everyone's lives event, there was a shred of time when our lives almost went back to normal. For the next six weeks we actually went back to school and took up familiar activities, such as homework and piano lessons and breakfast. But none of it was the same anymore, already. Somehow the word was out, that fast, that Polly and Daria and Amelia were the new It Girls. I wondered, a lot, at the time, how can you be the new It Girls, if nobody's heard of you and you live in Brooklyn, and you're not in magazines? I mean, none of it had happened, yet; the picture wasn't out. But the news was already out, that this thing that hadn't happened yet was happening.

It was like, Polly was still going to school all the time, but she didn't even pretend to do the work anymore. Daria's modeling career, which she had been vaguely pursuing, started to heat up, in a preparatory way. The big-shot agent who kept almost signing her actually sent contracts over to the house and called, for once, instead of just returning. Which was a total turnaround; for complete ages this agent, Collette Something, had been sitting on the fence because, while it is undeniable that Daria is a knockout, the fact is that she "started late," because eighteen is like sixty, in modeling years. But now that the *New Yorker* was going to put Daria on the map, the concern about how ancient she was evaporated, and Collette called to say the FedEx guy was bringing the contracts by and oh, yes—would Polly and Amelia like to come in as well and take a meeting?

So then that made Daria completely insane and not want to sign with Collette, and then Collette kept calling, and faxing over information about bookings she might be able to get for Daria, if Daria were actually one of her clients. Which made Daria mad, as she suddenly decided she wanted to be an actress, and not just a model, and Collette's bookings were beneath her. Mom meanwhile was fielding other offers from other agents who heard through the grapevine that the shoot was terrific, and could all three girls come in for a meeting, would that be possible? Polly and Mom and Daria got into huge arguments about the whole situation, as Polly, at the ripe old age of seventeen, didn't want to find herself in Daria's boat, being told she's too old to start a modeling-slash-acting career because she waited until she was eighteen. So she was ready to move. Daria now wanted to wait, although this might have been because she resented the fact that Polly was suddenly part of her career picture. Mom was endlessly moaning to people on the phone about how she wanted to "protect" her girls, and although I think she believed it, it was also clearly an excuse to buy enough time to get Polly and Daria on the same page because they needed to be behaving as if they were best friends when they finally did take all these spectacular meetings. I watched a lot of *Star Trek* reruns during these endless debates. Amelia took up a sudden interest in the piano.

Now, this piano thing was not completely out of the blue. She's taken lessons since she was five and had to stand up so she could reach the keyboard, and she's always been one of those kids who have talent but so what? You're impressed because they're pretty good, considering how little they are and all, but other than that it's sort of like a dog doing tricks on late-night television. Besides which, Amelia has a pretty reckless relationship with the whole idea of discipline so she doesn't exactly practice with anything resembling regularity. But now that everyone in the house had become obsessed with the idea of agents, and I was drowning myself in *Star Trek*, Amelia couldn't get enough of the piano. Which was vaguely annoying; you try watching *Star Trek* with someone pounding Beethoven in the room next door. But no one said anything, least of all me. We were all just generally unnerved as hell anyway, and Beethoven sort of articulates that in a very grand way, if you think about it. So she's practicing like a demon, and then she has this piano recital, and nobody goes except me.

Nobody went, except me. Which is, I think, another sign of how odd things were already. When your fifteen-year-old brother is the only one in your family who goes to your stupid piano recital? Something is definitely off, in spite of the fact that I probably was the only one who ever enjoyed those things anyway. I couldn't ever admit it, of course, but I always thought those recitals were sort of corny and great: All these little kids playing

27

Bach or the Beatles just terribly—there's only one or two of them who are ever any good, but the whole audience always cheers like lunatics, no matter how bad the kid is. And then afterwards everyone goes down into the basement of the school and the kids pig out on chocolate-chip cookies and cans of soda pop, then run around like maniacs and then after a while six or seven of the littlest kids crash and melt down and have to be taken home. It's strangely pleasant. But I have to say, even though Mom and Polly and Daria never appreciated the whole thing the way I did, they always showed up. Now, in preparation for everything changing, apparently, I was the only one there. And Amelia was good; she had practiced that Beethoven within an inch of its life, and it was loud and fast, so she had to really attack the keyboard to get it out, and she walloped it. Everybody cheered like lunatics when she finished, and she was all flushed and laughing when she took her bow. She didn't seem to care that nobody else in the family came; she mostly was just pleased that she had played so well. Her piano teacher, this skinny guy named Ben who had a huge crush on her, kept congratulating her and telling everybody how proud he was. And then I went up and gave her a big hug, even though I am her older brother, and she laughed some more.

So we walk home, and she's sort of humming the middle part of the Beethoven thing, and it's nice out, a little drizzly, but not cold at all, just springlike, so that the rain feels good instead of annoying.

"I never played that good in my life," she told me.

"No, come on," I said. "You play like that at home all the time. I'm about to blow my brains out, I hear Beethoven in my sleep."

Amelia laughed at this, even though it was rather lame. She was really jazzed. "I was good, I was really good," she said, mostly to herself. Then she kind of looked at me. "Dad says if I'm really good he'll get me into LaGuardia."

Okay. This piece of information just about knocked me out; I almost collapsed right there on the sidewalk. "Oh?" I say, completely casual. "When did you talk to Dad?"

She is oh-so-casual herself. "I don't know. On the phone a couple times. He said he was going to try and make the recital but he might be in Brazil, so it's no big deal he's not here. I mean, 'cause he's in Brazil."

"Oh yeah, I think I remember hearing about that." Ha ha, as if anyone ever knows where my father is.

"So he couldn't make it, but you were there. Not that, you don't have to tell him how good I'm getting or anything, I can have Ben do that." She is still being oh-so-casual, but I'm starting to get the drift of her plan here. As if I don't know when I'm being played by my own sister. "But will you, though? You will, right?"

"What, tell Dad you were good at the Garfield Lincoln piano recital? Sure. I'll tell him whatever you want. If I can find him, when he comes back from Brazil."

She pretends not to hear the utter disbelief and rampant sarcasm which has entered my tone here, and continues to blather on. "Thanks, Philip, 'cause you know it's really important to me. Thanks."

I'm still playing it cool with her, waiting to see how far she's going to try and push this. "Well, because, like, I mean—since when did you decide you wanted to go to LaGuardia?"

"Well, Ben says I'm pretty good, and he said that LaGuardia, you know it's not Julliard but it *is* the best high school for the performing arts and he thinks that my range is not just classical anyway, and I could keep up my other studies and still focus on the piano and I just started thinking about it and then I just wanted to play the piano all the time."

This is starting to strike me as obvious and pathetic. For all her talents, Amelia is absolutely the worst liar on the planet. I mean, she simply stinks at it. You have to stop yourself from laughing, that's how bad it is.

"So, since you've been talking to Dad so much, did you tell him about all this shit that's been going on with Polly and Daria and the *New Yorker*? Did you tell him about that?"

"He knows about it."

"So you told him."

"Everybody knows about it, Philip." She's starting to sound annoyed with me, which is a relief, because at least she's not putting on this weird I-Want-To-Be-A-Pianist Act anymore. "Where have you been?"

"Well, I guess I've been over here on the Planet of Total Morons; someplace you apparently own property," I tell her.

"What's that supposed to mean?"

"Gee, I wonder."

We walk on, in silence, getting rained on. The cool drippy rain is starting to get annoying, such a surprise.

"I don't care what you think. I'm going to LaGuardia," Amelia announces. "Ben thinks I'm really good, and Dad can get me in."

"Dad would do anything to mess with Mom's big plans to

30

turn all three of you into beauty queens," I announce. "And Ben has a boner for you. And you can't decide you're going to be a concert pianist when you're fourteen. You have to have some lunatic parent decide you're a genius when you're six or something, and then they torture you to death making you practice eighteen hours a day until you're Mozart, and then *maybe* you get into the most famous school for the performing arts in America. You're going to LaGuardia. Give me a break."

"That is not how it works."

"You know it is."

"Ben says—"

"And you called Dad? Are you insane?"

"I love the piano. I'm really good at it. I'm going to LaGuardia."

"Aside from the fact that that's impossible, Mom won't let you. If she finds out that Dad had anything to do with it, she'll put a stop to it before you've made it to the subway station."

"She won't be able to."

"Dad can't get you into LaGuardia."

"Yes he can, he knows the chairman of the board or something."

"So *what*?"

"That's how things are done in New York."

"You've gone insane."

"You just said I was good. I'm good on the piano. Ben thinks I'm really good."

"Ben wants to—"

"Could you not say that again, huh? I mean I found it really offensive the first time."

"I don't care if it's offensive or not, it's true."

"Since when do you know everything?"

"Yeah, okay, maybe I don't know everything, but I do know something about guys who want to bone your sister, and I also know you can't suddenly decide you're going to be a concert pianist just because you played the first movement of the *Pathétique Sonata* pretty good one day in high school."

"I'm going to LaGuardia."

"You're full of shit."

I don't know why I got so mad all of a sudden. I just did. And all the feeling just swell about what a good time we had at that stupid recital got rained right out of us. By the time we got home, we were both soaking wet and mad as hell and of course no one even bothered to ask Amelia how it went.

So the next morning I'm feeling rather hopelessly lousy, and I am in no mood to hear about fingernail polish and agents and modeling careers and lipstick shades at the breakfast table. I particularly am in no mood to hear about my idiot father who has of course run off to Brazil for who knows what reason. My head hurts and I'm tired and no one will look at me or even acknowledge that I'm sitting there eating a two-year-old lemon Zone bar, which just isn't enough—there's never enough food around our house because, in spite of the fact that all my sisters plus my mother are pretty much rail-thin, they're always afraid they're getting fat—and I am frankly just starving to death. So I'm thinking about how hungry I am, and why isn't there ever more food in our house, and I'm feeling a little light-headed and not fully paying attention, and then breakfast proceeds to go south, at approximately eighty miles per hour.

"My piano recital went great last night, in case anyone is interested," Amelia announces. It all seems innocuous enough to start; of course it does, it always does.

"That's terrific, sweetheart," says Mom, while she whips up some kind of inedible shake full of flax and ice cubes.

"Good for you, honey." Polly is all warm and fuzzy, in a completely self-absorbed way. "That's sensational."

"Great," says Daria, pouring herself a glass of water. Apparently she has decided to see if she can live on water; I don't think I've seen her eat any actual food since their big-deal photo shoot.

"I mean, I never played that good in my life. Or at least, that's what I thought, but then Ben said I've been playing really well for a while and that if I just keep practicing the way I have been, I could really be good." This is an approximation, obviously, of the conversation, but the tone is what I'm going for here. I mean, the whole thing sounded completely surreal to me, kind of way too bright and people kept saying things like "great" and "terrific" and "really really good," but it was hard to keep straight what was so good, like the thing everyone was talking about was just somewhere else, or maybe didn't even exist at all.

"Philip said I was great," Amelia continues. I roll my eyes at this, as it is strictly true but nowhere near the whole truth, but no one is actually all that interested in having me leap into this noteworthy conversation. Least of all Amelia, who is rolling along now, in her great and fantastic and really really good universe. Which leaves me sitting there, waiting like a dolt for the punch line. "Ben thinks I should maybe even be training."

33

"Training?" Mom says, her voice going up a little too high. My mother is not necessarily bright, but she is not necessarily stupid, either. She's starting to get wind that this little story about what a swell time everyone had at the piano recital isn't going to end well, as far as she's concerned.

Daria pours herself another glass of water. "What do you mean, training?" she asks. She is very cool. Polly is listening, also cool, while she scrapes the thinnest layer of tofutti imaginable along the inside of a hollowed-out bagel. No kidding, I would eat the bagels, except our housekeeper Lucinda has orders to scrape the insides out of them before I can even get a shot at one. Then she freezes them, these little skins of bagels, so that any time someone wants a damn bagel that's all that's available to you, frozen bagel skins.

So everybody's sitting around, hovering around the word "training," instinctively knowing that there's another shoe going to drop around whatever the word "training" is actually going to mean.

"Yeah," says Amelia. "Like for now I think he's just talking about maybe doing another lesson a week, but more practicing, you know, and then maybe in six months or something I'd be ready to audition for someplace really good."

The train wreck is picking up speed.

"Is that what you want to do, sweetheart?" says Mom. Her voice is so phony now you could put her on television.

"Yeah, I do. I really, I do." Amelia is getting good and firm. I think this plan of hers is a total crock but I also admire its strange daring. "I don't have to practice at home all the time, 'cause I know that probably could get really annoying—"

34

"Not at all," says Mom, tilting her head, poised.

". . . Ben says I can use one of the rehearsal pianos at school, he'll help me with that—"

"I think maybe I should have a talk with Ben before we let this plan get finalized, sweetie," Mom coos.

"It's just that if I'm really going to take this seriously, because he seriously thinks—"

"I'll call Ben and find out what he thinks, honey," says Mom. Polly and Daria are just watching now.

"Yeah, but—"

"I'm so excited for you, sweetheart! The recital must've really gone well. I'm so sorry I missed it."

"You got to talk to Ben."

"I will. Oh, and I've left a message with Mrs Virtudes about picking you up at two today. The appointment with Collette isn't until four, but I don't know what traffic is going to be like, the bridges are always such a mess, and I think she's enough of a pain, we don't want to start off on the wrong foot."

Amelia looks at the table. Polly licks her fingers, as if there's a shred of spare tofutti somewhere to be found. Daria sips her water. My stupid Zone bar tastes like straw.

"I can't go," says Amelia. "Ben and I have to talk about my rehearsal schedule."

"Don't be ridiculous. You just had a recital last night. You can take one day off from practicing, darling. You've been practicing so much lately the rest of us can hardly think without hearing da, da, daaaah . . ." Mom does her little musical bells laugh as a finish to this clever speech.

"I can't go, Mom. I can't go," Amelia says.

35

"She has to go," Daria tells Mom. She is not happy with any of this.

"Why do I have to go?"

"Collette wants to meet all three of you."

"I don't want to be a model. I'm a little kid," Amelia points out.

"I think you should leave that to her to decide," Mom smiles.

"Ben wants to meet with me. How am I going to—"

"Jesus." Daria is really disgusted now, and making no attempt to hide it. Which pisses Amelia off.

"What do you care?" she asks. "I'm not saying you can't go off and be some kind of idiot model. I'm just saying, I don't want to do it, and I especially don't want to do it today. I have something else to do today."

"What, be a pianist?" Polly is laughing at this, and she always has that attitude thing going, which doesn't help, when she laughs. It makes her look like she's sneering, which isn't necessarily what she means. Sometimes it is what she means, it's just hard to tell, all the time. And now she's got the spiky hair thing going too, from the shoot, so she's really got attitude now. Which means Amelia is starting to bristle.

"Fuck you," she says. "I'm not doing it."

Mom jumps up, shocked, *shocked* to hear such language come out of the mouth of her youngest daughter.

"That is quite enough, young lady," she says. "I won't have that kind of language in this house."

Amelia rolls her eyes, which doesn't help, as Mom sees it and puts her lips together, determined that her own child is not going to look down on her. "You're coming, and that's that."

"You can't yank me out of school for some stupid meeting with some stupid *agent*," Amelia retorts. "What kind of a mother are you?"

"What did you say?" says Mom. She looks like she might actually strike somebody.

This is stupid, I'm thinking. I'm also thinking, Amelia hasn't even played her trump card yet; she has yet to even mention the word "Dad" and this whole thing is already a mind-numbing mini-disasteroid.

At which point, Daria lets loose. She's not sneering, like Polly, nor is all superior and hurt and outraged like Mom. She's just straight out pissed off. "Believe me," she announces, "it was never my plan to drag my sisters along on my *life,* but now that I'm stuck with you, I'm not going to let either one of you screw it up. You're coming. Amelia, and you're going to keep your mouth shut and do whatever anybody tells you to do."

"For-fucking-get it," says Amelia.

"I've already warned you about that word, Amelia," Mom announces, like a queen.

"I'm going to LaGuardia next year; Dad said he could get me in," Amelia tells her. "So I have to practice and I'm not going into midtown to meet some stupid FUCKING agent."

Okay. This announcement has the hoped-for effect of silencing the entire room. Daria looks like she'd like to stab Amelia with something, but all she has in her hands is a glass of filtered water.

"She talked to Dad?" says Daria. She turns to Mom, filled with outrage. "She talked to Dad?"

Mom is no longer posing for the camera. "Is that what you did, Amelia?"

"I just said I did! Are you deaf? He thinks it's a good idea!"

"This conversation is over," says Mom. "I will let your father know he has nothing to say about—"

"About what? About me taking piano lessons? That'll look good."

"I don't care how it looks."

"He'll get custody of me," she announces.

Everybody stares at her. I start to sense once again that being a boy is a distinct disadvantage in this world. I mean, this plan Amelia's cooked up just so she can get out of being a model has levels I never even dreamed of.

"Your father is not getting custody of anybody. The courts made that clear a long time ago," Mom announces.

"Let her go. See how she likes it," Daria says. Mom turns on her, going white. This is apparently the worst thing anyone has said all morning.

"That's enough, Daria. That's enough out of all of you."

"I'm calling Dad," says Amelia. Like so many smart people, she simply doesn't know when she's lost. Which I could have told her, bringing Dad up would end any shot she had of getting out of this, which was never a good one anyway.

"I am NOT TALKING about your father ANYMORE," Mom hisses at her. It's impressive when she loses her temper, it really is. She's like Medea or something; you take it seriously. Even so, it looks like Amelia's about to go head to head with Medea, so I finally put my foot in.

"He's in Brazil," I announce. "You can't call him anyway, you told me yourself, he's in Brazil."

This silences everybody, and a sort of dread calm descends. Dad's in Brazil. That's that.

"Brazil, huh," says Polly, looking out the window. "I'd like to go to Brazil, sometime."

"Sometime, but not today," says Mom, shoving books together, pushing them at me and Amelia abruptly. "If you don't get out the door right now, you're going to be tardy."

"Mom—"

"We'll pick you up at two."

Amelia is going to make one last stab. "The stupid meeting's not till four!"

"You need time to change and do your face. You can't just show up for these things."

"I'm not doing my face," says Amelia.

"I'll do it for you," says Polly. "Eat it, Amelia. They want all three of us. You're not getting out of this." And she pushes us to the door, and shuts it behind us.

The elevator ride is grim. Amelia hates losing more than any person I've ever met.

"You were a big help," she tells me.

"I tried to help you last night," I tell her back. "It's a dumb idea."

"Why? Why is wanting to play the piano any *dumber* than being a model?"

"Because you actually have a *shot* at being a model," I tell her.

"Fuck you," she sends back. This use of the word "fuck" is a new thing with her. She does pretty well with it. I mean, she's not one of those people who doesn't know how to land it. It

39

sounds pretty authoritative, coming out of her perfect little rosy pink mouth.

Obviously I was not involved in the first big agent powwow. While Amelia was being dragged away from the Garfield Lincoln School and her stunning career as a glamour-babe pianist, I was finishing a physics lab which had something to do with creating alternative energy sources out of teeny-tiny waterwheels. It was sort of relaxing, truth be told, sort of like building a Lego castle and then seeing what happens when you pour water all over it. So I built my waterwheel, which was boring but fun, and then I went to soccer practice, which was just boring, and then I stopped for pizza on the way home, had four slices, and then I went home. No one showed up until nine-thirty, so it was a pretty good thing that I stopped for the pizza.

By the time they showed up, I have to confess I was dead curious about how it went. Although by then it's not exactly a big mystery, is it; if the stupid agent didn't want them, it's doubtful it would have taken her until nine-thirty to drop the boom. So I'm zoning in front of the television set, zipping the clicker coolly, as if I have no interest in anything whatsoever, when the four of them waft into the apartment. Mom leads the way, opening the door and turning to usher them in, cooing over all three of them like they were precious baby chicklings, or a hot piece of real estate.

"It's been a big night. All three of you should probably head straight to bed," she announces.

"It's nine-thirty, Mother," says Daria. Daria is all flushed and haughty; she's standing so tall she looks like someone cast a spell over her and she grew into a pope or something, like the woman in that fairy tale where the fish gives the fisherman too many wishes. Polly, on the other hand, looks short. This is the only thing I can think about for a minute—why does Daria look so tall and Polly look so short? Did they do something to them at the modeling agency, to make the threesome more marketable?—and then I realize, duh, that Polly took her shoes off because her feet had started to hurt.

"I think we should celebrate," she announces. She goes to the mini-fridge where Mom keeps the alcohol, and grabs herself a beer. Which all of us have done many times, just not in front of Mom.

But Mom doesn't notice, or at least she doesn't care to notice; she's still floating around the room like a dazed and happy flower, bobbing in a cool breeze on somebody's deck or something. Amelia tosses herself on the couch, next to me, rolling over the back and landing like a ton of bricks. Before I can give her a hard time about it, she is laughing at pretty much nothing.

"What a dweeb. What a dweeboid you are. What are you watching? I'm not watching *Star Trek*, how many times can you watch that stupid show? Give me the clicker." She grabs it off me and immediately concentrates on channel flipping even faster than I do.

"You know how many calories there are in a beer?" asks Daria. Polly laughs.

"I know exactly how many calories there are in a beer, and tonight I don't care," she says, waving the bottle in Daria's face.

"So it went good, huh?" I ask.

Amelia shrugs. "It was about what you'd think," she says. She

41

doesn't seem too bothered by it, though, and then she starts to laugh again, all flushed and happy and transfixed by the surreal shenanigans of some pink cartoon dog with a hole in its tooth. She's all flushed and happy, Polly's all flushed and happy, Mom's all flushed and happy, and Daria's just flushed—who can ever tell if she's happy? So it doesn't take a brain surgeon to figure out that all four of them are pretty well tanked.

Which makes me mad, frankly, although it's not like I don't believe in people getting tanked, or like I've never seen it or anything. It's not like I've never done shots of tequila in the laundry room of Jack Metzger's sister's apartment on Sterling. Amelia is tanked, and I've never seen her tanked and, the fact is, the last time I saw her she said she didn't want to be a model because she was just a little kid. I mean, you can't say you're a little kid one minute and then go and get tanked with your mother that afternoon. You can't watch cartoons, and be tanked. You can't do both.

This logic seems pretty irrefutable to me but, such a surprise, I seem to have no clear idea how to be the cool, rational, not-tanked person in a room full of tanked women. So instead I act like a big baby and grab the clicker from Amelia. "What are you watching?" I mumble, and I start to zip through all the channels again.

"Hey!" she says. She shoves me. "I was watching that."

"You're drunk," I say, quiet, like an insult. Which is relatively stupid, as Amelia is the one who snuck me up in the elevator and got me to my room, and later to the bathroom, without anyone knowing, after the tequila episode.

"I'm not drunk," she says, and then she starts to laugh like an idiot, like "I'm not drunk" is the most hilarious thing she's ever said in her life. I swear, she thinks this whole situation is just hilarious.

"What did you say?" asks Mom, all fake-startled and guilty as hell.

"Philip thinks I'm *drunk*."

"Don't be ridiculous, Philip."

"*Mom*," I say back. Like there's nothing else to say, really; sometimes, there just isn't, and this is one of those times. Not that she's going to give an inch.

"Today was a big day for everyone, and if you can't be happy for your sisters, then I think you might want to think about that."

"Yeah, sure, I'll do that, Mom," I tell her. And that's all I say about it. Amelia keeps giggling, and Mom goes into the study, probably to sneak another drink, because she's got liquor stashed in there too, and Polly and Daria drift back into their bedrooms to consult with the stars, and I find a *Star Trek* rerun, the one where Captain Kirk falls in love with an android and then she dies at the end of the episode because she learned that feelings hurt too much to live with. I swear, that show was really brilliant, it really just was, and I'm not embarrassed to mention it. I mean, I'm not one of those idiots who goes to conventions and dresses up like Mr Spock. I'm just saying. That show was not near as stupid as everything that's been on television since.

CHAPTER THREE

No one ever said Herb Lang was overrated, and the fact is, he isn't overrated. He's a very good photographer, even if he is a bit spooky in person. So the picture, when it comes out, is very hot. Daria the Ice Queen has a big smile on her face, her head is tipped back and she looks like joy, she just does. Polly looks like she's grabbing Daria and trying to push her out of the frame, which maybe could be a little too accurate, in terms of the reality of their relationship, but it doesn't look mean or competitive. It just looks nice, like a nice sisterly sort of thing to do. The spiky hair is great, the little green dress with the black beads, also great. She has a killer pair of heels on, also great. And then there's old Amelia, all the way on the other side of the frame, with her blue jeans and T-shirt, and those nutty little bare feet and little green toenails. She's sort of half in profile, head down, but looking up, right at the camera. And she just looks smart, and a little bit devilish and like someone you just want to know, who also happens to be so pretty you need to fall over. The whole thing is killer, there's no question.

When Mom took it out of the FedEx envelope, it was pretty wild. We were all sitting around the kitchen—I don't know why we always hang out in the kitchen, there's never any food there—but anyway we were hanging out in the kitchen, collectively on pins and needles, while Mom took her own damn time opening that FedEx.

"Just a minute, just a minute, would you please?" she laughed, turning away from Polly and Daria, both of whom were actively trying to rip it from her hands.

"Mom, it doesn't take normal people sixteen minutes to open a FedEx!" Polly screeched, still grabbing.

"Well, then I'm not normal," Mom informed her, elegantly cheerful. "I just want to savor this, is that all right with you?" What an act. I thought Daria was going to brain her with the blender. Amelia was sitting next to me, trying not to care, but even she couldn't stand the tension finally, and she practically knocked her chair over, bolting to the other side of the table so she could get a good look as soon as the thing was out of the envelope. It was kind of goofy and sweet, honestly; all of them were laughing and nervous and happy and shoving at each other to get the best look. And then they all saw it, at once, and I'm not kidding, they all just shut up. That picture shut them all up. Because it was impossible to look at it and not know that something was going to happen. You just couldn't not know.

This was like two days before the magazine hit the stands, that's when they finally sent us a so-called "advance" copy. I thought for sure they'd give us more preparation than that, but that old Collette apparently really had to pull strings just to get that much special treatment. Anyway, things had gotten pretty hot by then. In those six weeks while we were waiting for the magazine to come out, Collette set up a whole mess of meetings all over town with different ad agencies and magazines and stylists and publicists, TV execs, talk-show producers, it went on and on. Amelia spent the entire time kicking and screaming and saying "fuck you," and then getting dragged to all the meetings anyway. Which meant that she missed quite a bit of school, which meant that several of her teachers started calling to give Mom a hard time about it. No one particularly cared about Polly virtually dropping out; that was sort of understood as the sort of thing that was just going to happen, and Polly was always a little bit of a hell-raiser anyway, so truth be told I think the school was finally glad that she was taking off of her own accord. But Amelia was a freshman and known to be a fairly responsible little student, so the school got bent out of shape about her not showing up for algebra tests, and Amelia was bent out of shape, and Mom was bent out of shape. And then Ben the piano teacher got way bent out of shape, probably because, as I think I've mentioned, he had a completely illicit and illegal crush on her, which he had to pretend was, like, a more legal kind of concern about her development as an artist. So Ben called Amelia at home about six times, about missed lessons, and then he called Mom, who told him off, and then Amelia called Dad, who was back from Brazil, and he called Mom and expressed his supreme disapproval, and he reamed her out for yanking Amelia out of school, and Mom reamed him back, which just bent Polly completely out of shape, and sent Daria into a complete shrieking rage. So that's what life was like, up

47

until the day we got that picture in the mail and realized that, as weird as it all was getting? It was about to get worse.

The next day, it did. The phone rang. Mom picked it up, listened for no more than fifteen seconds, hung it up, turned around and informed everyone that they were going into Union Square to have drinks with a movie star whose name I cannot mention because he'd definitely sue me. This is a true story. One of the things that happen in New York, that people don't always put together is, there are plenty of famous people out there who would like to meet pretty girls who are about to become famous themselves. PR people and agents do this sort of thing all the time; it's their job to arrange these meetings between the famous and the nearly famous at a time when photographers might be around to snap some so-called candid shots of these exceptional encounters. So our friend Collette is somewhat on the ball, it seems, because Mom suddenly announced that Amelia, Daria and Polly had to go doll themselves up fast, because this major movie star was going to be holding court at W in an hour, and he wanted to meet them.

Which frankly floored all of us, even Amelia. She said, "Who?" And Mom said the name of this movie star again, we'll just call him "Rex Wentworth" for now, although we could just as easily call him Bruce or Arnold or George. So Mom said, "Rex Wentworth," and everybody just sat there. If that's the sort of thing that impresses you, you had to be impressed.

Although I have to admit that even now I'm not a hundred percent clear even on why movie stars actually are such hot shit. I have spent a good deal of time thinking about this and it continues to perplex me. As far as I can tell, they don't really do anything except parade around with machine guns or pistols shouting things like "Get in the truck!" Plus, when you check out their shenanigans when they're not on screen, you really start to wonder. You read Rush & Molloy, or Page Six, about movie stars shoplifting and trashing hotel rooms and smacking around their girlfriends or getting blow jobs from transvestite hookers, I mean, it's not like I'm saying there's anything wrong with things like that, but it's also not particularly something you have to admire. And then in the same issue you can read about how some studio handed over thirty million dollars or something, to one of these lunatics, so they can make some crazy movie that is just going to be so bad that your brain just starts to fry while you're watching it. And these are the people we're supposed to get all excited about, in America. I realize that I'm not saying anything particularly fresh here. But you have to wonder, over time, what the continued fascination is, you really just do.

Except that on the evening in question, all three of my sisters and my mother thought that meeting one of these guys was about the most mind-numbingly fantastic thing that had ever happened to them. They ran around like gorgeous birds, half-plumed, tossing shoes everywhere; even Amelia, who I would have sworn couldn't give a shit about shoes. But there she was, hungrily swiping a pair of strappy taupe heels off the floor of Polly's closet, and then acting all guilty when Polly walked in on her, having just ripped off a gold-sequined halter top from some reject pile in Daria's room.

"Do you need these?" says Amelia, as if it's actually possible to "need" strappy shoes with three-inch heels.

"Well, no, but you might try asking," Polly snips. "I *am* asking," snips back Amelia, to which Polly replies with the age-old witticism, "Whatever." So Amelia shrugs, pissed about something, but who knows what, since she was the one who actually got caught stealing red-handed, and she trips away haughtily, carrying off those noteworthy spikes. On the way back to her room she passes me, as I'm sitting on the floor of the hallway and have witnessed the whole ridiculous exchange.

"What are you looking at?" she asks, in the same snippy tone. Which I'm not sure why, if you're off to meet a movie star, and you're stealing shoes on top of it, you have to snap at people.

"Nothing," I said. I suppose I could have waxed poetic about how dumb it all seemed, but suddenly I just got real depressed. Not that I wanted to go with them, but not that I particularly wanted to spend another night alone channel surfing either. I was also wondering if I was going to be able to find anything to eat, as an actual dinner for me didn't seem to be on my so-called mother's agenda. The possibility that I might spend the evening doing schoolwork vaguely crossed my mind, as being too pathetic to be believed, while the rest of my family was off carousing with movie stars in Union Square. And that was pretty much what was going on in my head.

"So what's *your* problem?" Amelia suddenly yells. I mean it. She just started to yell at me. "I mean what, really . . . what . . . you really are, you know—forget it! Just forget it!" That's what she said, more or less. It was quite dramatic. I just stared at her, and then she turned red, threw the shoes on the floor, and went to tell Mom she wasn't going because Philip was being an asshole about everything.

I just want to make this clear. She's the one who was yelling. I didn't say anything. That is exactly how it happened. You can't make this crap up.

In any case, as per usual, Mom wasn't too interested in Amelia's protests. By then it was pretty clear that, for some reason, all three of them were the deal. You don't get just two sisters at any given moment, even though Polly and Daria together are not unimpressive. What people wanted was all three. Movie stars included.

So I ended up sitting in front of the television again, totally deserted by the whole female menagerie, eating the tail end of three bags of soy chips, two cans of Diet Pepsi Twist, and an orange and a banana. And then I got bored. I mean, of course I got bored. Everybody kept deserting me and I hadn't had a decent meal for three weeks, why shouldn't I be bored? And then I finally got tired of channel surfing, and so then I hacked around with the PlayStation 2 for about an hour, and I murdered about seven hundred aliens, and then I got mad, all of a sudden, and I picked up a six-thousand-dollar crystal sort of thing off the coffee table and threw it at the wall, where it made a dent but didn't actually break. Which may have been prompted by an hour's worth of murdering aliens on the PlayStation 2, but in all honesty, I think it was more of a someone-has-to-think-about-feeding-me sort of situation.

In any case, after this impressive display of impotent teen rage, I got bored again, put on my jacket, and decided to go out and stalk my own sisters.

It's ridiculously easy to get to Union Square from where I live. I'm a two-minute walk from the Seventh Avenue Station on Flatbush, and I picked up a Q Train right away. Then there's only five stops between Seventh Avenue and Union Square and the W bar is right there, just off the square, half a block up from the subway station. The point being that, I got there so quickly, the whole idea that maybe stalking my own sisters wasn't the brightest choice I could make never even occurred to me. I just spotted the bar, and walked right in.

It was hot in there. Not "hot" hot, just plain hot, like eighty degrees, the air recirculated so many times it just couldn't recreate itself into something breathable anymore. I didn't at first make it past the foyer, where there were like seven bachelors and bachelorettes, all of them squeezed into tight little business suits and looking like they were auditioning for one of those reality shows, where average people dress up like television stars and then pretend to be real in the most unreal circumstances some idiot at the network could cook up. So they were all squashed in there, in their great-looking suits, looking kind of uncomfortable and anxious, while this totally skinny girl in a tight black dress at a kind of mini-podium kept looking down at what might be a seating chart. Then she'd look up, and look over her shoulder at the crowded room, and then she'd sigh, and then she'd whisper to some passing person in another great suit, and then she'd laugh, carelessly, not worried at all about the sweaty crowd waiting in front of her, and then she'd look down at her seating chart again. All the bachelors and bachelorettes shifting on their tight shoes, and trying to act huffy, and it seemed to have occurred to none of them that this was, after all, a bar, not a restaurant; there is no seating, you can just shove your way into the room, push to the bar and get your own drink, can't you? It's a goddamned *bar*.

"Excuse me," I said to the first bachelorette, and I pushed right by her. She looked pretty annoyed at this, but that's kind of where she was even before I showed up. Anyway, I just slammed right through all of them, and went right to the podium, and said to Miss Little Black Dress, "I'm here with Rex Wentworth."

Well. Talk about the magic words. Little BD looks at me, startled, but then she stops, and thinks for a second. But I gave her pause. I mean, I did, after all, know that Rex was there, somewhere. That meant that I was potentially somebody who she really better not throw out.

So she looked at me, suspicious but cool, you know, not too rude but not friendly either, and once again she ran her eyes up and down me fast, clearly considering what I was wearing— a pair of jeans and sneakers, a T-shirt, a flannel shirt over that, completely normal for a teenager who could give a shit, but not exactly the kind of thing you would expect for a member of a movie star's entourage.

Just then, behind me, someone murmurs, "What'd that kid say? Rex Wentworth is here?"

Little BD gets a kind of look of panic in her eyes. She's in a bind now. She's got a weird cool loser in front of her, who's just loudly running around, asking for Rex, and the word is about to get out that Rex is somewhere in some back room in her crummy overrated bar.

"He's kind of waiting for me," I said. "Is there a problem?"

"What's the name?" she asks me, eyes narrowing.

"Philip Wentworth," I tell her.

It did the job. Little BD blinked, tipped her head to one side, briefly, trying out her memory about what Rex's family situation actually was, how many children he had out there, actually: Was it a possibility that I was Rex's son? Was that a possibility? Maybe I'm a nephew. She is looking down at another list, totally professional, seeing if the name "Philip Wentworth" has been written down anywhere so that she doesn't have to make a decision about anything, she can just let me in if this totally fraudulent name is anywhere at all; her brain is moving fast because she only has mere seconds to contemplate all of this before Rex will get wind that she kept his nephew/son/career-ruinous adolescent boyfriend waiting at the front door for no reason at all.

"There a problem?" I ask. "You want me to call his cell?" I reach into my pocket, pretending to have a cell. She looks up at me, very friendly, smiles. "No, of course not. Why don't you just follow me?" And with that she swivels and strides straight back into the promised land.

Okay, this all happened in about five seconds, and while it may sound like I vaguely knew what I was doing, I was actually pulling major shit out of completely thin air. I mean, I did follow this insane woman back into the bar, and I did my best instinctively to slouch and shrug and look around, bored as shit, but frankly the whole performance was a complete joke, because I was in truth utterly clueless. Little BD had hauled out of a pocket somewhere—where, I will never know, because that dress was too small to hide so much as a BIC pen—one of those giant walkie-talkie things that military personnel use when they're in the middle of the desert trying to coordinate some sort of crack offensive. And then she started murmuring with a kind of discreet determination into the speaker, "Hi, it's Shelly. I have someone here who claims to . . ." I was sort of slouching along behind her, acting like this was totally protocol, I was used to babes in black dresses talking in walkie-talkies and checking me out with the security team that constantly surrounds my putative father the movie star. Meanwhile of course I was more or less in a total state of interior panic. I mean, it did suddenly occur to me that I was now not actually stalking my sisters; in actuality, what I was now doing was stalking a movie star. And that's the kind of peculiar behavior in actuality which gets people tossed in prison.

So now I'm glancing around with casual desperation, wondering what bright idea is out there for me to just glom my brainless self onto, to get myself out of this, now that I'm in it, and Little BD is watching me carefully, as she snakes through the restaurant, and it is kind of occurring to me that in fact she never bought one bit of any of it, she's heading for some sort of back hallway, at the end of which there seems to be a kind of sinister back office, where three massive security-looking guys are clustered around a door, staring at the kid who is about to spend the next six months in juvie. I mean, these guys were not amused, and they were not kidding, either. The true insanity of what I was doing sank in. I stopped. Shelly kept going. The security gorillas all took a step forward, seeing quite clearly that I had decided to bolt in the opposite direction and make a terrible scene crashing back through the overdressed bachelors and bachelorettes, all clustered together in their misery. I mean, things were about to get way worse, when behind me someone yells, "Philip! Hey, Philip!"

The teeny little black dress in front of me stiffens as Shelly hears this, but, as she's swiveling, Amelia's already got her hands on my arm, and she's yanking me back into the bar. "Where are you going? There's nothing back there but offices," she tells me. Shelly, suddenly confused again, steps forward. "I'm sorry, do you know this person?"

"Yes, he's with us, with Rex, I mean," Amelia says, matter of factly. "Come on, come on, I'm so glad you're here, this is such a huge bore, it's hilarious that you came, what are you wearing, Mom is going to throw a fit . . ." Shelly and the giant security guys all relaxed and kind of grinned at each other; it's amazing what a pretty girl can achieve, without even trying.

So next thing I know Amelia has me by the arm, and she's dragging me back into the throngs of bachelors and bachelorettes, hopping a little every now and then, because she's so short, and she seems to be looking for somebody. "Come on, I'll get you a drink. Do you see a waiter with like kind of blue stuff in his hair? He's our waiter, you just tell him what you want and he brings it. Like anything. You just say, I'll have like a mango margarita and they bring it to you. I had one but I drank it too fast and I got one of those headaches in your nose. Can you believe that? Like is it not even noticeable to anybody that I'm, like, fourteen years old? And they're serving me margaritas? This is so stupid. Maybe now that you're here, Mom'll let me go home, I have so much homework to do. Hi, can we get another mango margarita?" She found the waiter with the blue hair, who was at the bar receiving thousands of drinks from about four bartenders. "Sure, absolutely, not a problem," says blue hair, and he turns back, calling suavely, "I need another Em Em."

56

Amelia grabs me by the arm and pulls me in the opposite direction now, still yakking. "Can you believe that?" she says, without even looking back. "So now they're giving out total alcoholic beverages to total teenagers, it's pathetic, someone should report these people. Rex is a complete drip, it's hilarious, you have to come meet him, what a jerk. How old do you think he is, forty or something? He's like got his *hand* down Polly's pants, I'm not kidding. What a sleezeball." And she shoves me into another room.

And there, sitting straight across the room, lit by moody little tubes of something approximating light, is Rex. Even in the dark you can tell that he has a tan, and he's leaning back on this big slick banquette, with six or seven people lounging around him, looking like Henry the Eighth, with one arm stretched out along the back of the banquette, and the other arm around Polly, his hand discreetly stuck down the back of her pants. It was spooky, really; he looked just like he looks in the movies, where he's always waving a giant weapon around and screaming, "Get in the truck!" But he had no weapon, and he looked real little. That's something I never considered when I thought about meeting movie stars . . . usually, when you see them? They're like four stories tall, on some giant movie screen somewhere. But when you meet them, in person? They're actually just sort of people-sized. Which makes the whole experience kind of surreal, if you haven't thought about things like that ahead of time. Plus, if the guy has his hand down your sister's pants, he looks significantly less like a movie star, and more like your average piece of shit asshole.

Not that Polly seemed to mind. She was leaning in and telling him some sort of secret, it looked like, and he grinned at what-ever it was she said, not like it was earth-shattering, but like it was a good minor joke, and he was enough of a mensch to give a small smile to this pretty girl less than half his age, while he meanwhile had his hand down her pants. He didn't actually look at her, but he was conscious enough of the social protocols that it was a definite smile. Mom, sitting across from the banquette, was deep in consultation with an enormous woman who was wearing something that looked like a giant green sack. She also had this major bead thing going on, strings and strings of them, big stone-like things, and crystals hanging off silver chains. She was seriously the only person in the room dressed worse than me, but Mom was hanging on her every word.

"Daria's pissed because Polly got to sit next to Rex," Amelia narrated. "She clearly doesn't know about the hand down the pants part of the deal. He tried it on me, and I shoved my elbow in his stomach. Then I acted like it was an accident so he couldn't get mad. What a creep. His last movie sucked anyway, I don't know why people think he's so hot. He smells, too: I think he went to the gym and then didn't take a shower. Isn't that gross? Plus all those guys who hang out with him? They're like total morons. I told Mom I wanted to go home like an hour ago— she keeps ignoring me. She thinks he's so great, she should try sitting next to him. I thought meeting a movie star would be cool but it is so totally no fun. How'd you get here, the subway? Let's go home."

"You think I could get some food first?" I really was hungry by this point, plus now that I had made it past all the different levels of security and screeners and fact checkers into the inner sanctum, I didn't want to just turn around and go home. Besides which, standing around and holding a huge drink in front of a bunch of adults who couldn't have cared less really does have a kind of weird thrill. Unfortunately, Amelia didn't have to fight her way in there past the gate keepers; she wasn't hungry and she was really bored. "We can go get some pizza," she said. "Come on. I got homework to do. I have a chemistry test tomorrow."

"Who's the lady in the green tent?" I asked.

"Philip, who cares? These people are creeps. I'm not kidding. This is no fun. We have to get out of here."

"You want to leave, and not tell Mom?"

"We'll tell one of the waiters to tell her. Or call her cell from the street. Come on. She won't care."

But a waiter with a giant sort of pu-pu platter of appetizers was heading across the room, toward the near end of the banquette, where the lady in the green tent and Mom were deep in consultation. "I've been eating pizza all week," I said. In retrospect, I wish I had just done whatever Amelia said. That is generally what I think about life anyway: Just do what the fourteen-year-old tells you, you know she's right. But I was hungry, and no one ever invited me to hang out with a movie star before. I wanted some pu-pu platter.

"Hey, Mom," I said, sliding into the chair next to her. Behind me, Amelia was hopping up and down, nervous. I pretended I didn't see her while I eyed the Chinese appetizers and bolted my margarita.

"Philip," Mom observed. "I'm surprised to see you, darling."

"Who's this?" said the woman in the tent, smiling. "Your son? You didn't tell me you had a son." This woman, whoever she was, had an incredible voice, musical and light, every syllable perfectly modulated with amusement and kindliness and intelligence. No kidding, it was startling, to hear this beautiful voice come out of a woman wearing a green tent, so I may have stared.

"His name is Philip," said Amelia. "He's come to take me home."

"Philip!" smiled the green ogress. "I'm Maureen. I'm Rex's producer." It was hard to see her face in the weird light, but her crystals and beads sparkled on her massive chest. The beads in particular were quite distracting, they were enormous, egg-sized pieces of amber, six or seven strands of them. The whole look was puzzling and a little magical.

"It's really nice to meet you," I said. "Um, can I have one of those?" I pointed to the pu-pu platter, which looked unbelievably delicious—golden egg rolls piled neatly on top of each other, little meats on little sticks, plump little dumplings. I can still remember the way it smelled, that's how hungry I was. My mouth was actually starting to water, so before anyone could say no, that's for Rex, I just grabbed some food with my fingers, and stuffed it into my mouth. It tasted delicious.

"Philip, *please,*" said Mom, handing me a napkin. Maureen the giant laughed, a beautiful bell of a laugh.

"Boys," said Maureen. "They're different from girls."

"Oh yes," said Mom. I thought, if this is the quality of the evening's conversation, no wonder Amelia is ready to bolt. But then Mom said, "Philip loves Kafka. Tell Philip about your great-grandmother, Maureen. Philip, you'll find this interesting."

Now, I can't remember the last time my mother worried about me finding anything interesting, and I also can't remember the last time my mother was interested in the works of Franz Kafka, so I knew immediately that this remarkable statement was for Maureen's benefit. But as long as they'd let me keep eating, I was more than willing to play along.

"Sure, Kafka's great," I said. "I wrote a paper on *The Castle* last month, for AP English."

"He's our deep thinker," Mom cooed.

"The heir apparent to, what was his name?" asked the ogress. She seemingly was not one of the people who cared about "The Terror of the New."

"Leo, Leo Heller," Mom smiled, gracefully dancing over the intellectual faux pas. Then she came out with a doozy. "Maureen's grandmother was Kafka's daughter!" she cried. "Franz Kafka was her great-grandfather. Can you imagine? Isn't that incredible?" She was all proud and giddy. Because I actually am the grand-child of a minor literary figure, or a majorly minor one at least, I do have some inkling of what it might be like to have a famous writer lurking in your pedigree somewhere. But, frankly, I was more than a little confused by all of this.

"Really?" I said, trying to sound impressed rather than incredulous. "Wow. Because, wow, I read, you know, that he died kind of, didn't he die, did he have kids? I didn't know that."

"My great-grandmother was a prostitute," Maureen said, with great dignity. "Most young girls of a certain class were, in Prague, at the turn of the century. Kafka was quite taken with her for a time."

"Wow," I said.

Exuberantly interested, suddenly, in Franz Kafka, my mother picked up the narrative thread of Maureen's saga. "He used to talk to her all the time about coming to America," Mom announced. "He wrote a novel about it, he was writing it, I mean—is that right?"

Mom looked to Maureen, who nodded benignly. "Yes, he was writing *Amerika*, he spoke to her about it all the time. She was full of his stories. When she became pregnant, she knew what she had to do. She didn't want to stay in Prague, there was nothing for her and her child there, it was a prison. And he could do nothing for her if she stayed. No one knew, of course, that he would soon be hailed as one of the greatest writers of the twentieth century. He had no money, he lived with his parents, you know the whole story."

"Oh yeah," I said.

"Philip, come on," whispered Amelia. She had no interest in Franz Kafka; at Garfield Lincoln, you don't do Kafka until your junior year. "We got to go."

I was still eating, though. "So they just came here. Wow. Huh. And then what happened?"

"Oh, it wasn't until long after that they realized," said Maureen. "In the thirties, it wasn't until then that my grandmother, and my great-grandmother, realized who Kafka was. My grandmother was a young woman, living in New York City, she came home one day from a café, where she had been meeting friends, and she had a copy of one of his books! Someone had given her a copy of *The Trial*, and she brought it home with her, and my great-grandmother saw his name, right there on the cover of the book, and she looked at my grandmother and said where did you get that? And my grandmother saw how upset she was and so she said why, what's the matter? What's the matter, Mama? And she told her. She was so stunned she just came right out and said it, she said, that man is your father."

"That is so amazing," said Mom. "I have goose bumps. And they never told anybody! That is even more astonishing."

"They tried," shrugged Maureen, bitterly accepting her fate. "No one believed them."

"So you're Kafka's, uh, great-granddaughter," I said. "That's pretty cool." I smiled politely. But Maureen narrowed her eyes. Now, it may be that occasionally a kind of skepticism sometimes creeps into my manner. I heard later, from Amelia, that in fact not only did I sound actively sarcastic, I also quite literally rolled my eyes before stuffing my mouth with some sort of fried shrimp thing. At which point she, of course, pinched my leg and started snickering. Such a surprise, neither Mom nor Kafka's gigantic offspring found any of this completely juvenile behavior from me and Amelia all that remarkably clever. "Kafka was one of the greatest minds of the Twentieth Century," the jolly green giant informed me, as if I needed to be informed, as if that were in fact what I was rolling my eyes about.

"I am . . . I love Kafka," I responded, my mouth full of gourmet Chinese food. Amelia, oh so helpfully, continued to snicker.

"Philip. Amelia. Please," whispered Mom, mortified.

"Never mind," laughed the giantess, waving her hand with gay dismissal of my hopeless social ineptitude. Instantly, Mom laughed with her, all that beauty queen charm eddying in new directions, right on cue. "Oh Philip, you're hopeless," she sparkled.

"And frankly I'm surprised to see you here, don't you have homework?" she asked, tipping her head toward the door.

"*I* have homework, Mom," said Amelia, renewing her mission to escape. "Philip said he'd take me home, you guys can stay, this is so total fun, but I really have to go study. I have a chemistry test tomorrow." This last bit was politely addressed to the magical ogress Maureen, who smiled benignly on the whole act. "It's just like a third of my grade and I *really* have to study." She was yanking on my arm, which I kind of enjoyed—it was annoying, I mean, but it was also nice to have someone paying attention to me for once, even under such bizarre circumstances. I stood up and grabbed a couple of dumplings and an egg roll to go.

"What an extraordinary girl," said Maureen. "Most girls her age would give their eye teeth to meet Rex, but I honestly don't think Amelia is all that impressed."

"Of course she's impressed! Good heavens, you should have seen us all when we got your call, what a flurry of nerves we were. And here's Philip, who decided to party crash I'm sure because he just couldn't stand his sisters having all the fun, isn't that right, Philip?" This sentence I could not even figure out, so I looked at my hostile mother and said, "What?" in an overtly teenage way that I was sure would work her last nerve.

Amelia butted in again. "He came because I called him, Mom," she lied. "I knew you wouldn't want me taking the subway by myself. This way you and Polly and Daria can stay, 'cause this is so cool. I really do think it's cool, I so love it, and please tell Rex I had such a cool time." She was laying it on thick now, with her hand on my sleeve, pulling. The ogress was watching her and, I have to say, she was not impressed. She was

64

kind of leaning back out of the light again, and all those crystals and giant beads were left sparkling on her chest, while her eyes were in shadow. It was quite peculiar, really. Amelia was, as usual, right; this party had a bad feel to it, as did Kafka's massive green great-granddaughter. I slammed back the rest of my mango margarita and stood. It was time to cut our losses and beat it out of there.

"Of course, I completely understand, Amelia. It's so lovely to see a girl with the right priorities," said the ogress, in her perfectly modulated voice. She held out her hand to Amelia, and gave her a friendly little good-bye shake.

"Rex!" she called, leaning back and smiling at him, "Amelia is saying good-bye."

The great man turned and looked at us. His hand was still down Polly's pants, and she seemed pretty happy, curled under his arm, but his interest had already started to roam. In retrospect, I have to say, I found this aspect of movie stars to be the most peculiar of all: They were bored with the girls they were screwing, even before they had screwed them. This guy had not even done my gorgeous and smart and fun sister Polly, who truly was gorgeous and smart and fun, in addition to being less than half his age. He planned to, and he was working on it, and he knew it was going to happen, maybe a couple times, even, and then he would get bored and dump her. But psychologically, he had already skipped the ride and gone straight to the boredom. And I'm pretty sure he didn't even know why. I don't know why everyone thinks it would be so great to be a movie star; aside from the fame and the money and everybody sucking up to you all the time, there doesn't seem to be a lot in it.

Anyway, as soon as the ogress tipped old Rex Wentworth off as to Amelia's escape plans, his future boredom with Polly peaked. She didn't even exist anymore. "No, come on, what are you talking about? Hey, where you going? Get over here, short stuff. You're not getting off that easy." Rex grinned, a really fun guy, just a swell fun camper, and he leaned out, away from Polly, and reached across the table to grab Amelia by the arm. In his swell-guy, fun-party mode, he was going to playfully grab her, I guess, make her sit in his lap, and tickle her, or something.

Amelia took a step back, so Rex's arm swung through midair.

Okay. A second before, old Rex couldn't have been less interested in what was going on at our end of the table; there were something like twelve people hanging on his every word, waiters coming and going, drinks and people laughing and talking about nothing, and he wasn't anymore interested in Amelia than he was in anything else. But boy, that little step back got to him. He looked at her, surprised, and then you could tell he really liked that. That she wouldn't let him grab her by the arm, and make her sit on his lap? He thought that just was so cool.

"Whoooa. Hey, what's that? Where you going? What's that, what's that?" He was on his feet now, reaching for her, forcing her to dodge him, making what looked like a game out of it. Amelia laughed at him, playing along, batting his arms away from her, and the hangers-on all started to laugh. Then old Rex grabbed Amelia and swung her in the air, just like somebody having a good time rough-housing with a little kid. She was kind of laughing and squirming, like a little kid, trying to keep it light, even though it wasn't light, the whole thing was creepy as hell. Rex started to whisper something in Amelia's ear, or maybe he was blowing in it, I don't know, she was smiling and wriggling and pushing his hands down, away from her chest, and he was holding on tight, enjoying every last bit of this. Polly was watching this with no expression on her face, looking more like Daria than like herself. Daria by this point was in the dark, you couldn't even see her, all the way down in Siberia at the far end of the banquette.

Someone snapped a picture. Rex swung Amelia into the air, grabbing her in between her legs, by her crotch, making like he was going to carry her off. And she bit him.

She did, she bit him. On the arm. And she must've bit him pretty hard, because he suddenly howled and dropped her, yelling, "Jesus Christ!" Everybody leapt to their feet and a couple of the hangers-on rushed to Rex's side, including Mom, even though Amelia was the one who got dropped on the floor.

"She bit me!" Rex yelled. "That little bitch bit me!"

Then there was a moment of huge chaos, people looking for napkins and ice water and smelling salts, during which Amelia rolled away from the table, got up, and took a few steps backward. She was mad and scared and totally confused; later on she told me that for a second there she thought maybe she could get arrested. For biting a movie star? That has to be against the law, at least in SoHo. She didn't mean to do it, she told me, but she just freaked, this total strange guy had his hands all over her, and she freaked. But for about ten seconds, at least, no one was paying attention to Amelia freaking. They were all obsessed with Rex, who was, no surprise, kind of a big baby.

"No, it's okay," he said, tough, like he had survived a gunshot wound, and wanted to make sure his men knew he could still lead the assault. "I don't think it broke the skin."

"You should have someone look at that, man, it could get infected," said one of his genius friends.

"It didn't break the skin, I said!" said Rex.

"It's gonna bruise, though. Wow, she really got you, man."

"Relax, it's not that big a deal," said Rex, magnanimous now that he had had his moment of making a big deal out of it. And then he looked over at Amelia, not very friendly, but ready to make up.

Amelia by this point was long gone. I was too. We ducked out during the mayhem and didn't stop running until we were on the Q Train, snaking our way back to the relative sanity of good old unhip, movie-star-less Brooklyn. We stopped for pizza and coke and, when we got home, I walked her through all the shit she missed in chemistry, while she was off taking meetings with agents and PR people, so that she had a shred of a chance of passing that test. Mostly I was walking her through all that chemistry so that we both could focus on something other than the disaster that was right around the bend. And sure enough, when Mom and Daria and Polly finally got home, Mom reamed us both. I've never seen her so mad; she was purple and kind of spitting, which Mom obviously never does because it isn't attractive, but she was really mad. At one point she threatened to ground us both, but we knew she'd never make that stick. The *New Yorker* was hitting the newsstands the next day, and drinks with Rex Wentworth was maybe the tip of the iceberg as far as their social life was concerned, so there was no use pretending to ground Amelia.

Later on, Polly snuck in to Amelia's room to tell her what happened after we left. I heard them giggling in there, so I snuck in too, and she told us how everybody had gone ballistic about Amelia and the fact that she was maybe unhinged, or had rabies or something. We all thought this was hilarious, but not as hilarious as the end of the story, when the mighty Rex decided that, after all, they *should* take him to the emergency room at St Vincent's, just to "make sure" he was all right.

My favorite part of the story involved Maureen Kafka, the green ogress, who really was all for dragging Amelia into court on grounds of assault—apparently you actually *can* get arrested for biting a movie star—until Daria pointed out that to a lot of people, it might actually look like Rex was the one who was doing the assaulting. Apparently that insinuation shut old Maureen up, and it also seems to have turned the tide on the let's-arrest-Amelia issue.

And it's the only part of the whole mess that I was sorry to have missed. Daria doesn't say much, but she's no idiot. None of my sisters are.

CHAPTER FOUR

"Rough-housing with the stars got a little rough Tuesday night at W, where pint-sized It Girl Amelia Heller took a bite out of Rex Wentworth," claimed Rush & Molloy the very next day. There was a huge photograph of Rex swinging Amelia through the air right before she bit him, and an unnamed source giving it up that Rex had to go to the hospital, although there would be no charges filed.

Meanwhile, everyone in America was paging through their *New Yorker*, and stopping to look at a spectacularly fun picture of three gorgeous redheaded teenagers, dressed in green, dancing and looking like fairies or princesses or mermaids or whatever your own particular female fantasy might be. Under the picture they ran the clever cutline, "Daria, Polly and Amelia Heller, granddaughters of lit giant Leo Heller, on the verge of their own breed of greatness. Herb Lang photographs the terrific trio in a loft on Spring Street, high above the isle of Manhattan, site of their grandsire's many triumphs." Cool, huh? But that old La Aura, the hair stylist, was dead right: Nobody really cared about who our literary grandfather was. What they really cared about was: "Which is the one who bit Rex Wentworth?"

School was hell. Everyone was screaming at me all the time. "Did your sister really bite Rex Wentworth? What's that about? Is she crazy? Awesome, man! Were you there? Did you see it? Why'd she bite him? Your sisters are hot. Are they all like, going out with movie stars now?" All the teachers spent the whole day digging me out from gangs of kids I didn't even know. I mean, the Garfield Lincoln School isn't exactly Stuyvesant; there are only sixty kids per grade level, so you pretty much know everybody in the high school by the time you're a junior. But kids I never even heard of were everywhere all of a sudden, swarming all over me like a pack of rats.

Polly actually made an appearance at school that day, because who in their right mind would miss this spectacular opportunity to be the center of so much attention? She totally enjoyed the whole ruckus, wearing her fishnets, posing in the hallways, laughing and tossing her new spiky do about like a total pro. She was brilliant. You really do have to give it up to Polly; she makes being famous look like more fun than anybody I ever saw. I mean, she was having a great time, until it sank in that the picture was losing first position to the biting incident, as reported in the *Daily News*. I passed behind her, in the middle of the chaos, and heard her explaining, in the most discreet terms, that it wasn't Amelia who was the center of the Rex Wentworth event, actually. It was *her*. "She didn't bite Rex— god, that whole thing is just, you know, the newspapers are always *sooo* full of shit," she bubbled, in a kind of edgy way. "They were just horsing around. He's really fantastic. I talked to him for something like three hours, Amelia was *leaving*. That whole biting thing was a total nonevent. He's not even upset about it! I talked to him, this morning he called me, we're going to dinner tomorrow? And he didn't even mention it." This last bit, obviously, was a terrific whopper.

Amelia's life was a disaster. She has a bit of a temper, as I've mentioned, so all the kids surrounding her and screaming questions about why she bit Rex Wentworth set her off about every two minutes or so. She never got to take that chemistry test; there was so much chaos in the chemistry lab they finally told her she had to go to Dean Morton's office. The chemistry teacher, Dr Nussbaum, was trying to explain to her that she could make the test up another day but that she needed to go see the dean and sort out the controversy. Amelia told me this later; she rather obsessively focused on being told that she had to go "sort out the controversy," because that struck her as being an especially stupid thing for old Nussbaum to say. And in fact, if you think about it, it *is* a pretty stupid thing to say to a four-teen-year-old girl who was being harassed by absolutely everybody in her high school, because she had bitten a movie star who was trying to feel her up. Anyway, at that point Amelia was so frustrated she started to cry, and then argue about how hard she had studied, and then she started babbling on even more, apparently, about how she's missed so much school and it wasn't her fault and were they all a bunch of fucking idiots, blaming her for this mess?

I'm not being euphemistic; she did in fact call Dr Nussbaum a "fucking idiot," which sort of finished off the question of whether or not she was going to the dean's office.

73

By the time Amelia got down to Morton's office, the whole situation—gorgeous redheads, the *Daily News,* a bitten movie star, screaming students everywhere—had exhausted the school so much that the dean instantly decided to simply send Amelia home. Which was not, technically, a brilliant solution, as the front sidewalk of the school was positively lousy with photographers, and had been since ten in the morning. So when Amelia stormed out the front door, alone, at noon, there were thirty or forty of them waiting there, crawling all over each other and ready to commit multiple acts of homicide on the off-chance that it might net them an out-of-focus photograph of the fourteen-year-old girl who bit Rex Wentworth.

I could see all of it from the third floor, where I was trapped in a Spanish lab. That dipshit Morton hadn't even arranged for someone to come pick her up; it says in our files that we're authorized to walk ourselves home, but wouldn't you think he'd have a half a clue?

The paparazzi went haywire. I mean, as upsetting as it had been to be mobbed by our fellow students all morning, they were rank amateurs compared to these bozos. They descended as one, shouting questions, grabbing, pushing, shoving their cameras right into her face, acting really like she was some sort of stupid animal in a zoo, instead of just a little kid. Amelia stood on the front steps of the high school, frozen, and then she totally just disappeared. I mean, one minute she was there, and the next minute she wasn't. It was like they had eaten her.

I bolted. I mean, what else are you going to do, just sit there and watch your sister get eaten? Señor Martine (his real name is Mr Martin, but he makes us call him Señor Martine) shouted something at me in Spanish, but I was truly in no mood. I made it outside in maybe ten seconds, but the situation was already way out of control. The shoving was unbelievable, it was like being at some insane British soccer match. Photographers were pushing and shoving and cursing wildly, and I had to literally pull at arms and legs and throw myself up against somebody to get him out of the way, just so I could clamber one or two inches further into the onion layers of photojournalists who had encrusted themselves around my little sister. People were screaming, "Fuck you, fucking asshole, get in line, fucker, hey who is this fucker?" while I pushed and shoved and yelled, "Amelia! Hey, Amelia, where are you?"

By the time I got to her she was just curled up in a little ball. Seriously, she was like all folded in on herself, a little turtle of a person, crouched down over her feet, her arms crossed over her head, down on the cement sidewalk. You got to wonder what's wrong with those guys, why they thought this would be a cool picture to take, a little kid so scared she's doing something that spooky. I mean, I wondered that about a minute later, but while I was surrounded by the crazy people with her, I was mostly just screaming at them to get away. Amelia was crying and hitting at me, because she didn't want to move, that's how freaked out she was, but I was pretty sure they'd just start stomping on her if I left her there, so I started dragging her back toward the front door of the school. They of course kept taking pictures and shoving at both of us. It was a ridiculous mess.

By the time we got back through the glass doors and into the security lobby, a whole bunch of teachers and students was gathering. Meanwhile, all those journalists were like in a feeding frenzy or something; it was like once they got started on the craziness they didn't know how to turn it off, so they actually tried to come in after us. Which finally turned into a kind of a showdown. Señor Martine, Dean Morton and Luke, the black guy who sits at the front desk and makes you sign in if you're tardy, charged the mob and started yelling at them.

"This is private property! I am asking you to leave! You are not allowed entrance to this building! This is a private high school!" yelled Morton. He was actually holding his arms out, sort of like he was being crucified, but more like he thought those photographers were actually chickens or pigeons or something he could just shoo away. "If you do not leave this property immediately, we are calling the police!"

This was not good enough for Luke. "Motherfuckers! Get out of here, you fuckheads! The police are coming to kick your ass—get out—GET OUT." He grabbed one guy, a kind of short, fat guy with a big beard and a huge lens, who was shooting wildly at anything and everything.

"Don't you fucking touch me, man!" the short photographer yelled. "I can sue you! That's assault!"

"You take another picture of these kids, I'll show you what assault looks like," Luke told him, sticking his finger in the guy's face. Meanwhile, two other photographers were deep in it with Morton.

"The police are coming. You are not permitted in this building," Morton droned. These idiots started to argue about freedom of the press.

"You want to do that? Show these kids that the press can be silenced? What's that teaching them? This is a free society.

76

This isn't fucking China, we're covering a legitimate story." Meanwhile the rest of the gang behind them kept clicking away.

It really was enough to make you sick. Luckily Luke is rather large, and when he gets mad enough to yell it's rather undeniable. "GET OUT OF HERE," he yelled. "I DON'T GIVE A SHIT ABOUT FREEDOM OF THE PRESS, YOU SHITHEAD, YOU THINK I WON'T HIT YOU, YOU TRY IT, MAN, JUST TRY ONE MORE STEP IN THIS BUILDING, THESE ARE MY KIDS. *MY* KIDS, MOTHERFUCKER."

Dean Morton cringed a little at that; obviously he was not thrilled that Luke was cursing so freely in front of all us fragile teenagers, but there was no denying that it was an impressive performance. And all of us fragile teenagers were definitely stoked that our security guard was willing to slug it out with all of the representatives of the free press that New York could spare that morning. Truth be told I think Morton was impressed too. In any event, he didn't say anything, and after they managed to get off another few hundred shots, the so-called protectors of all American freedoms finally took off.

Everybody got sent back to class and I got sent to the nurse's office, because I had a scraped-up face and a split lip. By the time they patched me up, Amelia had already been sent home, which really pissed me off. I mean, they couldn't wait and let us go together? But people don't think of these things. Anyway, the next day we all got the beginnings of a clue as to how serious the shit was that Amelia had stepped in. The many pictures taken by all those protectors of a free press were really quite impressive. And they printed all of them. Pictures of Amelia screaming, Amelia hitting photographers, Amelia kicking photographers, Amelia kicking me. Amelia curled up in a little ball on the sidewalk; they printed that one, too. A couple of those geniuses actually had video of the whole thing, which they showed on three local news shows, *Entertainment Tonight* and CNN, which, due respect to CNN, but there was in fact a war going on in Iraq at the time; you had to wonder why they actually cared about some kid who hit a couple of photographers in Brooklyn.

In any event, they showed the footage on television quite a bit, and the story that went along with the visuals went something like this: "Pint-sized It Girl Amelia Heller is burning through her fifteen minutes as fast as she can. Recently showcased in the *New Yorker* magazine, the fourteen-year-old heiress to a major American lit legacy has been spending her nights partying with the likes of film actor Rex Wentworth, who she allegedly bit in a scuffle at a Manhattan hot spot last week. Here she lets the paparazzi get a taste of her teen angst. An unidentified fellow student comes to her aid . . ."

The unidentified fellow student, that's me.

Polly and Daria were livid. Their moment in the sun had been completely obliterated by Amelia's shenanigans. Our home life now veered between long stretches of sullen silence and endless hours of screeching female rage.

"This is not about you, Amelia. None of this was ever supposed to be about *you*," Daria would hiss.

"I said, I didn't want to do it in the first place!"

"Do you know, do you have any idea of how long it's taken me to get my career to this point? Do you even have half a clue—"

"Oh, *what* career?"

"Look, people say that no publicity is bad publicity." This halfway optimistic opinion, or something like it, coming from Polly.

"People who have never had this kind of spectacularly shitty publicity say that! And it's not my fault! None of this is my fault! All of it is her fault, and she doesn't even care!"

"I care! I want to go to school! I can't even go to school, everybody hates me, and I hate everybody!"

This was occasionally punctuated by a series of slamming doors.

And in fact, she *couldn't* go to school—Collette called, the first morning, and put everyone in lockdown. Nobody was allowed to leave the apartment, and nobody was allowed to talk to anybody, either. Which put everyone in an even worse mood. The phone would ring off the hook until Mom finally answered it, and then she would hold the receiver tightly to her ear, cover her face with one hand and melodramatically whisper, "No comment." Then, infinitely bereaved, she would set down the receiver. It was quite an act and, as far as I could tell, gained us not one shred of legitimacy from the reporters on the evening news, who just kept reporting, snidely, "No comment from the girl's family. Looks like they're trying to keep this under wraps."

And then the anchor-idiot would say, "Little too late for that!" And they'd all chuckle. I mean, you really wanted to blow your brains out.

After three days of this I came home from school—the lockdown only counted for girl members of the family; nobody out there really seemed to give a shit, frankly, about the unidentified fellow student—to find Collette holding a major powwow around our kitchen table. In spite of how crucial she had become to everyone's lives over the past six weeks, this was in fact the first time I had ever laid eyes on Collette, and she was, frankly, pretty impressive. She wore one of those perfect suits—tight, curvy, both sexy and severe—and she was drinking ice water, and crossing her legs to one side, so that anyone who entered the room could see right off what great legs she had.

"All right, the fact is, Maureen Piven got out in front of us in every media outlet," she announced. "She had them all in her pocket within twenty-four hours, caught us absolutely flat-footed. She's brilliant at this, absolutely flawless. I would have warned you ahead of time not to take her on, but I had no idea Amelia would do anything as stupid as *biting* Rex Wentworth."

"He was—"

"Save it, Amelia. The damage is done." Collette clearly was not interested in discussion at this point, but the level of anxiety was pretty high. Mom leaned forward, wringing her hands.

"But why can't we even defend ourselves? It's not doing any good. We don't say anything and it just keeps getting worse and worse and worse, what they're saying about us, in the newspapers, on the television—"

"I know it feels that way," Collette nodded, not terribly sympathetic. "But you don't want to provoke Maureen any further. This is completely personal to her. Karl Rove could take lessons from Maureen, when she's in a mood like this. Did you guys do anything to piss her off? Besides biting Rex, did you say anything or do anything that I need to know about? Because we have maybe one shot to save this situation. I need to know everything."

Amelia glanced at me, worried, then looked away. I looked down. We were fast, but not fast enough. Mom caught the look, thought for a moment, then another moment. She can be stupid about some stuff, but on other stuff she's crackerjack. "Philip was rude to her," she said. Daria and Polly turned and stared at me. Amelia kept looking at the floor.

"I wasn't," I said. "I barely said two words."

"You were rude. She was telling us about her family, a story about her family, and Philip—"

"She said her great-grandfather was Franz Kafka!" I said.

Amelia's face twitched. She was trying not to laugh. Daria caught it.

"You're a moron, Philip," said Polly. "What were you even doing there, anyway? No one invited you."

"I was fucking polite! I was pretty fucking polite, if you ask me, about such a spectacular piece of bullshit!"

"He was polite about it, he really was, considering," Amelia chimed in.

"No one was fooled, by either of you," Mom snorted.

Really, the whole thing was ludicrous. It was suddenly my fault there were thirty crazed reporters in front of our building waiting to tear us all to pieces, because I didn't say, "Oh really?" with enough conviction when a giantess in a green dress told me she was the direct descendant of a hooker who had once slept with Franz Kafka.

"Oh my god," said Daria. "That's what happened? That's why they went after us? Because Philip was—"

"I wasn't anything!" I yelled. "I hardly exist around here, you can't dump this on me!"

"It doesn't matter," sighed Collette. "If that's what's behind it, the damage is done. She's notoriously sensitive, so if she thought Philip was playing her she was going to punish everybody sooner or later. It's just as well that we got it over with."

"Is it over with?" Polly asked, raising an eyebrow. "'Cause it sure doesn't look like that from where I sit. We're all under house arrest."

"You let the story have its natural life," Collette explained, standing and pacing now, like a drill sergeant. "I couldn't have you talking to the press because they want nothing more than to keep it all going—statements from you, statements from Rex, statements from Maureen—and she's just too good at this. You go to war with Maureen Piven, you're all dead before you've even started."

"You mean we're not? Dead?" said Daria. This was the news she was waiting for. And Collette sighed, apparently at our collective stupidity.

"No," she said. "Not quite yet."

Collette's opening gambit, as it turned out, was to drag the two offending dimwits into the belly of the beast, whereupon both dimwits were expected to throw themselves on the beast's mercy. I'm not kidding, that was the entire plan. We didn't even call ahead; she just tossed us into the back of her town car and the next thing I knew we were standing around in the waiting room of the swankest offices I had ever seen. I mean, this place was spectacular: Leather chairs, walnut paneling, a little Jackson Pollock action on one wall and a full southern exposure of Central Park on the other. And that was the *waiting* room. A skinny guy in a white shirt and tie sat in a tiny cubicle around the corner; he had no expression on his face and kept telling people on his headset to hold, while he simultaneously listened to Collette explain that Maureen would see us.

"But she doesn't know you're coming," he observed, with a kind of expressionless skepticism.

"No," said Collette, smiling politely at this little shit. "Nevertheless, as I said, I'm fairly sure that she will see us."

"Hold please," he said into his headset. "Take a seat, please," he told Collette.

Since she was already in a power struggle with him, Collette opted to stand, but Amelia and I slouched in that leather furniture obediently. I kept trying to catch Amelia's eye in some insane attempt to establish a kind of Vulcan mind-mold so that we might have something resembling a game plan when we went in and faced the Ogress, but no matter what I did she wouldn't look at me. "Knock it off, Philip," Collette told me, the third time I tried to get Amelia to communicate with me without actually saying anything. She clearly didn't want us cooking anything up. We were just supposed to go in there and suck up.

Which I was fairly sure was never going to happen, since Kafka's giant offspring kept us waiting just long enough for me to think this might turn into one of those stories about how they made you wait for two days and then said oh by the way that person isn't even here! We were there a long time; and then we were there even longer. The sun was setting gloriously across Central Park, in fact, when suddenly there she was, herself, in a purple tent this time—mauve let's say—again with those giant amber stones glittering on her chest.

"I'm so sorry to have kept you waiting," the giantess sighed. "It's just been a nightmare, I've been on conference calls about three different films all afternoon." Then she smiled happily, as if we were the most delightful interruption she could ask for on this busy afternoon. "It's so good of you to come by."

"Of course we wanted to come," Collette smiled back.

"Amelia, the picture, in the *New Yorker*! Wonderful. You must be so pleased," said Maureen as she opened the door to her office.

"Oh, sure, yeah. Oh! The picture. Yeah, it's good, I guess," said Amelia, completely confused. Who could blame her? They were being so nice. The whole thing was so weird you didn't know what to say.

"No. It's better than good. Herb Lang. He's a genius. He did one of my clients years ago: It absolutely put her on the map. It made her. As I'm sure it's going to make you," Maureen nodded.

I had the total urge to say "make her what?" but Amelia stepped on my foot. So instead I said, "Ooooow, you stepped on my foot, jerk." Which finally got Amelia to look at me, and shake her head and roll her eyes like, stop it, you moron. At which point apparently Collette knew that she'd better get us in and out of there fast, so she just launched in.

"We wanted to come by and see if there was anything we could do—any of us—about this terrible, terrible misunderstanding with Rex," Collette began. "Amelia feels just terrible about it."

"Oh," said Maureen, taking this in as if it were entirely surprising information instead of the complete reason we were even there. She looked at Amelia, a little snake for a moment appearing behind those sincere, kind eyes.

Amelia jumped a little bit, startled, as I was, by the sudden appearance of the snake. But she got right with the picture. "I'm really sorry, I really am," she said. "I totally did not mean to bite anybody. Wow. I just don't even know how it happened. And Philip and I also, you know, if you thought that we thought it was stupid that your great grandfather was Kafka? I so hope you didn't think that. Because it is really awesome, that you, know, that you—Philip was saying—"

It was clearly time for me to chime in. "Yeah, I think it's cool, I really do," I said.

Kafka's great-granddaughter thought about this, without responding, and suddenly turned to look out the window. There was a kind of creepy silence that settled in, while this enormous woman considered the intricacies of apologies, and what it means to make them, and what it means to accept them, and how long you should wait, in fact, before doing something so pedestrian. No one said anything. Just below, in Central Park, a couple of little kids suddenly bolted into the fading light of the sunset, and ran recklessly down the path, leaving their Jamaican nannies calling after them. They were all laughing, you could see it; the air was so clear, you could see them laugh. I totally wished I was out there.

"That story is very precious to me," Maureen said. "I don't tell it to everyone."

"Well, no, I mean, I totally understand that," I said. Which okay, that wasn't what I meant, what it sounded like I meant? It's just the whole thing was so stupid. "I mean, Kafka is really a great writer and it is awesome that he's, you know."

Collette leaned forward, crossing her legs fast, like a pair of scissors. "Are you cast yet, on *The Fury of the Titans*?" she asked pleasantly.

"I saw you on the news, Philip," Maureen announced.

At this point I was ready to blow my own brains out. I mean, I could not follow any of this. The only thing that was clear to me was that I was completely tanking and that the only safe bet now was to say as little as possible. I kept my head down, figuring that she hadn't asked a direct question—maybe that meant I didn't have to respond.

"Philip was on television?" said Collette, surprised.

"It's cute, he feels protective of his little sister," Maureen said. "Isn't that what he was doing when she got attacked by the photographers?"

This floored Collette, it really did. "What do you mean?" she asked, curious.

"He's in all the pictures," Maureen informed her. That giant ogress with the magic stones on her chest was literally the only person who had figured out that the "unidentified student" was me. Collette looked back and forth between Maureen and Amelia, still not getting it.

"He saved me," said Amelia, simple.

"Yes, it was very sweet, very sweet," said Maureen. "I have a brother, too. He sells auto parts out of a storefront in Astoria. Every other year he sends me a screenplay that he's written with one of his friends, every one of them worse than the next. My sister is married and living on Long Island. I hear from her when she needs money. But she's very sweet too. She has two hideously ugly daughters, they both want to be actresses. Do you want to be an actress, Amelia?"

Amelia squirmed like a six-year-old. "Not particularly," she said.

"No?" smiled Maureen Piven, all those stones winking on her chest. "I thought everybody did."

"I heard you were from Long Island, I didn't realize you still had family there," Collette purred, as if we were at a cocktail party. "They must be proud of you."

"I don't often speak to them," Maureen purred back. "The distance. You know. Where you're from and where you're going. They don't really mix."

"How did you manage it? I mean, how did you get from there—to here!" Collette wondered, astonished. "I've always wanted to ask, if it's not too personal."

"I stalked Sidney Lumet until I got him alone," Ogress laughed coyly, charmed to be asked to narrate the seminal event of her life's story. "He was waiting for a cab and I made a complete fool of myself, insisting that I wanted to work for him, that I'd do anything! He absolutely brushed me off but he'd had a couple drinks and I was pretty sure he wouldn't even remember what he actually said. So I showed up at his office the next day, and started making coffee. It took a week for everybody to realize he hadn't actually hired me, but by then it was too late, I was indispensable."

"You started by making coffee for Sidney Lumet!" Collette bubbled, elegant.

"There are worse ways to start in this business, as I think you know," Maureen noted. The two women laughed one of those "boy do we ever" laughs.

"It sounds like you were a totally different person," Collette smiled, both sucking up and narrating. "You really transformed yourself, didn't you?"

"Just like *The Metamorphosis*," I said.

We were all there to suck up, right? And she was the one all hung up on the Kafka thing. They all stared at me, like I was suddenly speaking a foreign language.

"You know, *The Metamorphosis*," I said. "The guy wakes up one morning and he's a giant bug, and no one in his family knows how to talk to him anymore?"

"Really?" said Maureen, unfriendly as hell.

"You haven't read it?" I asked.

"No, I missed that one."

"It's pretty good."

"I'm sure it is."

"I just meant, you know, you were like, a different person and your family understood you and then you transformed yourself and now you're like totally mysterious to them. That's all," I concluded lamely.

"Thank you for the exegesis," she said.

Okay, I happen to go to the Garfield Lincoln School, and I'm also the grandson of Leo Heller so I actually do know what "exegesis" means. "You're welcome," I told her, with a slightly edgy tone, to match her own.

"Is this you?" Collette cooed. "Look, Amelia, it's picture of Maureen with Ron Howard!" I was suddenly feeling like I was stuck in *The Castle*.

"Hey Collette, you know, I kind of have a lot of homework," Amelia said. "This has been really fun and I'm so glad to see you, Maureen, and I'm really really sorry for biting Rex and I'm especially sorry if I said anything that bugged you that night in the bar, and Philip is too, but we need to get home, okay, Maureen?" Even though she was saying all the right things, Amelia sounded even worse than me. She has no idea how to spin anything. Next to Maureen and Collette we sounded like a couple of rude teenagers, and the fact is, we were there to prove that we *weren't* rude teenagers. I actually saw Collette raise her eyes to the heavens for a split second. I couldn't say that I blamed her.

But Maureen was suddenly in a forgiving mood. She smiled, half to herself, and leaned back, letting the side-lighting play on her giant beads on her giant chest. I swear, it is no wonder I thought of her in the light of *The Metamorphosis*; she really did look like a giant cockroach, with all those beady eyes.

"Amelia means—"

"It's all right, Collette, I know what Amelia means. You too, Philip. No hard feelings. But perhaps you'd better go before either one of you opens your mouth again." She twinkled at us, benign. Who could keep track of this? I was getting whiplash. But the offer to leave came none too soon.

"Yeah, thanks," I said. "I really do like Kafka, I really do."

"Good," she told me.

And everything would have been fine if we had just gotten our butts out of there before Rex showed up. Really. We were out of there; we were all about to stand up and wave goodbye to this whole hideous interchange when the door swung open and the king himself walked in.

"Oh hey, sorry, Maureen, no no, stay, you know you can use

the place whenever you want, I just didn't know you were in here," he said, giving up the fact that this was his office, not hers, before he even saw that in fact Maureen was using his office to have a sit-down with the kid who bit him, along with her dorky brother. But of course we all turned to stare at him, and then he saw Amelia, who was unfortunately wearing a teeny little turquoise tank top over black jeans in which she looked awesome.

"Oh hi," Rex said. "Yeah, hi."

She didn't say anything. She just turned white.

"Nice picture. I mean, the thing in the *New Yorker*, that's . . ." Rex trailed off. He was totally giving himself away. Amelia looked at the ground.

"Thanks," she said. That was it. She was not too nice about it, either.

"Amelia and her brother came by to apologize about what happened at W the other night," Maureen narrated, expression-less. I thought it was weird because she had been so nice to us and now here was Rex and she was suddenly a block of ice.

"Yeah, whatever," said Rex. "Just finish it up, huh? I mean, it's okay for you to use this place, but I wish you'd clear it with me ahead of time." Maureen looked at him, sort of like a mother who is thinking about whether or not slapping her own kid is maybe a good idea. He looked back at her, like one of the shitty kids on the playground who's getting off on being a jerk. "Is there a problem?" he asked.

"Not at all," said Maureen, pulling out that dazzling smile. "As I said, we were just finishing up."

"Whatever," he said, and he grabbed the doorknob and turned to go.

And just as he did he snuck another look at Amelia. I saw him do it. And it was so clear, just in that one little sneaky look, that the asshole had the hots for her. I've seen it enough times, it's not like I'm likely to miss it. That guy was forty years old, at least, and he had the hots for my fourteen-year-old sister.

But anyway, then he was gone and we were going. So Collette reached over and held Maureen's hand meaningfully for a few seconds, smiling at her sincerely.

"I really appreciate your helping us through this," she said.

"Of course," said Maureen. I reached for the door.

"There's just one thing," she added. We all turned. Maureen, looking out the window, sighed. "It's wonderful that you came by and apologized," she noted. "But this really is so private. And the whole . . . event . . . wasn't private, was it? Was it, Amelia?"

"What?" said Amelia.

"I just mean," smiled Maureeen, "for an event *that* public—the apology will have to be public too, won't it?"

CHAPTER FIVE

The next thing we knew, Daria, Polly, and Amelia were on *Regis and Kelly*.

This took an endless amount of time to work out, even though it happened by the end of the week. Collette was on the phone with everybody in town for hours, but at first most of them were so mortally afraid of pissing Rex and Maureen off that none of them would touch us. So even though Maureen was the one who had insisted that the apology had to be public in the first place, it was apparently impossible to set up a public interview because that might make Maureen and Rex more angry, even though Maureen was the one who wanted it. It was like a Möbius strip of stupid logic that went on and on and on until almost out of the blue the whole situation flipped on its head and what we had was an exclusive on *Regis and Kelly*, the perfect chance to get those girls out in front of the public so that everyone could see that these were really very sweet and adorable teenagers, nothing like what had been reported by other media outlets. And, during this exclusive, Amelia would find the perfect opportunity to apologize to Rex, on the air, for biting him.

By this point, we were all just doing whatever Collette told us. Of course we were; we were in deep shit and the only way out, seemingly, was to let that shapely barracuda call the shots. Everyone even let her pick out the outfits they would wear, which for Amelia turned out to be a subtle variation on the blue jeans/T-shirt ensemble she had on in the Herb Lang photo. "We want them falling in love with you because you're such a great kid," she announced. "You need to wear something simple. No one likes a sexy fourteen-year-old."

"Please, this is America," Amelia observed.

"Cool it, Amelia," Collette countered, without blinking. "This isn't brain surgery. Regis and Kelly will just be lobbing softballs to you. Don't fuck it up."

There was not even any trouble when I announced that I was going, too. For an instant I thought there might be, because Polly and Daria and especially Mom were still really annoyed at me, having fully given themselves over to the notion that this was all my fault, because I let my voice get a little snippy when Maureen told that ridiculous whopper about Kafka. But before they could get started, Collette shut them up. "It's cute, he feels protective of his little sister," she noted, parroting the one insight she had gleaned from Maureen Piven herself. "It's wholesome, it's what you want to be selling right now. If he misses a day of school, is that a problem?"

"I don't know," said Mom, acting like this is the biggest problem she ever heard. "I'll have to call the school and look into it."

"Amelia never goes to school anymore, and you have to look into it when I want to skip a day?" I ask.

"Don't push your luck, Philip; I *said* I would look into it."

"Don't you have anything brown?" Collette suddenly asked, from inside Polly's closet.

"I'm not wearing brown on television, I'd rather be dead," said Polly.

"If you don't do what I tell you, you will be," Collette informed her.

"I have a brown silk Prada she can wear," Daria volunteered.

"The sleeves on that are a disaster," Polly sulked.

"Go get it," said Collette. Which Daria did. And Polly wore it, and looked great, even though it was brown, and the sleeves were really hideous.

They sent us a limo to take us to the taping. By that point the crowds of photographers had whittled themselves down to perhaps a half-dozen, but the ones left all had a lot more information and innuendo to throw about, so the ten-yard dash to the car was peppered with yelped questions about Polly's sex life, Daria's frustrated ambitions, and Amelia's temper. It was really interesting, what you heard was a kind of demented and thinned-out version of the truth—I mean, it sounded enough like the truth, with a kind of nasty spin on it, by people who didn't know anything, but must have heard something, from somebody who clearly didn't like us and wanted to hurt us. So by the time we slammed the limo door on those boneheads, all of us were a little spooked.

When we got to the studio Lynn the booker turned out to be a kind of skinny version of Maureen, poised and lovely and completely untrustworthy. She cooed politely over all the girls and handed us off to a PA, who was told to take Polly and Daria and Amelia to hair and makeup, and to dump me and Mom and Collette in the green room. The studio was big, or at least backstage was big, with long colorless hallways which turned back and forth and cut through each other with a kind of mazelike dedication to incoherence. Seriously, we just followed this person through one tunnel after another, to places that seemed less and less comprehensible; there were no windows and hardly any art on the walls, so there were just no signposts anywhere, and nothing seemed to have a relation to anything else. In all honesty, I think that PA was lost—I'm pretty sure we passed the same potted ficus three times—and everyone in my little tribe was getting even more tense because we were late to begin with. So no one was talking—we were all kind of just moving wordlessly through these blank hallways, hoping against hope that the silent PA actually did know where she was—when who should show up, literally, to save us, but La Aura.

Seriously, we turned a corner and there she was, hauling down one of those hallways, a big bag of hair junk slung over her shoulder, headed right for us.

"Hey, it's the *New Yorker* redheads!" she crowed. "How you doing, girls? Made it onto *Regis and Kelly*, you're coming up in the world! How you doing, how you doing, Amelia, I read about you biting that shithead Rex Wentworth, what a riot! I never laughed so hard in my life! You look great! Philip, how you doing? You need a haircut, man, doesn't anybody ever cut your hair?"

I've never been so glad to see anybody in my life.

"What are you doing back here, hair and makeup are right next to the stage. Have you met Regis and Kelly yet? They're real nice, but stay away from Lynn the booker, she's like the cunt from hell. Oh, sorry, I guess I shouldn't say that in front of teenagers, sorry, man, I am so sorry!" And then she roared with laughter, and kept talking. "Come on, let me get you to makeup—yeah, they called me up, said can you come in and do those girls from the *New Yorker* piece, the one who bit Rex Wentworth, and I was like can I do them! I love those girls, I did that shoot! Have you seen Herb, or Stu, since the picture came out? That Stu, what a piece of work, but boy the photo looks fantastic, you guys look fucking amazing." She just blathered on, turned us around, and led us back to the real world. I'm telling you, that woman is sensational. I'd marry her, if I were thirty years older, and she were straight.

Once we were back on track, with La Aura leading the way, people visibly relaxed, and we all remembered what Collette's orders were, with regard to the one big happy wholesome family act we were supposed to be putting on. Daria was the first one to get back on the family portrait plan; she reached over and took Amelia's hand, just to hold it while they were walking down the hall. Which made Amelia look up at her, surprised— then, even, for a second, grateful. Daria looked at her, out of the corner of her eye, and smiled. Which, I think, reminded Mom to do her part, too. "You look fantastic, Polly. I think that dress is lovely," she said.

"Thanks, Mom," said Polly.

We finally reached the hair and makeup room, and La Aura

shooed Daria and Polly and Amelia into the inner sanctum. Now we really were late, and the makeup people were a little frantic, because they had to do all three of them at once, and they were shorthanded. "Where have *you* been?" somebody snarled at La Aura. "Kelly needed a trim, and there was no one to do it."

"She's got her own person; come on, I was out saving your guest redheads," La Aura answered, still cheerful. "Some PA was taking them to Nebraska! Seriously, I was down near the parking garage, this kid is wandering around like Moses in the desert, hasn't got a clue where hair and makeup is. You can start on the little one, her hair doesn't need much more than a scrunch or two . . ." And she was off, spraying Polly with some sort of spritzer bottle full of product while she eyeballed that snaky cut.

I watched for a minute, before being ushered back into the tunnels in search of the green room. All three of them had people working on them, but Daria was still holding Amelia's hand. Amelia clearly liked it—at least she was holding Daria's hand back—and she leaned back into her makeup chair for a minute, and closed her eyes. I knew she was scared; she hadn't said six words in the car on the way over. For all the rush to blame Philip, I don't think Amelia ever once thought any of this was anybody's fault but her own. Even though she never wanted to be an It Girl in the first place, it was hard to mistake the fact that all the messes really started with her. And she knew, because Collette had drilled her, that she had to say the right thing right now. On television, in front of millions of people. No fucking up. That was the only way out, for any of us.

Then Daria leaned in and whispered something in Amelia's ear. Amelia smiled. Polly looked over, curious, watching this.

Daria said something else. Amelia opened her eyes, and bit her lower lip. Polly knew something was going on, so she leaned in to listen, too. It was just almost less than a moment, five seconds or something, all three of them huddled together in between the ministrations of all the hair and makeup elves. All four walls of this dinky room were mirrored, so the reflection did that strange thing and just went on forever, five thousand versions of my three sisters leaned into a little knot of female mystery and, in a flash of a moment, all five thousand of them cooked up some sort of strange unknowable event. It was an amazing sight.

"Polly, I need you! Laura, aren't you done with her yet?" someone bawled. And it was all over. They all went back to their own private style sections, and no one knew what was what until me and Mom and Collette were sitting in the green room—which by the way was not green—and the event happened.

So we're sitting there waiting when the show starts. This room is piled with food—bagels and four kinds of cream cheese, muffins, a fruit plate—so I'm eating, because I don't know when the next opportunity to eat will actually show up in my life; meanwhile there's some noise, people talking over the intercom and saying things like, "Five minutes," and "Mr Philbin to the set, please." It's all very cool and efficient. And then music starts and everybody looks up because the television monitors they have in there, for the green room people to watch, are hanging from the ceiling, just like they do in hospital rooms.

Somewhere in the middle of all the pre-show hum, La Aura decided to stop by for a couple of grapes and some coffee before she took off. So she was there too, chattering away, when the show started. "Don't worry, they're gonna do great," she told me, and anyone else who would listen. "I've done this show like sixty times, and Regis is so nice! Kelly too, you'd be amazed, they're nice to everybody, even the people who work for them. It's like they're on drugs or something. Only they're totally not, don't get that rumor started, they're just both really swell, your sisters are gonna do great out there. They make everybody look good on this show," she told me. "Hey, you look great! I saw you in the newspaper, slugging all those reporters, good job, kid, good job!" So that made a second person, besides Maureen, who recognized me as the unidentified student. "Pretty soon you're going to be as famous as your sisters!" La Aura crowed.

"I hope not," I said.

"Oh sure, everybody says that, but we all want to be famous. You think I don't want to be famous? Well, I do! I want my haircuts to be famous."

"Aren't they about to be?" I asked, tipping my head at the television set.

"That's right, by god, they are, man, they are!" she asserted. It was pretty easy to cheer this woman up. She watched the set greedily, like a little kid tracking Christmas presents under the tree. Regis and Kelly were doing their opening monologue chatter thing, but no one was listening; we were all just waiting for the haircuts and the girls. La Aura finally got bored, and turned to me. "Your sisters are really gorgeous, you know that?"

"I do," I told her.

"I bet you do," she said. Then she slapped me on the shoulder and laughed, "You need a haircut, man! You got some work to do, you want to catch up with 'em!"

"I don't want to," I repeated.

"Yeah yeah yeah," she grinned, dismissing this idea for the second time in thirty seconds.

"Here they are, here they are," said Mom, her voice a little high. La Aura crowed, "All right!" Collette leaned forward a little bit. I realized my palms were sweating.

They weren't actually out yet, but Regis was going through the introduction. And La Aura was right, he was real nice. "These are three girls—beautiful girls—"

"So pretty," Kelly interrupted. "Did you see them in the *New Yorker*?"

"Wonderful, the new 'It' Girls, that's what everyone is saying," Regis agreed.

"I wanted to be an It Girl," sighed Kelly. It would have been an annoying thing to say but, seriously, Kelly is adorable. "I wanted to be an It Girl, too," said Regis. "Do you think it's too late for me?"

"Well, *I* don't, but I think maybe some other people might have an issue with it," Kelly told him. There's no way to get annoyed at any of the stuff that comes out of her mouth, I'm not kidding. It's a very strange skill. Plus, she's real nice to Regis, too, even when she's kind of jabbing at him.

"Who would object? Would anyone here object?" he asked her.

"Reeg, come on, these girls are waiting, everybody wants to see them," Kelly admonished him. Then she turned and smiled at the audience. "Don't you? And don't you dare disagree with me!" The audience applauded.

101

"Yes, come on," said Mom, under her breath. Her face was real tight.

But on the set, everything continued to go swimmingly. "These girls, these exceptionally pretty girls, also have a big legacy in their family," Regis announced.

"They do," said Kelly, knowledgable.

"Their grandfather was a famous, what was he, some sort of critic, nobody likes critics—"

"No, he was a literary guy," Kelly protested. "An intellectual, a great—"

"That's right, a great great intellect who now has beautiful granddaughters. So let's give a big welcome to Daria Heller, Polly Heller, and Amelia Heller." And he looked over to the side of the stage, where three pretty girls had suddenly appeared.

The audience was clapping politely, but not too politely; there seemed to be real enthusiasm there. Later I found out they just do what they're told, and some people were standing in front of them, waving their arms wildly and making the applause happen. But it didn't matter; the applause was good, and Regis immediately went into introducing everybody.

"Now which one of you is Daria?" he asked.

"I'm Daria," Daria smiled. She's chilly, but she has a great smile. It makes her look like a movie star, it really does.

"And Polly—"

Polly raised her hand. "Here," she said. This got a chuckle out of the studio audience.

"Which makes you Amelia," Regis told Amelia.

"Yes," she said. She smiled, but not very well.

"Loosen up, loosen up," Collette told the TV. "Don't sit on

your hands. Jesus, don't *swirl*." Sure enough, Amelia was already starting to twitch, nervous, which made her tall swivel chair turn back and forth a little bit. Truth be told, her legs weren't quite long enough for the thing, so she was dangling a little.

But Kelly was taking over. "Here is the picture!" she announced. She picked up a copy of the fateful *New Yorker* and held it out, open, in front of her, so that the studio audience and, more importantly, the camera, could get a good look. And there they all were, in that great Herb Lang shot, dancing and looking ultra-cool. The audience applauded again.

"Unbelievable: How exciting is that, to have your picture in the *New Yorker*?" asked Kelly.

"It was really thrilling," Daria replied. It had already been agreed that Daria would be the front person, at least until the apology portion of today's show. This again was Collette's idea, as a subtle but unmistakable way of showing off what a good and healthy family the Hellers actually were. The oldest does most of the talking, until the troublemaking youngest sucks it up and apologizes to the movie star. Polly also had to sit the furthest away from the desk, as Amelia was being put in between her big sisters, so that it looked like they were protective of her. Polly was mad about these logistics—she's not exactly a shrinking violet—but, as I said, everyone was playing ball at this point.

"Herb Lang is just a genius," Daria reported, respectful and dignified. "I mean, we've all been such fans of his work for so long, and then they called us out of the blue with this opportunity to work with him. It was like a fantasy."

"And can you tell us a little bit about your relationship with the *New Yorker*? I mean, why did they call you?"

"Because they're gorgeous, Reeg," Kelly interjected.

"Yes, they are gorgeous—I can see they're gorgeous, I think everyone here can see they're gorgeous—but I want to know about the grandfather, he was some sort of intellectual—"

"Yes, he wrote for the *New Yorker* off and on, book reviews mostly, he wasn't on staff there or anything. He mostly wrote books and articles of, um, literary criticism."

"Brilliant, right?" said Reeg.

"Yeah," smiled Daria. "He wrote for a lot of different magazines and stuff about American literature, that was his field, and he, you know, he taught at Yale and Columbia for a while . . . sometimes I think he taught overseas, like at Oxford, and Cambridge, that sort of thing."

"The school system is so different over there, isn't it?" said Kelly. "I had a friend who went to Oxford on a Rhodes scholarship—"

"You have a friend who's a Rhodes Scholar?" Regis asked, raising his eyebrows.

"Yes, I do, I have lots of smart friends," Kelly responded, with adorable dignity. "You don't have to be smart for smart people to like you."

"That's clear," said Regis.

"Yes, it is," she grinned. "Anyway, she said that the whole time she was there, she mostly just sat around and talked to people about books. They don't have classes, they just sit around and talk to other smart people about books. Isn't that amazing? Because here, we have classes, right?" She looked at Polly and Daria for some backup here. They both looked back at her, uncomfortable, since neither one of them had any intention of going to college, and had not in a million years dreamed that this would be where the conversation with Regis and Kelly might go.

So there was a little lull for a moment. And then Polly suddenly had a brainstorm. "Granddad loved teaching there," she said sweetly, "but he hated leaving New York. He always said he didn't feel comfortable anyplace that didn't have a bagel shop on every block." This got another respectable chuckle from the studio audience. Polly wasn't allowed to say much, but she was making good use of what limited chances she got.

"He liked his bagels," Regis nodded, already a little bored with this. Well, who wasn't? "So, the *New Yorker* knows your grandfather—he's dead, is that right?"

"Yes, he died several years ago," Daria nodded.

"I'm sorry to hear that. So they know your grandfather over there at the *New Yorker*, they hear his granddaughters are beautiful and they put you in their magazine, why wouldn't they, compared to what's usually in there, I'd much rather look at a picture of three beautiful girls."

"I like the *New Yorker*," protested Kelly.

"Oh you read the *New Yorker*," said Regis, unbelieving.

"Yes I do," she protested, but making a little face to show she might actually be lying. "Well, I like the cartoons," she amended.

"I like the *New Yorker* too, but I like it better now that they're putting pictures of pretty girls in there," explained Regis. "Anyway, as I think everyone here knows already, this is not the only picture, of at least one of you, that we've all seen lately."

"No," said Daria. Polly smiled a little embarrassed smile; they were both playing adorable as well. Amelia looked at the ceiling.

"Yes, the press is really having a field day with what happened to you three . . . where was it?" Kelly wondered.

"At the W bar, they have a private room in the back, and we were at a party with Rex Wentworth and some friends," said Daria. "Maybe I should let Amelia tell you."

Regis and Kelly both looked at Amelia, who stopped looking at the ceiling and smiled tightly, embarrassed.

"Yes, Amelia, you've been a bad girl, and all of America knows it." Regis waved his finger at her, playful. He really is kind of brilliant. It was all so friendly and easy, getting to this hard place just didn't seem so hard.

"I didn't mean . . . I'm not really so bad," said Amelia. And she gave him a little smile, trying to enter the spirit of things.

"So what happened?" asked Kelly. And she leaned in. Down in the green room, Mom leaned in. Collette leaned in, those killer legs shooting out behind her. I think all across America, everybody leaned in. And Amelia shook back her head, pushed all those auburn curls out of her face, and swung her feet a little. She looked really young out there.

"I am so sorry for what happened," she said, getting that part out of the way immediately. "I didn't mean to bite anybody. And I'm sorry that I did."

"Good girl," whispered Collette.

"So it was an accident?" asked Kelly, raising her eyebrow a little.

"I . . . yes, it was an accident," said Amelia. Then, knowing that this truly did sound lame, she continued. "I mean, no, I . . . it's hard to explain." And she laughed a little, at herself, and the absurdity of the situation. "He—Rex, I mean—was horsing around, and he picked me up. And, I . . . I didn't, you know, I just met him that night, I didn't really know him, I mean, I knew who he was, of course, they had called and told us he wanted us to have drinks with him, but that was the first time we had met him. And, I, he was just horsing around. But then he kind of picked me up. And I got freaked out, I did. I mean, I didn't know this guy. Not really, as a person? And he's a lot older than me. And I, he had his hands, I know he didn't mean it, but his hands were, they were—I don't . . ." She looked up at the ceiling again, scared again, at a loss for words. The studio audience was silent as the tomb.

So was the green room.

"He was just horsing around," Regis volunteered.

"Yes, yes," said Amelia, smiling at him, grateful. "He was just horsing around, and I overreacted." And then she put her hand out, onto Daria's, which rested on the chair between them. "He's a nice person. I'm sure. It was all, you know, I just wanted to go home and do my homework," said Amelia. "And then the whole thing . . . I-I-I'm so sorry. I'm just, I'm sorry . . ." And she stuttered, and stopped herself again. This time she looked down, at her hand, which was being held by her big sister's hand, tight, as if to give her strength. And I swear to god, her eyes filled with tears. She was ducking her head, so people couldn't see them, but we saw them.

Daria reached over, and put her arm around Amelia's shoulder. Polly shifted and took Amelia's other hand.

Oh my god, it was staggering how impressive the whole thing was. The three of them out there, Polly and Daria's arms around their frightened little sister. They looked like three sorrowful angels, mourning the death of innocence in some painting in a church somewhere.

"Well," said Regis. "Well, well. I'm sure you didn't mean it."

"No," said Amelia, with a sad smile. "I really didn't." She slipped her hand out of Daria's, and wiped the back of it across her eyes quickly, bravely. She smiled at Regis and Kelly. They smiled back at her, sympathetic.

"Fuckin' creep," said La Aura. "Fuckin' prick. I'm glad she bit him."

Collette turned, sharp, and glared at her. It was a nasty look. I must have reacted because she caught my eye a second later, and pulled the look back into some other internal space. She shook her head and ran her fingers over her eyes and I knew that as good as that performance was, this was not how things were supposed to have gone.

"So what's up for you guys next?" Kelly asked, cheerful.

"I have a chemistry test I have to make up," said Amelia. Which seemed to strike everyone out there as funny, because they all laughed, and then they cut to the commercial break.

There was silence in the green room. Then, "I think that went really well," said Mom. She looked at Collette, anxious. Collette was now our designated guardian and guide through the dangerous rapids of public life; no one else's opinion meant anything to Mom anymore. "Yeah, terrific," said Collette. She still had that internal look, but it had shifted out of reaction and into strategy mode. It looked to me like her brain was computing things pretty quickly right now.

"Fuckin' asshole," said La Aura, still indignant. "That fuckin' creep, feeling up a little girl like that, they should arrest him."

108

"It really wasn't like that, that's not what she said," Mom smiled, dismissive; she obviously didn't think much of La Aura.

"It sure the fuck is what she said," La Aura shot back, defiant. "Those guys, they think they can do anything they want, no one ever says no to them. Feeling up fourteen-year-olds. He's like, what, fifty years old or something?" Rex would have loved hearing that. "She's a little kid!" La Aura informed Amelia's mother. "What was she supposed to do? I'm glad she bit him. Fucker. Motherfucker. You should take better care of your kids, lady. Stop making excuses for Rex Wentworth. And get this one a haircut, he's a mess." And with that, La Aura left the room.

Mom, of course, was deeply offended. "Well, that's ridiculous," she said. "Who is this person, anyway? A *hair* person?" She sneered the word "hair," completely forgetting for a moment that her daughters were all famous, basically, because they have really good hair. "I take perfectly fine care of my children, I'm a terrific mother," she continued, miffed. "That's ridiculous."

Collette wasn't listening; she was still computing. Since she wasn't getting any traction, Mom just kept talking. "Although I guess you *could* use a haircut, Philip! You're looking a little bedraggled these days. I think I have been a little forgetful where you're concerned." She smiled at me, sad, worried, trying to be brave.

"That's okay, Mom," I said. That was all she needed. She smiled, and then stood up, came over to me, and gave me a big hug.

"I think they did terrific," she said. "I am so proud, aren't you proud of your sisters? Didn't they look pretty out there?"

"Sure, Mom," I said. She was clueless; she really was. "They looked great."

CHAPTER SIX

The tide turned immediately—I mean, instantaneously—away from Rex Wentworth, bit by that crazy girl, and toward the poor suffering child who had been molested by the evil movie star. When we got home, the reporters were all gone. They weren't *gone* gone; Collette got two dozen requests for interviews that same afternoon. But the harassment part of today's media frenzy had been at least temporarily put on hold. No one wanted to be seen as the bad guys bothering that sweet sensitive girl, Amelia Heller. As we got out of the car, a couple of people on the street waved to us, and somebody yelled, "I saw you on television! You guys rock!" Daria and Polly rewarded them with big grins and waves. We went inside. The doorman smiled at all of us and told Amelia she looked good on TV.

Back in the apartment, the mood was high. Polly had recorded the show, so she and Daria went straight to the living room to watch themselves on television. Amelia kicked off her shoes and went straight to her room, even though Daria yelled to her to come in and watch. "I'll be there in a minute: Start without me," she called back. "Wait, wait, I want to see it too," Mom called, peeling off her heels. She dumped her shoes next to Amelia's on the kitchen floor, and hurried out of the room. "Come on, Philip!" It was all kind of exciting, and nice. People being happy again, after all the screaming and anger and disappointment of the last couple weeks; it was really nice.

But I didn't go watch it again. I mean, I saw it the one time, and it wore me out. Behind me, Collette was attacking her BlackBerry with an intensity that was frankly a bit unnerving. After the taping, when Daria and Polly and Amelia had gotten back to the green room, she hadn't said much more than, "Good work, guys. You looked terrific out there. Let's hope that does the job." And then she ushered them back out to the limo, where the general sense of relief erupted with a kind of giddy frenzy. There were giggles and hugs and Polly whooped like an Indian; Mom was laughing so hard she started to cry. At one point Daria had her arm around Amelia and she kissed her on the head and Amelia looked up and grinned at her. And Polly leaned over, and squished Amelia between them, and I knew the whole thing was an act, and Daria had cooked it up, and they were all three in on it. And when I looked over at Collette, who was also watching, I knew that she knew it, too.

Does this make any sense? It made sense at the time. Anyway, I knew that Collette was pissed with them, even though the whole thing went swimmingly, because Maureen was going to be pissed, even though she wasn't going to be able to say anything about it. What could Maureen say? Amelia did apologize. And she said a ton of nice things about Rex, and she didn't say anything that wasn't true. Amelia held up our end of the bargain. But she also got one over on them, which no one, in the long run, was going to like.

But Collette couldn't tell them that. No one could say anything. No one was going to be able to yell at anybody, or threaten anybody, or force any more apologies out of anybody for a while now.

I left Collette in the kitchen tapping away on her Black-Berry and went to see what Amelia was up to, hiding out in her bedroom. The door was open, and she was just lying there on her bed, looking up at the ceiling. She hadn't changed her clothes or anything, and she also hadn't made her bed that morning, so if you didn't know any better, you would have said she was just your average teenage slob, lying around and doing nothing, on your average afternoon.

"Aren't you gonna watch?" I said, dropping on the end of the bed.

"I was there, I don't need to see it," she told me.

"Yeah, it was great. That was quite a performance. I particularly liked the tears. That was a good touch."

She looked over at me on that one, a little annoyed, but not really; not yet. "What's your problem?" she asked.

"I don't have a problem. I was telling you. I really liked the show. You looked great out there. You really did."

"Good."

"You think it will get Kafka's great-granddaughter off our backs?"

"One can only hope," said Amelia. A slight smile ran across her face, fast, then went away again. But I was just worried,

113

that's why I said what I said. I mean, I wanted to be relieved? But I wasn't.

"I think it's probably going to piss her off."

"She wanted it to be public," she shrugged.

"Yeah, my impression though is that she wanted it to be like an actual apology."

"It was an apology."

"You practically called him a pedophile on national television."

"Are you defending him?"

"I'm not defending him, he's an asshole. I'm just saying that you were supposed to be making this whole thing go away. I mean, wasn't that the point? To calm everybody down?"

"Since when do you do what Daria says?" I asked. "We both spent our whole lives thinking she's a big idiot. Why all of a sudden are you doing what she says?"

"Look. I just told them what they wanted to hear."

"What *who* wanted to hear?"

"America. They asked me what happened and I told the truth."

"The truth? What are you even . . . you were out there doing some whole *Little Women* thing, Daria and Polly loving you up, like Meg and Jo hugging poor dying Beth—"

"Philip, chill out, would you? I did what everybody told me to do! And it worked. So get off my fucking back."

"Well, that's a lovely thing to say."

"Oh, you've never heard the word 'fuck' before?"

"No, I've heard it, I've heard it a lot, lately—"

"So what the fuck's your problem?" She wasn't even looking

114

at me, this whole thing was so boring to her. "I swear, Daria's right, you're jealous."

This was great to hear, as you can imagine. "Jealous," I laughed, even though nothing was striking me as particularly funny. "You think all of this is bullshit, so what am I supposed to be jealous of? The fact that your life is turning to shit, and you get to act like a moron on television?"

"I didn't ACT like a MORON," said Amelia, suddenly furious. "You're jealous because it's cool to be famous and no one even knows you exist. That's why you're always following us around and cutting school so you can hang out with us, even though nobody needs you, with all your . . . all your acting like you know more than everyone else."

"I don't—"

"No one cares, Philip! No one gives a shit what you think, isn't that clear to you yet?"

"Fine," I said. "Next time six thousand reporters try to stomp you to death, I'm just going to let them." And with this highly mature observation, I stood up and left the room.

Look, I don't care, really, that we all look kind of crazy and mean and stupid in retrospect. I don't think it was Amelia's fault that she said such a shitty thing, and I don't really think it was my fault that I said such a shitty thing back. Even when your lives are normal, teenagers say horrible things to each other, and then like within ten minutes or something everybody's forgotten it. At least, ten minutes later, Amelia showed up at the door of my room and told me that she thought she had left her chemistry book on my desk, which was completely untrue. And she poked around my stuff, and said she liked some ridiculous picture

115

I had scribbled on the back of some Spanish notes, and then she left. This was virtually the same thing as an apology from her. Which I accepted by saying something like, "I think I saw your chemistry book on the dining-room table." She said, "Oh, good, thanks," and left.

Polly and Daria and Mom watched the *Regis and Kelly* clip about six more times, and Collette fielded calls all afternoon. She turned down all requests for interviews, telling the papers and the news magazines and CNN and the evening news shows (all three of them) that "the girls really want to move on." And then she set up photo sessions with *Glamour, Elle, GQ, O, Vogue, Victoria's Secret* and *Ladies' Home Journal,* for all three of them.

So, by the end of the day, Collette was tired but, apparently, optimistic, in her wary, eagle-eyed way. She finally took her suit jacket off and, as she was wearing a sleeveless celery shell underneath all that armor, you could see her triceps, which were impressive. None of my sisters works out, as we have all been blessed with hyperactive metabolisms, so merely not eating keeps all of us in the stylishly wraithlike category. Collette, by contrast, clearly spent hours in the gym. So she was also skinny and gorgeous, but she looked like a warrior, compared to my sisters.

"*Regis and Kelly* helped us, there is no question," she told the troops. She sorted through her notes at the kitchen table and summarized for all. "Amelia's apology went a little farther than necessary, but so far that hasn't hurt us."

"How could that hurt us?" Daria inquired coolly. She was sitting at the opposite end of the table, and she kept looking off into the next room, as if Collette were some sort of servant who was giving her relatively unimportant news. Collette's facial muscles clenched for a second and then released, and I thought, well well. Collette and the Ice Queen don't like each other. Duh, there had to be a reason Daria would do what she did. And there you had it: Collette spent all those months making Daria wait on her indecision and then, when she finally moved, she insisted on representing all three of them rather than just Daria. They didn't like each other. This was getting interesting.

"It could hurt us," Collette explained, with a little edge of too much patience, "if Maureen Piven takes offense."

"Has she called?" asked Polly.

"No, she hasn't," said Collette, brisk. "Which could be a bad sign but I'm choosing to ignore it. I imagine they have their hands full over there, dealing with the press, who undoubtedly want to know how big a pervert Rex really is." Daria's lips twitched gently upward, toward a smile, not quite getting there. Amelia looked at the floor, fidgety. She was considerably less smug than she had been when I talked to her in her bedroom.

"I thought Amelia was really brave, to tell the story so truthfully," said Daria. She put her hand out, on top of Amelia's, in a little recreation of the whole noble sisterhood act.

"You told me to apologize so that's what I did," said Amelia. She pulled her hand back and stood, went to the sink. Mom looked around the room, confused by all this.

"But you said it was good, this is all good," she said.

"It's fine, it's terrific, Mom," said Polly, bored and intent to put the whole mess behind us. Polly is nothing if not pragmatic. She wasn't going to get lost in some stupid bit of power-playing with Collette; she was going to have fun. "Who did you say called for shoots?"

"Everybody," Collette replied. "You guys are lightning in a bottle right now. And nobody's going to fuck that up—that means you, Amelia."

"I did what you told me to do," said Amelia, sighing.

"Don't argue, Amelia," Mom snapped. Then her tone lightened immediately. "I'm sorry, sweetie, no one blames you," she said. "All this had much more to do with Philip than you. It won't happen again, we all know that."

I was standing in the doorway when this delightful barb got tossed my way. No one looked at me, not even Collette, who shrugged and said, "*No one* is allowed to fuck up again, for a good long while, and that means everybody. We barely scraped through this one, knock on wood, and the press isn't going to let you off so easy next time."

"Easy?" said Amelia.

"That's what I said," Collette shot back. "This isn't a game you can win, so play by the rules. Don't let them turn you into a joke. Some girls can survive it, but most don't. So no more biting. And any time a photographer calls out your name I want you to turn and smile and pose for him, as long as he wants. I don't care where you are, or who you're with, you are *always* to be polite to the press. You're in show business now and . . ."

The rest of the speech I didn't stay for; it clearly wasn't for me, and *Battlestar Gallactica* was about to come on the Sci Fi Channel. There was also a vague thought somewhere in my head that as long as I was no longer wanted to play the role of the protector of my darling sisters, maybe I should take a crack at catching up on some homework so I might actually pass one or two courses this semester. Not that anyone seemed to care anymore, as I said, about anything as stupid as high school. I sat down in front of the television set, turned it on, and started to flip. Then, after a while, when I realized that *Battlestar Gallactica* was not due to come on for another fifteen minutes, and there was nothing on Court TV worth watching, and I couldn't find anything decent on the Discovery Channel, or the History Channel, so I turned the stupid set off and stared into space for a while. Collette was still droning away in the kitchen, but there was no way I was going to subject myself to that nonsense anymore. And then I saw the telephone, sitting on the bookcase against the wall, behind the television. The cord was hanging down, as it had been for days, because it and every other phone in the house was unplugged in an attempt to keep us all locked in the pre-*Regis and Kelly* cone of silence. But this was post-*Regis and Kelly*. To my mind, that meant we could plug the phones back in.

So that's what I did. And the instant I plugged the phone back in, it rang. So I picked it up. "Hello," I said.

"What the hell is going on over there?" asked a not-so-familiar voice, furious. "I've been trying to get through for days, your phones are unplugged. Get your mother."

"Dad, hi," I answered, bright. "Gee, it's great to hear from you."

CHAPTER SEVEN

Perhaps you had begun to think that neither I, nor my sisters, actually have a father. But, in fact, good old Dad does exist, and he makes the occasional appearance, usually completely unannounced, and always in a thoroughly nerve-wracking style.

"Mom's going to have to call you back," I told him.

"Get her on the phone, Philip," he said.

Okay, there was no way I was going to do that. The whole situation with everyone had been so lousy for so long, and now everybody except me was finally having a good day. There was just no way I was going to march into the kitchen and announce, "Hey Mom, Dad is on the phone and he wants to talk to you." I just wasn't going to do it.

"She can't come to the phone, Dad, she's gonna have to call you back."

"This isn't a joke, Philip. I mean it."

"She's in the bathroom."

"Get your mother, or I'm coming over there," said Dad.

"Oh, fuck off, Dad," I oh so usefully told him back. And then I hung up the phone.

Okay, that was obviously not the correct way to handle the situation, but as I recall it felt pretty good at the time. And, in my own defense, I would like to point out that ten years ago, the guy did dump my mother because he was cheating on her with his secretary, which is ancient history, of course, except that it still gives us all a bit of leeway, whenever the opportunity comes up, to treat him shitty. Other relevant facts are, he managed to leave her, when he took off, with four kids under the age of ten, and he also apparently really tried to stiff her in the settlement, although the judge was not terribly sympathetic to the attempt. So, ever since the divorce, the checks have come like clockwork, but he himself has been pretty scarce. Now, he has a second and presumably better family on the Upper West Side—the new children are blonde, I believe—and so while telling him to fuck off was rude, it was truly not as rude as it might first appear.

Also, to give myself a shred of credit, I would like to point out that I fully intended to inform my mother that he had called, and that she should call him back. When the proper moment arose, I was in fact going to tell her that.

Unfortunately, the proper moment never did actually arise. The powwow in the kitchen went on and on and on. I unplugged the phone again, because I didn't want Dad calling back and harassing me. Then I returned to my channel surfing, which yielded back-to-back episodes of *Bonanza*, both of which I found strangely moving. Hoss and Little Joe kept flinging themselves into one battle after another to save each other, and to save Pa, and to save the ranch. I couldn't keep any of it straight but it seemed pretty riveting at the time, and I think I even choked up at some point, although who remembers why.

The relative calm was predictably short-lived. About midway through the second episode, just as Collette was wrapping up her strategy session, the intercom buzzed, and then continued to buzz rather insistently. Then someone started pounding on the door.

"Oh, goodness, all right, all right!" Mom laughed. And she opened the door before she answered the intercom.

She would have had to let him in anyway, is the way I ended up looking at it. There was no way Dad was going to drive all the way from the Upper West Side to Brooklyn, and then turn around and go home without saying his piece. So I do think the degree of blame which was instantly leveled at me was a bit extreme.

"Hello, Julia," Dad hissed, pushing by her.

"David," said Mom. She was so utterly stunned, it was probably lucky she could even remember his name. "David, hello! Girls, your father is here! David, this is Collette, the girls' agent."

"It's wonderful to meet you," Collette smiled, the instant professional. Just add water. "Your girls are terrific. You must be very proud."

"You think so, huh? You think I should be proud, watching them get up and spout utter crap on national television? I mean, that was completely humiliating, what the hell do you think you're doing, Julia, what the hell? That's all I can frankly think of to say. What do you think you're DOING?"

This performance was met with complete silence. I was watching from behind, from the doorway; no one knew I was there. Mom raised her chin, pretending to be taller than she is,

123

and affected the air of complete contempt which is one of her specialties.

"Thank you for your opinion," she uttered in crushing tones of ladylike condescension. "Forgive me, and the girls, if we don't choose to see things that way."

"I don't give a damn how you see it. Amelia, get your coat."

Okay, this was clearly intended as a bombshell, and it was in fact received as such. Amelia leapt to her feet, and looked around the room, completely confused and suddenly scared. Of course we knew immediately that he was threatening to take custody of her, but he did it in such a grand, phony way that there was no way he could possibly be serious. He sure as hell looked serious, though. I mean, I understood her confusion; what the hell was all this? Honestly, it was like watching afternoon television; it was entertaining as well as horrible, and it was happening in your kitchen!

The saga continued. "Mom?" said Amelia.

"Sit down, Amelia, your father has no right to be here or to order anyone around," Mom sneered.

"The hell I don't. I've been on the phone with my lawyers all day. They think my case is pretty interesting, in fact. The whole country just heard my fourteen-year-old daughter announce that her mother's been taking her to bars and handing her over to pervert movie stars until all hours of the morning. And I'm not even talking about the other shit that's been going on—paparazzi attacking her at her own school, when she's allowed to go, that is. I called the school? They say she hasn't been in a class for two weeks."

"That is utterly ridiculous!"

"I don't think so. Polly and Daria can do what they want; I know I have no say in what happens to them at this point. But I will not see that *child* paraded around New York City like some sort of underage hooker. AMELIA, GET YOUR COAT."

"I'm not going home with you! Are you insane?"

"She's not going home with you!" Polly shouted at the same time. She and Daria were both on either side of Amelia now; the holy trinity sister act was only a day old and it was already second nature, even when there weren't any cameras around.

"You get out of here now before I call the police!" Mom yelled. "GET OUT. GET OUT!" And then she raised her arm like a bad movie actor from the fifties. I'm not kidding. This all actually happened. Plus, they were suddenly all screaming at once, which ended up all sounding sort of like a flock of pigeons who were really mad at the bus that was about to run them down. So they were all flapping away, and squawking furiously. Dad just jabbed his finger at Mom, ignoring all of it.

"Go ahead and call the cops, get them over here, let's put them on the phone with the DA's office," he suggested. He didn't even raise his voice, that's how mad he was. "I'm signing out a warrant on you: Endangering the welfare of a minor."

"She didn't endanger me!" Amelia howled. "I wanted to do it! I wanted to do all of it, it wasn't her idea!" This was complete news to me, and in fact to everyone else in the room, but as far as lies go it was delivered with real conviction. I am quite sure that Amelia believed it herself.

"I don't care if you wanted to! You're coming home with me now."

"That is simply not going to happen, as I'm sure you're well aware," announced Collette, cool as a cucumber. She also didn't bother to raise her voice and, as with Dad, the tactic worked brilliantly. She had stayed out of the fray up to this point, casually watching it all from a sort of mini-perch on the kitchen table, but now she stood and took the floor. Silence fell over all of them. The momentum of Dad's sensational entrance and equally sensational announcement—that he had arrived to claim custody of a child for whom he had rarely exhibited even a passing curiosity—had somewhat dissipated in all the chaos. This was unquestionably Collette's moment.

"Why don't we go into the den and discuss it?" she asked. She held out her hand, inviting Dad into the inner sanctums of our apartment. Mom was completely shocked that anyone would even begin to deign to have a conversation about this. Dad was equally unimpressed.

"Look," he told Collette, almost but not quite keeping the sneer out of his voice, "I don't know who you are, and I don't care. I don't have to talk to you or anybody about this. That's my daughter and, as I said, I'm well within my rights to do what I can to protect her from people like you."

"I don't think you know enough about me to infer that I don't have Amelia's best interests at heart," Collette informed him. "From what I know of Amelia, it's quite clear to me that, in spite of the fact she is only fourteen years old, she does know her own mind, and she is absolutely not going to walk off with you simply because you say so. This is her home."

"A home I pay for," Dad interjected.

"Yes, just as you say. A home you pay for and provide for

126

her. A home you have up until this moment determined was in fact quite safe for her."

"I'm not the one who changed the rules," Dad spat.

I had no idea what that meant, but other people in the room did, I could tell. There was a slight pause before Collette continued and then she continued. "As you say. My point is— my question is, rather—do you really feel that calling in police and lawyers and perhaps—I only say perhaps—removing Amelia against her will, traumatizing her, separating her from her mother and her sisters, the only family she really knows, and performing this extraordinary surgery in the public eye—do you really feel that that is in her best interest?" There was another mysterious pause, and then Collette tipped her head, toward the den. "Let's go discuss this in private." And she picked up her BlackBerry, and headed into the next room.

After a moment, Dad followed. Since neither Collette nor Dad even bothered to glance back, it wasn't immediately apparent that Mom was going to be included in this conference, even to her. So she just stood there for a minute. Then at some point it occurred to her that maybe she should be involved in the discussion of her children's respective fates, even if just for the sake of appearances to the aforementioned children. So then she followed as well.

This meant that the four of us were finally left alone for once. Polly and Daria were really furious, which was no surprise; they're pissed at Dad when he's not doing anything at all, so the fact that he suddenly showed up and peed all over their parade was bound to get a response.

"What a complete jackass," said Polly. "I can't believe this. We finally catch a fucking break and then he has to show up."

The whole cursing idea obviously had taken hold of the whole family by now. She picked up her purse, pulled out a pack of smokes and lit up. The smoking thing was new with her too but, no surprise, she looked just great holding a cigarette.

"He won't get away with it, it's all posturing," said Daria, coolly running her fingers through her auburn locks like a James Bond heroine having a bad day. Both of them, apparently, increasingly had the whole act down. Every word that came out of Daria's mouth sounded perfect, and she tilted her head back with complete arrogance.

"I don't care if it's posturing or not; it's fucking annoying. I need a beer, anybody want a beer?" Polly bent herself in half to examine the contents of the beverage cooler.

"There's water and bagel skins," I informed her.

"Oh, that'll lower the stress level around here," Polly sighed. "I think my head is going to explode."

"I shouldn't have called him," Amelia moaned. "Oh, shit. Oh, shit."

"That was three months ago," Daria said. "Unless there's something else I don't know about?"

"No, no!" yelled Amelia, upset. "I just called him that one time, and he didn't even call me back!"

"You said—" Polly started.

"Oh, God, I lied," Amelia admitted. "He never called once."

"Then don't worry about it," Daria asserted, secure. "This is all posturing. If he was really worried about you he could've returned the call before he saw you talking on national television about movie stars feeling you up."

"Seriously," I observed. "*This* is what he finds offensive? What about all the crap they've been writing about us in the *Daily News*? Or announcing on CNN? That's okay, that you're out there biting movie stars and getting hammered for it, but it's *not* okay to go on *Regis and Kelly* and perform a heartwarming scene from *Three Sisters*?"

"This isn't a joke, Philip," Daria replied, narrowing her eyes.

"Daria, the last time you said anything funny was more than fifteen years ago—no one ever assumes you're joking," I said.

"You want to play it like this, that would be up to you," she responded.

"What is that supposed to mean?" I asked, suddenly sick of it all. "I mean, that's just the stupidest—what does that even mean?" I suddenly had the urge to throw something, but instead I just yelled. "This is ridiculous. All of it. She was supposed to apologize. And now not only is *Dad* breathing down our necks, those crazy Hollywood people are going to be pissed as hell at her, and in case you haven't met Kafka's fucking terrifying fucking great-granddaughter, she is not the kind of person who fucks around. And you just went out there and pissed her off . . . why, because you thought it was funny? This isn't funny!"

"Thrilling as usual to hear from the Voice of Doom, Philip," Daria observed, dry. "Why don't you go back to your cave and chew off your leg or something?"

"Whatever," I said, suddenly bored with all the Sturm and Drang. "Fuck all of it. Whatever."

Just as I said this, we heard the door to the den open. Everyone turned, to find out from the so-called adults what was going to happen next.

Okay, now I'm not sure my brilliant closing line, "Whatever, fuck all of it, whatever," was really the end of my argument with Daria. In retrospect, we had to be arguing for longer than that, because what was going on in the den surely took longer than the length of what I remember. It didn't feel very long, though. It felt frankly like no time at all.

Mom stood in the doorway, looking quite calm and even pleased with herself. "Philip, could you join your father and me in the living room?" she asked. This was such an unexpected thing for her to say that no one knew how to react for a second. Over her shoulder, I could see Dad waiting in the living room. He still had his coat on, and he was looking at the wall. Collette stood behind him, in the door to the den. She was on her cell phone, doing something: She had already moved on from all of this.

"Philip," Mom repeated.

"Why do you want to talk to me? I didn't do anything," I said. Really, it seemed so weird and oppressive; everyone was so quiet, all of a sudden, because all four of us were so surprised by the strangeness of her asking me to go into the next room, even though on the face of it there wasn't anything all that strange about the request. Why shouldn't I go into the next room? For a weird hallucinatory moment I almost did it, I shifted my weight from one foot onto the other, as if thinking about it and almost moving, and then out of the corner of my eye I saw Amelia shake her head, just a little bit. We all knew there was something up. She especially did.

"This is ridiculous," Mom sniffed, huffy. "Come into the living room this instant. I am not asking you again," she said.

"Why?" said Amelia. "What do you need to talk to him about? I thought Dad came over here to yell about me and all of everything, what does Philip have to do with it?" It was a relatively incoherent statement, but I certainly appreciated the support.

"This doesn't concern you, Amelia," Mom reprimanded her with the kind of stupid condescension she used on all of us when we were little kids. "Philip, I'm not asking again."

"Well, good, because I'm not going. If you have anything to say to me, why can't you say it here? I mean, what is the . . . what's the . . . ?" Mom was turning, not even paying attention; honestly, I'm as much good as a ghost sometimes.

"David, would you please come in here and help me handle this?" Mom said, utterly exasperated. "Philip is refusing to leave the kitchen. I think it's clear that we're making the right decision." And with that, she stepped back into the living room and ushered Dad onto the front lines of the confrontation, whatever the hell the confrontation was.

My father is, as I've said, rarely around, but when he shows up, he tends to cut to the chase. "You're coming home with me, Philip," he said. "Your mother and I both feel that, with everything that's going on now, you'll be better off with me and Sarah."

"What . . . are . . . you . . . talking about?" blurted Amelia. The rest of us were stunned into silence, but she was on her feet, her face was completely red and she was sort of laughing. Not laughing, but making that almost-laughing sound, that wallop of disbelief that comes out sounding like a laugh. "He didn't do anything! He has nothing to do with any of this!"

"That is categorically untrue, Amelia, and you know it," Mom told her.

"No one said anyone did anything wrong. This isn't a

punishment," Dad proposed, cool. He only loses his temper when he wants to make an effect. He's a businessman. There was no longer any reason to yell, as the deal had already been cut: They were giving me to him, as a kind of consolation prize for not getting Amelia.

"That's just crap, that's utter crap," Amelia blustered. "He didn't do anything. You can't kick him out. This is bullshit! You can't just come in here and take one of us! Mom! You can't just let him take Philip! It's my fault what happened, I was the one—"

"This is for Philip's own good, I just can't handle him anymore, not with everything else I have to deal with. He should be with his father, all of us agree."

"*All* of us? What, Collette gets a vote?" said Polly.

"Your mother and I are in agreement, and that's all that needs to be said about it," said Dad.

"That's a relatively new phenomenon. We're not even allowed to comment?" Polly snapped back. Polly gets smarter when she's angry, it's impressive. But she didn't have the opportunity to turn this into a fencing match, as Amelia was on a roll.

"That's not all there is to be said, what kind of bullshit is this?" she yelled. "You can't just show up out of the blue and just take him!"

"Amelia, this is no time for one of your immature fits," Mom snapped.

"Immature? You're calling me immature? You're giving him away! You can't give people away! You can't just give him away!"

"Oh, for heaven's sake—you see what I've been dealing with?" Mom noted, as some sort of confidential aside, to Dad.

"Philip, get your coat," said Dad.

"Stay where you are, Philip," said Polly, still mad enough to keep her cool. On this exceedingly rare occurrence that had put her and Dad head to head, it suddenly occurred to me where she got this peculiar skill. "They can't make you go."

This was a spectacular piece of information as far as I was concerned. Because it was true. If I just stayed where I was, what could they do? Pick me up and toss me out the door? Call the cops? Have the super come up and eject me from my own kitchen? None of these scenarios was even likely. Also, there were four of us and only two of them. Polly was suddenly functioning as my lawyer, informing me of my rights, and Amelia was howling with rage. In addition, you could tell from the way Mom was half flailing about that she was inches away from falling head-first into a muddled pool of confusion. So for a second it looked like the winds might shift my way.

Then Daria spoke up. "It's not necessarily a bad idea, Polly," she said.

Polly shot her a look and, let me tell you, I hope no one ever looks at me that way. It reminded me again that, as good as the loving sisters act was, Polly and Daria didn't especially like each other. "He's been saying some pretty extraordinary things," Daria continued. "He hasn't exactly been supportive of what's been going on here. While you guys were in the den, he actually—well . . ."

"He's our brother and he lives here with us," said Polly, definitive.

"That's not actually for you to decide, Polly, nor you either, Daria, although I'm grateful to hear that at least one person in the kitchen has a little common sense," Mom asserted. She seemed to be making a last-ditch effort to get everything to look like it was all her idea.

"There's just no place for him here, is there?" Daria said, with a faux kind of worried compassion that made me want to puke. It was just like watching them all on television again: She was acting one thing while doing another, and it was spooky, frankly, how good she was at it. "Collette just told us what we're looking at for the next six months. It's going to take everything we've got to meet this schedule and make sure that Amelia keeps up with her schoolwork. Mom needs to be with us, and we simply aren't going to be around. No one is going to have time to look after Philip." She turned her benign gaze on me. I felt like I was looking at a gorgeous fucking weasel.

"I don't, excuse me?" I said. I know it was lame. But it was the best I could do. I might have gotten further but Amelia was back in the fray.

"You're insane! This is all complete HORSESHIT," Amelia blurted. "You can't take him! Mom! Mom!" she pleaded. Mom looked away, indifferent, and Amelia's face turned red and then white and a blast of fear swept over her green eyes. The winds had shifted and we were definitely losing now. For a second it had seemed like our outrage might carry us far enough in the right direction, especially with Polly on our side; but then Daria messed with our heads just enough to confuse Polly, to scare Amelia, and to drop us somewhere else, where the sadness of it all could just suddenly overwhelm everybody, so that then we couldn't fight anymore. Watching your mother give you away.

It was so bewildering and horrible it just stopped us all in our tracks. That's how they pulled it off. I'm convinced.

"Daria's right," Mom said, all prissy and superior, so sure of her rectitude she was practically licking her lips. "Philip is going through a lot of things himself right now that I just don't have time for! Besides, we always felt that there would be a time when he would need to go live with his Dad. Boys need their fathers, especially in their teenage years. This isn't a punishment, I don't know why you're all acting like this is such a terrible thing. You should all be spending more time with your father. That won't be possible for you girls right now, but it is possible for Philip, so it's just the perfect solution to . . . to everything." She smiled brightly, as if she were back on that Miss America stage, talking about her dreams of world peace.

We were all so stunned by the stupidity of what Mom had just said, there was a moment of silence. My inexorable father looked at me.

"Get your coat, Philip," he said.

"I have school," I said. "I have homework." It was truly the best I could do.

"They have schools in Manhattan," he told me. "Get your coat."

"If he goes, I'm going with him," announced Amelia. Which was totally great to hear, except for the fact that everybody just completely ignored her.

"Philip, *get your coat!*" Dad snapped.

"I'm going too! He can't just take Philip! I'm going too!" Amelia kept saying. Everyone just kept ignoring her. It was so weird. When I turned, in the hallway, to look back into the

135

apartment, she was running after me, holding her coat. And then Mom just shut the door, right in our faces.

So that was what happened. I went to go live with my father, a man who I'd seen on maybe a dozen separate occasions since he left my mother when I was five.

There wasn't a ton of talk in the elevator. What did we have to talk about? Then, once we were past the doorman and out on the sidewalk, heading toward his black BMW, before he even said a word to me, he got on his cell phone.

"Hey, it's me," he said. "Listen, things didn't work out the way I thought. I'm bringing Philip."

There was a pause. He grimaced. "I know, but what was I supposed to do? I came over to get Amelia because I think her parenting is atrocious, and then she and this agent keep telling me that the problem is Philip and the real solution is getting him out of there. I would have looked like an idiot if I'd said no." None of this made sense to old Sarah apparently; she was yelling so loud that I could hear her through the phone from three feet away. Good old Dad got tired of being yelled at and cut her off. "I'll explain it when I get home," he said. "If the traffic's not too bad we'll see you in an hour. Bye." He snapped the cell phone shut and pulled out his car key, beeped the locks.

"She must be fucking delighted," I said. What else could I do?

Dad looked at me. "You may think it's cool to use that kind of language in front of your mother," he told me, "but it won't be tolerated in my house."

I didn't say anything. There was nothing to say.

AMELIA

CHAPTER EIGHT

Okay. It was just crazy. Just totally out of control, and then when they kept saying it was Philip's fault? Like, it was his own fault that he got tossed out of his own family, what for? Who kicks their own kid out? I was freaked, just completely out of my mind. One second he was hanging out in the kitchen and gabbing with the rest of us about how screwy it all was, Dad showing up out of nowhere and acting like, okay, I have to take Amelia home with me because she's in so much moral danger, like Dad cares at all about how much moral danger anybody is in, ever. And then the next second Dad is dragging Philip off, and they're all saying it's his own fault—that is the position that Mom and Collette and Daria and even Polly have chosen to take, although I know for a fact that Polly thinks it's nuts. She just gets tired of arguing and quits. And then she gets tired of that and starts to argue again. So she's not exactly reliable.

Anyway, that is what they're saying now, that Philip was such a psycho weirdo that he really was the problem, all the terrible screw-ups were his fault and that if he were less of a looney tunes none of any of it would have happened—like how can anyone seriously act like that's a true statement? I'm not saying he's perfect by any means and god knows he's been catastrophically stupid at certain junctures in this whole disaster, but for heaven's sake. And by the way my position remains: Before any of this started up, it was like, Daria and Polly; Mom, sort of attached to that; Dad in and out; and then me and Philip. No one really paid any attention to us at all, we were the afterthought all the time. And he— Philip, I mean, who else would I mean?—he is a really nice person. That's the thing no one ever even mentions, like it's irrelevant. But you know, when Dad took off, he took the dog. I presume no one has mentioned this yet. We had this dog, a big old black lab who nobody paid any attention to except Philip, who would feed her and watch TV with her next to him on the couch. The dog's name was Boffin, and Philip just loved that stupid dog. Then when Dad left? Mom was like, I don't want this dog, you take the dog. Like Philip had nothing to say about it. And he never complained. And then Dad took off, and he took the dog, and he never even told us when she died, that was just the sort of thing that happened in our idiotic family. We didn't even find out the dog was dead until like six months after it happened. And Philip just went into his room and shut the door and didn't even talk about it, not even to me. And I think about that sometimes, how much that dog meant to him, and how he never even complained. And, as I think you already have heard, he always came to my piano recitals. He never missed one, even when he was a teenager and it was ridiculous for him to show up.

So when Mom announced that Philip was supposed to go off and live with Dad and Sarah and their completely forgettable offspring, I was so mad. Mom, as you may have noticed, is a complete moron. So you don't actually have to really think about anything that she says, ever; you can pretty much just assume that it's completely and totally dumb. But this was beyond anything I ever thought she could do.

"We really feel that this is the best solution for everyone. Philip was more and more unhappy, and it just was totally clear to your father and me that he needed a man's touch to help him through a difficult transition time," she explained in this kind of whiney voice, after Dad had literally shoved Philip through the front door. I was particularly ready to faint over the "your father and me" reference, as in fact she and Dad never speak, I mean, blatantly never speak about anything, much less about what would be best for their darling children. I think the last time they supposedly consulted on anything was when their lawyers were screaming at each other over the divorce settlement. So, like, all these important statements about what's really best for Philip's happiness, as if she's ever imagined such a thing, are just crazy.

"That's just *bullshit*, Mom," I told her.

"I don't have to justify myself to you, Amelia," she huffed. "I am your mother, and my judgment is what matters."

"Like you even know what 'judgment' means!" I yelled. Which may have been too much; I admit I go too far. But why shouldn't I? What could she think she was even talking about, judgment? She just kicked her own son out of the house, for what? Why was he even being kicked out, what was the fuck…, point of that? And she's going to try and justify it? I mean, what do adults think, really, do they really think that we're all complete morons? "You can't let him take Philip!" I blasted. "He's my brother! You can't just give him away! Are you insane? Have you completely lost your mind? And if he's going I'm going too—you can't keep me here if you're kicking him out!"

"Amelia, this is so upsetting for all of us, please, please don't make it worse," Daria murmured. She was like a cat, sitting in the corner, so sad and pleased with herself that she was inches away, really, from just licking herself. I don't know why she hated Philip so much but she always did. I tried to warn him a couple times but he never listened to that stuff from me; I mean, he knew I was smarter than him, but his brain works pretty much the way all boys' minds work. They're like, yeah you're so smart, but I'm the boy, which means that secretly I know more. What a disaster. I would bother to be mad at him about it, because that's what sunk him, after all, was pissing off Daria, and I told him not to do it. But I can't be mad at Philip, I really can't. Getting sent off with Dad? That was just too messed up for words; we knew it when it happened to the stupid dog! So don't mistake me. I don't blame Philip. I'm just saying, it didn't help that he was always pissing Daria off.

Because Daria was now, like, working overtime to make all this look like something normal. "We're all exhausted," she sighed. "What a terrible, overwhelming end to the day. Are you all right, Mom?" She smiled at Mom, all sad and friendly. I just wanted to puke.

"Thank you, sweetheart, I'm fine . . . I'm not fine, I'm tired." She was all sad and friendly too. It was too much.

"I think we all need a rest," Daria mused.

"Yeah, no kidding," said Polly. "I'm going to bed." And she

stalked out of the room. Which got her nothing except out of the line of fire. Because Polly can't make an exit without letting everyone know what she really thinks, just with the way she walks. My point being, if you're not going to fake it, then why pretend to fake it? Why not just tell them what you think?

But when Polly left, that really was just like the end to it, it really was. Collette came clicking in, all business, acting I swear to god like nothing had happened and that, even if something had, she didn't know anything about it. "*Vogue* and *Elle* are both on board, if we can make it happen by the end of the month; they were both threatening to pull if we wouldn't give them an exclusive, but *Regis and Kelly* did the job, no one's saying a word about exclusivity anymore; these girls are on the map," she announced. "We're trading calls on the exact schedule, it's looking like they need you down at the *Vogue* offices tomorrow morning for fittings and some consults with their in-house people. I'm trading with people at *Esquire* and *GQ* as well and, believe it or not, I actually got a call from Agnes Vitale at *Vanity Fair*, but we have to consider that a long shot for now. She's a real cunt, pardon my French, and she's Maureen Piven's best friend, if you can imagine such a beast, so even if she intends to make this work she's going to need to torture me for another few months. When the heat on the girls cooks up a little hotter, I'll work on her then."

"I'm not doing it. I'm going to Dad. You can't make me be a model if I live with Philip at Dad's, you can't fucking make me do anything," I told her.

"Really, Amelia, your language has deteriorated, shockingly, in the past few weeks," Mom suddenly announced. "I simply cannot have you talking like a truck driver in front of publicists and photographers and everyone else we'll be dealing with in the coming months."

"Oh for heaven's sake, Mom, Collette just said 'cunt' in front of me. What are you even—"

"You're a public person now." Mom just sailed on, as if I had not bothered to interrupt her. "And while many people say that it's all right for women to curse, I am here to tell you it is not. It is not feminine, it is not elegant, and it demeans you and everyone around you. People may not say anything, but they know, in their hearts, that it reduces you. It undermines everything we are trying to achieve."

"What are you talking about, what we're trying to achieve?" I yelled. "We're trying to be famous. Who gives a shit if I say fuck?"

"I'll take care of this, Mom." Daria smiled and grabbed me on the elbow. "Come on, Amelia, let's give Mom and Collette a break. They've been working really hard, and it's been a hard day." She put her arm around my shoulder and gave it a friendly little squeeze. Frankly, it was not unexpected, but it was a bit spooky, how suddenly and thoroughly she transformed herself into this amazing phony. Mostly what Daria had been good at up to this moment was sitting in corners and pouting when she felt like people didn't realize what a big star she really was. For maybe five or six years now, she'd had this secret competition with Paris Hilton going on in her head, which she obviously had been losing, since no one on earth had ever heard of Daria Heller until, like, three months before this. But getting this close to what she actually wanted out of life definitely brought out the manipulative bitch in Daria. She coos, she smiles sadly, she prattles on about sisterhood and how much we all

144

love each other, she kicks my brother out of the house. It's like someone turned a switch, and the evil genius took over.

So she's shoving me down the hall and whispering in my ear, "It's late and everyone has had it and no one is interested in fighting anymore, Amelia."

"I'm going to live with Philip at Dad's," I told her.

"It's not going to happen. Trust me. So put it to rest and go to bed."

"I have homework," I sneered. "Remember homework? Remember high school? Remember real life?"

"Real life is for losers," she said, and I got to admit, she looked pretty cool when she said it. "You look terrible, you need an Ambien. Here." She ducked into the bathroom and started rummaging around one of her eight makeup kits, digging out her prescriptions. Then she pulled out a different kit, rummaged in that one as well. "Put this on your eyes, or they're going to look like hot-air balloons at six in the morning."

"What do you care what I look like? The worse I look, the better you look, isn't that how it works? Anybody checked in with Nicky Hilton lately? Uhhh, Nicky whoooo?" I said.

"Oh god, I'm tired. The fact is—listen to me—the fact is, I *don't* care what you look like," Daria informed me. "But everybody's got to behave until we get well past this utter disaster which, by the way, is the complete responsibility of you and Philip. We're almost through it. Today was a big step. And, honestly, once this show is on the road, I don't care what you do. You can finish chemistry or move to Brazil and take piano lessons and save the rain forests, whatever you want. But until then, we are all going to play ball." She opened a jar of green stuff and started to smear it on my eyes. "Fourteen years old, you look like Cruella De Vil," she said. "Now take that Ambien and go to bed."

This information—that I would be permitted to return to actual life and high school if I played along for now—was not news; it had already been explained to me before I went on that stupid talk show. This was the story, as I understood it: As long as the press was running things—which it was, in case anyone wondered—there was no way I could just disappear. Every last one of those tabloid weirdos were already too fascinated by this ridiculous bad-girl thing they said I was doing. However, if I played along and just pretended to be like, this girl who'd had a bad couple of weeks and so I bit a movie star and said fuck at inappropriate moments, but now I just loved being sucked up to by newspaper reporters and television talk-show hosts and models and actors and photographers and people like that—as long as I acted like I loved all this stuff for as long as I could stand it—then, maybe, they'd get bored by me. It was sort of like planned obsolescence—Philip explained this to me once: They deliberately build booby traps into DVD players and iPods, so that all of them just self-destruct at some point and everybody has to buy a new one. So acting like a boring good girl who just wants to have her picture taken all the time, hanging out with boring celebrities, that was supposed to be my planned obsolescence. If I really just got really boring, all those reporters would get, well, bored, and I would be allowed to just slink away. That was my understanding. It really was.

Now I had a new idea. "If I behave myself can Philip come home?" I asked.

"Stranger things have happened," Daria told me. "Go to bed."

146

So I put the green stuff on my eyes, and I took the stupid Ambien, and I went to sleep. And in the morning, I was going to call Philip, up at Dad's? But they got me out of bed at five-thirty, and threw me into a car, and then I was at some studio with hair and makeup people going haywire for an hour and a half, then the clothes people showed up and they had me and Daria and Polly changing outfits like crazed Barbie dolls for another two hours. They kept talking about how casual this all was—this was a casual meeting, supposedly, where we all got to know each other before the shoot at the end of the week; we were all supposed to be so relaxed and happy—but I'm telling you, all those fashion-istas are about the least relaxed human beings I have ever met. Anyway, every time I manage to find two seconds to pull out my phone and text Philip, just to see how he's holding up, Collette snaps, "Amelia, they need to try this camisole with those jeans," or Mom says something, or Daria or some stylist whose name I can't even remember starts whining about the shoes, whose idea was it to bring up a pair of clogs? Do they think this is L.L. *Bean*? And then I get yanked back into the river of chaos. And I don't want to say to anybody, you know, I have to call Philip, has anyone called Philip? Because I can tell that they haven't, and they haven't even thought about it, and that if I say something about just aban-doning him like that, they'll get all mad at me and it will just be worse and I won't be allowed to call him anyway.

By the time we got home, it was late afternoon. I muttered something about homework and snuck off to my room, and I did call him then. And I'm sitting there, listening to his cell ring in his room because apparently they shoved him out of his own life without making sure he had his stupid cell, of course they did. So then I called Dad's apartment on the landline, but that idiot Sarah answered the phone, and she said that Philip wasn't there, that he was off meeting with Dalton, and that she would let him know I called.

"Dalton, who's Dalton?" I said.

"It's a school," she replied, sort of mean and condescending.

"I know it's a school," I said. "I didn't know you could meet a school."

"Was there anything else you wanted, Amelia?" Sarah asked.

"Just tell him I called," I said. She hung up without saying good-bye. Which I'm guessing had more to do with Mom than with me. But sometimes I do think, even so. I'm fourteen years old, and they just took my brother, don't I have a little leeway? Aren't they supposed to be the adults?

Two days that week, I was allowed to go to school. Which wasn't, frankly, much more fun. Some things were better. There were only like two reporters outside my building now, and the school did something with the police so none of them were allowed to be there, either. Which at least meant that walking to school wasn't the scariest nightmare you could imagine. But once I got there, no one really wanted to talk about anything except me. Which I know sounds like fun? But honestly is kind of boring. Mostly of course what everyone wanted to talk about was the story I told on television about Rex Wentworth—that's what Philip always called him and, if you want to know the truth, it is a stupid name but it kind of suits him. Anyway, that's what everybody wanted to know: Did Rex really feel me up in a back room at W? The guys, the girls, the upper classmen, the janitor, the lady who puts the desserts out on the tray in the cafeteria. Even the people who sort of didn't want to look like they cared, like the teachers, they'd sort of hang around, whenever some dingdong just blurted it out. Did Amelia get felt up by a movie star? It was like news of the universe.

So, just by showing up, I was a bit of a disruption. And since I had to work so hard to get Mom to let me come at all, I didn't want to make a lot of trouble and get sent home, the way I did when all those photographers piled up on me. So I just kept trying to duck the question and get to class, or duck it and read a book, or duck it and eat my grilled cheese sandwich. This response turned out to be kind of dissatisfying to everyone so, by the end of the second day, people were being kind of mean. My friend Hannah Steinberg finally cornered me in the locker hall.

"What's the matter with you?" she hissed. "Are you like a snob now?"

"What are you talking about?" I said. I was pretty annoyed and tired by this point, and nervous about how much work I had to make up.

"You won't talk to anybody, you're like so stuck up about being a big star," she said.

"No I'm not," I said. "I just want to, you know, try and catch up on my classes."

"Oh please," she said, before I had even finished my sentence. "You love every second of this. Like everybody wants to talk to you but you're too good to talk about it, making out with movie stars—"

"I didn't make out with Rex Wentworth: That's crazy and you know it."

"I don't know it."

149

"I told you already, about six times—"

"Well, nobody in the whole school believes it and I don't believe it either."

"I don't give a shit what you believe," I said. It made me sick, listening to her, because Hannah is practically the best friend I have in the world and this was crazy, coming from her, that she didn't believe me. I mean, I told her what happened at that stupid bar that night, she knew that it was kind of nothing and just stupid. Why she was suddenly saying this stuff was just completely aggravating.

"Well, why don't you just tell people what happened?" she said. She was really mad.

"I did, I told *you*," I said. I was mad too.

"You didn't," she said.

"Oh brother," I said. "Now I'm a liar? Is that what you're saying, are you calling me a liar?" I hate that, I mean, I really hate that.

"I'm telling what people are saying, that you were making out with him—"

"Well, you know what happened, why don't you tell them—"

"It's not my job, you tell them! You won't say anything. That's why they think it! They wouldn't think it if you weren't acting like such a huge snob!"

"I just don't want to talk about it!" I said. "Why do I have to talk about it?"

Hannah got real nasty then. "All I'm saying is, people think you won't talk about it because it's a lie, that you lied because you were making out with Rex, and then he dumped you, and then you had to get back at him."

150

"Yeah, he did dump me, on the floor, because I bit him—this is crazy, I don't want to go over this again, you're all just full of shit, fuck you, this is just fucking bullshit—"

"Miss Heller, can I speak with you?" Suddenly Mr Renaldi, the English teacher, was standing at the near end of the locker hall. Which didn't surprise me; as I said, the teachers were all lurking, trying to hear what I was saying to people.

"Yes, Mr Renaldi," I replied, annoyed as hell. This whole school scene was suddenly a big drag.

"Your language is unacceptable, as I think you know," he informed me. "We could hear you all the way at the other end of the hall. If the middle school had been in the class change, many younger students would have been treated to your salty diatribe."

"My *what*?" I said.

"Don't give me that attitude."

"I'm sorry, what did you say? You don't like my attitude? Well, I don't like teachers hiding behind corners and trying to hear what I'm saying in a private conversation with my friend." Okay, this was not necessarily the smartest response I could have made, I realize that. But sometimes I can't help it. As if he hadn't been standing there, trying to hear what I was saying, and now he was yelling at me for saying it? Do they honestly think we don't know what crap it all is?

"Come with me, Miss Heller. I think we need to consult with Mr Morton on this situation." Which was his oh so clever way of saying, let's go to the dean's office.

So at the end of two days, I got sent home anyway. I tried to call Philip and tell him about it, but that idiot Sarah just said he was at his new school and he was in some afterschool science program and he wouldn't be home until six or seven. I told her I really wanted to talk to him, and she said that she had given him the message before, and that it was up to him to call me back. I would have told her there was no way that Philip was not going to call me back if he knew I had called, but I didn't think that would be a terribly useful thing to say, so I just asked if he had a new cell phone yet and she said that he would let me know if and when that happened and then she hung up. She did, she hung up! I didn't know what to do—they wouldn't let me talk to him, and they acted like I was crazy to want to, and then, on top of it, it made no sense to me that he hadn't called either. Why wasn't he calling? Then I thought, maybe he did call, and Mom didn't tell me, just like Sarah clearly wasn't telling him that I was calling. It all got screwed up in my head, who was saying what to who, and how to get the right story, or the right information, I just didn't know how to do it by that point, so I went and lay down in my room and stared at the ceiling, I just honestly didn't care by that point. I just didn't.

But I did think that Hannah should not have said that I was a liar. I don't do that. When Daria told me to cook up a big story about Rex trying to molest me, I told her to forget it, that all I would do is say what really happened. I just wasn't going to do it, I wasn't going to lie. The truth is scary enough for most people. As far as I can tell, that's the thing no one ever wants to hear.

CHAPTER NINE

So that was it with school, for a while. Sometimes I would think about how could that happen, that suddenly all the adults decide that a kid doesn't have to go to high school? And it seemed peculiar to me, but only slightly. I mean, I was sick of it anyway. And the bottom line was, Mom just didn't want to deal with it. Meanwhile, apparently, the school felt that I presented a serious disturbance to the other students—that's what old Morton told Mom; Amelia "presents a serious disturbance to the other students." When she told me that, I laughed, I really did.

"That stupid school could use a serious disturbance," I said, cocky as hell. "The students are all bored out of their minds. I gave them more action than they've seen in a hundred and fifty years." Polly snickered, but Daria glided across the kitchen and put her arm around me, all protective.

"Is this going to be a problem?" she asked Mom. "We certainly don't want any more public attention directed at Amelia's disruptive behavior—"

"I wasn't disruptive," I said, firm. "I was trying to do my

work, they were all bugging me, and that idiot Mr Renaldi was like hovering in a corner listening in on a conversation that had nothing to do with him, because he has the hots for fourteen-year-old girls—he's just a sick wacko. I'm telling you, I said three dirty words to him, the guy like got an erection, just standing there in the locker hall. It was the biggest day of his life, me talking dirty to him."

"That's enough, Amelia, that is hardly useful," said Mom.

"She's right, Mom," Polly said. "That guy is notorious—"

"Thank you, Polly, I don't actually need to hear what you and Amelia think about the poor man. The point is, the school has made it clear that they feel that Amelia's behavior is disruptive to their community and the stories that I'm hearing lead me to believe that Amelia isn't finding it to be a good environment either. Isn't that so, Amelia?"

"I don't know, Mom. I love it there. I have my piano, and my, my science is so important to me, I have so many friends there, who I just would hate to leave. I don't know, I-I-I . . ." I sighed. Okay, obviously this was a total act, but by that point I was just sick of her yakking on about nothing. I knew she wanted to yank me out of that school anyway, why did she need to go on about it and act like, Oh this was so serious? Why didn't she just pull the plug, since that was what she wanted to do anyway?

"Well, they are concerned and I am concerned, and that's what matters," Mom informed me, totally ignoring my phony protests. "Dean Morton and I agree that it's just not the right fit, at this time, and we both feel that for the rest of the year a home-schooling program would actually be more appropriate for you. They suggest that perhaps we can revisit this situation in the fall, but I'm really not terribly happy with how they handled this situation with either you or Polly—"

"Me?" said Polly, surprised. I swear to god, I think she had even forgotten she was supposed to be *in* high school. She's a senior, she's supposed to be getting her diploma this year and maybe going off to college, but like, all of that had just totally slipped her mind. Mom swept on.

"Dean Morton gave me the names of several excellent tutors, who will work with both of you to keep you up with your grade level," she said. "There's a whole terrific network of these people. Collette thinks it's really the only solution; she says all the working teenage models and actors she represents have just wonderful tutors and it works out wonderfully for everyone."

"That sounds terrific, Mom," I told her. "Because my education is so important to me. I mean, really, this sounds perfect! To be able to squeeze it in between modeling sessions, wow, it's the best of both worlds. Don't you think so, Polly?" I turned to her, with the biggest phony sincere smile I could muster, but she was done laughing at this nonsense. "Sure, whatever," she said, bored, looking off.

Such a stunning surprise, the question of tutors disappeared as soon as it came up. Education? Trust me, no one cared. So we moved on happily to the work of becoming cultural superstars. The *Vogue* shoot came and went without a hitch, then *Elle*, then *Glamour*, and then a bunch of other ones I can't remember exactly. But we were everywhere, for months, when you get hot it can go on for a long time, and we did everything—the really kid magazines, like *Seventeen*, and the really

155

totally hip ones, too, like *W*. That one was actually quite a scene. All these magazines knew what the other ones were doing—there were spies everywhere, everybody ratting out style secrets to their competitors; there's absolutely no honor among fashionistas—so the *W* guys knew totally everything about what the other spreads looked like. I mean, I was there, on these different shoots, and I didn't know half of what these guys knew. And since most of the other shoots were all relatively tame pretty-girls-in-tight-clothes kind of stuff, these *W* geniuses decided at the last minute to change their whole approach. Their big idea was: Weapons. I'm not kidding, they had pistols and rifles and Uzis, and even a bow and arrow, and a slingshot; that was in the whole pile somewhere. Which apparently they hoped to use at some point as some sort of a joke or something, who can tell?

So at the last minute they sprang these brilliant props on us, explaining that the spread was going be about these three gorgeous sister spies, who are sort of like Bond chicks, only there's three of them, and they're sisters, see? I swear, the stylist who explained the whole thing thought he was a major genius for coming up with this. He looked like he was about twenty-two years old and he was wearing the tightest pair of leather pants I have ever seen in my life. It was really pretty shocking and I don't know why, given his own personal fashion sense, anyone would give this guy any control, ever, over what other people might wear. His name was Denver, which I am not making up. So anyway, Denver has decided to mix and match pieces from a whole mess of collections, to build an "eclectic sex kitten" look, presenting me and Daria and Polly as "a coherent threesome of deadly femininity." That's what he said. He's also on fire with the idea of "narrative;" each spread will create a "narrative" about sex and death and fabulously over-priced shoes and jewelry and great skimpy tops. Which meant, I'm in a fantastic sort of postage-stamp-sized camisole with leather straps that criss-cross in incomprehensible ways, on top of these mauve harem pants that have tiny threads of lace and itty-bitty mirrors running down the sides. There are like seven different kinds of beaded bracelets snaking up my left arm, two or three beaded necklaces draping over the leather straps on my chest, and incredibly cool spiky sandals which also have really cute rows of beads dripping down the front of my feet. Plus, I'm carrying this really big gun that somebody tells me is an Uzi. Daria and Polly wear variations on the same island-pirate-princess-Arabian-nights thing, but Polly sports a littler silver gun, and Daria has *two* guns—one of which she's appar-ently supposed to aim at the camera, the other being strapped to her thigh with a really bizarre but also cute sort of leather garter thing.

I don't know where they got these strange clothes, but appar-ently they got the guns at a gun store. 'Cause at one point, I was looking at my Uzi, and I said to one of the assistant dressers, Nina, "Man, this thing looks real."

Nina replied, "It *is* real." With a kind of disgusted roll of her eyes. Like, what she wanted to say was, of *course* it's real, you fourteen-year-old moron.

Which okay, I have to admit, made me mad. Maybe if she had been a little nicer, things wouldn't have gone the way they did, but she was really pretty rude, and I'm thinking, okay, you're going to hand a real gun like this to a fourteen-year-old kid, and not tell her it's real, and then act like *she's* the stupid one?

So I handed her the gun back and said, nicely, "You know, I'm really uncomfortable with this. My mom would never let my brother play with guns? And I know she would not approve of this. Would you go tell Denver that I just can't be part of a photo spread that promotes, like, violence, like this? It's against my ethics." And I smiled at her, still really nice.

She blinked. I mean, she may have known I was messing with her? But honestly, there was just no way to say that. "He's not going to . . . uh, it's part of the concept of the whole shoot," she told me, a little more cautiously nice now. Like it suddenly occurred to her that she was actually talking to a kid. Not a little kid, but, you know, to some people, fourteen is actually still a kid.

"Well, I feel really strongly that I can't like, just even, I can't do it!" I said. "It would be so irresponsible of me! Part of what I'm trying to do is be a role model to other teenagers? And I'm just so worried about, you know, acting like weapons are cool and fashionable and stuff? Could you tell Denver?"

Nina blinked again. She just stood there and kept blinking at me, she was so terrified of actually delivering this message to that dimwit, Denver. But I didn't care. The fact is, I'm willing to go along with things up to a certain point and then I just won't go there anymore. And since I am always on the edge of that point, like all the time lately, it's not ever too hard to push me over it. If Nina had been nicer to begin with, I wouldn't have started messing with her, but now that I was in it, it completely made sense to me. Who on earth would give a real scary weapon like that to a little kid? Does no one think these things through? Well, obviously no one does, but once the question shows up it's just impossible to ignore it.

"It's not that big a deal," said Nina, desperate now. "There's no ammunition or anything."

"Oh my god, I hadn't even thought about that!" I said. "Oh, no, I can't even . . . there could be an accident or something. I mean, there are accidents all the time. What if I pressed the trigger and something happened, even though no one thought anything was going to happen? Isn't that what happened to Bruce Lee? He died totally by accident on that movie about crows—"

"It was Brandon Lee and that would never—"

"Oh god, I could never—if something like that happened, it would like ruin my life. Oh, god. I can't even touch it now. You have to tell Denver, I'm completely freaked out."

It's so weird when you get on these rides. This stuff is coming out of your mouth and you know it's total shit, but it keeps coming; it's like there's some weird spook inside you who knows exactly what to say, and you don't even know where it's coming from or who that crazy spook is. But the bullshit keeps coming. Really, it's quite unusual.

Nina still had no idea what she had unleashed. "It's totally safe, Amelia," she whined, trying her best to be soothing. "I'm not kidding, I wouldn't be here if it wasn't totally safe. None of them would! If something went wrong, there would be a huge lawsuit, you think the magazine is going to risk something like that? It's completely safe. And it's such a cool idea, that you guys are like spies on like a desert island with Tom Cruise or something, it's

159

fine! I think it's so hot. This whole spread is going to be so hot."
She smiled at me, a really good pal now. She was so hopeful and
sure that I was just going to suck this up.

"I just can't," I whispered. "I'm too nervous. You just have
to talk to Denver. I'll be in my trailer." I shook my head, like
really scared, and scooted off.

Okay. The rest of the morning was wild. I sat in my lousy
trailer and watched cartoons on television and every ten minutes
somebody else showed up; assistants to the photographer, and
stylists, and a couple of PR guys from the magazine, and Polly
and Daria, both of them mad at me, and Mom, really mad, and
Denver in a complete frenzy, snarling that no fourteen-year-old
girl was going to tell him how to design his photo shoot, and
he was going to walk if somebody didn't work this out. I mean,
he was really furious that I would dare to suggest that girls with
guns was not the sexiest idea on the planet. Brother. The thing
that was truly great about it all was, the madder everyone got,
the more reasonable I looked. I mean, I didn't have to do
anything except say stuff like, "I'm sorry but weapons like this
are just not cool. All those high-school shootings? Doesn't anyone
worry about that?" People would look at me and just blather
on, but you try coming back at logic like that. It was hilarious.

The best part was when Collette showed up and tried to
calmly explain to me why I had to do what I was told. "This
is a crucial job, Amelia, I think you know that," she began.

"Yeah, but you know, Collette, you say that all the time. Every
job is crucial, isn't it?"

"It is, yes, but I think you know what I'm saying. The past
several months have gone well, but that can change at any time.

160

They're ready to turn on you. If word gets out, at this point, while you're still building a reputation? That you held up an entire shoot for hours because you wouldn't come out of your trailer? The press will make mincemeat of you, all over again. I don't think you want that to happen."

"I hear you, Collette, I do," I said. "But, you know, because of what I went through, with people in the press getting so upset with me, before, I think it's just so important for me to really present myself as a good person, you know, who wouldn't do something like wave guns around in a photo spread."

"I would never ask you to do something exploitative, Amelia," she smiled, all phony and polite. She was better at this game than any of the others. Plus, she's persistent, old Collette. "It's not like we're talking nudity here. I wouldn't even entertain something like that."

"I just really feel that making three teenagers—because that's what we are, aren't we?—wave around all these big guns, I think that glamorizes gun violence in a way that makes me really sad. If you want me to talk to the press about it, I'd be happy to. I mean, if you think they might misunderstand all this, I'd be happy to explain to them—"

"No. Thanks, Amelia, I don't actually think that would help," she smiled. She took a short breath, sort of like she was bracing herself, and started out the door.

"Plus I want to see Philip," I added.

She turned and looked at me. Man, she was mad. And then she just shrugged, like she was suddenly oh so helpless. "Well, why don't we see how the rest of the afternoon goes?" she said. "And then we'll revisit that subject."

"No, I want to see Philip," I said. Which okay I wasn't as cool as I should have been I guess because then she just knew she had me. She just stood there and smirked. I swear, I knew that I had gone too far, because of that look on her face, and it was so mean, that they wouldn't let me even talk to him, that I couldn't keep it together, and I almost started to cry even though I know, I *know*, that when you cry then you lose. But I couldn't help it; it all seemed impossible, just impossible, that my life was turning into this totally weird thing and they took my brother. They took my brother.

But that was it. I lost. I was just a teary dope now. Collette stepped back into my itty-bitty trailer, gave me a big phony hug and said, "We'll talk about it later, honey. You've made such a terrible fuss about this prop situation, I'm not so sure now is the right time to talk to your mother about favors concerning Philip. Let's get through today and then see where we are."

Honestly, it was like being in some crazy prison somewhere. Psycho prison for teenage models, that's what it was like. Anyway, eventually the guns went away and we did the shoot. Denver was in a bad mood and Daria was really nasty—I think she had been looking forward to waving those stupid guns around—but then she got over it because Denver was clearly giving me the ugliest clothes to wear for the rest of the day. Word of the whole thing made it out to the press before we had even finished— such a surprise, one of those fashionistas ratted us all out; it was probably Nina, who started the whole thing—and this reporter showed up on the set to check it out. So then one of those PR guys spun it so fast in his direction you had to admire the sheer nerve of it all.

"No one's given us a second's worth of trouble today," he smiled. "Where'd you hear that, Lou? That's ridiculous."

"So you're not five hours behind schedule," said the reporter.

"Yeah, we're behind, it happens sometimes," PR dude shrugged.

"According to my source—"

"Who's your source?"

"According to my source, the kid refused to do what she was asked and hid in her trailer for half the day. Wouldn't use the props, wouldn't—"

"Hey. I'm gonna tell you what happened because I don't want some crazy version of this showing up on Page Six. There were some questions about props. One of the stylists had an idea, a kind of James Bond spy theme that he was thinking about pursuing. But we all had questions about it. These girls are teenagers. Is it appropriate to put, you know, semiautomatic weapons in the hands of teenage girls, glamorize gun violence like that?"

"Oh because *W* magazine is so concerned about—"

"You say we're not, and I'll sue you," PR dude grinned, with a little bit of edge, so reporter dude would get the point. "It wasn't an area we thought was appropriate. *W* feels strongly that we need to be responsible around issues of gun violence. These girls are role models."

"Oh please—"

"You asked for a comment, that's the comment. You print anything other than that? And we'll make you retract it."

He put his arm around reporter dude's shoulder and steered him to the door. Right past a table full of hardware—semi-automatics, automatics, my abandoned Uzi, the bow and arrow, all of it—just lying there for anyone to pick up and walk off with: That's how responsible those dingdongs at *W* were about gun violence. Whatever. Nothing ever made it into the paper. As long as as they couldn't trash me or Polly or Daria, I guess there wasn't much of a story.

Although Daria really took a while to get over it. When we got home, she started in on me. "If you ever, again, pull anything so unprofessional, on one of *my* shoots . . ." she began.

Mom was exhausted and pissed off herself, so she just went after the first target that presented itself. "It's not *your* shoot, Daria," she snapped. "There are three of you, remember? Amelia has rights, too." This was news to me, but I was certainly happy to hear it.

"Mom!" Daria looked at her, shocked at this betrayal. "We have tried and tried with her," she said, winding up for a good long rampage. "And she is just always difficult! Always! She deliberately tried to sabotage everything today, the way she's been sabotaging everything, all along!"

"You're being histrionic. Amelia didn't sabotage a thing," Mom said. Which, aside from the fact that she actually used a word like "histrionic," how novel is that, to have your mother actually defend you for once? It was so weird my jaw actually dropped. Which made Polly snicker. Unlike Daria, Polly was laughing at pretty much everything I did these days. But none of that made Daria any easier to live with, in the moment. The more clout I had, the less she had, there was no question that was how the equation was going to end up. And she was bullshit about it.

"I am soo tired of being held hostage by children and old

women," she retorted, just plain mean now. "I'm going out." And, with a staggeringly gorgeous turn, she swiveled on those heels and headed for the door. I have to admit that both Daria and Polly really know how to move on those spikes. I, on the other hand, still look like a retarded baby cow.

"Don't be ridiculous," said Mom. "It's eleven o'clock at night."

"That's right, Mother, it is," Daria snarled, grabbing her bag. "And if we didn't live all the way out in BROOKLYN"—she hissed it, like it was the dirtiest word she could think of—"then going out and having a drink wouldn't be considered a completely crazy idea, at eleven o'clock at night. Trust me, all over Manhattan, people are going out at eleven, and some even wait until eleven-thirty and then they go! To have a cocktail! Guess what? Some of them even have TWO." And having delivered this unspeakably brilliant exit line, she stepped into the hallway and slammed the door.

"That's ridiculous," Mom snapped. "Polly, go out there before she gets on the elevator, and tell her to go to bed."

"I'm going with her," Polly shrugged. She grabbed her bag and followed Daria.

"Well, I can't go with you," Mom said. "I'm not going anywhere."

"Nobody wants you to," said Polly. "Trust me." She opened the door.

"You're only eighteen years old!"

"I know how old I am, Mom. What's your point?" Polly said, unperturbed.

"I forbid it!" said Mom.

"I got to go," Polly shrugged. And with that brilliant exit line, she was gone, too.

Mom just stood there, completely at a loss.

"Hey Mom," I said. "Mom, can I talk to you about Philip?"

"Not now, Amelia," she muttered.

"Because I thought I could go up and see him," I said.

"I said not now, Amelia!" she hissed. "Haven't you made enough trouble today?"

So much for "this isn't Amelia's fault," I thought. So much for "Amelia has rights, too." When she snuck into her little den to drown her sorrows, I tried to call him, but the stupid machine picked up as usual. So I just hung up without leaving a message, and then I called again and didn't leave another message, and then I went into the living room and tried to find something to watch. A *SpongeBob* marathon was on, so I zoned out for about six episodes in a row, and then I went to bed. I was asleep when Polly and Daria got home at five in the morning.

And then that week? The two of them stayed out till five on three separate occasions. It was like, the dam busted, there's no going back.

I tried to call Philip two more times but nobody picked up. And I did try to ask Mom about it again? And she hugged me and sent me to wardrobe. I just want that on the record. It's not like I didn't try.

So things were happening really fast by this point—bookings were coming in by the dozens, and we were being invited everywhere, to benefits and fashion shows and parties and openings. Every day we were expected to show up somewhere, some lunch or dinner or cocktail thing, in addition to interviews and shoots. Collette kept saying that it wasn't going to be this hot for very long so we had to make the most of it. And there were guys everywhere, these great-looking guys, skinny, all of them, some of them kind of junior movie stars, some of them just like somebody who knew somebody at some magazine, all of them wearing three-hundred-dollar sweaters and narrow pants, and tossing money around like crazy for things like Cristal and bottles of vodka and pu-pu platters which no one ate, and jewelry—like suddenly everyone was giving us jewelry; guys we hardly knew would show up at these shoots and parties and corner somebody, me or Polly or Daria, sometimes you didn't know who he was after, or even if he had thought it through himself before he got there, there was just suddenly some guy handing you a snaky pair of silver earrings and asking if he could put them on you himself. Which everyone was pawing at our hair and our clothes and our shoes and our jewelry all the time anyway, what was the big deal, letting some stranger put earrings on you? It was really pretty wild for a while. You couldn't think about it, there was just too much going on. And sometimes you were just so tired, there was no way to think about anything except what the stylist was saying about your makeup or if it would be okay to let somebody trim up your hair, or whether or not they'd let you take home a cute sweater or something.

So things were really popping. Whenever I'd get sick of it all, I would figure out something that I could get all moralistic about which would give me an excuse to hide in my trailer for an hour or so, until the underlings worked it out. That trick worked so well the first time, I knew I had to keep it fresh or they'd go back to treating me like some kind of pet cat. It was better to keep them a little on their guard, that's what I figured. Then Daria started to act up, too, but she was less creative about it. She would just get all huffy about shaving her legs, or she'd throw a fit about nail polish, or some poor intern showing up late with her latte, and then she'd make everybody stew until she sailed onto the set, unapologetic, an hour late. Then Polly started taking ridiculously long lunch breaks, but she wasn't playing power games, she was usually in her trailer with one of those thousands of cute guys. One time I walked by and heard her. I think she really liked the guy, but still. She was never really very discreet.

Anyway, all that worrying about our reputations went flying out the window. And you know, such a surprise, it all worked out just fine anyway. There was no more griping from Collette about behaving ourselves so that we could get the press on our side, because the press decided pretty fast that the three of us were just loads of fun. Apparently Marlon Brando said something one time, about the only thing you can do to offend the public is to bore them. One of those dudes who was always hanging around the endless fashionista party scene told me this hilarious quote, and I thought, boy is that the truest thing I've ever heard. So I thought that was pretty funny, and this guy was telling me all about Brando and how smart he was, and he seemed pretty nice, and we were having a good time laughing about it all, until Polly came over, put her arm around me and looked at him with a big grin.

"Do you know how old she is?" she asked.

"Not really," he smiled.

168

"She's fourteen," said Polly, smiling herself. "How old are you?"

The guy blinked. "I'm uh, uh—"

"Let me guess. Twenty-nine?" said Polly.

"Not quite."

"Don't even try it, I already checked with your pal." She pointed to his friend, who was hanging out on the other side of the loft we were shooting in, pouring a martini for Daria. "That makes you, hmmm, let's see, fifteen years older than my little sister. Who is looking increasingly, to everyone, like jail-bait." I rolled my eyes at that one, but there was no point in even attempting a comeback, as Mr Wonderful had already beat it out of there. I looked at Polly.

"You want him for yourself, just ask," I told her.

"Hey. Amelia. Stop talking so tough. That guy was your age, right now, before you were even born," she informed me.

"Thanks for the math lesson," I said. "I wasn't going to do anything."

"Just making sure," she said, clearly not believing me. "There is a limit."

"Sure there is."

"I mean it, would you cut it out with the cynicism? You're a kid."

"I'm hardly a kid," I told her.

"Listen, I was thinking. We should go see Philip," Polly said suddenly. These were literally the last words I expected to come out of anybody's mouth. I mean, really. You could have knocked me over. No one had mentioned Philip for months.

"What?" I said. "Why?"

"Why? What did you just say to me, why?"

169

"They won't let us see him," I said.

"What are you talking about, of course they'll let us see him." Polly was surprised I even thought that. Which just showed, what did she know?

"I tried calling him a bunch of times," I told her. "That Sarah won't let me talk to him. And he never called back."

"He called, I talked to him," Polly said.

"You talked to him? When did you talk to him?" This floored me. Polly talked to him, but he didn't talk to me?

"He called last week."

"Why didn't he talk to me?"

"He didn't want to talk to you, he wanted to talk to me."

"Well, fuck that shit."

"What?"

"What yourself," I told her. "You know how hard I tried to get to see him, or at least talk to him, and he never once called back or tried himself—"

"Hey, Amelia, don't go there, huh? He wants to see you. We should go see him."

"I don't want to see him," I said. She raised an eyebrow or, at least, I think she raised an eyebrow. I couldn't look at her. But it was the truth. I didn't want to see Philip anymore.

"Why not?" said Polly.

"I just don't," I said. "I just don't."

"Well, I kind of think—"

Before she got any further, one of the hair guys waved at me. "They need me in hair," I said. "I have to go."

"Hey. Amelia," said Polly, short. She was kind of mad now. I didn't care.

170

"You said yourself, he didn't want to talk to me, he wants to talk to you. So you go," I said. "I think you should go. Tell him I said hi."

"It's his birthday tomorrow, you know," she said. Which made me feel sick for a second, I totally forgot his birthday. He never forgot anybody's birthday. But that was a zillion years ago. For some reason, the thought of seeing Philip made me panic. It was just not going to happen, it wasn't going to happen.

"So tell him I said Happy Birthday," I told her, and I went to have my hair shellacked. And I don't know what kind of a face she was making at me, as I left, because I didn't turn around and look. There was no way I was going to go see Philip. You can't be two people at once, you just can't. If anyone tells you that you can, take it from me, they're lying.

CHAPTER TEN

Then all of a sudden, one day, Collette descends. We were out in Central Park shooting a spread for the *New York Times* Style Section—collections with lots of flowing skirts and button-top shoes, flowers, corsets, boas, garters, Polly said we looked like Victorian hookers on holiday. Anyway, everybody was freaking out because the photographer changed his mind at the last minute and said we needed more backlight. So there were something like six hundred lighting guys around setting up instruments and umbrellas and every one of them was losing it in a sort of quietly professional way, because apparently the backlight thing is catastrophically stupid in Central Park in the middle of the day.

So we're all sitting around sipping mimosas while the lighting guys freak out, and Collette sort of saunters by, leans in to me, and says, very quietly, "Could I speak with you for a minute?"

I said, "Sure, Collette, what's up?" I mean, she came by and acted mysterious all the time, and usually it meant something stupid like *GQ* wanted us all to share a dressing room and they always treated women shitty over there and she just wasn't going to stand for it. She could get bent out of shape over pretty much nothing, so you couldn't take her seriously when she whispered, with that kind of urgent concern, into your ear.

"We have an interesting kind of interest in you," she said, as if this actually meant something. And then she looked up and looked around, like a very obvious and not very good spy. She was clearly trying to locate Daria and Polly, and to make sure they were not alert to her devilish doings at this particular moment in time. Polly was nowhere in sight—these long lighting breaks meant she was spending time in her trailer with her latest friend—and Daria was way across the set, being tended to by some stylist underling who was dissatisfied with the way her corsets had strung up. Mom was under a tree, watching. I could see that she was watching, and that this conversation between me and Collette was on some level her idea. But she was letting Collette handle it, behind Polly and Daria's back.

"Yeah? What kind of interesting interest?" I asked.

"It's an acting situation," she told me.

Okay. The word "acting" is like abracadabra, as far as I can tell, in model-land, even if you're not like just some freaky kid being dragged along for the ride. Because this is how it works: You go to these photo shoots and parties and fashion shows, and everyone treats you like a star, but then they kind of make sure you know that you're a second-class citizen because you're not an *actress*. Being an actress is actually considerably better than being a model, even if you're a supermodel. I mean, it would be cool to be as hot as Giselle, but it would be way cooler to be Scarlett Johansson. There's no question, actresses

174

are higher up the food chain than models. So obviously you would rather be an *actress* but, as soon as you become a model-who-wants-to-be-an-actress, you're pathetic.

So there was Collette, having said the magic words: "It's an acting situation." Ooo-la-la.

"What kind of acting situation?" I said.

"An off-Broadway play. They need a young girl, the lead of this play is apparently fifteen years old and they saw you on *Regis and Kelly* and they think you're very right for it."

"A lead?" I said. "Of a play?"

"Your mother thinks it's a good idea. She says you've done a lot of acting, and you're very good."

"Mom said what? That's . . . you know, Collette, I have to tell you, I'm sorry Mom told you that because that's kind of a big fat lie."

"There was some school play?"

"*Horton Hears a Who!* I was in the fourth grade."

"She said you had a huge part."

"Everyone in the fourth grade gets a part, that's the rule. They give everybody a part."

"But you were really good, she said. Besides, they aren't interested in you because of what you did in the fourth grade. They're interested in you because of what you did on *Regis and Kelly*."

"That wasn't acting," I said.

"I think you'll find that it's not, actually, all that different."

"How do you know?" I asked.

"I've represented a lot of people through the transition. People like to say that models can't act, there's a real prejudice against it, it's completely unfair to you girls. Modeling and acting are basically the same thing. I have complete faith in you, Amelia. Really, this is a terrific opportunity. I think we have to look into it. They're FedExing the script to your apartment tonight."

"Does Daria know about this?" I asked.

"Let's take it one step at a time. You look at the script, I'll find out what the offer is—although, I'm warning you, it won't be more than a few hundred dollars a week. It's the theatre, you do it for love. It's a terrific opportunity, Amelia. I'm really excited for you."

"What about Daria?" I said.

"I think you know how to handle that, Amelia. You're not a child," she informed me. Which basically meant, I trust you to keep your mouth shut until Daria finds out on her own, and we'll let her throw a fit then. Collette was pretty easy to understand, once you knew her language.

Sneaking the script past Daria turned out to be the easy part of this escapade. After they figured out the backlight fiasco— they moved the shoot into a really dense thicket of trees and shot through the leaves; it looked incredibly cool so that photographer turned out not to be as stupid as everyone thought— we finished the shoot and Daria and Polly went off to hit the scene with some choice members of the Heller fan club. I told them I was tired, which they were happy to hear, as dragging the fourteen-year-old out to clubs sometimes got a little dicey. Less than you'd think, really, but it's not like it was a complete non-issue. So they took off while Mom and I took the car back to Brooklyn. Mom didn't actually say anything about anything, on the ride. We just got home, she picked up the FedEx from the doorman and we both got into the elevator, where she

176

handed it to me. Then we quietly went into the apartment and I took it to my room, and I read it.

Okay, this play, as it turns out, is about a girl who was adopted, and her adopted parents are kind of crazy and drug addicts and politically they kept saying they were libertarians, which was apparently supposed to be hilarious but I don't know what a libertarian is, so I didn't get the joke. Anyway, these drug-addict libertarian parents decide that they want to find their daughter's birth parents, but the girl doesn't really want to—that's the hilarious twist, you see, everyone always thinks the adopted kid wants to find the birth parents and the adoptive parents are all threatened by that, but in this play, she's the one who doesn't care and they're the ones who do! And then they find the birth parents who are rich, as it turns out, and kind of stuffy, and politically completely the opposite of whatever a libertarian is supposed to be. And then all these adults are wacky and do silly things and the girl is smarter than all of them.

Okay, now first let me say that, even though I'm clearly no expert, I was pretty sure that this was not a very good play. I don't go to the theatre often, but it's not like I *never* go, so over the years I have seen some good plays and some bad plays, and this was more like a bad play. The characters all behaved in completely unbelievable ways and then said things that sounded like someone thought they would be funny but they really weren't funny, or they were only funny if you put them on a bad television sitcom and then put a laugh track behind them. So I thought, what a stupid play, who would write such a stupid play? And I went to the cover page, to see who had written it? And guess what, the playwright was a movie star.

I'm not kidding, the guy who wrote this stupid play was really a big-deal movie star—not as big as Rex, but pretty big. I truly thought, I didn't know movie stars were allowed to write plays. Which admittedly is a kind of dumb thing to think, but then again, it's kind of weird that this movie star had written a play. But it did answer the next question, which would have been, why would anyone actually *do* this dumb play? The answer being, I guess, you'd do the dumb play if a movie star wrote it.

Mom stuck her head in the door of my room, politely anxious, and said, "So what do you think?" It's a good thing I had bothered to check out the name of the writer, because I knew enough not to say, "It sucks!," which would not have made any sense to anybody, because, as I've already pointed out, it couldn't suck, because a movie star wrote it.

"It's kind of interesting," I said, making myself sound interested.

"Oh good! Well. This is exciting, isn't it?" Mom smiled. She sat on the bed and looked at me with teary eyes.

"Are you okay, Mom?" I asked her. She was acting sort of funny, patting my leg kind of gently. No one was being very tender with each other lately, so it was different, really different, to have her there patting my leg like that. It was actually kind of nice.

"You're just so grown up. My baby. Fourteen years old!"

"Fourteen," I repeated, like a moron. Actually, it did seem kind of surprising, once she mentioned it. So many things had happened in the past six months, it was truly startling to think, I'm fourteen? I'm only fourteen.

"You know what I was thinking we could do, just for fun

some day?" she said, getting all excited all of a sudden. "I was thinking, we'd go to Sephora and I'd buy you one of those silver kits, like one of those old-fashioned beauty cases? And then you and I could spend as much time and as much money as you wanted, just buying makeup, to fill it. Doesn't that sound like fun?"

I looked at her. This suggestion sounded so sad and insane, in the moment, that there was truly nothing to say in response to it. What was I supposed to do with a case full of makeup? In my previous life, I never had much time for makeup. And now? People were paid hundreds of dollars a day to make me up. What was she even talking about?

"We'll bring along one of your girlfriends, Hannah maybe, I haven't seen much of her lately. Maybe she'd like to come," she continued. "And then . . . and then . . . we could go to a movie, or have lunch at the Plaza," Mom laughed a little, more and more pleased with how this idea was shaping up. She continued to smile at me, delighted with the whole scenario. Honestly, I thought, is she hallucinating?

"Hannah and I don't really hang out anymore, Mom," I said.

"Why not? Did you two have a fight?" she asked. She seemed all worried now, like an actual mother might be.

"Well, she's, you know, she's kind of still in high school, and I'm kind of doing a lot of other things these days, so . . . it just doesn't work out as much," I told her, as if this were news. She nodded, thinking about it.

"You two have been so close for so long, Amelia. You should take care of your friendships. You realize how precious they are as you grow older."

179

She clutched my hands, like one of those pictures of Catholic saints my grandma on her side used to give us for Christmas to remind us that we were only half-Jewish. It all made me think, Oh brother. Mom's acting like a saint now? As if she hadn't thrown her only son out of her apartment and her life five months ago; never once, it seems, looking back. But there was no use being snide with her, there just wasn't. She was never really any sort of brainiac, and all the rubbing up with celebrity and controversy and the paparazzi and agents and movie stars had, it seemed, finally stupefied her into a sort of happy, weepy sap who couldn't do much more than flutter and smile and spout benign truisms from the seventies. It was like what was left of her brain had collapsed into all that dopey beauty-queen stuff they made her memorize back then, and she really believed that we could all work hard and use our perfect complexions and great hair to bring about world peace. I think that was about to pop out of her mouth, so I decided to cut to the chase before she had a chance.

"Did you want to know about the play, Mom?" I said.

She brightened instantly. "The play! Did you like it?"

"It's fantastic," I lied. Which, why not? Telling the truth gets me nothing at all. The lies seem to make everyone so much happier.

"Collette said it was a wonderful project. Did you see who wrote it?"

"Kind of hard to miss," I noted.

"He's so brilliant. It's unbelievable, that an actor that wonderful is also a wonderful writer as well. It's really thrilling that they're asking about you. This could change everything, you know."

"Wow, as if things haven't changed enough already," I said.

She laughed at this, as if it were really about the most clever thing she'd ever heard. "That's why they want you, Collette told me. The director admires your wit and intelligence."

Okay, now I have to admit that I was vaguely interested in this statement.

"He said that?" I ask, immediately wanting to hear it again.

"Yes, he thought you were just terrific on *Regis and Kelly*," Mom smiled.

"I wasn't all that witty on *Regis and Kelly*, Mom, mostly I just cried," I pointed out.

"You were adorable," Mom reassured me, as if "adorable" and "intelligent" were actually the same thing, instead of polar opposites. "I'm going to call Collette and tell her how much you love the play, and find out what the next step is."

The next step was what they called a "reading." If I had actually had any experience as an actress, this is apparently the sort of event that I would have known all about. Instead, when Collette called back and said, "They're doing a reading next week, they want you to be in it," I responded, "Sure, what's a reading?"

"Well, you know what a reading is, Amelia," said Collette, expertly deciding to blast right by this unfortunate confession of complete and utter ignorance. "It's when they gather a group of actors who they are interested in having in their play, and then they sit everybody around a table, and everybody reads their part out loud and so you get an idea of what the play might be like, by hearing all these people read it. I'm sure you've done table reads before."

"Maybe not so many, Collette," I told her, deciding this time to split the difference between a lie and the truth. "How much acting did Mom tell you that I've done, again? I just think that maybe she exaggerated a little bit."

"Everybody exaggerates, it's show business," Collette reminded me. "It doesn't matter, sweetheart, you know how to read, don't you?"

"Yes, reading I can do," I told her.

"Well, you sit at a table and you read your part, and you try to act it out a little, and afterwards the director and the producer and the playwright decide what direction they want to take things. That's really all it is," she said.

"What do you mean, direction, what is that supposed to mean?"

"They're making a lot of decisions right now, is what I mean."

"So this is like an audition."

"Is that a problem? You just admitted you have no experience of acting whatsoever. I do what I can, but wrangling an offer out of a major off-Broadway theatre for someone who's never acted in *anything*—"

"Relax, would you, I didn't say it's a problem, I'm not an idiot," I told her. "I just like to know what the rules are. Do I have to do anything else at this table read?"

"Just be yourself, Amelia, and everyone will love you," Collette asserted somewhat blithely, considering how many people up to this point really didn't like me at all, when I just "was" myself. "Oh, and I appreciate your candor, in private, but in public you might not want to mention how much acting you've actually done. No one really cares about all that. What they really want is just to see how well you can fit in. When they see how terrific you are, nothing else is going to matter."

Okay, frankly, this sounded like a little bit of a con to me, but then again I thought, it's show business, and it might be fun to get an acting gig. It certainly would make some of those snotty stylists sit up and be a little nicer to me. And an off-Broadway play which paid three hundred dollars a week, but was in fact written by a movie star, would be absolutely considered a first-rate acting gig.

"I'll do my best," I told Collette.

So, at the end of the week, I somehow managed to get myself to this reading. The theatre was in a kind of nasty section of the East Village, and even though I was a full-blown New York celebrity by this point, there was no car being sent for me; I was supposed to just show up. Because that's how cool they are in the theatre: *You* go to *them*. Collette and Mom couldn't come along because, Collette informed me, people don't do that sort of thing in the theatre; that's uncool as well. So I went by myself in a taxi, and even that wasn't cool. When I got there, a couple of people were standing in front of the theatre and, as I passed them to go inside, one of them said, "Whooo, check out the model, taking the taxi. No subways for this girl." Later on I found out that he only had something like six lines in the whole reading, so who cared, right? But it shook me up. It's New York City. Who would have thought that cabs weren't cool?

Inside, there were about twenty people milling around this tiny crummy lobby—the theatre was basically this completely run-down shack, which is apparently what many major off-Broadway theatres look like. So we're all crammed into this lousy lobby, and everyone else is chatting with each other, and looking like they all know each other, and they all completely know what was going to happen next, which I for one do not. And then for a full minute, every single one of these people completely ignore me, which was a feat, considering how many photos of me were plastered all over the city at the time. It was absolutely mortifying. I mean, I truly found myself thinking, what's the matter with these people, don't they know who I am? When for the past six months I'd spent half my time wishing everyone would leave me alone. But now that people were leaving me alone it made me both mad and nervous. I mean, it's not like they were *really* leaving me alone. What they were really doing was letting me know that they weren't going to suck up to me because I was a model and perhaps in fact I should be sucking up to them because they were real actors. Which, I knew enough about these situations to know that, as soon as I sucked up to anybody, or acted nervous in any way, they would be hideous to me and all my chances of ever making this work would be down the toilet before we even started. So I just stood there, in a corner by the door, terrified, but completely pretending to be hipper than thou, and I just waited them out. Finally, a skinny guy in torn jeans and a sort of crummy old polo shirt and wild black bed-head hair sticking out everywhere came over and put his hand out, to shake. Which also surprised me for a second, as no one does that in model land; everybody just kisses you on both cheeks, whether they know you or not. Three times if they're really big phonies, and want you to think they're French.

"Hi, Amelia—you're Amelia Heller, I'm guessing," slacker

dude says, in a really posh British accent. "I've seen your photograph everywhere, god, you're even more beautiful in person. I'm Edmund, I'm the director of today's festivities. Sam, Amelia's here, have you met Amelia?" And he turns and introduces me to my movie-star playwright.

Okay, his name's not really Sam. I can't tell you what his name really is because he will sue me if I do. So, we'll just call him Sam. And he's different from Rex; well, of course he's different from Rex. Rex is such a big old macho creep there's no way he would be caught dead writing a play. Sam is not a big old macho anything. He's sort of short, and he wears a kind of goofy baseball cap, backwards, even though he must be fifty years old. And he smiles, kind of shy and goofy, and mumbles something like, "Lovely, yes, so excited that you're doing this. Terrific, I've heard just the most wonderful things about you, really thanks so much for joining us."

"Thanks," I say, and I stick out my hand to shake, too. "I love your play. I think it's just fantastic." This makes shy goofy Sam just beam. The rest of the day old Sam sits in a corner and mutters things to Edmund while jabbing his finger into Edmund's face with a kind of dark rage, so I'm pretty sure the shy goofy thing is just one of many personas that Sam has up his sleeve. But I don't have to worry about that. With all the girls, for now at least, he's real nice.

"We should get this going, yeah, Sam?" Edmund looks around, distracted, as if he could care less whether this got going or not. This is another way modeling is different from acting: In magazine land, absolutely everyone is hysterical six hundred per cent of the time. But everyone in the theatre is so cool, they apparently don't care if they ever get to work. Of course, as I quickly discovered, this is actually far more nerve-wracking than all the screaming. I truly had no idea where to sit, what to do, who to talk to, or what happened next, and since I was so desperate not to appear like some kind of nitwit who didn't know what she was doing, I hovered aimlessly around with everyone else, acting like I couldn't care less what happened next, and feeling more and more certain that I was completely fucking up without doing anything at all. Finally, all the people who wouldn't talk to me drifted into the next room, and some of them drifted toward a large table in the center of the room, while others lingered around the table with the bagels and the coffee—the only thing that is the same in the theatre and modeling worlds seems to be the table with the bagels and the coffee, which all the skinniest women didn't touch here, either. I kept my eye on Sam and Edmund, who lingered with the best of them, until finally Edmund turned and looked around, perplexed, until he found me and said, "There you are, Amelia. Guys, this is Amelia Heller, she'll be reading Lucy for us today, fantastic, Amelia, let's put you next to Kristine . . . His attention drifted off me again, but a pretty woman with red hair looked up and smiled at me and waved, really nice, so then I had a clue at least about where I was supposed to sit, and for half a second I didn't feel like a complete freak.

"I'm playing your mother," Kristine told me, smiling, as I sat down.

"Which one?" I said, smiling back at her, feeling a slight wave of relief that someone was actually telling me something for once.

"Oh no no, I can't hear that—I'm your *only* mother," Kristine laughed, shaking her finger at me. Which just confused the shit out of me.

"I have two mothers, don't I?" I asked. "Isn't that the whole point of—"

"No, stop stop stop!" she cried out, waving her hands and laughing. "My character can't stand that you think that way." She laughed again. I was quickly starting to find all this reckless good cheer really annoying.

"Ignore her, she's got a complete fetish about staying in character. It's a *reading*, Kristine," said the guy sitting next to her, who leaned across her to shake my hand. He had this kind of thinning gray hair which made him look older, like maybe fifty even, but he had dimples and a kind of hopeful sadness around his eyes that made him seem young, too, so it was like he was young and old at the same time. "She's just being an actor, you can't take it personally," he told me, friendly, like he was sharing inside information. "Of course you have two mothers. Well, maybe not of course, that's your choice, however you want to see it. In any event, there hasn't been some sort of catastrophic rewrite no one told you about. I'm Reed, I'm playing your adoptive father."

"My real father, then," I said to him.

"God bless you, my child. You are a wise and wonderful girl, just as I raised you," Reed nodded, appreciating my feeble attempt to play their little game about staying in character. I grinned. As stupid and nerve-wracking and as full of shit as this all was, it was already about seven hundred times more interesting and fun than modeling. I was desperate for these people to like me.

But there was no way they were going to do that, there just wasn't, because as soon as we all settled down and started reading the play it became apparent to absolutely everyone, including me, that I was fucking awful. The play was terrible but I was terrible too, and the rest of them just weren't. I kept reading these dumb lines and they kept sounding stupid, coming out of my mouth, and then when everybody else read them they didn't sound stupid, they sounded sort of clever and complicated and both funny and sad and even wise, somehow. I swear to god, I had no idea, at the time, how anybody was pulling it off, but those actors were really good. And I sucked. I mean, I *sucked*, and then I sucked some more, and then because I knew how bad I sucked? I sucked even worse.

At one point, after it all got as bad as it could get, I found myself completely tangled up in this long speech; it was the longest one I had and I truly could not figure out what the hell the whole thing was even about, and I sort of stumbled over some of the words, which I shouldn't have, but then I got self-conscious because, as I said, I knew I was tanking and then it just snowballed, and I wasn't even making the sentences make sense—it was really horrifying, all of it, there's no other way to say it—but anyway, I finally got through it, and then I looked up, relieved just to be done, and I saw Edmund and Sam glance at each other. Sam had this look on his face like someone had just said the most insulting thing imaginable to him, or spit at him, or something; he looked completely personally outraged, and Edmund was rolling his eyes and shaking his head, pained, truly pained and mortified, he was even sticking his tongue out a little bit, like he had just eaten a bad oyster or something. It was fast, but it was unmistakable, what they were doing: They were making faces, at each other, about what a horrible actress I was, while I was sitting right there in front of them. And I thought, well, maybe I don't know how to act? But you two shitheads have no fucking manners.

Then there was this silence, sort of blooming around us, and Reed, the only one who had even attempted for half a second to be nice to the little kid who didn't know what she was doing? He kind of gently said, "Amelia, I think that's you." Which made old Sam and Edmund look over, because they hadn't been paying attention, had they? They were too busy making faces at each other about what a bad actress the little kid was. And they saw me looking right at them, and they knew that I saw them. And I thought, maybe they can make fun of me, because I'm just a model who doesn't know how to act? But they didn't ask me to do their fucking stupid reading because they thought I was such a great actress; they asked me because I'm a model, and I'm famous. And so then I thought, they're just as shitty as everyone in model land; they just think they're better but really they're worse because they're big fucking phonies who think they're artists, when actually what they are is big fucking phonies.

So I said, "Yeah, thanks Reed, sorry, I got a little distracted by Sam and Edmund making fun of how bad I am. Where were we?"

There was this terrible pause. Which, of course there was a terrible pause; that's why I said it, because I wanted there to be a terrible pause. And then Reed said, "Top of forty-seven, sweetie."

Okay, that "sweetie" that he added just about completely did me in, because in spite of being a complete brat in the moment, I was still scared shitless. But I was also still mad, so I just looked down, and launched back in.

And I don't know if I was really a lot better after that, or if everyone was so awake, now, because I had dared to call the stupid posh show-off director and the movie-star playwright on their bullshit. But the truth is, the play suddenly got really pretty good. Especially considering how bad that play was. The rest of the first act rocked. And the person reading the stage directions said, "End of act one," and everyone clapped and started to coo about how wonderful the play was, and I stood up and went to the bathroom.

I mean, the one thing I was regretting, at that moment, was that I hadn't waited until after the act break to mouth off. Because I just was in no mood for Edmund to come over to me and say, "*Listen*, Amelia, that is not at all what I was doing, blablablabla" with Sam right at his shoulder, mumbling politely, "Oh yes, you're great blablabla." I could see them, standing up and heading right over to me, with a load of bullshit right at the tips of their lying tongues and I was in no fucking mood. So I made a beeline for the ladies' room, and I hid in one of the stalls. And I stayed in there a long time. People came and went, chatting about nothing, because they knew I was in there. But I did not come out.

Finally, no one had come into the bathroom for a while, and I thought that probably it was safe. I had disappeared with enough fanfare, and I was late enough returning to today's festivities, so I could just come out of the bathroom, head straight for the table, and no one would try to talk to me, we would just get right back into the reading and get through this horrible mess and go home. So I stuck my head out of the stall, just as crazy Kristine stuck her head back in the front door of the restroom.

"There you are, they just sent me in to look for you!" she bubbled, much too cheerfully.

"Yes, I'm coming. Please, tell them I'll be right there," I said, excruciatingly polite. She was hovering with the look of someone who wanted to give advice to the pathetic teenager who didn't know what she was doing, so I turned on the water and started to wash my hands. I was in no mood.

Kristine, however, was not one to take a hint. She came up to me, and put her hand on my shoulder. There was no way to ignore this. I had to look up at her, in the mirror.

"Listen," she said, talking really fast. "You're not terrible. Especially after you said something about how hideous they were being, it really focused you. They've been trying to find someone who could do this part for months, and they're having no luck at all—partially because it's hard to find someone who's fifteen who can actually act, but also because there are huge holes in the writing—he hasn't a clue about what a girl that age might think about anything, he has problems with women in general, I'm sure you're stunned to hear it, and someone who's so young and in such a state of turmoil anyway, he just doesn't have a clue, so the things you can't figure out, some of them are not your fault. And of course no one talked to you before we did the reading, right? Did Sam, or Ed, take half a second to sit down and talk to you about who this person is, where the points of connection between you might be? I didn't think so. So listen to me, when you got mad you were halfway there. They wanted you because you're great looking, obviously, but there's also been so much in the press about how smart and edgy you can be and they think that that's who this girl is, even though none of the character, frankly, is on the page. So the madder you get, the better off you're going to be. I don't mean yelling, just what you were doing at the end of the act—just stay in that place where your intelligence is driving the scene; talk down to everyone. Keep talking down to us, even if it doesn't make sense to do it. Except in the last scene, with me, keep it simple, stay on me and you'll be fine. Here, your mascara's a mess, don't let them see you've been crying, they've behaved very badly and you give them nothing. *Nothing*." And with that she took a Kleenex, spit on it, and wiped my eyes off.

So old crazy Kristine turned out to be all right, too. She took me back in there, and she had her arm around me like we were the oldest friends on earth. "Here she is!" she called out, happily waving to everyone, like royalty. "It's my fault, I made her tell the whole story about that hideous Rex Wentworth. I've been so thrilled that someone actually bit that terrible actor that I had to wring every detail out of her. So it's my fault, it's my fault."

"No, it's fine, you ready, Amelia?" purred our bed-head British asshole director. He was putting on the charm again, what a lying phony.

"Yeah, great," I said, paging through the script to the top of act two. I didn't look at anybody. I was just trying to stay mad.

I was going to do absolutely everything Kristine told me to. Under the circumstances, why not trust the crazy actor?

And as it turns out, Kristine's advice was pretty fucking brilliant. The play still seemed terrible to me, and the things I had to say still didn't make a ton of sense, but delivering every line with a kind of dripping sarcasm somehow made them funny, and everyone started to laugh—at me, at my lines, the way I was delivering them, but then, at some point, they were just laughing at me because I started to do it, I started to act. I made faces, and I leaned in and zinged people, and I leaned back in my chair like I was bored with them all because I was a snotty teenager who thought they were all stupid, and then at the end, when I had my big scene with Kristine, she took my hand and talked to me real simple and direct, and I remembered even the last thing she told me, to stay simple, so that's what I did, and she was being so nice, and taking such good care of me, just the way she did in the bathroom, that I almost started to cry again, and then I stopped myself because I didn't want people to see how scared I really was, and then old Reed, who was playing my dad, leaned in, over Kristine's shoulder, and smiled at me, and let me know just quietly like that, that I was good. So then I almost cried again, and actually had to wipe one of my eyes with the back of my hand. The whole room was silent. And I said my last line, and then I glanced over at stupid Sam and old creepy Edmund, and they were not making fun of me now.

The stage-directions person said, "Blackout. End of play." And then everyone applauded, really loud and appreciative, and all of them started in on me, right away, how good I was, how I really "found" Lucy, how funny she is—no one knew how really funny old Lucy was until they saw me do it—I was a knockout, never heard the second act before, not really, that last moment was so vulnerable and Lucy is so funny! Edmund and Sam came up and congratulated me and thanked me with real pleased kind of smarmy dignity. The whole thing felt just great. Still, I decided I'd better beat it out of there while they still loved me, so before the tide turned I thanked everybody really fast and headed for the door.

Unfortunately, of course, there were no cabs in front of the theatre, so I just stood there, stupidly looking up and down the block for about four minutes. Which meant that everybody else drifted out behind me and I had to talk to them all again, so then I had to say good-bye twice, which I always hate. Finally, the six-line guy came up behind me and said, "Are you looking for a cab? You can't just stand in the middle of the block, you have to go to Third." Which I guess was his way of apologizing for being so snotty when I got there. At least, that's what it seemed like to me, because then he kind of shrugged and gestured for me to follow him, which I was about to do, when old Edmund stuck his bed-head out of the theatre and said, "Amelia, grand, I was hoping I might catch you. Sam and I were wondering if we could have a word."

I looked over at the six-line guy, who tipped his head, and got this kind of clever look on his face, like this meant something that he understood even if I didn't. He smiled at me. Then he turned and headed off. And I went back in.

CHAPTER ELEVEN

Such a surprise, Daria was a little upset when she found out that I was going to be the lead in an off-Broadway play that was written by a movie star. I thought, frankly, that she was going to faint; she turned kind of white and had to hold onto the kitchen counter when Mom decided to drop this bombshell like the cheeriest of good tidings, something we all would really want to dish about, first thing in the morning.

"I'm sorry, what did you say?" Daria said. She was staring into her cup of coffee, as if it were the one who had actually said the words.

"Amelia is going to star in a play, off-Broadway, that was written by Sam Vermillion!" Mom gushed. "It's amazing, really, they offered it to her after just meeting with her once!"

"They *offered* it to her?"

"Isn't it fabulous?"

"*Fabulous.*"

It was really pretty bizarre—Mom would say something, and it would sound like we were all going to Disneyland, and then

Daria would repeat it, and it would sound like we were being invaded by Iraq. Polly just stood in the doorway, looking kind of sleepy and confused. I mean, we had really been unexpectedly successful in our attempts to keep them both in the dark up to this point. They were completely blindsided.

"They didn't offer it to me, Mom," I said, feeling kind of embarrassed now. "I had to read, and—"

"You *auditioned*," said Daria, turning on me, icier now, more in control.

"It wasn't an audition, it was like a table read," I explained, trying not to sound scared. "They asked me to, you know, come in and do this reading, and that's why, it wasn't an offer, it was more like an audition—I mean, it wasn't an audition, but they didn't offer me the part until after the reading, it was like that," I concluded, lame as hell.

"Fascinating," noted Polly. She and Daria exchanged a glance. Of course they exchanged a glance; they were the team now, and I was the one who had betrayed them yet again. Polly reached for the coffeepot, and poured herself a cup, considering carefully what to say next. She settled on a sort of pissy, "Wow."

"It's sort of a bad play," I offered. They were both so quiet, that I felt the need to apologize for all of it. "I mean, the part is really stupid and the play is *so* stupid, it's like unbelievable how bad it is."

"I'm sure it sucks," Polly said. Daria just stood there. This was worse than screaming.

"You said you liked it!" Mom protested. "It's a big part. She's the lead!"

196

"Yes, you said that already, Mom," Polly informed her.

"Well, aren't you going to congratulate her?" Mom asked. "Collette says it's going to get a lot of attention. This is really a very big step for Amelia, it's just such an opportunity!"

"Yeah, congratulations, squirt," Polly said, not actually sounding like she wanted to congratulate anyone. "It's just a little surprising, Mom, that Daria and I are only hearing about this now. There was a reading and everything, Collette set this whole thing up, is that what you're saying?"

"Well, of course she did," said Mom, getting all ruffly, like an offended pigeon. Polly ignored the tone and kept right on going.

"Yeah, see, well, that's a little confusing. Like why we didn't know. Like, why didn't you tell us, Amelia, that you had this big reading? When was it?"

"Yesterday," I said.

"Uh huh, yesterday, and this has been in the works, then, for how long here? Huh? Amelia?"

"Just since, you know, last Friday."

"*Last* Friday!" she exclaimed, pretending to be surprised. It was horrible "You got a call about this a week ago, and you never thought it was worth *men*tioning—"

"It wasn't, if it didn't, you know, I didn't think I was gonna get it, so I didn't want to make a big deal about it—"

"Don't lie, you little liar, you're bad at it," she said, finally letting me have it.

"I didn't think I was going to get it!" I yelled. "I almost *didn't* get it, what would be the point of making some big stupid scene if it wasn't going to happen anyway?" It was good that

Polly was finally being mean, it gave me an excuse to yell, which felt better than apologizing.

But Polly just shot right back. "That's bullshit. You were hiding it. You were *hiding* it!"

"What is the matter with you?" Mom started. "If you can't be happy for your little sister—"

"Both of you," said Polly. "You both were hiding it. And Collette, was she the one who told you not to tell us?"

"You should be happy for Amelia. You should be celebrating."

"Yeah, Mom, that's why you didn't tell us. Because it's so fucking *swell*."

"I'm telling you now!" Mom protested, all indignant and parental.

"You should have told me," Polly said again, right at me. And she didn't stalk out of the room, which really is one of her favorite moves. And I was really kind of hoping for it, for once, I just wanted her to go so I didn't have to look at her angry face. Daria gets mad, who cares, she's just a selfish bitch anyway. But Polly is different, and she just stood there and looked at me, waiting for me to say something.

"I didn't want to make a big deal about it," I repeated, lame. I was just lame; I was so so lame.

"How much does this thing pay?" asked Daria coolly. Philip used to call her the Ice Queen; boy did he have that right. When she panics she sort of loses her mind for a minute, but just for a minute. After the initial panic she gets real smart, and the fact that Polly had gone off on a rampage for a minute had given her enough time to settle into a game plan. "Amelia, did they tell you how much they're going to pay you to be in this play?"

"Three seventy-five a week," I said. Which sounded as stupid as she knew it would. By that point, we were each making five figures a day.

"Well, I hope you aren't thinking some little play is going to interfere with work. We have a lot of commitments coming up and no one who's writing a check—a real check, I mean— is going to stand for that. And neither will I, by the way."

"Collette says—" Mom started.

"Yes, I'm interested in hearing what Collette has to say. This is business. If Amelia thinks she's going to abandon our commitments for some stupid off-Broadway play, Collette is going to hear from me about it. Obviously it would be a different story if she had a film, but a *play*?" Daria sneered. She had her cell phone out, and the speed dial was going. "Hello, Collette? Hi, it's Daria. Listen, I just heard Amelia's *terrific* news about this little play she thinks she's going to do? And I want to make sure you heard it from me first. If this interferes in any way with any of our major bookings? Polly and I are going to find ourselves a new agent."

"Don't you think you should ask Polly, before you start making ultimatums on her behalf?" Mom tried to sound all in charge but she just didn't pull it off. It was pathetic.

"It's okay, she can speak on my behalf, Mom," Polly countered. "Somebody has to."

"You both are being ridiculous!" Mom cried, suddenly overwhelmed and furious. It always works this way: She likes all the drama for about four minutes and then she just collapses. "This is terrific news for Amelia, and all you can do is complain! After everything she's been through, that you can't congratulate her, and be happy for her? I'm ashamed of both of you!"

"Shut up, Mom," I said. But I wasn't mean about it. I didn't want to behave badly; I just wanted everybody to shut up. That was not about to happen, though. Daria's voice was getting higher and higher.

"I don't want to hear it, Collette. It took four months to schedule the *Vanity Fair* piece, and I am not . . . oh at least that long, do not *even* . . . I'm not *talking* about the *in*terviews, and you *know* it! I am not, you are the one who changed the rules . . . listen to me . . . are you . . . *listen to me.*" She was shouting into the phone. Then all of a sudden she snapped. "*Nineteen is not old!*" she screamed. Only it wasn't like a scream; it was worse than that. I don't even know what it was. Which I couldn't believe Collette actually would say that to her, but I guess she did. Anyway, Daria was shaking now, actually shaking, and her voice too, but she stayed pretty tough.

"I'm just letting you know," she hissed, into the phone. "You go behind my back again, and you'll regret it." I expected her to snap the phone shut and throw it at the wall, but, for the second time that morning, a Heller girl held her ground. She didn't hang up the phone, she listened for a long moment, then she took the phone off her head and held it out to the center of the room so we all could listen to the sound of Collette now tap dancing wildly, and apologizing her head off, on the other end of the line. Daria glanced at Polly, checking in with her lone ally, and then put the phone back to her ear.

"Whatever, Collette. If this gets too complicated, we're finding new representation. Good, well that's good," she said, coolly

200

reasonable all of a sudden. "Okay, I'll tell them. Bye." She hung up and looked at Mom. "She's coming over for lunch," she announced.

"Really, Daria, I just think this is so . . ." Mom was at a loss for words.

"So *what*, Mom? You and Amelia have been lying to us. Under the circumstances, Polly and I are being pretty reasonable."

"The implication that somehow Collette and I do not have your best interests at heart is just—"

"It's just the truth and you'll have to live with the fact that I'm onto you. Both of you," Daria announced. And then she stood there, and stared at us both. And I thought, people kept making pronouncements, they keep throwing exit lines around, but nobody leaves. I just kept wishing somebody would leave the room and turn the fight off. If Philip had been there, he would've done it, he would have just slumped out of the room, like this was all too boring to be believed, and then I could have followed him, and we would have watched *Star Trek* or some other really boring old television show that he liked, and whoever was left in the kitchen would keep at it for a while longer, but the steam would have been let out, and eventually it all would have just been over. But Polly and Daria were definitely not going to leave, and neither was Mom, and I didn't feel like being the one to go, either; that just felt like losing, and even though I felt stupid and I knew I should have told Polly I was sorry, I also didn't think it was a good idea to admit to anybody that I was willing to suck it up and say I lost. More and more I was understanding that that is a big fucking mistake. I mean, Philip never cared about that stuff, and look what

201

happened to him! So I sat there. We all sat there. For a really long time.

Collette eventually came over to suck up to Polly and Daria and make sure they knew that my being in a play would give all *three* Heller sisters cachet, it showed we were serious players; besides, somebody had to be first, it may as well be Amelia who sticks her neck out, the critics will be nicer to her because she's so young, let Amelia take the brunt of it and pave the way for the better offers, much better film and television offers, which were going to pour in for Daria and Polly very soon. Somehow good old Collette managed to relate all of this without sounding in the least bit desperate; she sat there in the kitchen, in her tight little suit—she even wore suits on Saturday, which I found creepy, if you want to know the truth—and she blathered on, and we listened. When she wanted to, Collette could make everything sound perfectly dreamy: I hadn't betrayed them. I was just the front line of the fabulous new wave of acting work which was about to come hurtling at us from every corner of the show-biz universe. Daria and Polly bought it, even though they also knew it was mostly bullshit. And we all somehow made it out of that kitchen alive.

But Daria's point had been made: There was no way I was going to slink away from the three sisters act, even for some big old part in a play written by a movie star. So Collette was suddenly working overtime to make everybody's schedules "mesh," which was her oh so useful word for trying to figure out how Amelia was going to juggle two full-time jobs. Which was something that might have been possible in some other universe, where people like Daria and Polly would agree to

reschedule things even the teeniest bit, to accommodate my one day off a week from the play. Unfortunately, in the universe *I* lived in, Daria would instead say things like, "No, I can't move *Time Out* to Monday—that's when I'm having my Brazilian, and I can't reschedule, it's just impossible to get in to see Lope, you know how much trouble I had last time . . ." So the question of the day, every day, became: How is our Amelia going to be in two places at exactly the same time? Because Daria wasn't the only one who took the position that she didn't have to be flexible. There was really no one in model land who was particularly nice about it. The fact that Sam had written the play made an impression, as movie stars will, and that bought us some leeway. But Collette had to do an amazing amount of sucking up, to absolutely everybody, to make anything work at all.

I tried to stay out of it—I was ordered, in fact, to stay out of it, by Collette; that's how bad the whole thing was—but boy did I hear about it. Whenever I overslept—which didn't happen very often because Daria was a total fanatic about getting places on time, as usual—I heard about it from the stylists, and the photographers, and anybody else who thought they could get a shot in. So much for my fantasy that being an actual actress would make people suck up to me more. And my new actor friends—who took most of the hits, because they weren't paying me any money—weren't too happy either. At our first rehearsal, old bed-head Ed managed to work my situation into his opening remarks.

"We're really excited to be here, as I think you know, so I wanted you all to take a minute and congratulate yourselves.

Sam and I both worked hard at putting this cast together, and there isn't one of you who we don't think is just first rate, honestly, I couldn't be more thrilled with the caliber of the acting that surrounds me at this very moment," he announced. "Unfortunately, there are going to be some scheduling issues that we, ah, were not fully aware of even a couple of weeks ago. Miss Amelia Heller has come to us with a price attached to that gorgeous head of hair. So we're going to have to ask people to be patient. It's nothing that isn't workable, but there are definitely anomalies in the calendar, so to speak . . ." he announced. And then he went on to describe how we had to move the day off every week to make room for some big-deal modeling gig that I was required to be at, and also that they were going to rehearse the two-and-a-half scenes of the play that I wasn't in about seven times more than anything else, because there were so many days that I couldn't be there at all, in addition to the days off that I was demanding to have moved around. No one said anything—everybody was really nice about it— but they all definitely got a little tense. I didn't blame them. I barely made it through that first read-through without completely tanking, and now I was saying I wasn't going to show up at rehearsals?

But there was nothing I could do about it. We had big shoots and little shoots and even a couple of runway shows scheduled, and all of them had excruciatingly important fittings attached that simply couldn't be moved! It was completely mortifying, truth be told. Most of those good actors had somehow figured out how to survive on the spectacularly subhuman wages they were being paid in these bankrupt off-Broadway theatres. Telling them that their rehearsal schedule was going to be twisted into something resembling a pretzel in order to accommodate my twenty-thousand-dollar modeling gigs was frankly embarrassing. Especially since I was back to being not such a good actor after all.

The thing about acting is, of course, that everyone thinks they can do it. You watch people on television or in the movies and they're all fairly rotten, and you think, I can do that! Because it just looks like you get up there and pretend to be happy or sad, and do things that you wouldn't do in your normal life and everybody watches you and nobody has to be terribly good at it and it looks like fun. But the fact is, pretending to be somebody else, and making it believable; all the different things that person is supposedly going through? Is actually harder than you'd think.

And then, not only that, but in the theatre, you have to do a lot of it, in order, again and again and again. In movies and TV, apparently, they do the acting in bits and pieces and so you just have to make it through a few lines and then you move on to someone else's shot and you get all this time off to sit around in your trailer. So, apparently movie and television acting is more like modeling. But theatre acting is harder. For that you seem to need something everyone called "technique." There was a lot of talk about technique while we were rehearsing Sam's bad play. I know they all thought they were being subtle and nice, but they clearly were talking about me, and the fact that I didn't have any, although no one ever actually bothered to explain what "technique" actually is.

After a while, I stopped worrying about what technique was,

and just tried to figure out how I was going to pull this whole thing off. I mean, I had in fact told Collette that I didn't know what I was doing? And even though I went ahead and passed that reading-slash-audition, I never actually pretended even then that I knew what I was doing. But now I was in the soup, and truly, I truly did *not* know what I was doing. There were some rehearsals when I couldn't remember where I was supposed to be on the stage, or even if I was supposed to be on the stage, that's how lost in space I was. I got my lines down—I mean, remembering the lines wasn't actually a problem—but doing them right? Was a complete crapshoot.

This is like, one rehearsal:

I'm on stage, and Ed comes up. "Amelia," he says, "maybe if, there's a sense here, that your anger at your mother, the way she's manipulating everyone all the time, that's not something that you haven't noticed, right? Lucy is shrewd, she's onto everything, and I'm wondering if we can't add a tone of exasperation into this scene." Then he smiles at me, quite hopeful, really positive, even.

"You want me to be exasperated with her?"

"Just a touch, underneath the affection. I mean, she's a basket case here, you're not going to hit her while she's down, but if you could just add a color, I'm thinking it can kind of leak through in the middle of the speech, how really exasperating she can be and has been, like every fucking second of your life, and then of course you put a lid on it. I don't want you turning into Godzilla or anything."

"Godzilla was exasperated, that's why he took down Tokyo?"

"Right, right, mixing my metaphors. Sorry. But you under-

206

stand what I'm going for, right? I never want to lose the edge of her intelligence. Don't be too gentle here."

"Gentle isn't intelligent?"

"Just a slight bit more edge, that's all."

"Yeah, but she's crying."

"She's crying in a manipulative way."

"I can't hear this," Kristine says.

"Sorry, sorry, I think you know what I mean. Amelia. Let's just try it again."

So I do it again and then turn to look at Ed, who nods, thoughtful, and then he says something like, "Sorry, yes, sorry, Amelia, now maybe you could tell me what it is you think you're playing? Because I'm not quite . . . ah . . ."

"Exasperated, you told me to play exasperated, so that's what I did," I say.

"Yes. Sorry. I see, yes," he nods, looking perplexed. "Right, well, let's take a look at the scene from the beginning; maybe if we take a run at it, that will clarify things, right? Kristine, Reed, that sound good to you?" And Kristine and Reed nod, look down at their scripts—no one looks at me—and then we take a crack at it from the top.

That's a true story; I didn't make that up. And other things like that happened pretty much every day.

Ed was actually pretty polite about it, in a sort of quietly horrified way. Everyone was *so* polite, in fact, that I thought for sure I was going to get fired. I cornered Kristine in the bathroom one day and pumped her about it.

"Are they going to fire me?" I said. I frankly saw no reason to beat around the bush. Everyone was being so positive and nice all the time it was making my head hurt. That may have also been the double Ambien at night to help me sleep, and caffeine overdose in the morning to help me make it through the day. But mostly, I'm pretty sure, it was the excruciatingly good manners of all these nice people who were now being way too swell about what a bad actress I was.

"No, of course they're not going to fire you!" Kristine chirped. She was always particularly cheery when she was lying about something, so I knew she knew more than she was telling me.

"They should fire me; I'm awful," I said.

"No, you're really getting it," she told me. "For someone with as little experience as you have, it's remarkable, you have your lines down, and you remember your blocking, you're doing really terrific work."

"I'm terrible," I insisted. I was not trying to get her to tell me I was good. I just wanted someone to look at me and say, "Yeah, you suck." Sometimes you just want that, I don't know why.

But she wouldn't do it. "You're working really hard; everyone is impressed," she told me. "And I know that Sam is a little frustrated at the pace of how things are moving forward? But sometimes that's just the way it goes. Some plays come together the first week, and that's not good either. Then things fall apart during previews, and then the critics show up before you can get it together again. You should just pray that that doesn't happen!" she chortled. "The process is always different, but everybody knows what they saw at that read-through! People know you can do it! You just have to believe it yourself!"

"Yeah, thanks, Kristine!" I chirped back at her. "You're right.

I do, I just have to *believe* in myself, I don't need to know how to *act*." And I admit I put some edge on it; all that exasperation that Ed kept harping on to me about was right there when it wanted to be. Kristine blinked a little, hurt. I shouldn't have been so mean, I know, but I was really whipped at that point, and really tired of absolutely nobody telling me anything useful.

"Well," she said, with a big tonal shift in her attitude, "I do know that they're really happy with all the publicity you've brought to the production. So I don't think you need to worry about being fired." And with that—because she's somebody who still knew how to exit on a really good exit line—she swept out of the room.

And it was, at least, something of an answer. They weren't going to fire me, but it wasn't that they really thought I was ever going to be any good. They just liked the fact that the press was all over me and, consequently, all over their stupid play.

Which was true, the press really *was* all over the fact that I was in their stupid play. I hadn't noticed it at first, because they were usually all over me anyway; it wasn't that big a change, to tell the truth. But somebody at the theatre sent a press release out and it got in all the papers, the *Times*, the *Post*, the *Daily News* all ran it as a squib in their gossip columns. So the first day of rehearsal there were a half-dozen photographers outside the theatre snapping pictures of everybody, which was not necessarily the best thing to have happened, as nobody was expecting it. Ed showed up wearing torn jeans and a dirty sweatshirt, and the *Daily News* ran a picture of him smoking a cigarette and looking like a slob, which clearly annoyed him.

But pictures of me going into the theatre, and leaving the theatre, and walking down the sidewalk on the way to the theatre, started showing up everywhere. Everyone seemed to find it fascinating that the kid who bit Rex Wentworth was in a play off-Broadway. It was even on the news one night—someone caught footage of Sam chatting me up while we walked to Third Ave—and then they added old footage of the Olsen twins and Lindsay Lohan with Christian Slater from about three years ago, so suddenly I was in the middle of a big piece about teen supermodels and movie stars in the Big Apple. Which I thought was kind of stupid, even though Mom and Collette loved it. Daria and Polly didn't watch.

Even the mighty *Vanity Fair* got in on the act. They finally came through with a big piece on us, which apparently cost Collette a pound of flesh, but as I said it came through, and it was big. This snaky writer showed up at our apartment and made a big deal out of all three of us—really the guy was so smooth, you felt like he was your best friend like the instant he walked through the door—and then he asked all sorts of astonishingly personal questions which Daria and Polly and Mom answered without even blinking. It was unreal; the guy would say things like, "So you were pregnant before you got married?" or, "What about the divorce, what was that like?" and Mom would happily tell him anything he wanted to know. She especially gave it up on Philip. "Oh, it was awful. When the picture came out, in the *New Yorker*, and the girls started getting so much attention, Philip couldn't handle any of it. He was acting out at school and egging Amelia on, trying to get her to act out as well. He was completely out of control; I was terrified!"

Which was both kind of not true, and stupidly indiscreet. But this writer was so handsome and compassionate, you just wanted to tell him whatever bullshit you could, to make his story about our fabulous family even more fabulous, because you knew that's what he wanted, too.

"Were there drugs involved?" he asked Mom, after she gave up that totally phony lying confession about Philip.

"I didn't know. I hope not, I just can't say for sure," she sighed. "His father is doing his best to get him in line. I'm praying that he has better luck than I did."

"You were Miss Tennessee!" announced our new best friend. "Tell me about that." Polly went white. She has a complete phobia about Mom's moment in the sun; she thinks it's hopelessly unhip and that, if it gets out, it will ruin us all. But Mom just laughed, and Daria laughed and talked about how she used to think that was *sooo* glamorous when she was a little kid, like, weren't we all so silly, and then Mom and Daria and Polly gave up a ton of dirt on old Dad, some of which even I didn't know. It was quite a love-fest.

I probably would have gotten sucked in as deep as everyone else, but there were so many subjects that were danger zones with me that I had been ferociously overprepped by Collette not to let anything out of the bag. Part of the reason this whole thing had taken so long to set up was that she was absolutely adamant that the whole Rex Wentworth fiasco was utterly off-limits, as per her deal with Kafka's scary granddaughter. So when this guy turned all that bizarre charm on me and said, "What do you want to say about Rex Wentworth? Any regrets there, Amelia?" I knew not to give up one word.

"I can't talk about that," I said.

"It's something that really won't go away, isn't it?" he smiled, full of compassion for me and my difficult situation.

"Can't talk about it," I said.

"Wow, they've got you prepped," he laughed.

"I'm going to get some water, okay, you want some?" I asked.

He thought this was utterly delightful. "Wow, you're tough," he said, all sunny admiration. "You're right, there's no point in dwelling on the past. The future, then. I understand that you're acting now. Tell me about that. It must be thrilling to work with Sam Vermillion." Seriously, it's like all these magazines give a shit about are movie stars; like they're the only people of interest on the entire planet.

Anyway, part of the deal with the *Vanity Fair* guy turned out to be that he wanted to "trail" us through our exciting days and nights at fashion shoots and parties and nightclubs. This meant that he just would show up whenever he felt like it, and pretend to be one of our friends, while pumping people around us for more indiscreet information which would make his fabulous piece on the fabulous Heller girls even more fabulous. Most of the gang down in fashionista-land were totally on board with this, as magazines and gossip and hype are more or less the entire reason they get out of bed in the morning. But to most of the impoverished actors in Sam's terrible play, the *Vanity Fair* thing was truly new and amazing territory. When Ed announced that a writer from *Vanity Fair* was going to be trailing me through rehearsal one day, all my new friends acted like they thought it was a big joke. Of course *Vanity Fair* would join the rush to make a big deal out of the teenage model who thought she could act! They were really not very nice about it, except for Sam, who took me aside and asked me if I felt comfortable with this writer and said he was going to put a word in with the editor to make sure that this was handled properly. He was really nice about it, even though I was pretty sure he was more worried about what the guy might say about his play than he was about me. Anyway, mostly people just acted hipper than thou, like they thought *Vanity Fair* was a pretty stupid rag, but then they all dressed up on the day that the writer was showing up, and they strutted around and posed beautifully, even when they weren't working on a scene. And to give them their due, not one of those actors said a mean thing about me. I read the article later, and all of them, behind my back, told that guy that I was an amazing girl and a terrific young actress who had remarkable depth and intelligence for someone my age. Like, I know that most of them resented the hell out of the fact that I was getting so much attention, when I could barely walk and talk on that stage at the same time. But they sure knew how to sling the shit, and make it sound convincing, too.

So all that stuff was going on, and then our billboard went up, in Times Square.

Okay, now, I admit that I knew that this was going to happen. We had done a shoot for this really hot line of slip dresses from Anthropologie something like four months ago, and they told us they were going to use it for a billboard somewhere. It was a very cool shot, simple but good; they had all three of us in this vertical arrangement—me on the bottom, looking off to the right, with my head hitting the midpoint of Polly's stomach, then Polly standing in the middle, looking straight at the camera, and Daria right above her, looking off left. So Daria and I were in profile, in opposite directions, and they had about eight fans blowing so there was hair going in every direction, including up, since Polly's was spiked and gelled and totally punked out. I swear to god, there are very few people who can pull that off and not look like a total flake, but Polly can because she's got more attitude than anyone I've ever met, and besides which her eyes are so green you get kind of overwhelmed by them for a second. So she's smiling at the camera like a witch; she looked completely hot, and behind her Daria was on this teeny stepstool, so that her chin could clear Polly's spiked hair, which meant that to keep the three of us tight in the shot they had to have her holding onto Polly's chest from behind, and me holding onto Polly's thighs from the front. I mean, we were really clinging to each other, and the slip dresses were hardly any clothes at all and nobody had any underwear on, so it was a little like being asked to make out with your sisters. Which was sort of creepy, but we all decided just to relax about it, so mostly nobody got too uptight except some of the gaffers who seemed to be having trouble focusing, quite frankly.

Anyway, as I said it was a very good shot and they had said it was going to go up on a billboard in or near Times Square, and every now and then Collette would call with an update about it. And probably she had even called like that week. But honestly, I was working on my lines and my blocking and truly trying to just figure out how to act better. By that point, I really did not want to be the person who ruined this bad play for everyone else. So that is what I was thinking about, not some stupid billboard in Times Square. And besides which, I had no idea that a billboard in Times Square is something that is even bigger and more astonishing than, say, having your picture in the *New Yorker*, or biting a movie star.

So one day I come into rehearsal, and everyone is there, murmuring amongst themselves, like something really sobering and important has happened. Like when the Pope died, everyone talking in hushed tones because these are serious days. So I dumped my stuff on one of the ratty old seats in that ratty old theatre and I looked at Reed and I said, "What's going on, did something happen?"

And Reed said, reassuring, "Nothing, nothing! No, nothing! Kristine was just telling us that she saw your billboard in Times Square. We just didn't even know it was happening. It must be really exciting for you."

He smiled at me, very polite, but a little formal, too. He was kind of acting like his feelings were hurt; like I had kept some big secret from him and that maybe now he thought I was kind of untrustworthy, in addition to being such a catastrophically bad actress.

"Oh!" I said. "Is that up? I totally forgot about that."

"You forgot about it?" Kristine laughed, again way too cheery. "Well, now that it's there, that's going to be a little hard to do. It's eight stories high."

Edmund entered, looking like he had a hangover, and immediately came over. "Are you talking about Amelia's billboard?" he asked, eager to get in on this. "I saw it last night, my god, it's spectacular. Well done. It's gorgeous. Can I meet your sister? Which is the one with the spiky hair? My god, she's hot."

"Polly," I said.

215

Kristine took charge. "How old is she, eighteen?" she asked.

"Yeah, she's eighteen and Daria's nineteen," I said, uncomfortable.

"Eighteen, Ed," Kristine warned, wagging a finger at him. "Eighteen."

"That's legal, isn't it? She's allowed to vote!" he grinned. "She's a model. Eighteen is much older in model years; she's definitely old enough to date."

"Well, it's very exciting, we're very happy for you" said Reed, still formal, and even a little sad. "Congratulations." Then he picked up his script and went onto the stage, where he sat on the pretend couch in the pretend living room, and pretended to study his lines.

All morning, while we were working, he was definitely acting differently toward me, kind of avoiding my eye and stuff. And I did not want him to be mad at me. I didn't know why he would be, but I just felt terrible, like I had made a big mistake without even knowing what it was. I mean, I liked that guy, I really did, and there weren't so many people that I actually liked anymore. So I just went up to him, on our lunch break, when he was sitting by himself in the house, and I said, "Are you mad at me?"

He looked at me, kind of surprised at this. "No," he said. "Of course not."

"You won't even look at me," I said. "All morning."

"I'm not mad, Amelia."

"Because I didn't tell you about the billboard?" I asked him.

"No, no——" he started to try and explain himself, but I was so worried, I just rolled ahead.

"Yeah, like you think that I didn't tell you about that billboard on purpose or something? Or that you think that maybe I think I'm better than you; I don't talk about things because I think I'm such hot shit?"

"No," he said.

"Yeah, well, the thing is, I just don't like to talk about all that stuff," I blathered. "I don't think I'm better than anyone. I just think all that shit is just shit, not that it's *shit,* I don't want to be *ungrateful,* I understand that it's important and everything, but you know it's also just not that big a deal, it's just not. It's just a billboard."

"Just a billboard, in Times Square," he said, with kind of a sigh. "That is an extraordinary point of view. You know that, don't you?"

"Well, I know it doesn't happen to everybody, I'm not saying that," I said.

"No, it doesn't," he said back, raising his eyebrows, like that was such a fucking mega-understatement.

"Look, what am I supposed to do about it?" I asked him, getting kind of mad. "I mean, really. Maybe I just don't care. Did you ever think of that?"

"What do you mean, you don't care?" he asked me. He sort of crinkled up his nice little sad face, thoughtful, like he was really hearing me and taking in what I was saying. I mean, all of a sudden, somebody was actually listening to me. Which I got to tell you, was pretty fucking novel, at that point. It was so novel that in fact I almost started to cry.

"I just don't care," I said. "I don't care."

"Amelia?"

"I don't care," I said again. What a lamebrain. I finally had someone actually listening to me, and all I could say was nothing at all. So the two of us just sat there for a minute, with me trying not to cry, and him just thinking, I guess. I don't know. After a second, when I had it more together, he said, "Can I ask you a question?"

"Why not," I said.

"Shouldn't you be in high school? What grade are you in?"

This was so out of left field and so completely the right question to ask, I almost started to cry again. But I didn't. "I don't know," I said.

"You don't know?"

"I was a freshman last year, but they kicked me out of school because I was causing so much trouble," I told him. "I mean I wasn't deliberately, but it just was every time I showed up something bad happened. Then they said I could do all this modeling, and have a tutor and stuff, and it would be the same thing as being in high school, but I never got a tutor, there's like no time. So, I'm just, you know . . ."

"You know that's illegal," he told me, very quiet. "You're, how old are you? Fourteen? Your parents have to see to it that you're educated. You're not allowed to just skip high school."

"You're not going to tell somebody, are you?" I said. "Because that's the last thing I need. They all got so mad at me, all this stuff happened, I didn't, please don't tell anyone. No one cares. Trust me, no one cares! I have a big billboard in Times Square, who's going to care if I . . . you know, high school, who cares . . ." I trailed off. I really was ready to just kill myself. I didn't have so many chances anymore to really talk to anybody at all, nobody wanted to just talk, so I was sorry that I was blowing it. But that old Reed just sighed.

"I have two kids," he told me. "So these things just occur to me." This surprised me, he seemed so young. But he was playing my father, why wouldn't he have real kids of his own? Sometimes you just get yourself so confused that the most normal things just don't even cross your mind.

"Look, my mom is fantastic," I said. I just felt like such a terrible person all of a sudden; really, she's my *mom*, and I didn't want him to think that she was fucked up or anything. "She's on top of it. Besides, you know, I'm old, I'm not like a kid, fourteen is . . . it's not a kid," I told him.

"No, I know," he said, and he sighed again. "Well, I'm not mad at you, okay? But you know, you're wrong about what you said. Having an eight-story billboard in Times Square is not nothing. It is a very big deal."

He was right. We all made a field trip to Times Square, after rehearsal, to see it. It was Ed's idea, and it turned out to be kind of festive and nice. Me and the rest of the cast crammed into a couple of cabs and ran uptown and stood right in the middle of Times Square, where the streets all come together and there are about seventy zillion people everywhere, and there I was, with Polly and Daria, eight stories high, on top of the Virgin Megastore, just hovering over the whole scene like, I don't know what it was like. It wasn't like anything you expect to ever happen to you in your life, seeing a picture of yourself, so big up there. Everybody cheered and whooped and laughed, like it was a really cool thing, to have your own billboard in Times Square, and some of the tourists figured out that I was one of the girls on the billboard, and they asked to have their pictures taken with me. So then Reed and Kristine and Ed and the whole rest of the cast got in on the act and we just stood there, in the middle of the universe, having our pictures taken with grinning strangers from all over the planet, and it turned out to be a very good day, it really did.

CHAPTER TWELVE

Of course, some of those tourists turned out to be media sharks, and they called the *Daily News* and the *Post* and anybody else they could think of, and pictures of all of us horsing around in Times Square made it into a half-dozen newspapers and TV talk shows. Sam hadn't been around for the fun, but they called him for a comment about the billboard, which he described as "truly one of the most amazing things I've ever seen in my entire life," so that quote from our movie-star playwright made it into the articles, too. In short, we were all over the newspapers for a couple days, and by the end of the week, the entire six-week run of our not-so-good play was completely sold out. So then they added a three-week extension, and that sold out too, before we had even started previews, and before any critics had gotten anywhere near the show to tell everybody whether it was any good or not.

So the people who ran that theatre were pretty pleased with me, and all those actors I was now hanging out with thought this was a sensational development as well. Each and every one of them hated the critics like crazy; they just thought they were the dumbest and most hideous creeps on the planet, even including people like Osama bin Laden. But now it didn't matter what the critics thought about us, because there was a billboard of me in Times Square, so our show was suddenly so famous it didn't matter; we were a hit even if they hated us. So everyone was in a pretty good mood about that, and people seemed to care less that I was still pretty much stinking up the room whenever I tried to act. And, since they were all a little more relaxed about it, then I loosened up too, and then I was maybe only seventy percent awful, instead of being really just a hundred percent unforgivably bad.

And I have to say, for the record? Even being a bad actress was totally a gas. People maybe think they want to be actors because they think it might be fun to be famous and have everybody watch you and pay you a lot of money and then suck up to you all the time, but I had all that when I was modeling, and it wasn't all that much fun. Acting, real acting, like in a theatre? *That* was fun. I'm still not sure why. Maybe it's because you get to be somebody else who is actually having an interesting life, instead of being yourself, having the life you are having. I mean, I'm not saying that I was not having an interesting life; obviously my life is pretty fucking fascinating, or I wouldn't be asked to run through all this for you. I would have to say that objectively my relatively short life has not exactly been dull. But there was something that was just such a relief, frankly, about not being me, about being somebody else. It was very relaxing, and some days I would end up being so tired, but in a very good way. So I really did think it was fun, and I definitely wanted to keep being an actor—not because I thought it would be cool to be Scarlett Johansson, but more because it was just fantastic to do it.

In addition, all those other actors were really pretty nice to me, even when I was lousy, because they *didn't* think of me as some big-shot model; they mostly thought of me as a teenager who didn't know what she was doing and maybe needed some help. Reed wasn't the only one. Everybody was more or less very decent and protective of me at one point or another—like Kristine, that first day, in the bathroom—and then the longer we were in the soup together, the more like just a little club of nutty friends we all got. And it was such a gas, really, to be in this club with these somewhat crazy but also somewhat nice people, trying to make sense of what everyone agreed was a real stinker of a play.

Then we started previews. Which means that audiences come, before the critics write about you, and they pay, and they watch your play, and you have a few weeks to figure out if people like the play and if they don't like it you have rehearsal in the afternoon, and you try to fix it. And that was okay, too, because pretty much everybody thought we were hilarious. I'm not kidding. That dumb play had people rolling in the aisles, they were laughing so hard at all the stinky jokes. Kristine told me that that always happened with comedies: You forget how funny they are while you're working on them, because you're just thinking about everything you have to remember, and then when people come and laugh it's good to remember that you're in a comedy! She was really encouraged. And Reed said that it happened sometimes, stuff that you're doing you don't think is funny but an audience does, and it's better this way than the other way, when you think you're a riot but the audience doesn't laugh at all. And everybody kept taking me aside and asking me if I was taking care of my voice, and teaching me things like how to drink tea with honey and lemon before and after every show, and be sure to take a nap in between the matinee and the evening shows, because otherwise you wear yourself out. And Ed and Sam would take me aside every night and tell me how great I was; they were both incredibly careful, now that people were coming, to make sure that I felt good and wasn't completely freaking out.

The whole thing was just a complete gas. The lights would go down, and then up—the play started with Kristine out there by herself and she had virtually nothing to do, and even so they would start laughing. Reed and I were waiting in the wings at that point, and the first time it happened, he looked at me and shook his head.

"She's a complete whore," he informed me, like this was a good thing. And then they laughed again, still before anyone said anything, so he looked at the stage, determined. "So it's like that, is it?" he said. "All right, young Jedi, watch and learn." He glanced back at me, and then he went out there. And then he did something—he made a face behind Kristine's back, and they all laughed at that too. And I was so scared and overwhelmed and also laughing at Reed and Kristine, that first time, that I almost forgot to go on. But there was a costume person there who nudged me, and I went out, and I remembered my lines and my blocking and, even though I wasn't as good as the rest of them, the audience laughed at me plenty and I'd run off stage and someone would be there to rip off my clothes and put another costume on me in no time flat, so that I could make my next entrance, and when you were out there you couldn't see anything really except the other people on stage with you, under these bright lights, and the dust motes, I remember seeing them sometimes, and behind them in the dark this huge group of people listening and watching and laughing; and then, at the end, everyone applauding wildly while you stood there and took a bow. It was just the most fun I have ever ever had; it really was.

Collette came the first night, but no one else was allowed to come until we opened. She had hired a publicist, finally, this gay guy named Darren who told us that the goal now was to "maximize" every press opportunity, which meant that Daria and Polly couldn't show until opening night, when the national entertainment press would be there, in addition to the New York press. Apparently "national visibility" was now the goal, that's what I heard Collette say to Daria at one point, I can't remember where or when, even, because I just did not care one whit. I was out of it, and in my play. So I really wasn't listening. I mean, I think I thought I had escaped. I don't remember what I was thinking, frankly. I was thinking about my play. It was like nothing else mattered.

I said something to Reed about it, one night, while we were just hanging around the green room. He was reading a magazine and he held it up to show me a picture of myself, with my sisters, in another shot for Anthropologie. They were doing a whole campaign for those slip dresses. The pictures were everywhere.

"Oh, stop it," I told him. "Who cares?"

"It's just a nice picture, I think it's a nice picture."

"It's shit," I said. "Being a model is really just . . . it's not real. It's just shit."

He looked at me, surprised at this. I was definitely being more myself lately, with Reed and Kristine and everybody else. I felt more relaxed, like it was okay to say what I was actually thinking, instead of making things up all the time. It felt good to just tell the truth about all the modeling bullshit.

"You really don't like any of it?" Reed asked. "The fame, the glamour, the enormous wads of cash they are presumably hurling at all that hair?"

"That's it, frankly, it's mostly the hair that they seem to like." I shrugged. "I just don't want to do it anymore, I want to be an actress." He looked surprised again, and I got embarrassed. Let's face it, I had become one of those idiot models who wants to be an actress. It was kind of mortifying, but what could I do? It was the truth. "I mean, I know how bad I am," I told him, feeling more and more embarrassed, because he just wasn't saying anything. "But I can learn. I can take classes. I'm young, I have time, I can—"

"Of course you can, I think it's a terrific idea," he told me, making it sound like the worst idea imaginable.

"I can't help it," I said, now completely blushing. I knew I sounded like a total lameo. "I don't want to do anything else."

"I know, I know it feels like that," he said, putting the magazine away. He leaned in and started talking real quiet, like he was telling me a big secret. "And I know what you're going through, right now. When you're in a show that seems to be working, even when you're in one that's terrible, you feel fantastic, like your life has a purpose and that everything is in the right place, and you can't think about anything except the show, and getting to the theatre, and doing the show, and hanging out afterwards, talking to people about the show, and it feels like the world is bigger than it ever has been before. That's what it feels like. Right?"

"Yes!" I said, relieved to know that I wasn't making this up.

"It's not real," he told me. "The world isn't bigger. It's just replaced, somehow, with this other world, and it's a *good* world, I love it too, I can't do anything else; but the fact is that being an actor is a terrible life. The stuff we have to do, between all this? Going from one audition to another—people are horrible to you, you get rejected all the time, people you can't stand get all the good jobs, the critics say horrible things about you, other people win all the awards, you don't make any money; and the worst part is you're out of work almost all the time. This thing? That feels so great? You hardly ever get to do it. And it's like a drug. Once you're hooked, that's pretty much it. You're an addict. We're all addicts. And when you're between fixes? When you're not working? Trust me. It's awful."

"But do you think I'm good enough?" I asked him. Everything else that he said didn't matter. I heard them complaining in the green room all the time about how hard it was to be an actor, so what? What did I care? I just wanted to keep doing it.

He shook his head; he knew he wasn't getting through. "I got to be honest, what I really think is that you should be in high school," he told me. "What are you going to do if you change your mind at some point and want to do something else? You won't even have a high-school diploma. You might want to go to college someday."

"College?" I said, kind of laughing. It just sounded so weird, like something people did on a different planet. He looked kind of surprised and really sad, then.

"You're pretty smart," Reed said. "And . . . I'm sorry. I guess I just assumed kids want to go to college."

It was so weird, it really was. Like for a second everything seemed really like maybe I was two people. Because I remembered my chemistry class and thinking about things like the atomic weight of lead, and Avogadro's number, and covalent bonds, and being kind of good at that stuff, like doing good on the one test I actually took. But now I couldn't remember what Avogadro's number was. Or why anyone would need to ever know it.

"I don't want to go to high school," I told him. "Why would I want to go to college?"

This sort of made him sad, but he always looked sad. Then he sort of laughed, in a sad way. "What do I know?" he said. "The way things are going for you, they'll probably snap you right up. So what do I know? Forget high school. You're going to be a star."

CHAPTER THIRTEEN

That Reed was pretty smart. Everything he ever said to me came true. The critics came, and everybody was really uptight for a few shows, and then we had this big opening, with a party in a restaurant, and photographers everywhere, and Daria and Polly came and everybody made a huge big deal over all of us, and all of Sam's movie-star friends came, and they all asked to meet me, and I got my picture taken with half of the celebrities in New York City, and Ed flirted wildly with Polly, even though he knew she was half his age, and Mom hugged me and told me how proud she was, and Collette hugged me too—which was not typical Collette behavior—and whispered in my ear, "Get ready for a ride!" And then the next day we all woke up with champagne hangovers and the phone was ringing off the hook. Because the headline of the review in the *New York Times* was: "Gorgeous Hair, and She Can Act, Too."

I mean, the *headline*, of the *review*, was about *me*.

Now, the fact is, when you're acting in a play you're not supposed to read the reviews. That's what everyone else had already explained to me: Reviews just make you too crazy, and actors are crazy enough to begin with. So that's what I was going to do, I was going to Not Read the Reviews. And then Collette called, screaming, at six in the morning, and read me the *Times* review over the phone.

And it was really cool. I mean, this guy said really nice things about me. He said I was "lively and fresh," that I had an "innate wit" and "natural spontaneity which lifted a sparkling comedy into the blithe world of farce." He talked about how it was my first time on stage but that I was a natural, and although I clearly was someone who would have an enormous future in film, that he hoped to see me on New York stages for many years to come.

And the headline said, "Gorgeous Hair, and She Can Act, Too."

He said other things that I did think were pretty stupid. He actually said terrible things about Reed and Kristine, that Kristine was mugging shamelessly and Reed was trying to keep up with her, and they both were unbelievable, stuff like that. He also liked Sam's stupid play, which he thought was delightfully acute, and hilarious with a sorrowful undertone, pitch perfect, stuff like that. So I understood why you weren't supposed to read those things, they're pretty nutty. But this particular critic said I could act, so I didn't much care, frankly, that he was stupid about everything else.

The phone just kept ringing all day. It was really so exciting; all these people I barely knew kept calling all day to congratulate me on how great that review was and how excited I must be. Sometimes people would call Mom, and sometimes people would call Polly and Daria and tell them how exciting it must be for everyone, which was fine because by then Polly and Daria were not mad at me anymore anyway. They finally had a couple of modeling gigs for just the two of them—*Victoria's Secret* had just hired them to do this angel/devil spread, which was going to be big, apparently, and had no role for a fourteen-year-old sister—so they were just relaxed and giggling and happy, too. Polly gave me a big hug and swung me around and called me squirt and started taking pictures with this digital camera she was packing now, so then we had a whole mess of pictures of the four of us dancing around the kitchen in T-shirts and underwear, because that's all we wore all day, and every single one of us had gone to bed the night before with our makeup on, so we all looked like raccoons, with huge circles of mascara and eyeliner smudged all over our faces.

So when I got to the theatre for the half hour, I was pumped. I no longer worried about acting all hip and downtown, so I actually took a cab instead of the subway, and when it unloaded me at the front door of the theatre, Ed was waiting there.

"Hey Ed, there's a hot picture of you and Polly in Rush & Molloy, did you see it?" I asked him. He grinned, took a drag on his cigarette and dropped it to the ground, half smoked.

"Yes, actually, I did manage to look at it; she's gorgeous and I am as usual woefully underdressed," he acknowledged. "Listen, Amelia, you didn't happen to read the review, the *Times* review I mean?" He looked up at me, a little too casual, as he stomped out his cigarette.

"I didn't mean to read it," I said. "I wasn't going to. But . . . then all these people called all day, and told me it was great, so we ran out and got it. I mean . . . it's great, isn't it?"

"Well, actually, yes, terrific, terrific for you, sweetheart, and well earned. Well done," he told me, lighting another cigarette. "And the play was also treated rather well, so we're all quite happy. But the fact is, he was rather hard on some of the other actors, didn't you think? Kristine especially has taken it hard."

"Did she read it?" I asked, confused. "I thought she didn't read them."

"Yes, well, people actually say they don't read them quite a bit more than they actually don't read them. I'm afraid the position that they shouldn't be read is more theoretical than practical."

"Did Reed . . . ?"

"Pretty much everyone has read it, yes, and I did want to give a heads-up that there are some rather hurt feelings, as you can imagine, so just a heads-up. Really, though, well done. We're all quite pleased for you. It was well earned, you've worked really hard. So anyway, good job, dear." He really could lay it on thick when he wanted to.

I went backstage, to my dressing room. Those dressing rooms were all right on top of each other, and kind of knocked together in a sort of beehive-like construction of sheet rock and exposed wiring. Really, it's ridiculous how crummy those old off-Broadway theatres are; everything around that place always looked like it was on its last legs. Anyway, those dressing rooms were so small and the whole place was so old and icky, we all usually kept all our doors open, so that we could talk to each other, while we were putting our makeup on, and doing our hair and generally getting ready for curtain. But that day, everybody's door was shut. I mean, every single one of them was closed, and nobody was talking to anybody. It was like a morgue. And then the show started really *off*—they were just silent out there;

there were like no laughs at all for about two minutes. But then things started to roll, and they started laughing, and then they laughed a lot and we got really great applause at the end of act one, and at the end of the play the applause was fantastic and most of the audience even stood. So I thought that would maybe make everybody else feel better, and that maybe they would talk to me, but they all ran to their dressing rooms then, too. Seriously, everyone completely dashed off stage, and slammed their doors in my face. It was horrible.

So I sat alone in my dressing room, feeling really lousy, and then I thought, I have to go talk to Reed about this, he'll be nice, and we'll just talk about it, and then it will go away. That's the way it always works with that guy. So I finished changing into my street clothes, and I didn't even bother wiping off all the makeup or taking all the crap out of my hair, and I went to knock on his door.

I didn't end up knocking, though, because his door was sort of cracked, just an inch, and Kristine was in there with him, and she was crying. Okay. I know you're not supposed to listen at doors? But I don't believe that anyone on the planet, in my position, would not have just listened at that door. So of course I listened.

"She's terrible," Kristine sobbed. "I can't believe it. She got the whole review and she's terrible."

"I know," said Reed.

"We had six laughs. In that opening? There were always six, at least, doing next to nothing we had them, there was no mugging involved, how dare he say we were mugging, and now they're not laughing, no laughs. None!"

"They'll come back, you know they will," Reed soothed her.

"No. No. Now, they're laughing at her, because that idiot told them she was great and now they'll laugh at everything she does out there, and she's *terrible*," she whispered. "And she's going to get everything, now. They're just going to hand her everything, and why? Because she has great hair? It's ridiculous. I can't pay my rent. I am an actress. And she's *terrible*, am I wrong about that? She's terrible."

"She's a nice kid, but she's pretty bad," Reed acknowledged.

"I don't care if she's a nice kid, she's awful, and she's going to have a huge career now. I hate this business, that fucking prick, he's in love with her billboard, that's why she got that review and he's not even straight! I could understand it if he wanted to fuck her, but he's not even straight, what on earth is the *fascination*? Now all you have to do to be a star is have *great hair*?"

"Amelia, there you are!" Ed suddenly boomed, behind me. I cringed. Behind the door, there was a sudden and complete silence. So I knew that they knew I was standing out there listening, too. "There's a bunch of people waiting in the lobby, want to say hello," Ed announced. "Reed, are you in there?" He knocked on the door, and Reed stuck his head out, brilliantly casual and at ease.

"No more notes, Ed. Not tonight," he joked. Ed grinned, and chuckled, the big phony.

"All right, I'll save them for tomorrow," Ed promised. "Your fan club is out in the lobby, just wanted to let you know. Oh, Kristine, there you are. Terrific show. I know you're worried about the opening, darling, but don't. It was just off tonight, it'll come back. Really, they adored you. Everyone's waiting in the lobby to tell you how brilliant you are. Sam's here, he was raving, you should have heard him, you're a genius, that's his position. Mine too."

"Thank you, Ed," Kristine said, quite meaningfully. She didn't even look at me, and I was standing right next to him.

"We'll be right there," said Reed. And he shut the door, firmly, also without even glancing my way.

Okay, so my feelings were hurt, so I didn't try to talk to those guys that night. And then so much kept happening—I mean, just agents and producers and all these famous people kept coming to see the show, and wanting to chat me up, and do interviews, and have drinks with me, and flirt with me, and talk to me about other projects and LA, when was I coming to LA, we should have lunch, you're terrific, when are you coming to LA—it just went like that night after night after night, and I just never got around to talking to Reed. I mean, it's true that I shouldn't have been listening at the stupid door of his stupid dressing room, but he shouldn't have been saying rude things about me, either. He could have apologized too. But nobody did. And so that was just the way it went.

Until Brian Redgrave showed up.

Brian Redgrave is not his real name. We keep having to make up names for these movie stars so we don't get sued but, the fact is, I have nothing mean to say about Brian Redgrave. Not only is he a big-deal movie star, he is also just one of the most amazing actors in the world, and he came to see me in my play, and he waited in the lobby afterwards to tell me how good I was. No kidding, I hadn't even bothered to take my makeup off because I didn't think anybody important was there that night, and I was in my dressing room pulling on my jeans and a sweatshirt because I was just going to get a cab and go home. And then the stage manager knocks on the door of my shitty little dressing room and says, "Amelia, Brian Redgrave was at the show tonight, he's waiting in the lobby to say hello to you." And then she smiles and walks off.

Okay, that backstage area is a total shoebox with cardboard walls sort of only half-separating everybody's dressing rooms. Truly, that day when I was listening to Reed and Kristine kind of trash me? The door didn't actually need to be half open; everybody can hear everything back there anyway. So I'm just like sticking my head out of my dressing room and staring, with my jaw like hanging to the floor, at the back of the stage manager, who is walking away all cool as if she just said something completely normal instead of, "Brian Redgrave came to see you," when the door to everybody else's dressing rooms all pop open at once.

"What did she say?" said Reed.

"She said Brian Redgrave came to see the play," I said.

"He came to see *you*?" he asked, like this was the craziest thing he ever heard. I didn't hold it against him. It was the craziest thing *I* had ever heard.

But we all went up to the lobby and there he was: Brian Redgrave. He looks pretty awesome in person. Most movie stars don't, they kind of shrink up a little and it's so weird to see how short they are that you kind of don't think it's all that great, in general. But Brian Redgrave is so tall and so awesome he just did not disappoint. He's British too, but not like kind of sloppy British like Ed; he's more like the King of England kind of British. So then he holds his hand out to shake my stupid hand, and he says, "Such a pleasure to meet you. I really enjoyed the show. You were first rate, you really were."

"Thanks," I said. "Wow. I mean, like, thanks. That's I mean, like, thanks." Okay, I totally turned into a babbling moron, that's how cool I thought all this was. And the fact that Reed and Kristine and everyone else thought that he was so cool as well, and they were watching all this? That didn't hurt. So I'm feeling pretty fucking awesome, and I'm sure I was about to say something else totally boneheaded, when this enormous woman comes up behind him and smiles at me.

"Yes," said Kafka's giant great-granddaughter. "It turns out our little Amelia is quite a talent."

You could have knocked me over with a stick. Maureen Piven was there with Brian Redgrave. She shook her finger at me, like I was some sort of disobedient pet. "The last time I saw you, you insisted you weren't interested in acting, Amelia. But I knew you would change your mind." She turned and sparkled up at old tall Brian Redgrave. "I told Brian I thought you might be something special," she twinkled.

I was totally speechless. This whole thing was now both awesome and fucking bizarre. Last time I saw her, I was pretty sure that woman wanted to cut my heart out, and now she was doing, I had no idea what she was doing. So I think I was standing there with like my mouth hanging open like a complete dope, when Kristine stepped up and held out her hand, like a princess.

"Mr Redgrave, I hope you don't mind, I just wanted to say hello and tell you what a genius I think you are," she smiled.

"Thank you; you were just wonderful," he said, shaking her hand. "Just terrific work. The show is so charming." They gushed at each other politely about what geniuses they both were, and then she introduced Reed, and he gushed politely about what a genius Mr Redgrave was, and Mr Redgrave gushed about what a genius Reed was, and then everybody gushed about what a genius I was. Which was not as corny as it sounds, it was really pretty swell.

"Are you heading home, or would you like to come out for a drink?" Maureen asked me, after the gushing sort of died down.

Which again, I was like, Why is she being even a shred nice to me? According to Collette, this woman completely hated my guts. And now she was glancing up at Brian, all sparkly again; it was totally clear that she was inviting me to go out for drinks with her and Brian Redgrave. So apparently I just stared at her with one of those HUH? faces that you make when you're completely stumped. Seriously, I just could not figure this ride out.

And then I felt this little tap on my arm, so I turned, and Kristine was there, and she smiled at me and just touched my arm, very calm. She did that once on stage when I forgot my lines. They call it "going up"—you "go up," and then while you're up there you don't know what to do and everybody else on stage has to kind of cover for you and help you out until you come back down again. So this one time, I "went up" and she reached over and petted my arm, just for a second, and looked at me really kindly, and it kind of focused me, you know? And then I remembered my line.

So that's what she was doing while I flipped out and tried to figure out what to say when Brian Redgrave and Kafka's great-granddaughter said do you want to have a drink with us: She touched my arm. And it focused me.

"Do you want to come?" I said to Kristine. "It might be fun. Reed, you want to come have a drink with us?"

Okay. Which absolutely was totally genius, if I say so myself. Both of them beamed at me. Maureen the giantess was a little surprised and I think not so happy that I included them, but Brian Redgrave seemed to think it was a swell idea, so we all went out to this teeny little Italian joint on the corner and he bought three bottles of red wine for the table and everybody drank too much and by the end of the evening Reed and Kristine were my friends again. And Brian Redgrave seemed to like me fine, and even Maureen the giantess seemed to like me all right, although that might have been the red wine.

So things were really fun again, doing the play, and being famous for once for doing something that you kind of liked, instead of being famous for getting mad because everybody was making you do things you thought were stupid. Then one night, Ed showed up at my dressing room at half hour, and slumped into one of the bad folding chairs that passed as furniture in that dumpy theatre, and he started thumbing through this huge pile of scripts which was sitting on my dressing table.

"Wow, CAA, ICM, Endeavor, very impressive," he observed, with a sort of snide, raised eyebrow. "Anything any good?"

"They just want to talk about stuff," I told him, putting on my eyeliner. "A bunch of meetings, that's all."

"A bunch of meetings, well done, you are quite the little hot tamale." Sometimes he really was too cool for school.

"What do you want, Ed? I have to prepare, okay?" I said.

"No, certainly, absolutely . . . Jesus, Jonathan Demme?" he asked, reading a title page. "I love his work," he said. "Are you

239

meeting with him?" And he suddenly looked so sad and vulnerable, I was sorry for being so snippy, I really was.

"I don't think so," I said, trying to be a little nicer. "You know, I think it's just a casting person. I don't know."

"Wow. He's good. Is it a good part?" he asked.

"I haven't read it yet, I don't know," I told him, embarrassed now. Sometimes everybody in show business seems so sad, underneath all the bullshit, I just can't take it. "It's almost five, Ed," I reminded him. "Did you want to ask me something?"

"Yeah," he said, tossing the script aside with this ridiculous kind of fake I don't care thing. "So listen, are you going to the Herb Lang opening tonight? It's supposed to be a really hot party. Can I be your date?"

He didn't get to go along when we all had drinks with Brian Redgrave, and I was totally feeling sorry for him at this point, so I didn't care that he basically just came out and said he wanted to use me to get into a good party. "Sure, Ed," I told him. "Just keep your hands off my sister."

It turned out Ed was right, that old Herb Lang retrospective was a hot ticket. Half the Whitney was blocked off, this show was huge, supposedly there was going to be something like two hundred photographs there. Darren and Collette had a big powwow about whether or not the Heller girls should arrive as a threesome, but since I was going to be so late, running up from the theatre after the show, they decided that Polly and Daria should make a grand entrance without me. I'm pretty sure the real reason was that Darren and Collette were now working overtime to reconfigure the sister act as a twosome, since it was pretty clear to everyone that I was about to splinter off into acting land. But they kept making up these stories about logistics so that nobody's feelings got hurt.

Anyway, Darren had Prada send this incredible gold silk goddess dress over to the theatre, so that I had something great to wear, which I thought was stupid, because I was getting sick of everybody else dressing me by this point, but he insisted. He also was sending a car. I told Ed about the Prada number and the car, so he decided to make a vague attempt to dress up himself and he ran home during the show, where he found half an Armani tux that someone had lent him at some point. So we got to the museum, had our pictures taken by a bunch of bored photographers, and entered what was maybe the swankest party I have ever seen, and by that point I had been to plenty of swank parties. Everybody in New York was there, socialites and politicians and hip-hop musicians and actors and models, of course. Everybody who had ever had his or her picture taken by Herb was there, and there were quite a few of us, and then everybody else was there, too. I was really grateful Darren had covered my butt with that Prada arrangement; I really was.

Ed stuck by me like glue for a while, which I was glad for, because about a zillion people pretty much descended, like I was a big piece of raw meat or something. Everybody wanted to talk to me about Sam and the play and what I was going to do next, and Ed fielded the questions because he really loves all that shit. So I just stood there for a while and let everybody else talk, and then Ed said, "Isn't that your sister?" And he nodded toward the other end of the room, where you could barely see Polly through another crowd of about a zillion people. So I said, "Eddddd . . ." and I shook my finger at him, which made everybody laugh, as lame as it was, but I let him drag me out of that crowd of losers because I was already feeling claustrophobic and sick of it all. Anyway, Ed waved down Polly—he apparently had no intention of obeying my request that he keep his hands off my sister—and Polly grinned, acting like she was glad to see both of us, so what did I know?

"It's about time you got here," she said. "Nice dress, where'd you get that?"

"Darren had somebody from Prada send it to the theatre," I shrugged.

"Go Darren, you look amazing," Polly told me.

"That's good, where'd that come from?" She was wearing this really tight little black number, which made her look like she weighed about three pounds. Plus somebody new apparently was doing her eye makeup; she looked like a cat.

"Darren," she said. "That guy knows his shit. Daria's in a white sheath, very fifties Hollywood. We made quite a splash when we showed up."

"You look . . . stunning," Ed gushed. When he wasn't being too cool for school, he was actually kind of adorable, for a thirty-six-year-old British has-been.

"Thanks," said Polly. "What a scene, huh? Yikes." She looked around, those amazing eyes raking the crowd, like she was looking for someone. "You say hi to Herb yet? He was just here."

"You know Herb Lang?" Ed gushed a little more.

"Well, he did us for the *New Yorker*, god, that seems like a thousand years ago, doesn't it?" she asked me. "He's got one of

242

us from that session, all the way in the back. You should go see it, it's unbelievable. Like six feet high or something, it's a pretty good shot."

"That *New Yorker* shot? He included it?" said Ed. This was all so hot and inside and happening he could hardly contain himself.

"Don't faint, Ed, the night is young," Polly told him, laughing and laying her hand on his arm. "Let's get you a drink." She started to steer him toward one of those little bar stands that litter these events. "It's all the way in the back, just go straight," she yelled to me. So I split. The crowds were thinner back there anyway, which meant it wasn't as hot and disgusting and scary, and as long as I kept moving no one could really corner me and say stupid things. I passed Daria on the way. She was wearing this unbelievably stunning floor-length white sheath, and she was standing next to a shot of Mrs Astor, and there were something like six guys in tuxedoes surrounding her. So she looked like she was having as much fun as she ever did. I kept moving.

And there it was. This huge picture, black and white, huge, really, it took up an entire wall, this incredible picture of all of us, dancing, and happy. And it was all of us. I forgot that he did that, but he did, he took some pictures of all of us, back then, and it was one of those, me, and Polly, and Daria, and right there in the middle was Philip, in this big goofy oversized shirt—this shirt he wore all the time—sort of flying about him, his arms were up and he was looking down, lifting one of his feet high in the air, like he was concentrating really hard on this totally goofy dance move, and I was laughing at him, and Polly was behind him, kind of blocked by that big shirt, but she was

243

laughing too, and there was Daria looking over Polly's shoulder, curious and alert, trying to see, and the whole thing was so beautiful and full of life, that I just started to cry, not really cry, but like when tears just come to your eyes and it's a big surprise, like some part of you is crying and you didn't even know? And then I heard someone else crying behind me, like this picture had done the same thing to somebody else and they were crying too, not loud, but definitely a sad sound, like someone gasping for air, and I thought it was myself, for a second, because it was so much like what I was feeling, and then I realized it wasn't me, it was someone else, so I turned around to see who it was, and it was Philip.

It was Philip. He was right there, behind me, standing in the middle of that empty room, looking at that big picture, and crying. He looked terrible, just awful. Oh my god, he just looked so sad and so awful. So I went over and put my arms around him.

That's what I did.

POLLY

CHAPTER FOURTEEN

I had to get them out of there. I mean, the place was crawling with photographers. Amelia was pure junk food to the press by this point; her every move was catalogued and printed in six different places eight times a day. To catch her sobbing all over her insane big brother in the middle of the hottest party in Manhattan, who knows what that could have turned into, but it would have turned into something, they couldn't leave the kid alone. So I grabbed that loser Brit she kept trying to dump on me and dragged him over to where they were standing and crying; I think I was hoping the two of us, skinny as we both were because that stupid Brit is just a rail, might be big enough to create some sort of human shield and then no one would be able to see both Amelia and Philip completely losing it in front of that giant picture Herb took of the four of us dancing.

"Hey Philip! It's so great you're here!" I told him, real firm but quiet, and then I put my hand on his shoulder and I just said, "You got to get it together, both of you, there's seven thousand people here and you cannot lose it like this in front of seven thousand people they will put you on the front page of the *Daily News* so help me god, and then who knows what will happen. Get it together now. I mean it. Now." Admittedly this wasn't genius but it seemed to work, at least on Amelia, who sort of shook, like an animal almost, like she wasn't in control of her body, but her body was going to get it together because it knew it had to even if she didn't.

"It's okay. I'm okay. I'm okay," she said, but she really was shaking, it was a little spooky to watch. She took Philip by both hands and said to him, "We have to go. Okay? Come on, Philip. You're okay. We'll go get a coffee, okay? You want a coffee?"

Unfortunately, Philip couldn't even talk. I think for a second he tried but he couldn't get words out, he just kept crying. Amelia was barely holding it together anyway and the fact that Philip couldn't stop crying was unnerving as hell. That stupid Brit sort of shuffled, like he was embarrassed, and just ducked away, completely useless, or maybe he just felt like this was none of his business and he wanted to give us privacy. Privacy, what a joke, I wanted to tell him, there was nothing private in our lives, you can watch it in person or see it on Channel Two at eleven! Whatever. I looked around, coolly frantic, hoping that maybe Daria would show up and have a clue on how to handle this; she and Philip never had much use for each other, but she has a good head in a crisis. Who knows where she was, though, off being the White Princess somewhere, surrounded by throngs of dazzling New Yorkers. We were so deep in the museum, like really one of those galleries that's just way in the back, and I had no idea how to get any of us out of there without facing the mob. Which would have been awful, because Philip was not coherent, he just wasn't, and the nicer Amelia got with him, telling him that she would take him home and make him coffee, and they'd watch *Star Trek*, and get some pizza, the more he cried. It was very bad. I mean, there have been worse things we faced—all that shit over Amelia biting Rex, and then when the press went after her in front of the high school, that all probably was worse than this. But it didn't feel worse. Being stuck there in that spectacular party with Philip just losing it felt really pretty desperate.

Then all of a sudden there was this kind of spooky, disembodied voice right over my shoulder. "Do you need help, my dear? How shall I help here?" I turned around, and ta-da, there was Herb. Herb Lang himself, and behind him that loser Brit. I don't even know what that guy's name was, he directed Amelia's bad play, but I never managed to hang onto his name the three times I met him. Anyway, I don't know why he got it into his head that Herb would be the one to solve this, but that's apparently what he decided and then he went and got him. And it turned out to be a completely brilliant move. Herb at least was kind of large, he's not fat but he's definitely a sizable guy, so the first useful thing he did was he actually blocked the view of the meltdown from the hovering crowds which were beginning to gather. The second useful thing Herb did was completely ignore Philip's nervous breakdown.

"I'm glad you could make it. Do you like the picture, my dear?" he asked me.

"It's fantastic, Herb. Congratulations, it's really such an honor to be included in the show, it's all so beautiful, you must be really proud," I told him.

"The little one, you just arrived, yes? I saw you come in, everyone making such a fuss, I thought you were a movie star. How do you like the pictures?" he asked Amelia.

"Can we go?" Amelia asked me, ignoring him. For such a smart kid she is almost retarded sometimes.

"Herb, Philip's a little upset," I told him. "Is there anyplace he could sit down?"

"I think he's all right," said Herb. "It's flattering, to an artist, to see a person who can be so moved by my work. I hope that is not too selfish for me to admit that," he smiled. "You like the picture, Philip?"

Philip nodded. He still couldn't talk. Herb pretended not to notice.

"I told them, at the *New Yorker*, this is the one; it was by far the best shot of the day," Herb said, looking up at it. "They didn't care. They wanted color, they wanted the sisters, not the brother, it was too much to argue with them, I wasn't interested. I'm glad you like it. I like it, too." He put his arm around Philip's shoulder and the two of them stared up at the photograph, together. And slowly, Philip stopped crying. The two of them just stood there. Then, after a minute, Philip actually put his head on Herb's shoulder. Herb looked down at him, and smiled. Then he looked over and smiled at me too.

He has a good smile, Herb. He's not a young dude, but there's no question he's a sexy guy. He came onto me after that shoot, like a lifetime ago, which I thought was pretty bold. I was kind of surprised and a little freaked out by it, frankly—I mean, I was still in high school, for crying out loud—so I passed. But when he saved us, at that opening, with Philip losing it like that and me at my wits' end, I sort of wished I had done it. Let's face it, since then I've been a whole lot more forthcoming with guys who weren't near as reliable.

Anyway, once Herb got Philip back to planet earth, it was relatively easy to get out of that museum. What turned out to be the hard part was everything else.

The first problem was even deciding what to do next. Get in a cab, stand on a street corner, walk two blocks and get a slice of pizza—the dumbest things were suddenly impossible to decide. Daria and I had a limo for the night, but when I called the guy, it turned out he was off somewhere picking up gypsy fares for extra cash; he was at least thirty blocks away. So I'm sort of screaming at him on the phone, and then that nutty, overly helpful Brit wants to know if we should call Daria and get her out here on the sidewalk, since he assumes along with the rest of New York that Heller girls are *supposed* to travel in threes, but then Philip goes all buggy and starts to kind of mutter like one of those crazy people who are like, really nuts.

"That's great. Let's call Daria. That's a fucking awesome idea, she'll probably try to have me arrested. HEY DARIA!" he suddenly yelled. Like completely the opposite of what we were trying to do, which is just get out of there with no one looking at us. Amelia took his hand to kind of comfort him, maybe, or else it was to keep him from bolting back inside the museum and making a spectacle of himself. He looked at her, and shook his head, like she just didn't get it. "I just wanted to talk to you, like what's so fucking awful? What is so fucking awful?" he asked, upset. Which she totally didn't get until later, so right at that moment all she did was hold onto him, which was so the

251

right choice; I did not want her blowing a gasket on top of Philip blowing a gasket, which would have been just the end of everything. Finally, the overly helpful Brit hailed a cab and we all piled in, including him, which meant there were four of us in the back seat, and even though we are all quite thin, that's ridiculous.

But there we are, squished together like teenagers trying to go clubbing, and the Pakistani cab driver says, "Where you going?"

Amelia says, "Brooklyn, Park Slope, take the Manhattan Bridge and go straight up Flatbush to Grand Army Plaza."

And I say, "Wait a minute. We can't just take him home."

"He's coming home," Amelia snaps at me.

"Mom will flip out."

"Fuck Mom," Amelia retorts.

"I'm not going back there," says Philip. He's all the way against the other side of the cab, leaning against the window, sinking, it looks like, but as long as he's not in full meltdown mode, I figure we're still on the up side of the equation.

The cab driver yells back at us, "Brooklyn?" If we had told him anywhere except Brooklyn he would have taken off by this point, but they all hate driving over that bridge, so he clearly thinks he might be able to dump this fare.

"Just hang on a sec," the helpful Brit tells the cab driver. Then he checks in with me, like we're secretly in cahoots here, taking care of this together. "Is that where you want to take him?" he says, under his breath. He's got his back against the door of the cab, but he's sitting sideways, like there's just not enough room and that's why we had to squash together and

252

why he has to put his arm around me, as if guys haven't been trying that move on me since I was ten. Whatever, it comes with the territory, and sometimes I dig it, but in that cab, at that moment, I found myself thinking about cockroaches.

"Brooklyn, yes, we're going to Brooklyn!" Amelia hollered. She was holding Philip's arm and clinging to him. His head was against the glass. "It'll be fine, Philip."

"It's not fine," he said. "I just wanted to talk to you. What is the big fucking damn deal? Huh? Polly? Did you even tell her?"

"Tell me what?" asked Amelia.

"We can't talk about this right now, we have to get out of here!" I told them. "You don't want to go to Brooklyn? Where do you want to go? You want to go to Dad's?" It was a bone-headed thing to say. Philip just turned to look at me, over Amelia's shoulder, and he looked so sad. He didn't even answer, he just looked out the window.

"Brooklyn," snapped Amelia, leaning forward and trying to talk directly to the cab driver. "Grand Army Plaza!"

"Hang on, Amelia, would you just shut up for a second?" I said to her.

"I will take care of Mom," she told me, very stupidly sure of herself.

"Mom is not going to just go along with this!" I told her back. "She'll flip out and make a scene, which is the last thing Philip needs, just look at him, and then you know what'll happen next? She'll call Dad, who will come out to get him first thing in the morning and then Dad will be even more shitty to Philip than he's already been, which you might know something about if you had bothered to even try talking to him once or twice in the past six months. If we take him to Brooklyn, Mom will send him to Dad, so just shut up for a minute, and let me think this through," I told her. I know I was repeating myself but sometimes you have to, to get that kid to listen.

"Hey, I can't just sit here," announced our cab driver. And he wasn't wrong about that—those photographers were sniffing around the outside of the cab, peering in, starting to snap away; although what kind of a photograph they thought they were going to get (Wow! Four people in a cab!) was beyond me.

"Well, where are we supposed to take him?" asked Amelia, like she was offended by my stupidity.

"Who gives a shit," said Philip. He gave the finger to one of the paparazzi who was sticking his lens through the window at us, and sure enough the guy started snapping away.

"Philip, stop it!" I tried to reach over Amelia to hit him, and she shoved me, so they all got pictures of that too.

"How about a cup of coffee?" the helpful Brit suggested suddenly.

"Yes, coffee," I said, now desperate, to the cab driver. "Could you take us to the Lower East Side?" I went for my cell, while the cab driver shrugged and pulled away from the curb, took a right at the corner and headed down Park.

"Why are we going to the Lower East Side?" asked Amelia, still all bossy. "He needs to come home. We can handle Mom and Dad. What happened with Dad? What's been going on? Did Dad do something to him? Philip, did Dad do something to you?"

"They won't let me watch television," Philip said, sort of tired of it all. He was really sliding down now, someplace way

254

inside, which made me kind of long for the moment he was yelling and giving everyone the finger.

"You got an address?" the cab driver called back.

"Just a second," I told him, because the person I was calling had just picked up the phone. "Hey, it's Polly," I said. "Are you doing anything? I got Philip and Amelia and some Brit I don't even know in a cab with me—can we come see you?"

So that's how we all ended up in this crazy hairdresser's apartment. I have to take a second to backtrack, so you can understand why she was who I called. Her name is Laura Munroe, and she did our hair on that first shoot, the one for the *New Yorker*, and then again, she assisted the girl at *Regis and Kelly* when we were on the show that day. She was actually the person who cooked up the whole upscale punk look I've had going since then, so I'm not likely to forget her, but what was news to me, when I went and took Philip out for his birthday, was that he was kind of obsessed with this person. He was much more animated that day—he was really glad to see me— and he was trying to put a good face on, so he was being kind of bright and conversational, although you could tell even then that things weren't going so well for him. I was trying to be really nice, because this whole situation with him basically disappearing from his own life was so fucked up that I couldn't figure out what to say anyway. Unfortunately, Philip wasn't my turf, really, so when it happened, that he got kicked out of the house? I more or less expressed my opinion and then stayed out of it. I truly thought Mom would feel too guilty to go along with this nonsense for very long, or that

Amelia would make such a fuss she would somehow take care of it and get him back, but they both just totally dropped the ball, which was exceptionally poor behavior, if you ask me. Which is why I stepped into the breach and took him out to dinner on his birthday, even though up till this moment Philip and I had virtually nothing to say to each other. I mean, *he* called *me*—he got my cell-phone number from this kid at Garfield Lincoln who I dated for about three minutes—but it was my idea to take him out to dinner. I just mention this here because it turned into such a huge fucking point of contention, who was calling who, during those weeks that Philip was disappearing from his own life. The fact is, he called me because he wanted to talk to Amelia, but when they rushed him out of the house he left his cell phone and then they never gave it back to him so he didn't have her number. And then he left a bunch of messages on the phone at home which she never got, because we were never there and apparently Mom never passed them on. And Daria apparently did at one point take a call from him, and she also apparently told him to stop calling, which was massively fucked up if you ask me. Anyway, he finally skipped out of Dalton one afternoon and went and hung out at Garfield Lincoln, to see if he could talk to Amelia? But by then she had been yanked out of school. Which he found out about by talking to this character who, as I said, I dated for three minutes, but who also still had my cell number on his cell.

So that's how he finally got hold of me, which he only did, as I said, because he wanted to talk to Amelia. But by then she didn't want to talk to him. Which, as I also think I already pointed out, was surprising and fucked up, but everything in retrospect was pretty surprising and fucked up.

So there we were, figuring this all out, just me and him, having dinner at some Italian joint on the Upper West Side, and we're both trying to be real nice because this situation is so hideous, and we're trying to pretend like it's not because, honestly, we don't have much to say to each other, and what we ended up talking about was this hairdresser person. She had made a big impression on him, those two times we met her, and he was wondering if I had seen her since then, as if models and hairdressers just naturally ran into each other all the time in the course of our lives in New York City. Actually, I guess that's not such a dumb thought, it's not that big a circuit, frankly, but the fact is I hadn't seen this particular hairdresser since *Regis and Kelly*, so that's what I told him. He couldn't get off it, though; he felt somehow that it was really necessary to hunt her down and have a conversation with her. So eventually I called a makeup person I was pretty friendly with, and I described this hairdresser—she's kind of distinctive, really—but she didn't know her, so we discussed hair people in general, and she gave me the name of someone else, who had some thoughts and after about four or five calls we had tracked this Laura down.

"Hey, is this Laura?" I asked. Philip shook his head, earnest and a little upset, and he started saying something like, "Her name is 'Laaara, it's Laaaara,' I really couldn't figure out what his problem was, so I just kept talking. "This is Polly Heller, do you remember me?"

"Sure, Polly, god are you kidding?" she shouted. She's one of those people who shout a lot. "How's your hair holding up?

You need a cut or something? I don't like the thing they did in that *W* spread, you looked ridiculous, you want my opinion, you need a cut." Okay, it's possible that some people might find that sort of thing offensive, being told that your hair looks like shit in a major magazine spread? But I thought it was kind of entertaining, and besides, she was the one who had cooked up the whole look, I figured she had a right to be a little bit proprietary about the cut.

"No, my hair's fine," I said. "Listen, I was talking to Philip, my brother, about you, do you remember Philip?" Really, this is how it went, which was odd, I admit, but somehow in the moment it didn't seem so odd, mostly because Philip was so eager to talk to this person. So that seemed to make it make sense.

She seemed to think so, too. "Oh, yeah, Philip, how's he doing? Does he need a haircut?" she asked, but it was kind of a joke, not like she was trolling for work, just sort of like that's the friendly thing hairdressers say, when you have them on the phone.

"Philip actually could use a haircut, but that's not why we're calling," I told her. "It's his birthday, and we were wondering if you'd like to come have a drink with us."

"Really?" she asked. "Great!" She sounded like nothing would suit her better than having a cocktail with some kid she barely knew. "Yeah, I can do that. But if it's his birthday, shouldn't we have cake?"

Well, she was right, of course, so that's what we did. She was down in the West Village with a private client—a lot of hair people moonlight by going to rich people's homes and giving a trim or a blow-dry in your kitchen for like four hundred dollars a pop; it's quite a lucrative gig for your average hairdresser. Anyway, that's where she was, so we went down and met her in a bakery a couple blocks away from where she was doing this rich person's hair. She got there before us so she had them take one of those really small cakes and squeeze Happy Birthday Philip in icing-writing on it, and then she had them put a couple of candles around all the squished letters. She was waiting for us outside, on this little bench, by the time we got there.

"Well, this is a kick, getting your call like that out of the blue, I didn't expect *that*!" she announced. I wanted to say, who would? But she had moved on already to lighting the candles on this little-bitty cake, with a little-bitty BIC lighter. "I didn't know how old you were so I just tossed a bunch of candles around here. How old are you, Philip?"

"Sixteen," he said. He didn't seem to think this whole scene was terribly odd, either. I don't know why I did; lots of weirder things had been happening to my family for months. But it just seemed quite unusual, to be sitting out there on a little bench on Bleeker Street, lighting candles on a cake, with a person I barely knew, for my brother, who I also barely knew. It was dark by then, so the candles looked pretty on that little cake. The streetlights were on, and the air was good, so our haphazard and pathetic birthday dinner had quickly, it seemed, morphed into something much better than it started out to be.

"Sixteen?" said Laura, with a kind of look at him. "Isn't that one of the big ones?" Clearly, the question behind that question was, Where the hell is the rest of your family? Your sixteenth birthday, why are you spending it on a street corner with someone you hardly know? But she didn't say it. As I got to know her later, I found that she's not the kind of person who generally holds back; she can be ridiculously direct. But that night, she did the polite thing, and didn't ask.

So we sat there and ate cake and she talked and talked about her nutty private clients and the people who came into the salon where she worked part time, and how she had a crush on Sharon Stone, but how she really thought Sela Ward could use a decent haircut. She asked how Amelia and Daria were doing, and I told her, fine, and I left it up to Philip to tell her how he'd been kicked out of the family in such a peculiar way, and sent up to the Upper West Side to live with our invisible father and a completely different family, but Philip didn't say a thing. He just listened and ate cake. At one point she was telling some story about her two dogs, and how she did their numbers, she was into some numerology thing that I completely could not follow, and I'm not sure he could either, but he laughed, finally, at some dumb thing the dog did which proved, in her mind, that numerology is completely accurate when it comes to predicting a dog's personality and life journey. And I laughed, too, because suddenly it all seemed more weird even than I had thought.

Eventually it was time to go. We were all heading in opposite directions—Laura to the Lower East Side, me to Brooklyn and Philip back uptown to the Upper West Side. So Laura took off, and Philip was climbing into a cab, and even though we were going in opposite directions, I got in with him. He looked at me, surprised, so I just shrugged. "Hey, I'm in no

260

hurry, I'll ride with you," I said. He didn't protest and in fact he seemed pretty pleased, so I felt like I had room to come out and ask.

"How is it up there, living with Dad and Sarah?" I said.

Philip just shrugged. "Dalton's kind of hard," he said. "There's a lot of homework. And Dad's on this big Jewish kick. Sarah converted so they can raise their kids Jewish, so there's like, I don't know, a lot of Hebrew stuff. These endless temple things, services, everybody talks in Hebrew and rocks back and forth, stuff like that."

"And Sarah and Dad make you go, with their adorable little blonde Jewish children?" I observed.

He didn't even smile at this poor joke. "I'm not allowed to talk to them," he said.

"What?" I asked. This sounded so bizarre, I wasn't sure if he meant what I thought he meant.

"They don't want me to talk to the kids," he said.

"Why not?"

"They've decided I'm a drug addict."

"A *what*?" Now *that*, I thought, was truly preposterous. The kid came home drunk one time from some other kid's house, but other than that his drug of choice was *Star Trek*.

"Everybody at Dalton's a drug addict," he explained. "At least, that's what the parents all think. They're like, obsessed. So I'm like, why did you send me there, then? If I wasn't a drug addict to begin with, presumably all the peer pressure would get to me eventually, right? So if I'm a fucking drug addict now, whose fault is that? It was your bright idea to send me there."

"What'd she say to that?"

261

"When I piss her off, she just starts screaming. You know. About Mom being so lousy and you guys are all being paraded around like prostitutes . . ."

"She said that?"

"She's loads of fun. Dad totally traded up, believe me."

"Well, what does Dad say, what does—"

"He doesn't talk to me. Outside the yelling, nobody talks to me," he said. "And there's no TV."

"They don't have a TV?" I asked him. "At all?"

"Sarah thinks it's bad for your brain," he said. And he went back to looking out the window.

It sounded so different, so utterly foreign, like a totally different country to me, from what it was like to live in our family, that it scared me to hear him describe it like that, so plain. "Are they ever nice to you?" I asked. It was the only thing I could think to say. He looked at me, like, don't be such a moron, Polly, and he didn't answer. And then we didn't talk any more.

So, I understand that more gruesome things have happened to other people, but this is the gruesome thing that happened to my little brother, in the middle of everything else that happened to my family, and somehow I seemed to be the person left in charge. Which was unexpected to say the least, as I'm not precisely the person who it immediately occurs to people, Let's consult her in a crisis. People think about me in other contexts, like when you think, Who would I like to fuck? Generally my name makes the list. Which explains the presence of the overly helpful Brit in the middle of this catastrophe, when Philip showed up and had a nervous breakdown at the opening of Herb Lang's retrospective. But that night, in spite

262

of my lack of credentials, I was the one in charge, and so I called that hairdresser on the Lower East Side and took everybody down there.

And, I have to say, as good as she was with the spontaneous birthday party scenario? She was positively brilliant in these far more dire circumstances. Philip was still relatively catatonic when we arrived, so Amelia almost had to carry him in. Laura's apartment was not in the best neighborhood; you had to get past three buzzered doors to even get into her hallway, which was sort of poorly lit with nasty green fluorescents, so everything looked grim and tired, with kind of old newspapers and flyers on the floor—stuff people in the building were too lazy to clean up. Her apartment was nice and clean, though, but real small. You went through a teeny kitchenette and then onto a marginally larger room, which had a couch and a bed and a television and a little table by a mirror, where she apparently sometimes cut hair or did color for friends. She had two dogs, but they were small as well, just itty-bitty little kind of yappy mutts.

"Hey, how you doing? These are my dogs Olivier and LaCroix, I told you about them, hey boys, this is Amelia and Polly and Philip—hey, Philip, what's wrong?" Laura asked, immediately focusing in on the kid, even though I hadn't told her anything except that we had to come by.

"He's just kind of upset," I told her. Laura jumped right on board, bright and matter-of-fact, not panicking.

"Yeah, I can see that," she nodded. "You want some tea, Philip, how about I make you a cup of tea? Say hi to the boys, Philip, guys stop jumping on him. Behave yourselves. Anybody else want tea?"

"I'd love some, thanks," said the helpful horny Brit. "I'm Edmund, hi," he added.

"Yeah, I'm Laaara," she told him, glancing back at Philip. He was right, she pronounced her name funny, I was saying it wrong. I remember thinking that, kind of stupidly, while I looked at him, sitting on this couch, unable to talk, letting those little dogs lick his fingers while Amelia held onto his arm. I followed Laaara into the kitchenette, which gave us about four feet of distance from Philip and Amelia, but it was all the privacy I was going to get, so I took it. The helpful horny Brit looked like he was about to follow us, to get in on the powwow, which I so did not want to deal with—I mean, even though he had been intermittently helpful all night, he still seemed kind of cockroachy to me, and I did not want this guy any further on the inside of our real lives. So I took him by the hand and I looked into his eyes and I said, "Listen, Philip looks like he hasn't eaten in days, can you go out and get a sandwich or some pizza or something? Just anything, cookies, anything." I was so quiet and earnest, I needed him so badly, it was truly what he was living for at that moment, and so he touched my face—I swear, he touched my face, that old dude *sooo* thought he was getting laid that night—and then he went out to hunt and gather for me. Which left me alone in the kitchen with someone who I thought might actually be useful, so I told her the whole story.

Even before I finished, like, right when I was in the middle of describing what happened at the museum, with Philip showing up and losing it, Laaara went back into the other room and sat on the couch next to him and put her arm around him. She was both cheerful and mad at the same time. "Hey, Philip!" she shouted. "What the fuck is this story? They kicked you out of your own house? That sucks, man! That just completely sucks, I don't know how you stand it, and you didn't even call him?" She turned on Amelia, like on a dime, it was all part of the same sentence. "Well, shame on you I say, he was there for you, when you were going through your shit, and you really let him down, that's not okay, you know, to do that to your brother, he's really a nice guy."

"I did try to call him, I tried so many times—" she started.

"You quit, though. You quit trying. Shame on you." It was pretty awesome, how directly this came out of that hairdresser's mouth.

"There wasn't anything I could do."

"Bullshit." Laaara was not going to let her off, even though everyone else had. "At least *she* showed up for his birthday—" she tipped her head at me— "I did, too, and you could see even then he was in trouble, that was months ago, you don't just abandon people. You're a kid, I guess you don't know better, but you should. You should." Amelia turned all red; she knew this person was right.

"It's not her fault," said Philip. Which of course he would let Amelia off the hook, even though he shouldn't, but what are you going to do? At least he finally was saying something.

"No, it's your shitty parents' fault, both of them, and I'm not excusing that, it fucking sucks what they did. You're going to need to be in therapy for the rest of your life now, is what I'm predicting, your fucking parents are completely insane," Laaara declared.

Okay, it was in fact pretty funny the way she said it, and

thank god it made him laugh. Because he did, and then he kept laughing, and for a second I got worried because I thought he might start to cry again, but he didn't, and then Amelia looked at me, and she was so relieved and grateful that *she* started crying and it was then that I decided to forgive her. We were all in a mess, that's all, really, that you could say about any of it at that point. It was just one big fat stupid mess, and there was just no way any of us really knew what we were doing, there really wasn't.

CHAPTER FIFTEEN

So we stashed Philip in Laaara's apartment. It was her idea. "Fuck them, they don't deserve you!" she shouted at Philip. "Why should you go home to either one of those bastards, they don't take care of you. At least if you stay here for a while, you'll get a decent haircut!" And then she roared with laughter. I was starting to get what Philip saw in this unusual person. She really was pretty entertaining, and her solutions to problems had the added charm of actually working. At least for the time being we had found a place that Philip could stay where someone would be nice to him, and feed him, and let him watch television and give him a haircut.

Obviously he couldn't stay there forever, although it seemed pretty cozy that night. Suddenly it just felt like none of us had paused, for one second, through all of it, we had been just swept into this river of chaos and there had been no letting up; but now here we were in this little cave on the Lower East Side, drinking tea with this hairdresser and her two little dogs. I thought that maybe we should keep it to ourselves, for a while, that we

267

knew where Philip was, even if Mom and Dad didn't, just to make them sweat a little bit about what may have happened to the kid and also so that we could keep going back to this oddball cave whenever we felt like it. But when I tried this theory out on Laaara and Amelia and Philip, none of them bought it.

"They won't care," said Amelia.

"Besides, what if they called the cops?" asked Philip. "Laaara could go to jail."

"I'm not going to jail," said Laaara. "They're going to jail for child abuse and neglect and what else can we slap them with? Being fucking selfish nasty fucking pricks, how many years can you get for that?" She roared; she was one of those people who think their own jokes are hilarious.

"They're not going to call the cops," I said. "We'd end up in the *Daily News*, and Mom's too afraid of lousy publicity."

"We'll just talk to her," Amelia said, kind of cold and quiet. She was still holding onto Philip's arm and she had her head on his shoulder, and she was looking at the floor, but she definitely had something up her sleeve. And I was not interested in any more secret plans.

"What, what are you up to?" I asked. "Amelia, what are you doing? What do you think you're doing? What do you mean, talk to her?"

"I mean, talk to her," she shrugged. "She has to let him come home, we just have to explain why."

The buzzer rang. I had totally forgotten the loser Brit, sent out to forage for food. Amelia stood, and ran to the door. "It'll be fine!" she said, determined as shit. "It might take a day or two but she'll let him come back, and then, until then, he can stay here. He'll be fine here. Won't you, Philip?" Philip looked up at her, smiling and relaxed finally, and I thought, well, he's not completely fucked up by all this, he's still basically the same old Philip, completely in love with his little sister. And then I got distracted by the arrival of the helpful horny Brit, who had brought three pizzas and beer and donuts, of all things. Not that anyone could eat any of it without getting completely bloated, but it was a sort of grand friendly gesture. I was so grateful to that cockroachy Brit that I let him kiss me before I got into the cab home, and I even let him stick his tongue down my throat. Why not? It didn't mean anything to me and he really had bailed us out of some truly dicey situations all night; after all was said and done, he really had helped. A little tongue seemed a small price to pay.

The following day was predictably rather hysterical. We didn't get home until four in the morning, so Amelia and I slept in until about noon. Mom and Daria were still in the kitchen having black coffee and melba toast—it was their idea of brunch. So there they were, lounging around in T-shirts and underwear, nibbling on their melba toast and sucking down the black coffee, when Amelia and I dragged in.

"Morning," I mumbled.

"We saw Philip last night," Amelia announced. "He's a mess and he has to come home, and if you say he can't, I'm calling Child Welfare and telling them that you and Dad forced me to quit high school so I could be a supermodel. And I'll make sure it gets in all the newspapers, too."

Okay, now obviously this is not the way I would have handled things.

"What did you say?" said Mom, all haughty. It's possible she was trying to see if she maybe could get the upper hand just by tossing around a lot of attitude, but I think it's just as likely that she hadn't actually heard what Amelia said, because Amelia was so upset she was talking really fast so it actually was kind of hard to understand the words.

"He's a mess. He's having a nervous breakdown, Mom, he cannot live with Dad anymore. That bitch Sarah won't even let her kids talk to him. And that's not even the point, you don't kick a person out of his own family, you just don't do it," Amelia continued to blurt. "And I'm not going to say any more than that, except that you have to bring him back, now, and if you don't, well, then you'll be sorry." She was running on instinct, which meant that everything she said had a very compelling kind of force behind it. When she got like this, you could really see why people think she's a star. It's because she just is.

"That is not your decision, Amelia," Daria interjected coolly.

"And you're a bitch too, because he called here and you talked to him and you didn't tell me, so I don't have to listen to anything you say either, Daria," she announced.

"You're hysterical," Mom sighed. She still thought she had the upper hand, so her creepy attitude was careening all over the kitchen. "And you're just a child, so—"

"If I were a child, I would be in school, wouldn't I?" Amelia hissed. "And if you think I'm not going to do what I just said I was going to do? You are so wrong. You bring my brother back here, or I'm blowing the lid off all of it. And I'm blowing the lid off Dad, too. I know you guys think I don't know about what he did to Daria? But you all talk too much, all the time, right in front of me, and you always did, even when I was a little-bitty kid, and you gave your son to a known pedophile, that'll play great in the *Daily News*, oh they'll love that one—"

"Shut up! *Shut up!*" screamed Daria. So, I thought, my initial observation that Amelia was starting out with the big guns turned out to be not entirely accurate. Turns out she had much bigger guns in her arsenal, and she was not afraid to use them.

After a good deal of screaming on everyone's part—except my own, why bother?—there was enough of a lull for me to put in my two cents.

"I don't know what you're all yelling about," I said. "Philip is not going back there anyway. He's gone. Got it? Dad has misplaced him, and we have him. So you can go along with this and be nice about it, or not, but Philip's not going back either way."

"What are you talking about? Polly? Are you telling me, are you, are you a *party* to this?" Mom was aghast at the very thought.

"Yeah, Mom, I'm a party to it," I said. I liked that phrase, "a party to," for some reason it really sort of got down to what was up. "You can call Dad, he'll tell you, it's true, Philip's not up there. They don't know where he is. So then you can call the police, which will get into the news because we're so famous now, it just will. And then once it's in the news, a lot of other things might get in the news, depending on how mad Amelia is, I guess. I didn't know she was that mad, I mean, I never told her that stuff about Dad, I would have kept that off the table, but I'm not her, so I can't help you with that. Anyway, that could happen, I guess, if you guys take the position that Philip really needs to go back up there and live with Dad and Sarah and those two little kids no one will let him talk to. Don't you think that's creepy, though, that Sarah won't let Philip talk to those kids? They live in the same apartment, for fuck's sake. And I'm telling you, Mom, they have been not nice to Philip at all. Just really, I don't think."

"Philip has given you an earful, I'm sure, about how 'not nice' they are. Did he also manage to tell you he got suspended from Dalton being verbally abusive to the teachers? And—"

"That just means he said fuck a lot which, why not, this *is* fucked!" Amelia was yelling again.

"And striking another student, I don't suppose he told you about that, or the drugs—"

"Drugs? Oh, 'drugs,' ooo, Mom, people are offering me *and* Amelia blow every night and you could give a shit!"

"That is simply untrue and if I thought it was true, I most certainly would intervene. Now you are making things up, to hurt me. After everything I've done for you." Mom was getting all teary now.

"Could we stay on the subject?" I said. "Philip is a mess and they're not doing anything except making it worse!"

"They asked him to have some self discipline at home," Mom started to blather again. "And I know that Sarah was concerned, we all were, that he would be a bad influence, the way he has been here—"

"Bad influence, that's crap, he was fine until you kicked him out!"

"He needs—"

"YOU DON'T GIVE A FUCK WHAT HE NEEDS!" Amelia yelled.

"I will not have it," said Daria. "Things are finally going right, I won't have him back here, I won't, Mom—"

"FUCK YOU," Amelia yelled.

Honestly.

"It doesn't matter, it doesn't matter," I said. "It doesn't matter. It doesn't MATTTTTTEEEER!" Who knows why this worked, but somehow it did, or maybe they all just wore themselves out with the yelling and not listening. In any event, they all just kind of stopped screaming at each other to stare at me. I think it worked because I was the loudest. Who knows.

"It clearly didn't work out for Philip to be up there, so he's not going back. So you know, what I was thinking, was maybe we could get Collette to talk to Dad about this, for us. I mean, I know you don't like talking to him. And you know, Collette, she was here when the whole thing went down, anyway so, even though she's our agent, she's also part of the family, more or less . . ." Okay, this part made me want to puke and I was the one who was saying it, but the fact is I knew that Mom and Daria would shut up once I suggested Collette should be the one to handle things, and I was actually right. ". . . so I say we call Collette and run this by her and see what she thinks, and then, you know, get Philip back here as fast as we can. That's really what I think."

This was when the screaming really stopped. I mean, it had already stopped when I started rambling, but now there was a different sound in the silence. It was the kind of silence where you can hear your opponents thinking different thoughts;

seriously, you could practically hear both Mom and Daria re-evaluating what their position was going to be. Amelia had presented them with an impossible ultimatum, and I had presented them with a way to cave to her ultimatum while simultaneously preserving their refusal to cave. I'm telling you, in that moment, I was pretty impressed with myself.

"It doesn't matter what they think," Amelia started to tell me, and I literally raised my finger into the air, to silence her too.

"Shut up, Amelia," I said.

"I think—" started Daria.

"You shut up too," I said. "I'm calling Collette."

Which is what I did. I had enough sense to go into my bedroom to make the call; there was no point in rubbing their noses in it. Besides which, Collette was not amused, as I more or less predicted she would not be.

"Where is he?" she asked.

"Well, you know, Collette, we really don't know where he is."

"You don't."

"Collette. What if the cops think, you know, if it got out to them that he's missing, and they put out an APB or whatever those things are, and then they discovered that we knew all along where Philip was, they might think we were playing games with the law, and that would look terrible in the press. So no, we don't know where he is."

"I see."

"Yeah. But we're pretty sure he ran away because he can't stand living with Dad, and he needs to come back home. He really does."

"Has your father been hitting him, say, or molesting him, sexually?"

"Not to my knowledge, but he still needs to come home."

"Why?"

"Because it's not working out up there for him."

"Your brother is a difficult boy."

"No, he's not."

"It's very possible that he's finally getting some necessary discipline, Polly, and he doesn't particularly like it. I think you need to consider that before you start making rash demands about his return to the maternal fold."

"Philip is not the problem."

"That's news to me. I heard he was there last night, he crashed the opening?"

"He didn't crash it."

"He certainly wasn't invited, how did he get in?"

"I don't know, but Herb seemed pretty glad to see him."

"There were some terrifically charming photos of you all in a cab, with him flipping off a photographer, I've been working for hours to keep that one out of the *Post*."

"Can we stay on the subject?"

"This is the subject, Polly. You didn't make too much of a fuss when your parents decided to send him away. I'm kind of wondering why you're so interested now."

"My parents didn't decide that alone, Collette, as I think you might remember." She was pissing me off now, so I got kind of clippy with her. "My question is, why you took such an interest in the whole thing, why you wanted him out of the way and why you want him to stay out of the way now? And why you wouldn't even let him talk to her, because I know that that was not Mom's idea."

"That's ridiculous."

"Bullshit."

Okay, I was suddenly real fucking sick of Collette, as I think you may have noticed. I was also sick of myself, for just going along with her bullshit for as long as I had. But I still had to get her to take care of this. There was nobody else to do it.

"Maybe we should talk about what's happening next, instead of what happened a long time ago," I said.

"That might be wise," she sneered, real fucking frosty and condescending, like she couldn't believe she was being forced to talk about this stuff with an eighteen-year-old kid who knew nothing.

"Cut it out with the attitude, would you?" I snapped. "Like you actually knew what 'wise' means. Need I point out, you're a fucking *agent*?"

This was perhaps not the smartest thing I ever said; however, once it was out of my mouth, I just had to keep going.

"The real point right now is, this thing had to happen," I said. "You need to call Dad and explain to him, we all want Philip back, and we've heard it's not working out for him up there, and we hope that Dad sees that this is what's best for everybody, because if he makes a big fuss, we're afraid it'll turn into a big public fight and terrible things could get said in front of newspaper reporters. They all really like Amelia and, for that matter, they like me too, and Dad needs to understand the power of the press in a situation like this. Can you communicate that to him?"

"Can I speak with Amelia for a second?"

"No, you can't, she's real upset right now," I told her. "She's maybe even too upset to make it to her matinee, that's how upset she is."

There was a pause at this.

"That would be a shame," said Collette.

"It fucking well would," I replied.

"Why don't I call your father right away, and get this taken care of, so that she doesn't have to worry anymore?"

"That would be great, Collette, thanks a bunch."

So that's how Polly learned how to play hardball. It felt both great and lousy at the same time, to tell the truth; it felt like when you pick up some really fabulous dress off a rack, and it fits great and looks amazing, but the color is maybe just not perfect, and it costs a fucking fortune, and you just can't decide if that color is great or terrible, and so you buy it anyway, and then you wear it once and you feel just restless all night, because you realize that the color is, in fact, wrong, it's just dead wrong, and you look awful instead of great, and you spent all that money and now you can't even take it back. That's exactly what it felt like, it really was.

The rest of the day was undeniably shitty. There were endless phone calls flying about: Collette calling Mom, Dad calling Mom, Collette calling Daria, Collette calling me, Dad calling Mom again. I honestly thought after a couple hours of this nonsense that they would wear themselves out and just throw in the towel—they all clearly knew that they were not going to win this—but there was just no way they were going to cave before they'd really made us suffer. Amelia had a five-show weekend, so she got to

277

duck all the drama and go wait it out at the theatre. But I got to live through every miserable second of it.

Finally, Monday afternoon, Dad sent a car service over with all of Philip's stuff in it. It was what Mom did when she kicked Philip out—she just dumped all his stuff in a town car and sent it away. So that's what Dad did back. The whole thing was so fucking unceremonious you really wanted to puke. Because when the car got to our apartment? Amelia and I went down to help the doorman unload it, and there was just stuff tossed everywhere, schoolbooks and papers just dumped on the floor of the car, along with his T-shirts and gym shoes, and he had this little cardboard box with a couple of arrowheads in it, they had just tossed that on the floor too and the lid came off and we really had to scrounge to find those arrowheads because Amelia was in a panic; she said it would have killed him, really, to lose them. I don't know. The whole thing wasn't even unceremonious, it was just nasty, and I know they were more mad at me than anybody else, but still I was glad that we waited to go get Philip until after his stuff got there. It would not have helped, if he'd seen that.

So then Amelia and I got in a cab, and we went down to the East Village and picked him up. He already looked a lot better. He was sitting on the couch, watching television and letting those two little dogs jump all over him. I remember he used to do that with our dog, Boffin, who was this big old lab who was just a pain in the ass; that dog was like a hundred pounds or something and she wanted to jump on you all the time, which was absolutely ridiculous except, as I recall, Philip seemed to enjoy it. In any case, he seemed pretty content to have those two little yapper dogs hopping all over him now. Laaara had given him a terrific haircut at some point over the weekend, and he had grown a couple of inches while he was gone, so now he looked almost like a man. Except for the fact that every now and then something would happen on the television that would crack him up, and then he'd laugh really hard, which you don't often see grown men do.

While Amelia was going to tell Philip it was okay to come home now, that crazy Laaara looked at me and tilted her head toward the patio door; she had this tiny little patio attached to her crummy apartment. "I need to talk to you," she said.

So I followed her out there. It was not a great little patio by any means—mostly sort of broken-up concrete and dirt, and some empty old pots that had dead plants in them. "This is nice," I said, mostly to be polite, but she brightened right up.

"Isn't it?" she said. "I was so lucky to get it. I have to share it with three other apartments, but they're hardly ever out here so me and the boys get it to ourselves mostly. It's so great to have a little bit of a garden in New York, isn't it?" I thought, this person is quite insane, she actually thinks she's lucky to have this unbelievably shitty little patio.

"He seems to be doing a lot better," I said. "I have to thank you, it was really incredibly decent of you to let him stay here for a few days. And that's a really good haircut you gave him."

"Yeah, thanks, you should let me cut your hair," she said.

"I will, I'll call you," I said. I was kind of tired, by this point, and I didn't have much more in me. I wanted to get Philip home, and get over the last hump of Mom and Daria having to say hello to him, and I didn't know what that was going to be like, but I wanted to just get it done. Unfortunately, Laaara had a few things on her mind.

"Listen, I have to tell you, your brother's not in really great shape," she said. "Are you guys doing anything for him? Like, is there someone for him to talk to? He talked to me a little bit, but he really needs like some major therapy or something."

"Yeah, I'll mention it to Mom," I said.

"You got to do more than that; you got to make it happen," she told me. She was getting real stern real fast, this basically flaky hair stylist. "I'm just going to come out and tell you this, because I think that maybe you have it in you to be a good person. And you know, I didn't think that, the first time I met you—you seemed like just your average self-involved shithead, you know what I mean?"

"Hey, don't hold back," I said.

This made her laugh. "Yeah, right?" she said. "How's that for a kick in the teeth, when you really did the right thing, I mean, it's good that you stepped up for him, and brought him here, that shows me that you care about him, but I'm just saying, you know, you're going to have to do a lot better. I mean, I understand that you're not really the person at fault here? But someone has to take care of this, and it looks like you're the only person in line for the job, am I wrong about that? So what are you going to do?"

"What do you mean, what am I going to do?" I said. "I'm not, I mean, I'm going to take him home and, you know, I'm not going to let Mom kick him out again, is that what you mean?"

"Yeah, I mean that, and I mean other things. What about his school?"

"He's going to his old school, they're fixing that."

"And therapy?"

"I'm eighteen, what do I know about that stuff? You know what? Wait. The school has a therapist. He can talk to her."

"And what are you going to do about your sister?"

This was a bolt out of the blue, as far as I was concerned. "Amelia?" I said. "Not that it's any of your business—" now I was being rude to someone who had really helped me out, but she was getting pretty pushy— "but Amelia can take care of herself."

"That's not what Philip says."

"He's got a hero complex, he's in love with her."

"You think that's what it is?"

"You don't?"

"I think they're both kids."

"Oh, look—"

"All I'm saying is—"

"Don't lecture me about my family," I said, pretty sharply.

"I'm not lecturing," she said, kind of sharply herself. "But I helped you out, you know, you came to me for help, and that gives me the right to ask a few questions."

"Yes, it does," I said, feeling both mad and regretful at the same time. "I'm sorry, I'm tired, okay, I been working like a crazy person for days to solve this one crisis and you're asking me, What? What am I going to do for Amelia, to-to-to help her out of this? I can't help her out of any of it. She's worth too much money. There's nothing I can do."

I didn't even know I thought this until I said it but, as soon as it came out of my mouth, it was the most true thing I had ever heard. Laaara stared at me, just, you know, kind of completely appalled.

"She's worth too much *money*?"

"Just look at her," I said. "I mean, look at what the press does whenever she shows up. Look at the things that happen around her. She's worth a fucking fortune, they're not going to walk away from that, from any of it. I don't know why you think I have any control over any of this. I did what I could for Philip, but Amelia's on her own."

"If that's true . . ." said Laaara.

"It is true," I said. "It's just the truth." I must've sounded pretty tired when I said it. I sure felt tired. I mean, this person is in the business, and she was acting like it was oh so awful, what I was saying. When the fact is, nothing I was saying was really news.

"Then you have to do better. You just do," she told me, real mad now. "You're not allowed to just stand there and whine and say there's nothing I can do."

"I'm not whining," I started.

"You're whining," she said. "That's your sister and your brother in there! Those two are good kids, I met them at that shoot all those months they're both really good kids, you have to protect them! You have to be a lion, you have to be a mother lion protecting her cubs! 'Cause if you don't, if you decide you're just some idiot party girl doesn't give a shit about anybody else, just wants to get her picture in the newspaper and get laid, that's who you decide you want to be? What happens to them is on you."

I swear, that weekend, I worked my brains out taking care of everybody and doing the right thing, and I just kept getting my ass kicked. It was enough to make you want to say to hell with this and go back to being a selfish fucking prima donna, it really was.

CHAPTER SIXTEEN

We got past Mom and Daria, who were polite if not effusive at Philip's return and, the next week or so, Amelia and I were pretty careful about getting him back in his room and more or less mimicking his old routines—school, homework, obsessively watching bad reruns of seventies television. I made sure that there was food around the house for him to eat, the guy was really way too thin, even for a family of thin people. And for a while Amelia came right home after her show every night, just to be with him and to watch cartoons, or something on Nick at Nite. She even started playing the piano again, which she hadn't done in months, because he asked her to, but it put her in a bad mood because she wasn't as good as she used to be. Still, she was working hard to behave herself and things were kind of settling down again, and then Collette insisted, after about a week of this, that Amelia get back into the game.

As it turns out, that bad play she was in was only running for another two weeks, and Collette wanted to capitalize on it. So she was sending all sorts of agents and managers and producers and directors down to see the play and take Amelia out afterwards, for drinks and late supper, to "get to know each other" so that they could "talk about other projects." Amelia was kind of reluctant at first, as I recall, because she didn't want to leave Philip at home by himself all the time, but you could also tell that these other projects that Collette was selling her on were actually pretty enticing to the kid. I don't know if Amelia was really any good or not as an actor, but it was clear that she liked it, so sooner rather than later the enticement was going to overwhelm the reluctance. And sure enough, within the week she was making dates to go out with producers and a couple of these studio guys who were in town from the left coast.

So that was going on, and then one night she came home at like four in the morning. Which, okay, I realize that I often stay out that late? But she's fifteen. I mean, I don't want to sound like a prude, because I'm clearly not, and it wasn't because of what that crazy hair stylist said, but you have to ask yourself if that's the smartest choice going. Half the time I wasn't sure it was the smartest choice for me, and I was never the sort of person Amelia was. When this whole thing started, she didn't want anything to do with any of it; she didn't want to even do the *New Yorker* thing. And then whenever we were out for drinks with some hotshot, she was always complaining about wanting to go home with Philip because she had homework. Seriously, this is even before the biting incident. I thought Daria was going to choke her half the time, because Daria never wanted me along on her ride, much less some whiney 'tween like Amelia. And now the kid's going out for drinks till four in the morning?

So one night I just showed up at the theatre and tagged

along. Like, why not? She was going out with some indie director who trust me, was happy enough to have me there. And Amelia was glad to have me, too. No one really thought much about it, least of all me. So we ended up in the downstairs bar at the Soho House, which was nice, and he ordered a martini for himself, another for me, and then he said to Amelia, "What would you like? Champagne, a cosmopolitan?"

And she said, "A cosmo, that would be great."

Which, honestly I was going to let pass; trust me, it's not like I've never seen the kid drink. But some part of me was just feeling irritable lately around some of this crap. I mean, what is the assumption, that a cosmopolitan is an okay drink for a fifteen-year-old kid because it's got like a shred of fruit juice in there, along with the triple sec and the vodka?

So I laughed and put my arm around her and said, "Do you know how old she is?" Which really is the question that shuts everyone up. Because the fact is, they all do know how old she is, even when they're pretending not to.

So Amelia kind of rolled her eyes, and said, "Do you know how old *she* is?" Which I'll give it up to the kid, was not a bad point, in a state where the drinking age is twenty-one.

So then I rolled my eyes, and said, "What kind of sparkling water do you have on tap?" Which was not a very good joke by anyone's book, but people laughed anyway, and we ended up listening to this dude yak on about his movie, which he had no financing for, and was probably never going to happen, and we made it out of there by midnight, stone-cold sober, the both of us.

In the cab, on the ride back to Brooklyn, Amelia yawned

and said, "Thank god you were there, that guy was so boring." And then she fell asleep. Honestly, she was really exhausted all the time, around then. She was always sleeping till noon.

I was not planning on making a habit of this, believe me. That guy was in fact a real snore, and it was also a bit of a snore that I couldn't have a martini and got stuck drinking Pellegrino all night with Amelia. But the following two nights, when I wasn't there, she ended up dragging in after three, and I thought, boy, there really is no one driving the bus around here; there just isn't. So I went back to the theatre, to tag along again and get the stupid kid home at a halfway reasonable hour, and Collette was there. And she had, along with her, this giant woman wearing an enormous green muurmuur with about six thousand yellow stones strung across her chest.

Amelia saw them first. For one minute she's waving at me with this kind of grin, because she actually was glad to see me— I got a lot of points for saving Philip, so we were more or less on the same page at this point—and then she just kind of blinks and looks past me, and goes white. This is a kid who nothing freaks out. So I turned around and see what she's looking at, and it's Collette, with this huge woman who looks like a cross between Jabba the Hutt and an enormous green Popsicle.

I got to Amelia first, so we had three seconds to share info. "Who the hell is that?" I asked.

"It's that Kafka person, Rex's manager," she hissed. "It's the second time she's been here, I don't know why." And then she smiled and held out her hand. "Collette, hi! Maureen. How nice to see you." It was very smooth. She was more or less catching onto the niceties by this point.

While everyone was shaking hands and cooing, I tried and failed to catch up. That night in the back room at W, I was pretty involved with Rex, who had his hand down the back of my pants most of the time we were talking to each other, so I confess I don't remember meeting anyone else, and I had no idea what Rex's manager actually looked like. And then, why would Collette be with this person, since it had been rather my understanding that they loathed each other? At least, as I recalled, there was certainly a lot of loathing going on around the *Regis and Kelly* episode. At this point in my thinking the politely smarmy introductions were more or less finished, so I just thought, Oh well, it's all show business. Who knew what they were cooking up?

But, on the other hand, whatever they were cooking up was clearly something I was not supposed to know about, because neither one of them was too thrilled to see me. The giant green muumuu lady smiled brilliantly and cooed an introduction to a third party, some film director she was there with, who reacted to me the way guys do, kind of like he was instantly in heat, so I didn't catch on right away that they really wanted me to get lost. Collette, however, didn't even smile when she said hello; she just looked over my shoulder right away, like there was somebody more important out there somewhere, anywhere, that she would much rather be talking to. And then at the restaurant, she pretty much flat out ignored me, even though we were seated next to each other. I didn't have much choice in the matter, so I just ignored her back and tried to pay attention to the nonconversation that was sparkling around me.

"Do you come down to the theatre often, Polly?" smiled Jabba the Hutt.

"Just now and then, when nothing's going on," I shrugged, sipping my Pellegrino. Even Collette kept trying to pour alcohol into Amelia, so the "we'll have water" act was still in full force.

"Nothing's going on for you?" asked Jabba. "That doesn't sound right."

"No, I mean, there's a lot going on," I amended, sounding lamer than I wanted to. "We have a very big *GQ* shoot coming up, Daria and I are looking forward to that," I said.

"Ah, *GQ*!" smiled Jabba, with a condescending curl of the lip. "Lovely. Although I rather suspect that *GQ* will no longer be good enough for our rising star, Amelia." She sparkled, smiling at Amelia like some kind of poisonous fairy godmother, then turning and looking at the shiny shiny Los Angeles film director. He smirked and checked in with me, to see how I was taking all this. I thought about smacking her, then I thought about ordering a martini, then I smiled, coy.

"Absolutely not," I said to her. "It is an extremely filthy lingerie shoot. Definitely too hot for a toddler like Amelia. But I have a feeling that you might enjoy it. Should be right up your alley. Real X-rated stuff." Amelia snickered and Jabba got a kind of evil glint in her eye for a second. But then she laughed lightly and raised her glass, like nothing ever bothered her.

"Touché," she purred.

Not too long after that, Collette asked me to come outside with her so that we could have a smoke. Which I knew was not going to be the charming little friendly event that she made it sound like, but I thought maybe I should find out what was up with her. So we're there on the sidewalk, and she's firing up a Camel light, and offering one to me, and then she says, "Polly—

can I mention something?" very quiet, sort of awkward, like she's all embarrassed.

"Sure, Collette, what's up?" I said back, dragging on my Camel.

"How do I put this?" she smiled, still so embarrassed. "I don't want to hurt your feelings. But it looks, really, *awkward*, that you're sort of trying to steal some of Amelia's limelight. A couple of people have mentioned it to me."

"Steal her limelight? What are you talking about?" I asked.

"You did this on Tuesday, didn't you? Invited yourself along, when Don Nigro wanted to talk to her about a project?"

"That guy doesn't have a film, Collette. He was all over the place pitching, but even I could tell he doesn't have a shred of financing."

"That's not actually the point, Polly."

"Why are you sending her out for drinks with that woman, anyway? She's Rex Wentworth's manager. She can't stand any of us. She particularly can't stand Amelia."

"Maybe that's just what you'd like to think."

"Oh, what is that supposed to mean?"

"It seems clear to everyone—I've heard this from a lot of people—that you're maybe a little bit . . . jealous?"

"Everyone, everyone who?"

"You know I can't tell you that."

"I don't know that, if people are saying shit behind my back—"

"What do you think is going to happen? These people have come to see Amelia, and talk to her about projects that are really about *her*. They're excited about *Amelia* and . . . you show up. No one knows what you're doing here."

"It used to be we didn't go anywhere without each other, what's the big deal, I want to have a drink with her once in a while now?"

"You're not exactly drinking though, are you?" she laughed.

"You know, technically, I'm not old enough either," I said. "But why you don't just tell me what the big deal is; I want to hang out with my sister."

Collette sighed at my stupidity. "Don't play coy with me; you were never that interested in 'hanging out' with Amelia before," she said. "But that's not the point either. I don't think you're jealous, I've known you for almost a year now, and I can see that that's not part of your character. But I do think your behavior in this instance is not as smart as it might be. Now, I can take care of this, but it has to stop immediately, and I mean yesterday. This isn't a joke. The people who saw you down here on Tuesday—one of them is, unfortunately, a member of the press, and he said that it was really kind of desperate and pathetic, the way you invited yourself along on her meeting with Don. I just don't want this to go any further."

Okay. "One of them" in the *press* have mentioned that he thinks I'm "desperate and pathetic"? People do actually say that shit in my world, and they mean it. And then it gets in the magazines and then everybody talks about how desperate and pathetic you are and then your bookings start to evaporate and only losers think you're hot. At least, that happens often enough that you have to consider it a possibility.

So Collette saw me take this hit, and then she tried to comfort me. "I did what I could for all of you; you know I've worked really hard and I believe in all three of you girls," she sighed.

"Frankly, I would have much preferred it if it was you or Daria who had broken out, but that's not the way things went. It was Amelia. So you're going to have to step aside while I make this happen. You'll get your turn." And she smiled at me, so phony, that I swear, it all became so clear to me, right then, that she was playing me, and assuming that she could just scare me enough that I'd go away, and she and that Maureen person could do what they wanted, whatever that was, with Amelia.

"Huh," I said, sort of startled about what was going through my head. "Thanks for pointing that out, Collette. I'll think about it. But another way to look at this might be, the kid's only fifteen, I'm her big sister, I'm here to keep an eye on her, make sure nobody orders her a martini, or offers her a line of coke or something that's basically going to hurt her. Maybe I'm not trying to suck up publicity. Maybe that's why I'm down here."

"Amelia can take care of herself," Collette informed me.

"She's surrounded by sharks and liars and people who want to use her," I told her. "She *can't* take care of herself."

"Then I will take care of her."

"Except you're one of them, Collette, so that won't quite work, now, will it?"

Okay, now *that* I should not have said; I knew it even when I said it. And it startled her, it really did. It startled me, too.

"I hadn't figured you for a sentimentalist, Polly," Collette informed me.

"Me neither," I said, dropping my smoke, and heading back inside. "So we're both surprised now, huh?"

CHAPTER SEVENTEEN

Okay, so by the time we got home that night, both Mom and Daria were fully armed and waiting for me in the kitchen. Daria went first.

"Are you insane?" she snapped.

"Yes, hello to you too," I said. "So may I presume that taran-tula we call 'our agent' has called, maybe even before we left the restaurant?"

"She says you're acting like a fool," Daria said, nostrils flaring. Sometimes she can't help herself, she has Mom's taste for bad melodrama. "Everyone is laughing at you."

"What are you talking about?" said Amelia. I hadn't told her anything about my little chat with Collette—what would be the point?—so this was all news to her.

"Collette says that Polly has been crashing your meetings, and that it's quite awkward for everyone," Mom told her.

"Oh that's nuts," said Amelia, rolling her eyes and heading for the door.

"Not according to Collette. She says people have been

complaining and it's actually hurting your chances of landing your next acting job, Amelia. We all have to take this seriously," Daria said.

"Well, no one said anything to me about it," said Amelia.

"She was trying to be discreet. She thought if she talked to Polly about it, Polly would do the right thing. Apparently Polly told her off."

"You did?" said Amelia. "When did this happen?"

"I didn't tell her off, I just said she's a liar and a shark and a user," I said.

Amelia laughed. "You said that?"

"This isn't funny, Amelia," Daria told her, still trying for offended outrage. "This is a very serious situation. Collette says that Polly's behavior is extremely inappropriate, that she's trying to take over as your agent, at these meetings—"

"What meetings? We go out for drinks."

"Besides, Collette is a first-class bitch and she's also a first-class liar, you can't believe a word out of her mouth," I repeated. "This isn't opinion, this is fact."

"You think you don't need her anymore, is that your position?" Mom countered. "Because that can be arranged. She's threatened to quit."

They clearly thought this would be the thing to silence me. I mean, I was floored, frankly, but it wasn't by Collette's cleverness so much as it was by how stupid they were, letting her play them like that. "Get real, Mom," I laughed. "We're the biggest meal ticket she's ever landed. She's not going anywhere."

"She's serious, Polly," Daria spat. "You get it together or she's dumping you *and* me."

"You and me," I repeated. "You and me?"

"Yes."

"But not Amelia."

The speed of the conversation was definitely slowing down, as we all took this in.

"That's nuts," said Amelia.

"I'm afraid not," Daria countered. "She's very unhappy with the way Polly treats her; she says she was also terrifically rude about this whole thing with Philip, which was obviously none of her business, really, but she did what she could to help and you just keep . . . apparently, her feeling is that you keep insulting her and it's not worth it to her. To keep working with us. If you're going to treat her that way." Daria sounded real breathless, suddenly, like she was having an asthma attack. She used to have them when she was a kid. They went away when she was eight but then they came back again when the divorce thing was going on, and she had to keep talking to shrinks about all the stuff Dad had been up to, so I thought that was maybe what was happening, the asthma was coming back. But then I realized that she wasn't having trouble breathing, she was just so fucking mad at me, she could hardly get the words out. And I didn't blame her for a second. Not that we were ever the Bobbsey twins but, even as different as we are, Daria and I were always on somewhat the same page. Now it was like that was just over and done with, and I was the one who had ended it, and I hadn't even paused, or bothered to explain to her why.

"Okay," I said, pausing for the first time. Maybe she deserved an explanation. Maybe so did stupid crazy Mom. "Okay. I have, in fact, gone down to the theatre twice to hang out with Amelia after the show. Why is that such a big damn deal?"

"She's fine, Mom," Amelia said. "These guys are all into like movies and babes and stuff, you think they don't like it that Polly's there? Are you kidding me?"

"Collette says it's inappropriate," Mom insisted.

"Why?" asked Amelia, seriously confused.

"Yes, why? Why?" I said, trying to get this conversation on something resembling a more rational train track. "She's only fifteen years old. Why can't I be there? Or why can't Mom be there?"

"If you get too difficult, they don't like it," Mom explained, getting mad. "You're not stupid, Polly. You know this."

"How is this difficult?" I asked. "Why does she need to get rid of me? Why did she need to get rid of Philip? 'Cause I wasn't there, in the room, when you gave him to Dad? But I'm betting that was her idea. Did you ever ask yourself why?"

Mom's eyes widened, startled, for just a second, so I knew I had her.

"You're jealous," she said.

"I'm not jealous, Mom. Answer the question. Whose idea was it to get rid of Philip? And why wasn't he allowed to talk to her? He called her all those times and you and Daria both, you wouldn't let him talk to her! And Dad didn't tell Philip that she was trying to call him, either. And you took his cell phone. So they really couldn't talk, they really, you really—"

"That is hardly what happened," she sputtered.

"Whose idea was it?" I said. "Was it your idea, or Dad's idea? Or was it Collette's?"

"Mom?" said Amelia, kind of quiet and worried.

"Your sister is being ridiculous," Mom told her, like she was talking to a three-year-old.

"Just answer the question, Mom," I said. "Whose idea was it? It was Collette's idea, wasn't it, because she was tired of Amelia fighting all this-this-this-*crap* . . ." I never thought of it that way before, but in the moment it sure looked like that to me. "And she wanted to just sell the three sisters act and Philip was messing that up because he and Amelia, he just made that harder. And so you gave him away, because he was in the way, you gave your own kid away, didn't you? For money, or convenience—"

"Leave her alone," said Daria.

"I'm not leaving her alone. We never asked and I want to know. What happened, why did Philip—"

"We have been over and over this!" Mom said.

"Answer it. Whose idea was it to—"

"Hey, Philip, you're still up!" Amelia stood up, fast, and went to the door. I didn't know how long he was standing there, and I don't think she did either. He looked kind of sleepy, and he was squinting a little, like the light in the kitchen was too bright. But he was so tall, taller than all of us now. For a second it seemed like he was gone those six months he had just grown non-stop. So he stood there blinking in the doorway, looking like a giant kid, but also kind of like one of those really young marines who you see on television commercials talking about getting the job done in the middle east. Like, you didn't want to hurt his feelings? But you also didn't want to piss him off.

"I heard you guys talking," he said.

299

"We just got back from the theatre, well, we went out for drinks afterwards, with some creepy movie people," Amelia said.

"They were creeps?" he asked.

"I don't know, they were probably all right, who can tell? I'm going to bed." And with that, she left. Philip left too. He didn't have a lot to say to the rest of us ever; now it was like he couldn't even imagine pretending to talk to anyone except her. And since no one had bothered to pick up a phone and call a therapist, it seemed better than having him snarl at everyone, or lie around in a depressed stupor. Which seemed to be the choices, if she weren't around.

So me, Mom and Daria were left in the kitchen. Nobody said anything for a minute, but it was a very lively silence. It was like we were all speeding down the same river, but we were on different rafts, fighting different kinds of rapids. Daria was all worried about losing her agent, and what that might mean. She worked so hard, before any of this happened, to get an agent; it took her almost a year and a half, with people kind of half-signing her, saying they'd rep her as a favor for a while, she was already eighteen and that was too old to be starting, shit like that, she heard all of it. So of course she was scared, that was why Collette said she was going to dump us, to scare her. Mom, meanwhile, was in her own little battle with what remained of her conscience, thinking about how she threw out her only son and turned him into the walking wounded, and I'm pretty sure that what she was working on was how that simply wasn't her fault. None of this is her fault, that was usually the sum total of Mom's thought processes. And then there I was, the new source of everyone's problems. If Collette really did follow through on her threat and dump me and Daria, it most definitely would be my fault, no doubt about it. And maybe I was making it all up, anyway, that Collette had some stupid diabolical plan for controlling Amelia, like who was I kidding? We'd been out on the scene for a year, all three of us, and we had survived it—it was even a blast most of the time, clubbing and hanging out with rap stars and riding around New York drinking champagne in big old limos. What was I making such a big deal about, if Collette wanted to make some money off Amelia and the kid ended up doing some of the things I had been doing all year, why on earth was that such a supposedly lousy idea?

Well, because it just was, I thought. She's still a kid. And she was better off hanging out at home, trying to play the piano for her brother, she just was. And for that matter, she should be in school.

"*What?*" hissed Daria. That's how I knew that I said it out loud, in addition to thinking it. That's how screwy that whole situation had gotten, I couldn't tell when I was thinking or talking anymore.

"Well, don't you think Amelia *should* be in school?" I said. "Like, once this play closes, maybe we should talk to that old Dean Morton, they might take her back at Garfield Lincoln now that she's . . ."

Daria didn't wait to hear the rest of the sentence, she just stiffened that spine of hers and left the room. Mom looked up to the heavens, completely baffled, shook her head, held out her hand to silence me, and then she left as well. Oh, brother, I thought. I must have said that out loud too, because Mom glanced back at me, sharp, with one of those "if looks could

301

kill" looks, before she stalked off to bed. So then the other person left in the kitchen was me, on my own little life raft. The whole thing was a complete drag.

The next morning Collette called early, before ten, with information about a couple of photo shoots that we already had on the books. Daria took the call, wrote down the general stats for the first shoot, which was scheduled for a couple days after Amelia's play closed, and then she passed the phone to Amelia.

"She wants to talk to you," she said.

So then Amelia took the phone and said, "Hey, Collette! What's up?" Then she listened for a second, nodded her head a couple of times, looked at the ceiling, a little bored, and said, "Okay. That sounds great, thanks. See you." And then she hung up.

"She didn't want to talk to me?" I said.

"She didn't say, so I guess not," Amelia told me, raising her eyebrow, like, a little paranoid, maybe?

I looked at Daria. "She say anything to you? Like, is she keeping you and just dumping me now?" I asked.

"She didn't say," Daria replied.

"She's still dumping both of us, then," I said.

"We didn't talk about that," Daria said. "Since she's sending contracts over for next week's shoot, I rather doubt it."

"You didn't doubt it last night."

"No, I didn't, last night she sounded like she meant business," Daria responded, completely cool-headed. It really is unnerving when she does that, and she knows it.

"She's not dumping anybody," Amelia said. "She told me last week that she was thinking about dumping you guys and I said if she did I would quit too. She's not going to do it."

Daria looked at her, surprised, and then she turned pink.

"She tried this on you last week?" I repeated.

"Yeah, and I told her to forget it," she said.

"And you just didn't bother to mention this last night."

"It didn't come up," she said. "Besides, I thought it might piss you off."

"I'm not pissed," I said.

"You're acting kind of pissed."

"I'm not pissed!"

"As I said, she's sending over contracts," Daria repeated. "So I guess that settles that question. No one's being dumped after all."

"So what did she want to talk to you about?" I asked Amelia.

"Nothing," she said. "If you want to talk to her, why don't you call her?"

"I don't want to talk to her."

"Well, then what's the problem?"

"Nothing's the problem. You said something was great, what was so great?"

"For crying out loud," Amelia yawned. "Just something about how I don't have to go out for cocktails anymore, after the show. She said that she was trying to get some people down there, for the closing weekend, but they had to fly back to LA, so I'm just supposed to meet them sometime next month, when they come back. So that's good, there's a cast party the last night and I don't want to miss it. So that's a big relief that these LA losers took off, good riddance." She poured herself a cup of black coffee and looked around the counter, sort of hazy. "Is there any melba toast around here?"

It seemed improbable, to say the least—one second Collette's snarling at me on street corners, threatening to cut us loose; the next second it's all, have a great weekend, I'll send the contracts over. I knew she was up to something; I just truly could not figure out what, but she never called back, either to Mom or Daria or Amelia or me, for that matter. Which left me trying to be supersleuth all day, following everyone around, listening in on phone calls, I even broke into Daria's email account, I know her password, even though she doesn't know I do. But nobody called, nobody emailed, nobody texted, nobody did anything. I thought about calling Collette on a pretext and trying to cleverly wring some information out of her, but I knew that would merely give away how dead curious I was about what she was up to, and I doubted I'd get anything out of her anyway. So I just spied on people all day. Amelia messed around on the piano, then the new contracts arrived, then Daria did a papaya mud mask, then Amelia tried on a new color nail polish on her toenails, then Mom phoned in an order to Fresh Direct, then Amelia decided she didn't like the new nail polish and so she took it all off. After about three hours of this I thought my head would split.

Finally, Amelia was taking off, to go to the theatre. When she walked out the front door, she yelled back to Philip, "I'll be home by eleven for *Star Trek*, don't watch it without me, it's the Tribbles episode and I want to see it!" It was really pretty nice, frankly; he grinned at me and dutifully went back to the living room to program the Tivo. Daria was already out for the evening with some gossip columnist that Darren set her up with, and Mom was having drinks by herself in the den, which was more and more of a favorite pastime with her. I cracked a beer and thought about calling a couple of lighting guys I knew who had good parties in Tribeca; one of them shared a loft with this Czech supermodel who was never around but she had amazing booze stashed all over the place, and the view on their roof was really good. So that's what I was thinking about doing, when the phone rang.

Honestly, if I had known it was that horny Brit, I wouldn't have answered. I'd been dodging calls from him for weeks, ever since our night on the town after Philip's nervous breakdown. But the caller ID on the phone said the call was coming from Amelia's dressing room, down at the theatre, so I picked it up.

"Amelia?" I said.

"No, god, hello, oh Polly, is that you? Fantastic, I was hoping I'd get you, this is Edmund," he said. "How are you doing?"

"Hello, Edmund!" I said, trying to drum up some phony enthusiasm. "I didn't know it was you, I thought it was Amelia! The caller ID says it's her dressing room."

"Right, I'm down at the theatre," he said. "I heard from some of the actors that you'd been coming down this week, to go for drinks after the show, and I wanted to see if you were coming tonight, it'd be so great to see you."

"Oh, I wasn't, I don't think I can make it tonight," I said. "And you're there tonight? I'm so sorry to miss you."

"Oh. That's too bad," he said, trying not to sound too disappointed, and sounding terrifically crushed anyway. "Sam's coming, I really thought you'd like to meet him."

"Sam? The playwright?" I asked, nodding to myself, as if that old Brit was in the room with me, watching this bad

305

performance. "I did meet him, at opening night, didn't I?" I vaguely remembered this kind of sad-faced ex-movie star shaking my hand and checking out my cleavage; that's the most I could remember about Sam.

"Yeah, he's bringing his friend, Rex Wentworth. I know Amelia had a bit of a rough time with him whenever that was, a while ago I suppose, but I guess that's why I thought you'd be here, for moral support or something. I know how much you worry about her and your not-so-little brother—what's his name again?"

"I'm sorry, what did you say? Rex Wentworth is coming to the show tonight?"

"Yeah, he's coming with his manager, apparently. I thought for sure you knew, what with everything that happened, and . . . Christ," he said, catching on. "Does Amelia know?"

CHAPTER EIGHTEEN

By the time I got to the theatre, the show had already started, and Edmund was on the sidewalk having a smoke, waiting for me. He shook one out of his pack and offered it before I even asked; he truly had the act down, that he could predict my every need and whim, as if we were partners in these escapades. And who am I to say he was wrong? "I gave the other actors a heads-up, to keep it to themselves who was coming, so nobody's told her. Everybody wants her to have a good show," he said as he lit my cigarette. So once again he saved the day. It hadn't even occurred to me that absolutely everyone down there would know that Rex was coming and that one of them might just blurt it out to her. So that horny Brit may have been overly helpful, but overly helpful was apparently what I needed, that's how many messes me and my family kept stepping in.

"They all know?" I said. "Who told them?"

"Actors just know when somebody big is in the house—it's in their DNA," he shrugged. "Sorry, I don't mean to be flip:

Most of them talk to Sam or me, or their agents. I heard from Sam that Rex was coming to check Amelia out; there's some huge part for a teenager in his next film and they think she might be right for it. The director's already seen her, wasn't he here last night?"

This really was enough to make my head explode. "Rex Wentworth wants Amelia in his *movie*? Are you fucking kidding me?" I said.

"No, why, she's really quite good, a lot of people are coming to see her, it's not utterly crazy that he might want to cast her," he told me.

"She called him a pedophile on national television," I reminded him.

"Come on, that was a long time ago," he reminded me back. "And she didn't actually come out and say 'pedophile,' as I recall; it was a good deal more subversive, what she actually said."

"He almost sued us."

"Did he really?"

"No, but he should've. Trust me. That old Rex Wentworth is not here to give Amelia some big fat movie job, this is bad, this is really bad," I worried.

"You know, you are even more beautiful when you're being neurotic, if that's possible," he told me.

"Oh stop flirting," I said. "I'm in trouble here."

"I can't help it," he said. "I keep thinking about that night, when you kissed me. I can't think of anything else, you've ruined me, I'm under a spell, you've got to kiss me again to get me out of it, I'm begging you." He kept blathering on while he leaned in and kissed me. It was rather sudden, and I was in no mood; however, I have to admit that this kiss was significantly better than the last one.

"You dropped your cigarette," he told me.

"Did I?" I said. "Oh well. Oh well. How's that spell, did we take care of that?"

"We might need to try again," he said, moving in for another go round.

"Oh my god," I said, trying to get a grip while I came up for air a second time. "I have to talk to Amelia, I really do."

"She's only halfway through act one, we've got another twenty minutes," he said, and his left hand was kind of sliding under my shirt in a very pleasant way. "Besides, as the show's director, I don't think my star should be given any information during the interval that might interfere with her second-act performance." And before I could put up any more of a fight, we were back at it. I know, I know, but this guy was growing on me. He was actually pretty good looking and he'd helped me a lot, in very surprising ways, over the last couple weeks, and besides I was tired of being a mother lion. I'm eighteen years old, and making out on a street corner in the middle of the East Village with this guy I was starting to dig was just fun.

Which, you know, a lot of guys would have tried to push what was going on into something more; grabbed a cab and dragged me back to some crummy apartment, or tried to get me to do it in some prop room at the theatre. But that old Edmund knew not to push. I may be a slut, but I'm a slut who was growing a conscience, and I had to get to my sister before Rex did, but not before the show finished, because he was right, if we told her in the middle of the play it might flip her out too much right before she had to go out there and do more acting. Anyway, instead of trying to get me off in some darkened alleyway, that helpful Brit took me down the block to a coffee shop, and bought me dessert and a latte. There was considerably more kissing involved, but on the whole the guy was really a gentleman.

About ten minutes before the play usually ended, he scooted me back to the theatre and snuck me in the side door, where there was a stairway down to under the stage so you could cross over and get to the dressing rooms without people seeing you. So the next thing I knew, he was setting me down in Amelia's inky-dinky dressing room. It was truly a tiny space, covered in mirrors, with open lightbulbs everywhere, and the counter was crowded with dying flowers, note cards and makeup—just piles of it, foundation and shadow, eyeliner and lipgloss.

"They do her makeup in here?" I asked, looking around. I mean, the light in there really sucked.

"You're adorable," he told me, moving in for another round of kissing. "It's the theatre, darling. Amelia does her own makeup."

The place didn't look so great to me, frankly. Every other time, when I picked her up, I waited out front, in the lobby, which was just kind of plain and white, nothing very fancy but kind of funky, in a good way. But this little dressing room was really kind of skeevy. The walls were dirty, high up above the mirrors, and the floor was just painted concrete. The light switch was one of those open boxes, on the wall, with a big fat wire running out of it, snaking up above the doorframe. And it was dead hot in there, with all those open bulbs in that tiny space. Seriously, it was nowhere near as nice as any other place we'd worked; it just wasn't in the same category. But there were little notes posted everywhere, "Break a leg!" "We're so proud of you!" "To our own 'Lucy,' it's been great to watch you on your own quest for self-knowledge!" It was very friendly and corny and sad and crummy at the same time, and I had one of those strange moments where you think maybe you don't know as much as you think you know. I mean, Amelia was always so demanding, so sharp and full of edges. This little room really wasn't anything the kid I knew would be interested in.

"Hey," she said, standing in the doorway. She was in this goofy costume, clips in her hair, this kind of Midwestern teenager Gap-wear, so she actually looked like a totally different person who was surprised to see me in her room, and not necessarily in a good way. "What are you doing here?" she said. I couldn't tell if she was mad or just startled, but she was definitely accusing me of stepping on her turf; it was like she thought that just by being there I was reading her secret diary. That's really what it felt like.

"I have to tell you something," I said. I looked over at Edmund, who just nodded and left. That guy really did know how to pick up a cue. Amelia squeezed by him in the doorway, smiled up at him in a kind of annoyed way, and then she shut the door.

"Your lipstick is a mess," she informed me, handing me a tissue. "You and Edmund been having a good time?"

"Listen, we have something we have to deal with," I said, wiping my lips off. "Rex Wentworth is here, he came to see the show tonight."

Amelia turned and looked at me in the mirror.

311

"How do you know?" she said.

"Edmund called the house, he told me," I said. "Rex is a friend of your playwright—those movie stars all hang out together, you know that."

She started messing with her hair, trying to shrug this off. "So he's here with Sam, it's got nothing to do with me," she said.

"He's here to see you," I told her. She kind of blinked. "There's some movie he's doing—they're saying there's a part for you in it. He came down here to check you out. He's going to be waiting in the lobby for you."

"You know this for sure?" she said. "I mean, Collette said, she told me no one else was coming to see me anymore; she said . . ." She stopped herself, knowing that we both had been had. "Shit. Fuck. Just fuck it," she said, sitting down.

"I'll be with you," I said. "We'll just go out there, say hello, and go home."

"It's not going to be that easy, and you know it," she said, now really yanking at her hair clips, like they were hurting her head.

"We can do it, Amelia, we can just go home. Philip's waiting to watch *Star Trek*. We'll just tell them that we have to go and walk away from it."

"Are you nuts?" she hissed at me, mad now. "After what I did? We have to do what they say. They want to say hi, and good-night? That's great. But if they want to go out for drinks, we're going out for drinks. Get a clue. I'm not allowed to piss on Rex Wentworth in front of his friends. We're going to do whatever they tell us to do."

There was a knock on the door. "Amelia? Are you in there?" someone said, kind of quiet and urgent. She wiped her eyes really fast with the back of her hand, not that she was crying, but like to make sure, and then turned and cracked the door just a tiny bit, so whoever it was couldn't see how upset she was.

"Yeah, I'm here, Kristine. It was a good show tonight, wasn't it?" she said, trying to be real positive for this person.

"Ed told us not to tell you before the show, but I had to make sure you know. That old creep Rex Wentworth is here. He saw the play tonight with Sam, and he's waiting out in the lobby to talk to you," she said. I could see part of her, even though she couldn't see me; she seemed to be the actress who played one of Amelia's mothers in this terrible play, the one who had adopted her and was really her mother but then flipped out and felt like the kid should find her real mother, something like that, it was all kind of convoluted but she was the nice one, as I recall. "Do you want someone to go with you, so you don't have to do this by yourself?" she asked, pretty concerned. Amelia shook her head.

"My sister's here," she said.

This Kristine person looked back at me, shoved in the corner of the dressing room, and you could tell she didn't think I was going to be much use in this situation. She looked back at Amelia, checking her out, sort of like a real mother would. She put her hand on Amelia's arm, real light, and kept talking to her as if I wasn't in the room. "Are you all right?" she said, quiet, but sort of like, don't kid around with me now. Which I thought was nice except for the fact that it made Amelia burst into tears and grab hold of her and cry and totally fuck up her makeup.

She just cried and cried, and this actress held onto her and said things like, "It's okay," and "I know, I know," and "shh, it's all right, you're going to be fine, you're a star, you don't have to be scared of them!" There really wasn't room for her to step inside and shut the door, so the whole meltdown could not have been less private. Behind them, I could see a couple of other people gathering, wanting to help, but also not wanting to interfere because this Kristine was doing a good job of letting Amelia cry it out on her shirt. Then, when she finally calmed down, and was quiet for a minute, one of them came forward, this young-looking older guy, and he murmured something about is she going to be all right, and Kristine nodded, and he touched Amelia's shoulder in a nice way, and she let him hug her and then Ed was hovering behind them, and he checked in with her too, and that went on for a while and I just sat in the corner and watched it, feeling like a complete intruder, instead of the person who was going to get the kid through this.

Finally, Amelia shut the door, sat down and reached for a bag of cotton pads and a bottle of some squirty type of makeup remover she liked. I tried it once and I thought that stuff was junk, but she really liked it, and in the moment it suddenly occurred to me that what she liked was the fact that it squirted. You could see that she enjoyed it, in a very simple way; there was something comforting to her, in doing the little squirty motion, and I got real sad, just sitting there and watching her do it. Her face was a mess and because of all the crying she looked so young, almost like she was ten or eleven years old, but that other part of her, the one that knew how to be a tough girl, was coming out again and taking over. "I'll be ready in a second," she said, all business. It made me feel lousy, frankly; I thought, all those other people here get to see the kid who will burst into tears, and I'm her sister, and I only got to see that because I invaded her turf. This is the person she thinks she has to be with me.

And who's to say she's wrong? That was the way things were with us by then; we were the ones who had to get the job done. I reached over, grabbed some of her lipgloss and went to work on my own face. There were going to be photographers involved at some point this evening, I was pretty fucking sure of that. Both of us needed to look hot.

By the time we made our entrance into that crummy lobby, we both looked like supermodels. And there was quite a crowd gathered to greet us. A couple of theatre underlings were hovering needlessly, pretending to put things away while they also pretended not to notice the mega-movie star in the middle of their dinky lobby. That giant Jabba the Hutt woman was there, wearing that same old green muumuu, looking again like some kind of giant poison Popsicle. Collette was there, elegantly sucking up to the Popsicle, and Ed was slouching around, trying to chat up Sam, the pathetic aging movie-star-slash-playwright. Meanwhile, that old pathetic aging movie-star-slash-lousy-playwright Sam was cold-shouldering Ed, because he was infinitely more interested in sucking up to Rex, the real movie star, who stood in the middle of all this action, glowing, like a god. He was cleverly underdressed, in a pair of blue jeans and an old T-shirt under a kind of shapeless browning suede jacket, and on his head he wore a baseball cap, backwards. Now Rex is absolutely a good-looking guy, and he's in terrific shape—he clearly spends hours a day at the gym—but he's absolutely on the nether side of forty. And he's dressed like a sixteen-year-old punk. It was all *sooo* very cute.

Ed spotted us first. "Here they are," he announced, taking a few steps forward in a kind of proprietary way. A few days ago I would have found it creepy that he was taking over again but, now that I'd spent half the night making out with the guy, it seemed like a perfectly appropriate move for him to make. Besides, Amelia was still his actress, at least until the show closed on Sunday. So he held out his hand in a kind of friendly gesture that brought us into the room, simultaneously encouraging Rex and his entourage to take a step forward themselves. "Amelia, you know Rex. He was just telling us how terrific he thought your work was," Ed announced, in his poshest tones. Honest to god, I was so grateful to that silly Brit for being so smooth at this terrible moment that I was half convinced I was falling for the guy.

"Well, thanks," said Amelia, all fresh and friendly. She smiled at Rex her best little guileless smile. He smiled back.

"Seriously, you were so great," said Rex. "You're so funny! I mean, your timing is just unbelievable."

"I just say Sam's words. He's the one, he makes us all look like we know what we're doing," she smiled some more at Rex and, simultaneously, the entire room. Seriously, it looked like a conversation, but all of it was really more of a performance; Rex would say a line, and then Amelia would say a line, and the ten people surrounding them, me and Ed and Collette and Jabba and all the theatre underlings would listen and watch and heave a collective sigh of relief that it was all going so well. In the corner of the room, a photographer magically appeared and started to snap photos. There was only one of him, which meant that he had been tipped off with a promise of exclusivity, which meant that he was one of Darren's guys over at Rush & Molloy. Which also meant that this little exchange was pretty much guaranteed to get major play there—you don't get an exclusive on something like this unless you're willing to commit, ahead of time, to running the thing in a big, spectacular way. I was betting on a lead, a full-page photo and story, at least.

"Oh god yeah, the play is terrific," Rex nodded. Sam chuckled, completely gratified that the staggeringly important movie star was saying nice things about his staggeringly stupid play.

"It's been such a thrill to do. I'm so sorry that it's ending," Amelia said.

"When's the end of the run again?" asked Rex, with barely a glance at Sam, who surely had already told him eight times that his stupid play was closing tomorrow.

"This weekend," Amelia said.

"But you've been running a while?" Rex inquired, again sincerely curious about facts he had already been told.

"Almost three months," Amelia responded, smiling again, as sweet as pie. "We extended twice already but the theatre has another show coming in, I think that's why we have to close, isn't it?" She looked at Sam and Ed, with the perfect little lilt of a question in her voice for the big authoritative boys who were in charge here. And I thought, she really is a pretty good little actress; the whole performance was flawless. It brought to mind the act she turned in for Regis and Kelly, which was, as you know, utterly and hideously memorable.

"I saw the terrific notice you got in the *Times*," Rex said.

"I got so lucky," Amelia said humbly. "The first time I was being reviewed by the *New York Times*? I was terrified. That critic was so kind."

"I don't think so," Rex said. "You're terrific in this, you really are."

Poison green muumuu Popsicle lady, I swear I never could remember that woman's name, said, "Well, we're going out for a drink, aren't we? Amelia, are you joining us?" And there was a kind of fluttering noise at this as people shifted, like a flock of birds suddenly realizing as a group that it is time to migrate. Amelia turned to me, politely checking in while communicating to everyone there that I would most certainly do what she wanted. "That sounds great!" I said, smiling at her, then smoothly turning and smiling at the whole room. The photographer clicked away.

"Wonderful," said green muumuu Jabba. "There's a car outside, I think."

Collette didn't say a word. She was there, but she politely hovered, taking a back seat with consummate grace and accommodation. She and I didn't even glance at each other; our petty little feud fading in the presence of this major negotiation. What was so unspeakably brilliant about the whole scene, of course, was that neither Amelia nor Rex had to even ask or answer the question of shall we go out and have a drink? Other people did that for them.

The rest of the evening offered more of the same. Rex and Amelia politely traded respectful sound bites, and their respective entourages respectfully took note. Ed spent the whole evening maneuvering to get a seat next to me on the divan at the discreet club that green muumuu Popsicle lady had arranged for our affairs of state, but it took him all night to manage it, so I didn't have to deal with someone putting his hand up my shirt until rather late in the evening. And while I didn't exactly mind, given what Ed and I had managed to negotiate ourselves that night, I also needed my wits about me, and I couldn't give other matters the full attention I felt they deserved. Collette and muumuu lady chatted and glittered and propped up the conversation whenever it was lagging, and Rex and Amelia kept a polite distance from each other as they traded boring sound bites in their most professional manner. In short, we all managed to make it out of there intact.

Which I felt completely proud of, frankly, after Amelia and I collapsed into a cab on the way home. We were both so relieved that the whole thing was over, and that we had made it out of there without insulting that idiot Rex in yet another unforgivable way, that we just started snorting and laughing like lunatics. That old idiot Rex had spent half the time at the club telling Amelia that there was a "great part for you in my next film, I think you'd really be unbelievable, I'm going to have my people send you the script tonight and I want to talk to you about it right away." So she kept nodding and agreeing that that sounded wonderful, she was "so honored that you would even think of me, I can't thank you enough, of course I'd love to read it, if you think I'm right for it, I'd be honored!"—like it

319

was all so earnest and phony, I swear we could not stop laughing. Could he possibly be serious? She called him a pedophile on national television, and now he's offering her a part in his big old stupid movie?

Obviously, Amelia and I were just punch-drunk because neither one of us, once again, even got a sip of anything alcoholic all night. We fell over Philip first, as he was still waiting for us in the living room.

"Oh my god, you are not going to believe what we just pulled off!" Amelia shrieked, falling onto the couch. "That shithead Rex Wentworth came to the play tonight and NOBODY TOLD ME and I had to go out for drinks with him, it was HORRIBLE, and now he wants me to be in his dumb movie! Can you BELIEVE it?"

Philip slouched up, rubbing his eyes with the back of his hand; he had fallen asleep and was a little slow on the uptake. "Rex Wentworth?" he said, like it was a kind of funny word in a different language that he only half remembered.

"We went out for *drinks* because we're such great *friends* and he thinks I'm such an unbelievably brilliant *actress*," she continued, laughing. "I swear to god I am not making one word of this *up*. What a maroon. What a nin-cow-poop. What an ultra-*maroon*."

Philip was yawning. "Was Kafka's granddaughter there?" he asked.

Which made no sense at all to me; it sounded like he was stuck in a dream and not waking up properly. "Kafka's grand-daughter?" I said.

"She thinks Kafka is her great-*grand*father," Philip snorted. "I

320

kid you not, she's got it all worked out in her head, that she's the *grand*daughter of some Bohemian *hooker* that Kafka slept with—"

"Kafka slept with hookers? I should have paid attention in English, when did this happen?"

"Yeah, right? That's what she was telling us, that night Amelia bit Rex, that Kafka was her grandfather, or something; that's what they got mad at me for, 'cause I made a face, you remember this, it's why I got kicked out the house, 'cause I raised my eyebrows when this giant woman in a green dress told a fucking whopper about Kafka and a hooker, where have you been?"

But he was laughing while he re-explained this; we all were; we were really losing it now, quietly, we thought, because no one wanted to wake up Daria or Mom.

"I think she looks like Jabba the Hutt, I've been calling her Jabba the Hutt in my head, don't you think she looks like Jabba the Hutt, or some science project, some science project gone hideously awry, in that green dress?" They both were laughing so hard, they had to stuff their faces into pillows to keep from being obscenely loud. Seriously, it was stupid? But it was also such a relief.

"Did I hear you say Rex Wentworth was at the play tonight?" Mom said brightly, from the doorway.

Talk about a damper. We all turned to look at her, and she smiled at us, like Mom's on Planet Ten again. There was no, "what's this about?" or, "you all are making a lot of noise, could you keep it down?" or, "what's so funny, this late at night?" And there was no way she had just heard about old Rex's appearance that particular second, was there? We were well into making fun of the Kafka Popsicle person by the time Mom appeared in the doorway. So I knew right away that Collette had called, and tipped her off, on what was going on, and that Mom was in on it.

Amelia looked at Philip, making sure that he knew that she knew this was about to turn into utter crap. Seriously, those two were like identical twins by this point, the type who understand each other telepathically because they just do. Philip barely glanced at her; he was staring at Mom, and his lips were just slightly parted, like he wasn't feeling very well, although just a second before he had seemed fine.

"Yeah, he showed up," I told her. Daria was kind of hovering there behind her, in the doorway to her bedroom, trying to listen in and stay up to date on developments, I guess.

"You were there?" said Mom. "I thought Collette told you not to go."

She was real fucking frosty. Nobody was laughing anymore.

"Mom," I said, sick of this fast. "Someone had to go with her. That guy is kind of dangerous."

"You think everyone is dangerous. You're in some paranoid fantasy; you're so jealous of what's happening for her you're creating all sorts of negative interpretations for the most wonderful things, all because they're not happening to you, they're happening to your sister. You should be ashamed of yourself."

"Yeah, well, I'm not ashamed of myself, and you know why? Because Collette lied to her, and lied to all of us, and set it up so that Amelia would have been there, like alone, with that asshole—"

322

"He wants to offer her a part in his film! I hardly think that makes him an 'asshole.' Maybe you're the *asshole*," she hissed.

"Whoa, what did you say?" I said. It truly is a remarkable thing to have your mother speak to you like that. I thought, she must be drunk; she has to be.

"I wanted her there, Mom, I was really glad she was there, I really was," said Amelia, quietly trying to be reasonable.

"You don't know what you want," said Mom. "You're too young to understand what Polly is doing, you're so innocent and good, you are, Amelia, you can't see how she is undermining everything that could be happening for you."

"Mom, that's just crazy," I said.

"Is it?" she countered, puffing up her chest like some sort of insane pelican.

"Oh for crying out loud, I am not doing this again," I said. "I'm going to bed. In case you wondered, the kid did a fantastic job. I didn't ruin anything because she was dazzling. And I'm not going to let you and Collette just throw her to the wolves, I'm just not. So both of you can get over yourselves and deal with it." It was damn late by that time, and I needed some sleep. So I was just walking away from the fight, squeezing past the new, completely spooky version of Mom, who was snorting and flaming in the doorway there.

"Come on, Amelia, you need your sleep, too," Mom cooed. "Tomorrow's a big day." And she went and fluttered over the kid, who was looking at Philip in a kind of worried way, because he had just gone away again; it was spooky the way he kept coming in and out of reality. He wasn't looking at her, or anybody anymore; he just picked up that remote and started

323

channel flipping again. So Amelia let Mom usher her off to bed, and Daria disappeared in her doorway, and so did I, and Philip just stayed out there on the couch, a worried ghost of a person who knew, like I did, that things could really go south fast now that Rex had shown up.

The script for Rex's movie showed up at our doorstep the following morning, a Sunday delivery, before ten a.m. Which honestly I could not figure out how they made that happen, unless Collette had told them to send it over before we even got to the theatre that night. Whatever; the fact is, the script showed up early, and Amelia read it right away, making fun of the whole thing the whole time, laughing about how stupid it was, reassuring Philip that she was all right, and that old idiot Rex was such a dweeb, sending her his stupid movie, what a stupid part, while she simultaneously fell in love with the stupid movie and the stupid part right in front of our eyes.

Philip was sitting in the living room, trying to do some lame bit of homework in front of the television set, but it was clear that he couldn't focus on the homework, or the television; he just kept glancing across the room to where Amelia was slouched in the easy chair, reading and complaining about the script.

"Shut up already," he finally said. "If it's that bad, stop reading it."

"It's like a spectacular car wreck, with flames and dead bodies, you can't take your eyes off it," she replied, not even looking up.

"It's not like you're going to do it, what do you have to read the whole thing for?" he asked.

"I just told you, it's riveting, how bad it is," she snapped, impatient.

The phone rang. Daria picked it up and handed it to me, announcing, "It's Darren," in a kind of bored undertone. So before I could enter this fray with Amelia and Philip—coming in on Philip's side, I might add; I didn't like what I was seeing in Amelia either—I had my own load of shit to deal with.

"Listen, doll, have you seen the *Daily News*?"

"Not yet, Darren, did we get in? There was somebody there from Rush and Molloy last night but I can't imagine that he made the deadline."

"You'd be surprised what they can pull off with a hot story, honey; the picture is huge. You and Amelia both look adorable, and Rex too; it's just a really great shot in the lobby of that hideous little theatre, so that all is just fantastic but look, honey, I don't want you reading it okay? I am taking care of it. I am so mad at those guys, I don't know where they got that garbage, but they are *sooo* off my list unless they print something utterly fabulous about you and Daria within the week. Within the week, this will be addressed. You don't fuck with me like that, you just don't."

Obviously, this didn't make me feel better at all. "What does it say, Darren?" I asked.

"It's not bad. Well, it is bad but it's not as bad as it sounds. That's why I don't want you to read it, it just sounds bad, but it's really ridiculous, even the way it's phrased is just crazy, it really is, I am so mad at them!"

"Just spill it, Darren, what does it say?"

"And the picture is what people are going to remember, which is fabulous."

"Darren, you tell me or I'm going out and buying it." I was actually having heart palpitations. I hate this side of things, when people say mean things about you in the paper and there's nothing you can do about it, and you know that millions of people are reading these terrible things and thinking horrible thoughts about you. It completely sucks; it really does.

"Okay, this is what it is, but seriously I don't want you to worry about it, I am absolutely taking care of it. The article is mostly really good; it says things about Amelia and her successful run in the play and the celebrities who have been coming to see her in it, including of course Rex Wentworth, who she had a tussle with earlier in the year, blah blah blah, which both of them seem to be happily laughing off, as he came to see her performance because she's under consideration for his next picture. That part is really quite good, they wouldn't let that out if they weren't inches from making an offer, trust me."

"Darren, I am going to fucking kill you if you don't stop spinning this and tell me what the fuck they said!" Everybody was looking at me now, and Mom even had a kind of smirk on her face. I was on her list now, so she was giving herself permission to enjoy it when I got upset. It was incredibly aggravating, on top of an already aggravating situation.

"All right, I just don't want you to get upset, as I said, because I can handle this. Basically the asshole writer—what a *cunt*, he is *sooo* off my list—he added a line about how, that your career

326

isn't shaping up the way you hoped so you seem to be content to, um, be the Entourage."

Okay. In show-biz language, "Entourage" means "loser." That's literally what it means; it means you have no life so you just run around and suck up to your famous friend or sister who pays for everything and likes to have you around because you feel familiar and you're willing to pretty much just do whatever she tells you. "Entourage" is you have no life of your own and you have no pride either; you don't mind that everybody sees you as a parasite.

When I didn't say anything for a second—I was fucking reeling, I got to admit it—Darren kept ranting. "The whole thing is utterly ridiculous and spurious and I am looking into where he got it," he huffed. "Somebody clearly planted that piece of trash and I am going to find out who, trust me. This is not over by any means."

"I'm not the Entourage," I said, sounding, I am sure, truly pathetic.

"Honey, you have to ignore it! That's why I don't want you to even look at it. You have to put it behind you and think about what you have. You and Daria have a huge career already with or without Amelia; for example, might I point out you have that huge lingerie shoot for GQ tomorrow. There are dozens of girls they could have gone to but they wanted you, they fought for you, and they didn't even ask for Amelia, I might add."

"She's fifteen, you can't put a fifteen-year-old in underwear in GQ," I noted.

"Don't be ridiculous, they've already done it. But they didn't want her. They want you, and Daria, together; and I've already been on the phone with the stylist and they have something really special planned, and I will be there to make sure it all goes fine, and I've been talking to GQ all morning and they are really in love with you. So this trash is over before it even got started."

"If this trash is over, why have you been talking to GQ all morning?"

"Darling, you know as well as I do that there was gonna be a little bit of fallout. And I handled it. This is a major spread for them; they just wanted some reassurance that you weren't, you know, on a slide."

"On a *slide*? Because I went out for drinks with my sister?"

"Oh, this is exactly what I did not want to happen," Darren sighed. "I did *not* want you upset. What I do want is, I want you to take the weekend and relax. I have two all-day tickets for the Bliss spa, and I'm sending them over right now and I want you and Daria to spend the whole day—*the whole day*, not part of it—treating yourselves like queens. I want you both rested and relaxed and looking fabulous for the shoot on Monday. Can you promise to do that for me, please? Can you promise?"

"Is this your way of telling me kindly that I need to stay away from Amelia?"

"This is my way of telling you to go to a spa, and *also* to stay away from Amelia. Amelia doesn't need you looking like her Entourage, Polly, you know she can take care of herself. And we need to take care of you. That is what we are doing now. We are taking care of *you*."

So I hung up, and I stood there, and I thought, well, that

old hairdresser didn't tell me this part. She didn't tell me what you get for trying to be a mother lion. You get turned into the Entourage.

DARIA

CHAPTER NINETEEN

It's not like she wasn't warned. Polly *was* warned, and many times; she was very specifically warned. There are rules in this world, as there are in any world. If you follow them, you are rewarded, and if you don't, you are punished. This isn't brain surgery. Antagonizing someone as powerful and vindictive as Maureen Piven was simply a stupid thing to do. And then antagonizing your own agent, the only person you can really rely on to protect you from someone like Maureen? Even stupider. And all these claims, that she—Polly I mean—was trying to "protect" Amelia? Don't they rather overlook the fact that Amelia *wanted*, rather badly, everything that Polly was supposedly protecting her from?

Let's recap, shall we? Amelia did tell Philip—and Mom, and Polly, and me too, as if I were interested—how absurd and ridiculous that ridiculous screenplay was. But that's not what she told Collette, or Rex, either, when he called later that day to ask what she thought of the script. Contrary to her initial ravings about how stupid the whole thing was, she told him she thought it was brilliant. And she loved the character of Nina, the determined teenage girl who has to go into the jungle with her father to save her mother, who has been captured by poachers. How thrilling that Brian Redgrave was on board to play the villainous swine who led the poachers and how wonderful the plot twist, that he was secretly in league with Islamic terrorists! And she was so excited and nervous about telling him all this brilliant news that she did not even bother to hide in her room while she took the call. She sat right at the kitchen table while Philip and Polly, her two would-be protectors from the evil Rex Wentworth, watched her bubble.

She hung up the phone. We all stared at her. Really, there was nothing else to do; the transformation from "it's just the stupidest thing ever" to "I love it!" would give anyone whiplash.

"What are you doing?" said Philip.

"What?" said Amelia, caught. I hate it when people say that. "What?" I always think, you have to be kidding me, that's the best you can do, "What?"

"What are you doing even talking to him?" Philip asked.

"Of course I'm talking to him," Amelia said, all edgy and proud. I know there has been a lot of noise from the rest of my family about how edgy and proud *I* can be. The complaints, I assume, are not phrased as kindly as all that. But let me assure you, in the pride department, no one outdoes our little Amelia. She knew she had been caught, and stupidly caught. She had just come home from her final Sunday matinee, and she was flushed and excited and restless. Presumably she had been drinking since Polly wasn't there to impose prohibition on her. In fact, no one had gone to the theatre with Amelia; she had been on her own all day, once Polly got branded the Entourage, and sent to the Bliss labs to decompress. Philip had wanted to go with her, because he as well as Polly now believed that Rex was lurking everywhere, or Maureen Piven, or Collette; all of them lurking, apparently, waiting to snatch Amelia up. But she was having none of it. Oh, and now she was chatting up Rex, on her cell phone, in our very kitchen. Not on the land line, on her *cell*. If one were so inclined, one might be tempted to ask, how on earth did he get her cell-phone number?

"I'm talking to Rex," she announced, mostly to Philip, speaking to him as if he were some sort of boring half-wit, "because he and his director wanted to have a meeting with me tomorrow morning, to discuss the script, and their shooting schedule, if I'm actually interested in the project."

"Tomorrow morning." Philip couldn't believe it. Amelia changed tacks; instead of facing off with him, she decided to suddenly go all casual.

"Yeah, we're having coffee at the Four Seasons," she said. "It's no big deal. It's just a coffee. I'm sure they're talking to two hundred girls for this."

"Oh, you think they're having coffee with two hundred girls? I don't think so. I don't think so." Mom laughed with delight and hugged Amelia.

"Cut it out, Mom," said Amelia, but she was trying not to smile, like she was delighted herself but pretending that she wasn't.

"Well, good for you," I said, reaching for enthusiasm. "I guess Hollywood actually does come calling, once in a while."

"I guess so," she said, still trying to pretend, for the sake of

335

the skeptics, that this wasn't the hottest thing that had ever happened to her. "I have to go figure out what to wear. The part . . . this girl is really not like a city person, she's not sophisticated at *all*, so I don't want to show up wearing Prada or anything, but it's the Four Seasons so I can't exactly show up in jeans. Maybe I'll call Darren, he'll know what to do. Do you think it's too late to call him? It's Sunday night, I don't want to bother him if he's on a date or something."

She looked at me for advice, for once. Why not? Darren came on after the play started up, and she didn't really understand how to work with a publicist yet. Well, she didn't really have to; the press followed her around like a pack of wild dogs whatever she did. "Try his cell, I'm sure he'll pick up," I told her. "He *so* will not want to be left out of this."

"Are you kidding? You're *going*?"

I turned and looked at Philip, who was leaning against the doorway, sincerely disgusted with all of us, but mostly with her. Amelia looked at him and blushed a little, going all pink and rosy around the corners of her cheeks; sadly for her, she looked stunning when she blushed, so it never bothered her that much when it happened. "Of course I'm going," she said. "I mean, obviously I'm not going to get it. But I can't just not go."

"Yes you can," he said. "Just don't go. This is Rex Wentworth we're talking about, remember? He's trying to, he wants to, he isn't doing this because he likes you! He's still just bugged that you beat him!"

"Philip, it's just meetings, with other people there," she started, not wanting to get into this at all, and certainly not in the very moment of her dream coming true, but he rolled right over her.

"No," he said, furious now. "You beat him, you did. It made him mad the first time when you just wanted to leave his stupid party that night, that night in the *bar*; all you wanted to do was go home and do your homework and even that bugged the shit out of him because you wouldn't just do what he said! Even that was enough to piss him off! And you think he wants you to be in his movie? You said yourself, TWO DAYS AGO, when he first showed up—two days ago, that was a completely insane idea, that's what you said!"

"That is not what I said," Amelia started, but he was implacable.

"Yeah, you did." Polly had kept her mouth shut through all of this, so far. I'm not sure why. If anyone had a right to feel betrayed, after everything she had done to presumably "protect" Amelia, it would be her. But, as I said, she perhaps should have asked Amelia, at some point along the line, if she actually *wanted* to be protected.

"I was there, you were scared to death when you heard that guy was stalking you," Polly reminded her.

"I hardly think Rex is *stalking* me." Amelia rolled her eyes.

"He wants to—you know what he wants! You're not a moron!" Philip was increasingly out of his head.

"He wants to talk to me about being in a movie!" Amelia insisted.

"I was there! The first time he saw you, the first time, all you wanted to do was go home and do your chemistry and that was it; it pissed him off that you wanted to leave, he wanted to get you then, just because you wanted to leave, what kind

337

of crazy person does that? And then you bit him, you—"

"We all remember what happened, Philip—"

"You don't act like it. And then when we went to that office and he looked at you then, I could tell—he just has a boner for you, god—"

"Would you stop saying that?"

"You know it's true! It's what you do; you walk around this city there are pictures of my sisters everywhere that are all about giving boners to . . . like everybody I go to school with is like jacking off to pictures of my sisters!"

"That is enough, Philip," Mom hissed.

"You're being so stupid, like you actually think that he means what he says now, he wants you in his movie, are you crazy, why do you believe that, it's all just a big lie—"

"It is not! He wants me in his movie because I'm good! I'm good at this and you just don't believe in me, you want me to go backward and be just your stupid sister!"

"That's—oh god. I *only* believe in you and I don't want to go back, I just want to go. We should go, right now, we should go, go . . . to Ohio. Everybody. All of us. Even Mom. We should go to Ohio; we should have gone before any of it started but we could still do it. You're the one, you said, we should go to Ohio—"

"What are you talking about, you crazy loser?"

She clearly thought this would shut him up, but she was wrong. "You know what I'm talking about," he said. "You know he's lying. He doesn't want you in his movie. He's playing a game with you, him and that giant Kafka woman. They don't mean what they say! The lies have totally taken over those two; they're not even thinking in terms of what the words mean, they're not even trying to teach you a lesson, they just want to, they don't even want to just hurt you because that would be too simple. What they want is worse, even, and you're just walking into it, why, you would give up everything, everything you ever were or knew or wanted to be, give it all up so you can be in some stupid *movie*? Where you get to run through the jungle and say things like 'Get in the truck! Save me, *Dad*'—like Rex wants to play your father, *I don't think so*—'save me, go, run, give me the gun!' That's what you want to do with your life? You used to play Beethoven on the piano. Now this is what you want? You're going to let him get you, because this is what you want? *Get in the truck . . .*"

Okay. I can't truly vouch for much of this. What he said was something like it, I think; it rambled and turned around and there was this inexplicable refrain about Ohio. It was all truly strange but somehow you could follow it, and it sounded both crazy and true, and Amelia sneered at him and told him he was paranoid and needed therapy, and he got madder still and told her that she was an idiot and she deserved everything bad that was about to happen to her. And then Mom yelled at Philip and said that if he didn't start behaving himself she'd send him back to his father, and he said, go ahead, you're not a mother you're the devil's pimp, you'd pimp your daughters out to Satan himself if you thought you could get a good price, even a lousy price; you'd sell them out for nothing the way you sold me out for nothing, you corrupt crazy bitch. And Polly said, that's enough, Daria and I have a big shoot tomorrow and we had to get to bed or *GQ* was going to fire us both, we should all go to bed before someone says something really terrible. Although by that point it's not like there was anything worse that anyone *could* say. And then Philip stormed out, and Mom burst into tears and started sobbing that he really was impossible, it was such a strain having someone so unreasonable in the house, so moody and mean-spirited and even having him around was ruining everything.

And then, we all went to bed. There was nothing else to do.

CHAPTER TWENTY

The fact that Philip and Amelia think that I am a big drip is hardly news to me. I would like to point out, however, that at least I know what I want. I don't run around saying one thing and doing something else and screwing up everyone else's lives. I would also like to point out that not only do I know how to do the job I am asked to do, I also seem to know how to clean up the messes other people create. Amelia's big moment on television? That was, in fact, my idea. And it worked, didn't it? She got more out of that little bit of theatrics than she ever got out of throwing fits anytime she felt like it. And, by the way, sending Philip off to live with Dad wasn't actually my plan, although I will admit I didn't see anything all that wrong with it. It simplified things, a lot, when he was gone, and by that point we all needed some simplification. I was always clear about what I wanted, and when Philip was gone, that became a lot easier to accomplish. So no, it didn't bother me. It didn't particularly bother me when he came back, either, because by then things were more or less moving ahead in a good way. As long as the train was moving forward, I was fine.

When Polly created yet another disaster, by mouthing off to Collette and Maureen Piven, I was, yes, upset. Why wouldn't I be? How many of these ridiculous messes did everyone expect me to clean up? Honestly. I never asked to be the problem-solving sensible sibling; it is truly a thankless position and frankly not all that much fun. No one ever appreciates what you do, and they also never take responsibility for having created a mess in the first place. But they don't actually walk away from it all either, do they? It's not like anyone was walking away.

The following day started well before even the hint of a sunrise for both Polly and me. I of course was up at five, and had finished showering and putting lotion on my eyes, face, elbows and feet when they rang up from downstairs to say that the car was here. At which point I stuck my head in Polly's door and told her that the car was here. She mumbled something about being "completely fucked up on two Klonapin," but she was coherent enough to roll herself into some sweats and make it down the elevator to the limo, where she promptly fell asleep again. There was obviously no traffic, so by six they had both of us in makeup chairs in the back room of a truly spectacular penthouse in midtown.

As you may have noticed, photo spreads are no longer merely photo spreads. I honestly don't know when it started, but largely these magazine pieces are now constructed to communicate some sort of fantasy narrative which tells some sort of fantastic story about people having fantasy lives. For instance, this particular shoot, for *Gentlemen's Quarterly*, was about how every master of the universe lives in spectacular sky-high apartments with wraparound views of New York City. Perhaps we can take a peek at what a day in the life of one of these fellows might look like! And then the ad copy has one line, perhaps, about the master of the universe, and then it moves on to report on the retail price of his amazing suits as well as all the little thongs and corsets that readers will doubtless want to buy for the beautiful girls who happen to be lounging around such a place. Which is where Polly and I would fit in to the photo spread.

They were planning on doing three or four shots with just me and Polly in different thongs and bras and bustiers and negligés, and then several more with the two of us and a male model, who was supposed to represent the master of the universe. He would be wearing suits, as I said, while Polly and I posed beside him in our dazzling lingerie. The male model was somebody named Roger something—I had never heard of him—but he wasn't supposed to be showing up to makeup until one; they were scheduled to do Polly and me first, and then the shots with him later in the day.

Right away, though, there was something off. Roger wasn't there yet, but they had already sent the car for him, because he needed to shoot out by two. It wasn't clear if Roger's people had insisted upon this shift in the schedule, or if the stylist was the one who changed his mind, but the fact was that Roger was showing up any second and they only had two chairs, which happens sometimes when they're shooting in someone's apartment. So they raced us through and sent us straight to wardrobe. By six-thirty, Polly and I had already been slammed in and out of camisoles and bras and rhinestone v-strings and mesh thongs

343

and g-strings and hot pants (which were inexplicably "in" that month) and a pair of pink poinsettia satin bikini briefs that were fastened with ribbons at the side, so your partner could just untie them with a flick of the wrist, rather than watching you wriggle out of them when it was finally time to do the deed. It was all unfortunately less amusing than it sounds, because none of the underwear seemed all that fresh and Polly was in a terrifically foul mood. She hadn't had enough time in the makeup chair, she was tired, and she knew everyone was watching her and waiting to pounce on any shred of unprofessionalism because someone had written snotty things about her in the *Daily News*. So she was snappish, I was getting tense, the clothing was dull, and then at about seven a.m. one of the wardrobe assistants managed to inform me, in whispers, that "the fantasy bra and thong" were being kept in a portable safe in the next room.

"Really?" I said, not quite understanding what she was actually talking about.

"Is someone getting me a fucking cappuccino or not?" Polly asked. "And what the fuck is a 'fantasy bra and thong?' " Everyone in my family swears like a sailor, even though it gets you nothing, if you ask me.

"Oh my god, they didn't tell you?" said the wardrobe girl, breathless. "I knew they were being real careful about who knew, because of security, but I thought they'd tell the models at least!"

"Tell us what?" I asked. Her whole air of awe and wonder was starting to annoy me. No one likes to hear that a wardrobe assistant knows the big secret that you don't.

"The fantasy bra and thong, from the Mouwari collection. They're made of thousands of diamonds, set in white platinum.

I haven't seen them? But both of them have a sixty-carat diamond set in the center: in the bra it apparently hangs between the breasts, and on the thong, it hangs over the center of the . . . center."

"You've got to be kidding me," Polly said.

"No, god, that's why they had to change the shooting schedule, because they want to keep security as tight as they can when they finally bring them out. They're clearing out all unnecessary personnel and adding three private security guards: the insurance company insisted on it."

"Some security guard is going to watch me scamper around in a diamond bra and thong?" Polly asked, yawning.

"What makes you think you're going to be the one wearing it?" I said. I was just kind of matter-of-fact about it, not mad or anything; we'd been through so many of these shoots together by this time there was simply no point in getting all worked up over some idea that one or the other of us was going to be wearing cooler clothes. I know that some girls get into that, but given how many other bizarre things we had to worry about, we usually didn't bother with mundane competition anymore. So the wardrobe girl got all worked up but I assure you I did not.

"Oh no, they're putting one on each of you," she said, like this was a terrific compromise. "You're wearing the bra" this to me— "and she's wearing the thong."

"Yes, of course, the slut gets to wear the thing with the diamond over the center of the center," Polly observed.

"Oh no they're not slutty at all, they're just magnificent," the wardrobe girl sighed. "You can't believe how beautiful they are."

"So you've seen them?" I asked, slipping into a see-through kind of filmy pale rose thing that covered up nothing even though it was apparently supposed to be some kind of bathrobe. "I thought they were in a vault."

"Yes, I mean, they are in a vault, I've just seen pictures," explained sweet and breathless wardrobe girl. "I'd love to see them, but I'm one of the ones who has to clear out! Oh well, you'll have to tell me about them."

"So how much are they worth?" I asked.

"The bra is worth ten million, but the thong is a little less, I think. Eight? Something like that."

Polly started to laugh. "And here I was, thinking this whole shoot was going to be just a kind of boring semipornographic celebration of redheads crawling all over men in suits; just your same old same old," she said. "Wow, was I wrong."

"Eighteen million *dollars*?" I said.

"Right." Polly grinned at me. "Somebody out there made underwear that costs eighteen million bucks? You could buy a country for that amount of money, couldn't you?"

I wasn't fully paying attention to her, frankly, at this point; the filmy thing that I had put on was a bit confusing—there were hanging little ties in the oddest places, and I was trying to figure out what attached to what. So I was looking at myself in the mirror and pulling at all this pink chiffon, when, all of a sudden, Polly put her arms around me.

"You look like an angel in that thing," she said. It was so surprising, really. I looked at her in the mirror, expecting to hear the rest of some cynical bit of banter about angels and sluts, but it didn't come. She really was just looking at all that

346

pink chiffon with a kind of wonder. "No kidding, Dari. You look really pretty." And for a second she looked pretty too, and I remembered playing dress-up when we were kids, and how much she liked running around pretending to be gypsies and mermaids, and, for a second, honestly, I felt like crying without quite knowing why.

"You look pretty, too," I said. This made her smile, suddenly, like that was the best thing you could say to her, and she looked like a teenager. Which I guess she still was, who remembers?

Right about then, Roger showed up. He stood outside the door and called, "Everybody decent?" which, given general manners on the sets of fashion shoots, marked him instantly as a complete gentleman. Once we assured him we were all decent, even though we were wearing nothing but underwear, he stepped in and said he just wanted to say hello and introduce himself. The guy was, no surprise, so handsome you literally had to just stop and stare at him for a moment, no matter how rude it seems. He had those kind of shocking blue eyes and lots of dark brown hair and a square face and all those other attributes that sound boring when you describe them but when they come together in the most unspeakably fabulous way imaginable nobody can speak for a second. I know that in my family we all spend a lot of time thinking about female beauty, but for my money there is nothing on earth as beautiful as a gorgeous man, there really isn't. Anyway, Roger was already dressed to the nines in blue pinstripe, which I had thought until that instant was utterly over, and part of his hello message included the information that they were ready for us on the floor, whenever we were ready.

At the beginning of the day, it was actually a very good shoot.

Roger was pretty relaxed about how stupid it all was—him being fully dressed while Polly and I were virtually naked—and he was very professional. It turned out that he was gay as a post—again no surprise—so even though he was manhandling both of us like crazy he never got too excited, so to speak, which made things move considerably more smoothly than they might have otherwise. And then some of the shots were kind of fun, too; the stylist actually had the wit to set up one that was loosely based on Manet's *Le Déjeuner sur l'Herbe*, which portrays two fully dressed men having a picnic out in the woods with two almost naked women. So we got to lounge and eat grapes and drink wine and stare at the camera, as opposed to just writhing around Roger like sex-crazed redheaded nitwits.

Anyway, the assumptions of this shoot being that Polly and I would be wearing lingerie while Roger was wearing business suits, I was in fact pleasantly surprised that the morning went as well as it did. Roger was a lot of fun and I was kind of sorry to see him go, when they actually made the deadline and shot him out by two. Nobody really had thought that we would pull that off, so they gave us an hour for lunch while they relit for just the two of us. Polly stretched and yawned, like a cat.

"Did you bring your cell?" she asked me. "I left mine at home, and I wanted to call Amelia—see how breakfast with that big creep Rex Wentworth was."

"Do you think that's a good idea?" I asked her.

"Don't start, Daria," she said, and with that all the good feelings of the morning kind of drifted off a bit.

"I'm not starting anything," I said. "I just don't want you to get into trouble."

"By calling my little sister to see how her morning went?" she said. "Yeah, that's really crossing a line." I honestly was so tired of the whole thing I was about to give her the stupid cell phone, when Darren showed up.

"Oh my god you look fabulous," he gushed, which made Polly laugh.

"Shut up, you only have eyes for Roger, which I know is why you're even here," she told him.

"God I've had a thing for him ever since he did the Gap ads, I used to tape pictures of him to the inside of my glee club binders," he sighed, looking around like a high-school teenager trying to spot his crush.

"Well, tragically, you're too late," I told him. "They switched the schedule around and shot him out. He left ten minutes ago."

"I know I know," he said, dismissing this as old news.

"You know?" said Polly, bored and interested at the same time. "If you knew, why didn't you tell us?"

"Well, it just happened at the last minute, is what I heard," he said, dismissing the question with a flick of his wrist. "Listen, you guys, there's something else that's come up. I just got a terrific phone call from publicity, and some of the higher ups here at *GQ* are going to be stopping by this afternoon, to say hello and to thank you for your work," he started. "They've heard through the grapevine how well the shoot is going, and so they asked them to send the proofs right over, digitally, obviously they can do that now, so everybody in editorial has already seen just the first initial proofs and they are just totally thrilled. *Thrilled*, they are over the *moon*. Anyway, some of the top people said they wanted to come over and say hi, which should happen by four or four-thirty. So this is great news, guys, it really is, and I just wanted to let you know personally who it was who would be coming by so that you had the heads-up."

"Oh for god's sake, Darren," Polly said. "Cut the crap. Those shitheads in editorial just want to come over and watch me and Dari writhe around in our underwear. This isn't a peep show. That's so creepy, you've got to be kidding me."

"Polly, now, that's not what this is, that's what I'm telling you," he started.

"Come on, I'm not stupid!" she said, working herself into a little bit of a lather. "Guys in suits standing around and salivating and trying to flirt with you between shots: it's really worse than boring, it's hideous, and we don't have anything on except this Frederick's of Hollywood bullshit, and those guys want to come over and watch? Ick, double ick, I'm not doing it. No way."

"I'm sure that Daria doesn't mind," Darren started, turning to me and raising an eyebrow, with a sort of shocked grimace, like he was trying to communicate, silently, would you please go along with this please? Because of course that is what they always count on, Daria will behave herself and go along with it and then everyone else will have to behave and the problem will just go away. But I didn't feel like it. I don't always agree with Polly, and her behavior is often abysmal and self-destructive. But at this moment I thought she frankly had a point.

"I do mind," I told him. "I mind very much. I think it's poor form for them to ask. Tell them no."

"I can't do that," Darren said.

"You're our publicist, you do what we say," I reminded him.

"And as your publicist I'm telling you, I don't think it's a good idea for you to ask me to tell the editors of GQ magazine that you don't want them to come over and thank you for your work. I am just not going to let you do that, and most of all I am not going to let Polly do it. You don't want to be making trouble right now, when we have a lot of damage control already on our plates here."

This was not much fun to hear, as I'm sure you can imagine. Polly blinked.

"Sorry, sorry," she said. "I forgot."

"Then tell them it's a security issue," I said. "Around the whole diamond bra and thong business. I thought the insurance company had this place locked down. That's why Roger had to shoot out early. There aren't supposed to be any extraneous personnel, that's what we were told. Not by you, by the way, I wanted to ask you about that, Darren—why didn't we know about this?"

"*I* didn't know about it, obviously; they didn't tell anyone. I didn't find out until they sent me over here! But obviously it's fabulous news, this is going to be huge, for both of you. The Heller sisters in GQ, wearing the Mouwari fantasy bra and thong, you cannot ask for anything hotter than that. You don't want to know how many girls wanted this shoot, and you have it and I am not going to let you blow it. Everyone who will be coming by this afternoon will behave like complete gentlemen, I promise. I will not let anyone step even one inch out of line."

"You're staying too?" Polly asked.

"Absolutely, and I will guard your somewhat questionable honor, Polly, with my dying breath," he promised.

"You better, you crazy queen," she told him, as she left to follow some makeup person to the back for a touch-up.

I was about to follow her myself when Darren stopped me.

"Daria, could I talk to you for a moment?" he asked. He looked at me with a sort of seismic I-have-a-secret grimace.

"What is it, Darren?" I asked.

"Maureen Piven is coming by," he told me.

"What are you talking about?" I asked. He was looking over his shoulder again, with one of those theatrical gestures that makes sure that everyone in the room could see that he was making sure no one could hear. "Maureen Piven? The movie producer? Why is she coming here?"

"Apparently Polly invited her," Darren said, making another face. "At least that's what she's saying."

"That . . . is . . . ridiculous," I told him. "Polly loathes her. And my understanding is that she loathes Polly. I think she loathes all of us, Darren, why would you let that woman come to our set?"

"I'm not letting her do anything! And I hardly think she loathes you. She's been pulling favors for you all over town. The way I heard it, the fantasy bra and thong—which is major, darling, that they're dripping those diamonds all over you two—that was her doing."

"Then you did know about it," I pointed out.

"I knew it was possibly in the works because Maureen was making some phone calls on your behalf. I am only repeating what I heard, and I don't want there to be any misguided fuss about this," he warned me.

"Darren, stick with me here," I said. "Honestly, some days

it's like everyone assumes that you're nothing but a sort of gorgeous stupid cow. Maureen Piven—"

"Maureen Piven has lots and lots of friends, and she pulled a lot of strings to get those diamonds over here, and she's bringing some rather significant European buyers with her, and my understanding is that one of them is interested in talking to you about some of the Paris runway shows, based on Maureen's recommendation. So I don't think you know everything, Miss Smarty Pants Gorgeous Stupid Cow."

"Maureen Piven is bringing someone from Paris? To talk to *me* about doing a runway show?"

"So you might deign to be interested in something like that?" Darren raised that old eyebrow again.

This all sounded too far-fetched to be believed, but show business often is. "What does Collette say?" I asked.

"She says, be nice to Maureen, that is what she says," Darren told me.

"Can I talk to her?" I asked.

"No, you can't," said Darren. "She's with Amelia in meetings all day, something else that Maureen has helped out with enormously. So no more career suicide, especially not from the one Heller diva I can count on to act like a rational adult. I want you to be nice to Maureen, I want you to be nice to *alllll* the GQ boys, and I especially want you to be nice to our friends from Europe when they show up. And Polly has to be nice too. That's your assignment. I love you, you're gorgeous." And with that he kissed me and tripped away. He really was just a terrible queen, but a terrific publicist.

I went back into wardrobe. Polly was curled up on a cot

under the makeup table. She cracked an eye, just barely. "What was that all about?" she asked.

"I don't know," I said. Which, as it turned out later, was simply true.

When the oh so grateful editors at GQ showed up, the atmosphere changed considerably. Of course they thanked us profusely, but suddenly we really were in the kind of creepy men-in-suits-girls-in-bras situation that we had been play-acting at all morning. And while they were complete gentlemen, there was no question about why they were there, and it wasn't to thank us. Polly actually shines at moments like this; her attitude is an asset when guys are standing around and drooling: It makes her a little cockier, whereas I tend to get a little annoyed and tense. As Darren had requested, I was the consummate professional, but the room simply was not as relaxed as it had been in the morning, so it took longer to get a decent shot. Which meant that tempers got higher and we needed more breaks which also meant that we had to put up with talking to the guys in suits even more than we already didn't want to. So the situation was already a bit of a high-wire act by the time Maureen put in her appearance.

Polly was, of course, the one who spotted her first. The cameras were clicking and we were rolling around like nymphomaniacs getting all hot and bothered while we waited for our lord and master to come home, and she just . . . stopped. It took a second for everyone to catch up with the fact that she had stopped, as it does sometimes, but I knew something had happened because I was in the shot; I was on the couch with her, and I could see her face, and feel her freeze. She was staring past the frame of the picture, out into the apartment, where all those *GQ* boys were watching and drooling. And then she reached for something, I couldn't tell what.

"Polly, sweetie, is there a problem?" the photographer asked. He was a kind of round guy named Henry, utterly clueless about anything except light.

"What's she doing here?" Polly asked, and I realized that she was using one of the throws on the couch to cover herself. "Get her out of here." She turned around, on the couch, putting her back to the camera and stopping everything dead. I looked off. Maureen was there, with two staggeringly well-dressed men in their forties—the guys from Paris presumably. Maureen smiled at me, and waved, then leaned in to talk to the suits from *GQ*. The room was really not that big; there was a good chance she had heard what Polly had said—not that she gave any indication of it.

"They said you invited her," I said quietly, to Polly's back. Polly turned to me, with a frightening look on her face, puzzled and furious. For a moment I thought she might hit me.

"What is the matter?" I said. "That's what Darren told me. He said you invited her."

"You and Darren knew she was coming, and you didn't tell me?" she asked. I didn't reply; I didn't think I needed to. "That's sweet."

If she expected an apology, she wasn't going to get one from me, not after what she'd been pulling for the past three weeks. "This is a situation of your making, and I'm trying to get us through it," I said. "Did you invite her or not?"

Polly shook her head, laughed a little to herself, and pulled the throw around herself, tight. "That woman is a real cunt," she told me, but quiet, so no one else could hear. She looked at poor silly Henry, who was patiently waiting for us to finish our conversation. "We're done, Henry, you got the shot," she said, and then she stood up, still wearing the throw, and walked off the set, back to wardrobe. Henry looked at me, pissed, and I smiled at him, my best smile, stood up, and went to him.

"You do have it, don't you?" I asked, putting my hand on his shoulder. "It's been a long day and we haven't even started on those diamonds."

"I just don't like behavior, you know that," Henry snipped, getting a little of his own back.

"And you haven't gotten it," I reminded him. "She's just tired. I think we all are. This isn't the best shot anyway; they're not going to even use it, Henry. Come on. You know what they said about her in the *Daily News*. She's been upset all weekend."

"She just better watch herself," he warned me.

"I'll talk to her," I said.

"You, I like," he smiled. Which by the way is what they all say at the end of a shoot. At home, they all think I'm a bitch. On a set, I'm the one everybody likes.

Before I went back to wardrobe to talk to Polly and prepare for the grand finale, I took a moment to say hello to our special guests. Maureen was wearing an emerald sheath, with large crystals hung down the front. I don't believe that anyone has mentioned it yet, but she is quite an elegant and beautiful woman, and her manners are impeccable. I really barely knew her, frankly; the last time she and I had spoken was that hideous night when we went to meet Rex Wentworth at the W bar and Amelia behaved like an animal in a zoo. I knew that at this point

Maureen had had run-ins with just about everyone else in my family, none of whom seemed to care whether or not they pissed her off. I also knew there was an enormous amount of damage control to be done.

"Maureen, hi! We're so pleased you could stop by." I smiled, and leaned in to kiss her. I went for both cheeks; as long as the French guys were there, why not?

"Thank you, yes, my meetings finished early today, luckily," she smiled and kissed me back. "Jean-Claude, Luc, this is Daria Heller." She raised her arm, including them in our conversation.

"It's a pleasure to meet you," I smiled.

"No, the pleasure is ours," said one of them, in one of those perfect French accents. "We are so pleased to see you, and the diamonds."

Because of the diamonds, the whole place was already in the middle of a major reshuffle. I was ushered off to wardrobe and, as promised at the beginning of the day, all the extraneous personnel were asked to leave the set before the safe was even unlocked. Back in wardrobe, another little drama was exploding, as Polly was giving Darren an earful.

"What do you mean, you're taking off? You invite Maureen Piven, who you and I both know, you *know* she was the one behind that hideous piece in the *Daily News*—"

"I *don't* know that—"

"Yeah, well, I know it. And then you in*vite* her to my *set*, to watch me take all my fucking *clothes* off—"

"You were the one who invited her!"

"It doesn't matter who invited her, she's here now and she's

357

not going anywhere and do you think we could just get through this?" I asked. "Wardrobe and security people are scampering everywhere and, call me crazy, but I was actually hoping that for once we might make it through a little bit of a misunderstanding without ending up in *allll* the newspapers in the nation: How's that for a nutty thought?"

"A little bit of a misunderstanding? Is that what you call this?"

"Oh honestly, Polly, could you stop staring at me like I'm some kind of monster? Honestly," I said. "You nearly cost us our representation four days ago, and you didn't think there was anything wrong with that, and now I'm suggesting that we just finish the shoot, and you're acting like I'm out of my mind!"

"Do you know what she's done?"

"She hasn't done anything! We're the ones who keep doing things!"

"This is wrong, this is all wrong," Polly told me.

"I'm sorry, sir, but we can't bring the diamonds out until the floor has been cleared of all unnecessary personnel," somebody announced. Polly turned, furious, to find a security guard—a complete idiot in a uniform, at least—in the middle of our dressing room, staring at Darren.

"What are you doing in my dressing room?" she asked.

"I'm just doing my job."

"Your job is to invade my dressing room?"

"The insurance company says—"

"I don't give a fuck about your fucking insurance. He stays," she announced.

"It's all right, Polly," Darren interjected.

"It's not okay, Darren," she said, raising her voice so the whole apartment could hear. "They're throwing everyone out because of security reasons. Meanwhile any shithead who wants to show up and get an eyeful of me in an eight-million-dollar thong is allowed to come on in. If I want you here, you stay. And if you go, I'm not wearing any fucking diamond fucking thong. And you, get the FUCK out of my DRESSING ROOM." The security guard was obviously about making a response to this diatribe, but Darren heard what I heard, and shoved him out the door. However she had gotten herself there, Polly had just gotten over her rage at Maureen Piven and she had agreed to continue the shoot. As long as Darren could work it out with the insurance people that he was not an unnecessary person, we would actually finish the day.

I didn't want to push it, but I needed to make sure that this was the end of the tantrum. We sat in silence for a minute, while everyone outside the little wardrobe room started shouting at each other.

"So you're okay with this," I started. "Because she's not leaving; she's apparently the person who arranged for us to be wearing those diamonds in the first place and she's—"

"She's a bitch, and so are you," said Polly, looking at me in the mirror. And it was so far from where we started that day that I didn't know what to say. There was nothing *to* say. It was just where we were.

When we returned to the set, wearing million-dollar under-wear under actual bathrobes, Darren was happily ensconced among the editors and their tan buddies. Polly and I drifted over, as expected, to be polite and lovely to our waiting oglers.

"Hello, Darren," she cooed, letting him kiss her on the cheek.

"Does it feel fabulous to have millions of dollars' worth of diamonds dripping all over your precious treasure box?"

"It feels itchy, is how it feels," Polly said. This, of course, made all the men laugh.

"My associates have been begging me to introduce them," said Maureen, turning her dazzling smile on Polly. "This is Jean-Claude Metier, and his associate, Luc Bernot."

Jean-Claude and Luc murmured their appreciation for our beauty, and the fact that we were allowing them to stay and watch the shoot, as if we had any choice in the matter. It was all very European and elegant and we said, of course, what a pleasure to have you here. And then security whisked us away. They were nervous as bees.

"So who the hell are these guys?" Polly whispered, pissy, under her breath.

"Some sort of international bigshots," I said.

"Probably crooks," she observed.

"They're hooked up in the fashion industry," I said. She looked at me, shook her head.

"So what else do you know that I don't know?" she asked.

"Apparently they're interested in buying these things," I told her.

"Oh, cut me a break," she said. "What a line." And with that, she dropped her robe.

The room went silent, as I disrobed as well. Seriously, there was a kind of awestricken hush. For a second I thought, that's right, the two of us are damn good-looking girls, and we both have great bodies, but that didn't even last a second, to tell the truth. All those men weren't looking at us, and, trust me, there was plenty of us to look at. They were looking at the diamonds.

There were diamonds everywhere. The bra was molded out of tiny strips of white platinum, every inch of which was encrusted with thousands of tiny diamonds, and all those thousands of diamonds curved together in this sparkling pattern that kept turning in and over itself and looked sort of like snowflakes and sort of like wings and sort of like two hearts which barely overlapped at the center of my breastbone, framing right there, between my breasts, one giant, impossibly perfect pear-shaped diamond, which was so big you had to ask yourself if it was fake. Of course it wasn't fake; we all knew it wasn't fake, just as we knew its identical twin, which hung over Polly's so-called treasure box, was also not fake. She was strapped into the thong version of the snowflake-wings-heart diamonds, although there was less of an attempt, with the thong, to cover up as much territory. And although I held the rest of my robe in front of that part of my anatomy that wasn't covered in diamonds, as usual Polly saw no reason to be as discreet. She never does.

So, quickly enough, all those boys were looking at both us and the diamonds, together. GQ being GQ, they all seemed fairly pleased that Polly was so willing to bare all up top and, because they were GQ and not *Penthouse*, they were equally happy to honor my reluctance regarding the rest of my anatomy, so that part was easy enough. Because the diamonds were so heavy, we couldn't do the shot lying down, as they would have squashed my chest down to next to nothing, but they liked us hovering near the bed, so they had me leaning against the headboard, with my lower half discreetly draped with cleverly arranged sheets. Polly, on the bed, stretched out across a pile of pillows and stared boldly at the camera, utterly naked except for all those dazzling and itchy diamonds all over her crotch. And so that was the shot, and they clicked away for a while, and all the men watched and murmured amongst themselves, with Maureen Piven surrounded by them all, watching as well, having arranged the whole scene, apparently. It was actually quite strange, and I was happy enough when the photographer looked up from the back of his camera and said, "I think that's it. Nice work everybody."

I was tired, and so was Polly, so when we put on our robes and went to say good-bye to our fan club, neither one of us was exactly thrilled to hear Maureen announce, "Jean-Claude and Luc were just mentioning how much they'd love for you two to have dinner with them and I said, I feel very sure you're free this evening!"

Polly tensed up a little bit. So did I. "Well, we're pretty tired," she smiled. "We've been up since five."

"We promise, you will be home before you turn into a pumpkin," said Jean-Claude, or Luc—I couldn't tell which was which. Darren was smiling at me a little too tightly, which I correctly interpreted to mean, You are not permitted to say no to this great offer I have arranged for you.

"Maybe just drinks?" I said politely to Polly. "It would be great to unwind a little."

"Lovely," said Luc or Jean-Claude, whichever one was the other one. "Our car is downstairs."

Polly looked at me out of the side of her eyes. She took this as another betrayal, and maybe it was, but the fact was, those guys came to see me, and quite honestly I had those Paris runway shows in the back of my head, and I was not going to let them get away. Maureen watched Polly watch me, I could see her do it, and she thought it was funny, I could see that too, and I didn't care. I was thinking of Paris, and how this might be my ticket out of the endless sister act, and I wasn't going to blow it. That's what I was thinking.

"We'll be right out," I smiled. Polly stalked off.

To give him his due, Darren followed us back to wardrobe, to give Polly a little lecture and make doubly sure that she knew, as I did, not to fuck this up. "They're fabulous and *huge*, internationally, *everyone* knows them. Jean-Claude has a yacht in San Trope, his parties are *in*famous, this is going to make that thing they printed in Rush and Molloy look like the trash it is, they are *sooo* going to have to eat their words."

"Has anybody heard from Amelia?" Polly asked. "I was going to call home on our lunch break but didn't get to it. Did you hear anything about how her meeting went?"

"I don't know, I had my cell off, I'll check it out but I'm sure it went fine. That is not your concern," he warned her. "I mean it, Polly. This is a gift from the gods and I do *not* want you fucking it up. You be nice to these guys. Daria, you're in charge. Make sure that they take you to someplace fabulous, nothing too public because that looks desperate—no, on second thought, just leave it up to them. Wherever they want to go will be ex*qui*site. And call me. Call me when it's over, I want to hear all about it."

Because I think ahead, you have to in this business, I had a really sweet little Yves St Laurent sundress in my shoulder bag, a good shade of lilac. All Polly had to wear were the jeans and sweatshirt she'd rolled into at five in the morning, but she was saved by the exiled wardrobe girl who was allowed back in to help pack up, who found a brilliant mauve camisole which looked great over jeans, in spite of the fact that it was still, essentially, underwear. That wardrobe girl also dug up some really spectacular strappy little spikes, so both of us looked fantastic by the time we made it to the limo where our zillionaire Euro-trash escorts were waiting with two chilled bottles of Cristal.

Things were actually all right for a while; the guys were charming and flirty in a good way, the Cristal was a relief after such a long day, and they had their driver just take us around the city for a while before deciding to stop off at a stunning private club down in Tribeca, quiet but definitely on the map, where we were photographed going in by four or five different photographers. Which was good for Polly's ego—finally, something was, that day—so she relaxed a bit and joined the small talk about wine and clubs and yachts. One of those guys really did own a yacht, and he seemed pretty eager to show it to both of us, the next time we happened to be in the south of France.

So all was going well enough until we actually got inside this swank club. Jean-Claude and Luc were apparently quite famous in the private club circuit, and they had a lot of people they needed to check in with, most of whom were also snaky-looking playboy types. All of them seemed appreciative of the fact that the European fashion royalty had shown up with two of the Heller sisters, which was gratifying and flattering to everyone involved, but the tone had somehow again shifted, the way it had been inexplicably shifting all day. We found ourselves on an overstuffed and decaying couch in a darkened corner, where Jean-Claude or Luc, one or the other, ordered another bottle of Cristal and lit up a smoke. My head was starting to hurt from all the champagne, but I was still trying to keep up my end of the conversation.

"This place is fantastic, I've never been here," I smiled. Jean-Luc or Claude, whatever his name was, was whispering something to one of the barely clad waitresses. The other one was checking his BlackBerry.

"I wonder what it looks like in the light. I'm always curious, what happens when they turn the lights on in these places?" Polly laughed. Neither Claude or Jean or Luc was even paying attention now. Now, they were talking to each other, right in front of us, in French. Like we weren't even there. One of them said something, and the other one offered up a little laugh, dragged on his cigarette and looked away. It looked for a second, even, like he was checking out that scantily clad waitress, thinking about whether or not he might be able to score with her. Polly and I, exhausted after a really long shoot, having been dragged down there at the last minute by men who watched us lie around in diamond underwear all afternoon, may as well have been invisible.

Polly leaned in and whispered to me, "Let's go home."

"I don't think we can," I said. "They already ordered the champagne, I think we have to at least get through the bottle."

"Come on, they're being assholes," she whispered. "We were nice to them, we let them show us off, let's get out of here, I'm wiped, and we still haven't talked to anybody at home about what went down with Amelia."

"She's fine," I said, annoyed again. And then I leaned forward, to say something to one of our hosts, who were still murmuring to each other in French.

This, frankly, was where the whole evening turned. Because the thing that the zillionaire French Euro-assholes had not counted on, or even considered as a possibility, is that I am actually fluent in French. As you may have noticed, none of us is exactly dumb; we are, after all, the grandchildren of Leo Heller, the guy who came up with the devastating idea that Americans are actually not in love with new things, we're scared to death of them. Old Granddad was pretty smart, and so are all of us, including—perhaps especially—me. I simply never felt the need to show off my brains because I always considered it rude. And when you look the way I look, and the way Polly looks, and the way Amelia looks, no one actually cares whether you're smart or not, do they? So no one really paid all that much attention to the fact that, aside from Polly, who never studied, the rest of us just basically sailed through school. At the very least, I sailed through French. I even won awards.

And so I had just leaned in to say something nice to them, in French. And before I could say anything, they looked at me, and then the two of them started talking about which one of them was going to have me back at their hotel and what he was going to do to me before the second one took his turn. And then they laughed, because they thought this was so cute, to talk about me like this in front of my face, because of course since she was a stupid American model there was no way that she would understand a foreign language.

Polly had not a clue what was going on. The waitress had arrived and was opening the champagne; she didn't understand a word of the French either, so she was quietly going about her job.

"Here, let me," I said, reaching up and taking the bottle. Jean/Luc/Claude smiled at me, clearly enjoying the idea that the gorgeous girl who they watched naked and dripping in diamonds all afternoon was ready to start servicing them right there in a club where all their friends could watch. So I opened a thousand-dollar bottle of champagne and poured it on their heads. They both started screaming, enraged, in French, and I screamed right back at them, also in French. Polly just stared—it was taking her a little while to catch up—but when I leapt to my feet and shoved one of them, with both hands, while insulting him in his native tongue, he reached back, cocking his arm like he might hit me. At which point she picked the half-empty champagne bottle off the floor and swung it at him. He howled with rage, although I mostly think he was being a big baby, as she didn't hit him *that* hard, considering what he said about her as well. In any event, before things went any further, a couple of bouncers came over to settle things down and, essentially, throw us out on our pretty little behinds.

CHAPTER TWENTY-ONE

I didn't stay angry for very long. While they were throwing us out the door, I started to laugh and laugh, and, even though we were creating the kind of scene I've always abhorred, nothing could get me to stop laughing. Really, it all struck me as so absurd. I was laughing and screaming and laughing, and behaving in ways I've never behaved before, and the paparazzi were getting pictures of all of it, and I didn't care at all. I even started blowing kisses to them, while Polly shoved me into a cab. Which of course they loved and, later, when they printed the whole thing up in the papers, that's the picture of me that they ran, blowing kisses to them all from the window of a cab. I don't know why people act like the press is so impossible to handle. I think they're just like anyone else—they want you to love them. And they're very sweet when you do.

So, at that point, I thought we were looking at a good end to a long day. I still had to tell Polly what those Mediterranean assholes had been saying, which made her mad, and then she was mad and I was laughing, and then we both were laughing and, by the time we got back to Brooklyn, it even seemed that she and I might start half liking each other again. Not liking, exactly, there was always too much competition for that, but it used to be that even when we hated each other, we truly understood what was going on in the other person's head. In any case, that night, in the cab, Polly and I were as close as we used to be, or even as close as we've ever been. In retrospect, I don't think we could have done what we had to do next, if we hadn't had that cab ride, where we just laughed and shouted out the window and laughed some more.

It wasn't all that late when we got home—maybe nine o'clock—and at first things seemed as normal as they ever get around there. Philip was watching television and Mom was somewhere—the den, or her bedroom, it wasn't immediately apparent, but her purse was on the kitchen table so we knew she was home. And Polly and I were tired, so we weren't still laughing like lunatics, but there was a sort of giddiness still hovering about.

Philip looked up, from the television, where as I said he was watching yet another endless rerun. "Where's Amelia?" he said. Quite simply, like he truly expected us to say something simple in return. Like, "She's picking up a copy of *Vanity Fair* at the newsstand," or, "She's downstairs, paying the cab driver."

Polly understood before I did. She bristled, like an animal. "What do you mean, 'Where's Amelia?'" she said. "How should we know?"

Philip sat up, as worried and upset as Polly was, and just as quickly. In retrospect it seemed to take me forever to catch up.

"Mom said she was with you," Philip said. "Mom said—"

"She's not with us!" Polly snapped, furious. "Why would she be with us?"

"Mom said she was with you," Philip repeated. "When I came home from school, I asked her, I said, where's Amelia? And she said, she went to your shoot, to watch your underwear thing, that she was . . ." He was on his feet by this point, looking around, as if the empty room would somehow explain things to him. Polly was ahead of everyone by now.

"MOM!" she yelled, barreling through the kitchen, through the living room, and straight into the den. "*Where's Amelia?*"

Philip and I were on Polly's heels, so when Mom looked up, all three of us were right on top of her. The den was her little inner sanctum, that's what she always called it, "My sanctum from the world!" which I always thought was an odd thing to say, since she truly loved the world as much as anyone I've ever known. She loved all of it—the shoots and fittings and meetings and runway shows and drinks with actors; when I was finally exhausted and constantly on my last nerve, Mom would be there smiling and waving and acting like the belle of the ball. She didn't care that it looked like what it looked like, an aging beauty queen pretending to be one of her own daughters. She just wanted to be there, and the only reason she ever stopped coming to absolutely everything, including some of my dates, was because Collette and I told her she had to cut it out.

So there she was, lounging on her floral couch, in her Gucci pajamas and mules, in her sanctum from the world she wanted, sipping orange juice and vodka and getting quietly soused, the way she did every night, when she wasn't out getting soused with her daughters at some club. She smiled up at us, and didn't seem to have heard the question.

"Well, look, it's everybody! How was the shoot at *GQ*? Collette said there was some big surprise that no one was supposed to know about! What was it? It must've been fantastic, even she didn't know the details!"

The Mouwari diamonds were already decades ago.

"Mom, where is Amelia?" Polly asked, firm.

"You said she was with Polly and Daria," Philip snapped. He was really angry. "You told me—"

"Please, don't use that tone with me, Philip. I am, after all, your mother." It was so strange—up until that very second I would have been on Mom's side; I usually was, because she was on mine. But now I could tell that something terrible was going on. I didn't understand it, but Polly was so upset, and Polly and I were, as I said, somehow, again, the team. So instead of dismissing every word out of Philip's mouth—which truly was my tendency, because for heaven's sake, it just was—I listened.

"You lied to me!" said Philip, not dialing it down one notch. "I asked you, I said, where's Amelia, you said she was with Polly and Daria, what did you do, Mom? Where is she? What have you done?"

"I will send you back to your father!" Mom shouted back. "I don't have to answer to-to-to a teenage boy—"

"Mom, stop it!" Polly said, insistent. "Where is Amelia, why did you lie to Philip, where is she?"

"She's fine! What are you all so upset about? Daria, please, tell them to leave me be. This is my inner sanctum, my sanctum from the world—"

She was completely drunk, that was clear. "Mom," I said, nice, because it looked like tone was going to be important here. "We just need to know—you guys, could you give me a minute with Mom? Just a sec, okay?" I pushed them forcibly back out the door, but left it open so they could hear. I didn't even know what I was asking. But this was the way it was going to get done.

"My head is splitting," Mom complained. "Everything I do, I do for my children, and then to have you come in and accuse me . . ."

"No one's accusing you of anything, Mom," I said, sitting her back on that silly couch she has, with the roses and the little Restoration people all over it. "We're just surprised—did you tell Philip Amelia was with us? Because she never showed up at the GQ shoot, she wasn't supposed to, was she?"

"I had to tell him something, or he would have just thrown a fit, the way he always does, he thinks he owns her, it's ludicrous," said Mom. "You know he would have gone down there and ruined everything! I did it to protect her, and him too for that matter; not that he even understands how ridiculous he looks."

"It was a breakfast meeting, wasn't it? That was more than twelve hours ago."

"No no, she's been in meetings all day. They love her, Daria, this is really happening for her!" Mom gushed. "And I know that might be a disappointment for you, sweetheart, but it shouldn't be! Your turn is next, I just know it is!"

"So, did you go with her, Mom?" I said.

"No, of course not!" Mom said. "I know you girls need your space." For a moment I wished I hadn't screamed at Collette

373

and told her to get rid of my mother, but then Mom finished her thought. "I did see her there, though. At the Four Seasons. I had an appointment at the spa, for a facial at eleven, so I stopped by to say hello."

"That was lucky!" I said. Behind the door I heard someone make a noise, a kind of snort, which I know she heard, but I just kept talking. "So it was going well, I guess."

"So well. So so well. The director is really smart, and he described the movie to me. Her part is *huge*," Mom told me.

"So they offered it to her?"

"No, they were reading her. They scheduled an audition, for the afternoon."

"This afternoon?"

"Yes, that's what I'm saying!"

"Okay—so how did that go?"

"Wonderful, apparently. Because Rex asked her to dinner after that."

Okay. I'm not someone who leaps to the negative conclusion, but I was starting to understand why Polly and Philip were flipping out.

"Rex . . . Rex took Amelia out to dinner? Did she call and tell you that?"

"Of course she did."

"And she was okay with that?"

"Why wouldn't she be? He's offering her a part in a major motion picture, why wouldn't she be just thrilled to have dinner with him and his director?"

"The director was there." That sounded a little better.

"The director and another actor, that wonderful British man who is in all the Harry Potter movies . . ."

"They were all going to dinner, all of them, with Amelia? And maybe Collette?"

"I don't know who was there," Mom replied. "I don't see how that's relevant."

There were sounds of a physical scuffle at the door; I think Polly was keeping Philip from rushing in and strangling his own mother. "Mom," I said, trying to stay on her side, or at least to keep her thinking that I was, "can we go back for a second? That might clarify a few things."

"I don't know what needs to be 'clarified.' Once again, none of you appreciate what is happening to Amelia. Heaven forbid she get a little support, or enthusiasm, from her sisters."

"No, I'm happy for her, I really am!"

"I see how happy," Mom said, starting to pour herself another drink. Somehow she's convinced herself that drinking vodka is not fattening. I think it's technically not a carb, someone told her that once, and it made a big impression.

"So did they actually offer her the part? I mean, is that why they were taking her to dinner, because there's an offer on the table?"

"Not yet, but they think there will be any minute. Any day."

"Any day or any minute?"

"I don't know the answer to that, Daria, please, why am I being grilled like this?"

"Sorry, Mom, I'm really sorry," I said, squeezing her hand, with affection. Like the press, it is easiest to get what you want out of Mom if you're just a little bit nice to her. "So that's why,

I guess, she had to have dinner with him. Because she wants the part, of course, and so of course she wants to be nice about it . . ."

"Why wouldn't she want to be nice about it?"

"So she told you she was going out to dinner with Rex and Collette, or Rex and . . ." Honestly, I knew that Mom knew more than she was telling. She's ridiculously easy to read.

"I think it was just the two of them, actually."

"Why do you think that?"

"She mentioned it. I think she was a little nervous about it, frankly."

"Really? And why do you think that?"

"Well, you know, she wanted to know when your shoot was finished, because she said that she might ask Polly to join them, but I told her I didn't think you'd be finished until well after nine. So then she asked me if I wanted to come along."

"She did?" My palms were starting to sweat. "But you, well, you decided not to? How come, Mom? You love hanging out with movie stars."

"Well, sweetheart, I didn't want to have to run back into Manhattan. Besides, you know how these things are. He's always liked her. And if he wants to be alone with her, who am I to get in the way?"

"YOU'RE HER MOTHER, YOU FUCKING MORON." This oh so useful explosion from Philip, at the door. After which he stormed back to his room.

Mom burst into tears. "Oh, it's been a nightmare having him back here, it really just has, I don't know why you insisted I take him back, Polly, I just don't!" she wailed. "He doesn't do anything except talk back to me. Honestly, I am going to send him back to his father, I really am."

"Mom," Polly said, from the doorway, really trying to make one last stab at this. "You have to tell us where Amelia is. Where were the meetings, or the dinner, who was with her—anything at all."

"You're jealous too," she said. "You just want to stop this from happening. Well, I won't let it happen!" she stood, wobbling, full of outrage. "I *won't*." And she wobbled past us, heading for her bedroom.

Philip appeared, pushing by her and almost knocking her down on his way out the door.

"Stop it, stop it!" she yelled at him.

"You stop it, you crazy drunk," he told her, and he left. I had no idea where he thought he was going—none of us had any idea, obviously, where Amelia actually was. We just didn't know. But Philip went anyway, slamming the front door to the apartment behind him, just as Mom slammed the door to her bedroom behind her.

"What do we do now?" asked Polly.

"I think we have to find her," I said.

Even though we were just seconds behind him, Philip was long gone by the time we made it to the curb. The doorman got us a cab, and we headed blindly back to Manhattan, and then we both started calling anyone and everyone to find out what anybody knew. Amelia's cell was off, we tried that first, and then we called Darren, who claimed not to know a thing in between wanting to find out how our date with the two creeps from the south of France had gone. And then I tried Collette, who was worse than useless.

"Daria, hi!" she cooed into the phone. "Wow, it's late! I heard the *GQ* thing was amazing. What did you think of all those diamonds? Wasn't that fun?"

"Yes, what a fantastic surprise," I cooed back.

"For me too. Even Darren didn't know until it happened. Well, you were there so I guess I'm not telling you anything you don't know. But he said it was fantastic and you went out with Luc Bernot and Jean-Claude Metier afterward, how was that? Those two are famously naughty boys. Are you still out with them? Where did they take you?"

"You know, we ended up having a drink and going home for once," I said. Polly kept making faces at me; I knew it was excruciating to keep this up but just yelling at Collette was not going to get us anything. Polly had been bullying her for weeks, and now she was not inclined to do us any favors. "But listen, Collette, we haven't heard from Amelia since late afternoon and we're a little concerned."

"Why?" said Collette. And that was it. Just, "why?" It made my skin crawl.

"Well, it's almost ten," I started.

"Nobody even starts on their appetizers till ten; ten is the new eight," she told me.

"I know, god, that's so true . . . Do you know where she is?" I asked.

"I don't, actually," she said. "Sorry."

"When was the last time you saw her?" I asked.

"Daria," Collette laughed. "She's fine! She's doing what she needs to do."

"And what's that?" I asked.

"Don't worry about it," she said. And then she hung up.

Polly looked at me, really worried. "She's with Rex," I said. "Collette says she's doing what she needs to do, and that it's none of our business."

Polly looked out the window.

"So where you girls headed?" said the cab driver. "Got a destination in mind yet?"

"No," I said. "Not yet."

"Well, you said Manhattan, this is Manhattan," he informed me, oh so usefully.

"Yes, I see, well, let's see, midtown? Tribeca? SoHo?"

"Well, which one?" he asked.

I was out of ideas. I couldn't think anymore, because it suddenly struck me that this whole thing was my fault. Philip had said that to me. No one else wanted this. And there was that one day, months ago, when he was just ranting at me in the kitchen, I didn't know what his problem was and I didn't want him around anymore because all he ever seemed to do was whine. And that's what he said: This is all your fault. Then Dad took him, which was fine by me, so I didn't think about it any further than that. But Philip was right. What he said that day. This was my fault.

I looked over at Polly. "I'm sorry," I said. I know it wasn't her, really, that I needed to apologize to. But it just seemed like it had to be said.

She wasn't paying any attention to me. She was on her cell. "Helpful Brit, I need help," she said, almost as if she were talking to a magician. "Amelia is out there somewhere with that shithead Rex Wentworth, and we don't know where he's taken her, and no one will tell us anything, and I don't know what to do, I don't . . . I don't—" Her voice was actually shaking at this point, she was so worried, but then she stopped talking and started nodding. "Okay. Okay. Yes. Okay," she said. "Call me back. Call me right back. Even if you don't get him, call me right back, right back." She hung up and looked at me, trying to act like some sort of commando and failing utterly.

"He's calling, he has this idea, that he can call Sam, the guy who wrote the play; he knows Rex, they're friends, and he can find out, he's going to tell him some sort of story, about how he and I were supposed to meet Rex and Amelia at Rex's hotel. For a drink. And he thinks Sam will know the hotel." This didn't particularly make sense, but somehow I understood it.

"Do you think that's where they are?" I asked.

"I hope not, you know what, I really hope not," she said, getting her edge back a little. "But it's a place to start, and that's better than—" Her cell phone rang and she answered it.

And in fact, that person she had called had the name of the hotel. It was very close to where we were, only blocks away. Polly yelled the address to the cab driver, who said, "Great!" and did an immediate U-turn in the cab, like this was completely normal—which it probably was for him. We were there in minutes.

"Who was that again?" I asked her, as we threw money at the cab driver and went inside.

"The Helpful Brit," she told me, as if this explained everything. "He's really fantastic."

At the hotel we hit a wall. Of course, no one would even

admit that Rex was staying there. They're trained to be terribly protective of people that famous, and we didn't have the code name that Rex would have used to register. Unfortunately, before we could start to wheedle, Polly lost it.

"Listen, you useless piece of shit," she started. I grabbed her hand and squeezed it. "Excuse me," I said, quite politely. "Really, I apologize, we're upset right now, there's a family emergency, frankly, and it's made Polly a little high strung. This is Polly Heller, and I'm Daria Heller; do you know who we are?"

"Yes, Miss Heller, of course I do," the clerk smirked. "I think everyone in America knows who you are."

"Good," I said, utterly polite. "Then you'll maybe understand that we in fact have a right to ask you to tell us if our sister Amelia—you know Amelia, as well, I think, if you know us—could you tell us if she has been here this evening with Mr Wentworth? We really need to get in touch with her. Because of the emergency."

The clerk continued to smirk. "I can't give out that information," he said.

"Listen, you fucker—" Polly started.

"Please Polly, let me handle this," I said, smiling at her much too brightly. Things were just starting to feel terrible to me; this desk clerk was smirking much too much. I knew he knew something and he wouldn't tell us because of whatever his terrible personal reasons were, he wouldn't, and I was trying not to panic, and to think as clearly as I possibly could.

"Maureen Piven," I said. "You don't have to put us through to Mr Wentworth, Maureen will do that for us," I said.

Polly stared at me. I didn't what she was thinking, that I

knew something that I wasn't supposed to know? I didn't; I just knew there was no way that Piven woman didn't know what was going on. She had her fingers in everything; that was clear by this point.

The clerk clearly resented his sudden inability to make us suffer, but he couldn't say no. "I can put you through to her voicemail," he said, very proper, picking up the receiver of the phone on his desk.

"JESUS FUCKING *CHRIST*!" Polly yelled. Which, as you might suspect, was not terribly useful.

"You're disturbing the other guests, and I'm going to have to ask you to leave, ma'am," he informed her, putting the phone back down.

"Oh my god," said Polly. "This isn't a joke, you fucking fool."

"Polly," I said, calmer and calmer. "Could you give me your wallet?"

This got both of their attention. Polly carries cash. I don't, really, never more than fifty or sixty dollars. But she has a more reckless spirit, so her wallet was the one I needed. I opened it and took out everything she had in there.

"How much is this?" I asked her.

"It's about four hundred," she said.

I tapped the bills together into a neat little pile. "I'm not asking you to break any rules, Fred," I told him. He had a name-tag on, with his name, Fred Stubing; maybe that was why he was such a nasty little man, because his parents had given him a nasty little name. "I'm just asking you to do your job. We're friends of Maureen's, and I guarantee you, she will be unhappy if you make it impossible for us to find her right now. We don't want to talk to her voicemail; we want to talk to her. Now, if you help us out we'd be happy to tip you handsomely, rather than have you fired for being an obstructionist shithead. Where is she, Fred?"

Fred took a moment before he politely took our money. "She's in the bar," he said.

CHAPTER TWENTY-TWO

And there she was, by herself, in a corner, underneath one of those idiotic spotlamps that illuminate nothing at all. She looked up as we approached and laughed an exquisite little bell of a laugh. "Ah, the cavalry has arrived," she smiled with infinite charm.

"The cavalry? Why do you say that?" I asked, smiling back and sliding into the seat across from her. I still had Polly by the hand, and I squeezed it very hard, forcing her to sit as well. I was somehow convinced, in the moment that, if I could get her to sit down, Polly would not begin to shout again. This was not a person that anyone could ever shout at.

"Well, I've heard through the grapevine that one of you at least is determined to keep our Amelia under a bushel," she smiled, managing to be both provocative and delightful at the same time. She waved her finger at Polly. "The Entourage . . ." she said, in a teasing tone, as if this would lighten the mood.

Forcing Polly to sit down seemed, for the moment, to be

working. She smiled and played along. "Oh, it's so awful what people say; all that gossip is so boring and dreary," she announced.

"It is, it is," Maureen agreed. "But I am surprised to see you here. Luc and Jean-Claude could have done you a lot of good, and it was not easy getting them to come out and meet you. I don't know that they would've, if I hadn't arranged for the diamonds as well. I worked hard making that happen, and I'm a little disappointed, frankly, that you didn't have the sense to take advantage of that, Daria."

"It's really wonderful how much interest you've taken in my career, Maureen," I told her. "I can't help but wonder why."

"I like to help people, I don't think there's anything wrong with that," she smiled. "Your family is obviously of interest to me. For many reasons. I hope there's not a problem with that."

"Not at all. In fact, that's why we're here, because we could use a little help," I said, matching her casual tone. "We're looking for Amelia. She called and asked us to meet her and Rex for a drink after dinner, but she forgot to mention the restaurant. She did say Rex was staying here, so we thought maybe that's what she meant. But I don't see them," I added, doing the neck swivel. "So they must be still at dinner. Do you know where she is?"

"I believe that Amelia is exactly where she wants to be," Maureen responded, with an elegant carelessness.

"And where is that?"

"If she wanted you to know, wouldn't she have told you that herself?"

"Oh for god's sake," said Polly. She really was at the end of her last nerve. I ground my fingernails into her wrist, willing her to be silent.

"She did tell us, Maureen, I wrote it down, and lost the slip of paper," I laughed.

"That was careless of you, Daria, wasn't it?" Maureen replied. She smiled a knowing little smile and sipped her cocktail. It was one of those blue drinks that sometimes look to me like there actually might be poison in there. For the moment, I wished there was.

"Amelia is still quite young, as I think you know," I said, and I smiled. Maureen smiled back.

"Are you telling me it's past her bedtime?"

Polly gasped at this. I glanced over at her quickly, and her face was terrible, her eyes were full of tears. She knew what was going on. We both did; of course we did, and Maureen knew we knew, and she thought it was funny. She thought it was funny that Rex Wentworth, who was forty-seven years old if he was a day, was off somewhere trying to screw our fifteen-year-old little sister. And I didn't feel like being polite to this ogress anymore.

"I think we understand each other, Maureen," I said, still ridiculously polite. I don't know how I managed it now; I really don't. "And, I hope I don't need to say the words 'Roman Polanski' to you more than once?"

"Meaning what?" Maureen sneered.

"Meaning, I'm not going to threaten you. It seems to me that a more efficient way for us to handle this would be for Polly and me to go directly to Mr Wentworth's room and retrieve our very very young sister as discreetly as possible. That is where she is, isn't it?"

"She went there quite happily, of her own volition," Maureen

387

smiled. "Rex had some thoughts about the script that he wanted to share with her, in private."

"Is that what you're going to tell the judge during sentencing?" Polly asked. Her voice was shaking.

Which Maureen enjoyed. "Collette told me how envious you've been of Amelia's success. I think it's a shame," she said. "This is a great opportunity for her, it's a dream come true. Do you really want to be the one who stands in her way?"

"We can call security, and make quite a fuss, or you could help us be discreet, it's up to you," I told her. "I think you know that we're not afraid of publicity."

Maureen looked off for a moment, thinking, then sighed, as if this whole scene just grieved her piteously. "This will ruin everything for her, you understand that," she said. "It was a lot of work, trying to keep you all happy and out of his hair, and you should know I'm not going to put myself out any further. Not one of you knows how to behave. I thought you might, Daria, but you're turning out to be just as bad as the rest. And Rex likes her, but he's not going to put up with this kind of interference from her family, it's just not worth it. You might consider Amelia for once. She wasn't really all that good in that silly play. In spite of the review, it could be years before she gets another opportunity like this. She is not going to thank you."

"Tell us where she is, you cunt," Polly hissed. There was a dreadful, shocked silence. Maureen turned and looked at her with smoldering outrage, as if she had never heard or used the word herself. She took a breath. She looked off. Honestly, I didn't know what we were going to do next; I was ready to actually leap on this giant person and go for her eyes; I was ready to start throwing drinks or screaming like a crazy person. But the instant before I proceeded to finally lose it, Maureen shrugged.

"Fuck him," she said. "I warned him. You don't want to know how many times I warned him. He never listened. And every year they just got younger." She grimaced, and then she laughed, as her mind shifted onto something that clearly gave her great pleasure. "It would serve him right. It would just serve him right," she said, deeply amused at herself and her private thoughts.

"Where are they?" I said, trying to keep my voice from failing.

"Room six eleven," Maureen announced, sipping her drink. "Although they've been up there for almost an hour. I don't know what you think you're going to stop."

We didn't bother with the idiot at the front desk; we went straight to the elevator, found room six eleven, and started to pound on the door.

"Amelia! Are you in there?" Polly yelled. "Open the door, it's Polly and Daria, open the door!" No one seemed to hear us for a moment, because there was a lot of noise going on inside, people shouting, and someone seemed to be throwing things at the wall. Polly kept pounding. "LET US IN!" she screamed. We heard glass breaking. Behind us the elevator dinged and somebody got out, but neither one of us cared about making a scene in public by this point. Why should we? We were tabloid trash anyway. If they were going to throw us in jail for being a public nuisance in a four-star hotel, so be it.

"Amelia! Open the door!" I yelled, yanking at the doorknob. "We're calling security if you don't let us in!"

"Get out of the way," said a male voice. And then I got shoved aside, quite forcefully, by a large man, who came up behind us and suddenly took over. He had a key card, which he slammed into the lock, while turning the doorknob and leaning his shoulder against the door with real urgency. I thought it was security, that somehow Polly had managed to alert security and, instead of arguing with us, they were just immediately doing the right thing, thank god. Everything was happening so quickly by that point, of course that's what I thought.

I guess "of course" is the wrong thing to say. Because it wasn't security. Improbably, it was Philip, who had somehow managed to get his hands on a key card, to get us into the room. I remember being so startled that it was him, because what was he doing there? How did he find us? And he was so tall. In my head he was always so short, somehow, thin and short and he slouched all the time; mostly all I ever think about Philip is what a nuisance he is, and that he should stand up straighter. And yet there he was, half a head taller than me, shoving me and Polly aside, and pushing the door open with his shoulder, leading the charge into the room. But there was really no time to think any of these thoughts; things were moving so fast.

The hotel room was a complete and utter mess. In other circumstances it would have to be considered the height of downtown chic, all subtle shades of blue and gray, graceful furniture, a couch and chairs, stunning flower arrangements; but the flowers were everywhere, and there was food on the floor. It looked like some sort of pasta had been ground into this gorgeous rug, and a chair had been overturned. There was an open bottle of some expensive beer that somehow had been left standing on the table just past the sitting area. All of this went into my brain quite quickly; it was like looking at a crime scene before you've located the body; all the details register, but that's not what you're really looking for, is it? People were yelling in the next room, or maybe it was Polly and I who were still yelling. Probably all of us were yelling, except for Philip, who shoved me into Polly and reached into his jacket.

And then, right there in front of us, was Rex. "What the hell is *this*, a family reunion?" he laughed. He was standing in front of a pair of open double doors, which led into the bedroom, and he was naked, except for the smallest pair of Calvin Klein underwear I have ever seen on anyone, aside from the most flamboyant of male models. Honestly, he was someone who clearly liked being naked, because there was no reaching for a towel or anything; he seemed positively thrilled, in fact, to have an audience, even if it was only us. Well, he had a great body, for a forty-seven-year-old man; he really did. And obviously he was used to having people look at it.

"FUCKING ASSHOLE," yelled Amelia, and a telephone hurtled out of the next room, and caught him right on the side of the head.

"God*dam*mit, you little piece of *shit*," Rex bent over and grabbed his ear, but when Amelia tried to bolt through the doorway, past him, he reached out and shoved her back in there. She had her clothes on but just barely; several buttons on her blouse were gone, torn off, and her skirt, a maroon Kenneth

391

Cole, was torn as well, all the way down one seam. You could see her bra under the torn shirt, and a large red welt forming just underneath, and there were actual scratches on her face, and the beginnings of a black eye. It was suddenly overwhelming, seeing her like that. I wanted to kill him, I really did.

"Amelia, are you all right?" Polly asked. "Get out of the way, Rex, GET OUT OF THE WAY."

"I'll be with you in a second, darling, there's something I need to finish here," snarled Rex.

"Bring it on, you fucking RAPIST," Amelia hollered. Really, the whole thing would have been much more horrible except she was clearly fine, aside from the torn clothes and the bruises. She was looking around for something else to throw at Rex, who, now that I got a good look at him, was clearly the worse for wear himself. He had a huge scrape on his neck and shoulders and there was a big bite mark on his arm. The thought flashed through my mind, *oh god, she bit him again; we'll never live it down.*

"I'm calling security," I announced, getting some sense of clarity back into my brain, an impulse to do something halfway useful.

"Be my guest," Rex tossed back. "Get them up here, so I can have every last one of you arrested." He actually threw me the phone, which of course I dropped.

"He tried to RAPE me," Amelia announced, as if that needed to be explained.

"You *wanted* it, you came to my room!" Rex laughed. "You ever hear of Kobe Bryant? Tell them whatever you want! Who do you think they're going to believe?"

"Get away from her, or I'll blow your head off," said Philip.

This was such a startling statement that of course we all turned to look at him, and, well, in fact, he had a gun. He wasn't kidding. Philip had a gun. It was of a significant size, too; black, with a nozzle that was quite long. I couldn't figure out why it was so big, until I realized it had one of those silencer things screwed onto it.

"Holy shit," said Polly.

"What the hell is that?" Rex laughed.

"Philip, put the gun down," said Amelia.

"Let her go, shithead," said Philip.

But Rex thought this whole thing was hilarious. "Woooo, a *gun*," he said, raising his hands and wiggling his fingers in the air, to show Philip just how scared he wasn't. "Wow, you got me; you got me. Take me down to the jailhouse, sheriff, you done saved the day. Christ," he sneered. "You think this proves you're a *man* now, can't have her yourself, so you got to save her from sex with someone who can. You're *pathetic*. You think I had to drag her up here? That's not really what happened, kid. I got witnesses. She was dying for it. Not my fault she likes it rough," he added, swaggering over to the table and reaching for his beer.

That's when Philip shot him.

Well, he didn't actually shoot him; he shot over his head. But he didn't shoot really very far over his head; it was pretty close to his head. There wasn't a big bang, just a kind of sizzling pop, because of that silencer, but the sound is actually kind of frightening, when you hear it up close, and since no one actually expected Philip to pull the trigger, and also since no one expected the gun to work, it was all quite impressive.

Rex hit the ground, immediately. "What the hell, what the hell are you *doing*?" he yelled, more annoyed than frightened.

So Philip shot him again. This time it went right over his shoulder and into the stereo speaker.

"Philip, stop it!" yelled Amelia.

"Hey hey HEY there are bullets in that thing!" Rex yelled.

"That's right, there are," said Philip. And he shot him again, on the other side.

Rex jumped. "Stop it stop it, what are you—stop it!" Philip shot the gun again, hitting the television screen right above his head. It was a plasma flat screen, so there wasn't any big explosion or shower of glass; it was all just punctuated with those little sizzling pops. But Rex was suitably cowed. "C'mon, man . . . c'mon! I didn't hurt her! What are you doing? I'm sorry, man, this is all just a misunderstanding, I didn't mean to hurt anybody. Please, come on, cut it out—don't, please, don't come on, don't . . ." He was sobbing now, because Philip was no longer pointing the gun over his head or just next to his leg or anything; he had taken several steps forward, and he had the barrel trained right between Rex's old beady little eyes.

"Please, please don't, please," Rex sobbed.

Philip stood there for a long moment, and he held the gun right there, and nobody said a word. Then, he very slowly took a step backward, and raised the gun into the air, like they do in the movies. "Get the hell out of here," he said. But he hadn't really stepped far enough away from Rex, who was still terrified, so Rex just stayed there for another long moment, looking back and forth between me and Polly and Philip, and then, since none of us were moving, he slowly scuttled himself backwards, like a crab, until he was close enough to the door to sort of slide himself up the wall, reach over and turn the knob, and then turn and bolt out into the hallway, all battered and buck naked except for the tiniest pair of underwear I have ever seen in my life.

"Help, help, he's trying to kill me!" Rex screamed as he ran down the hallway.

Polly went over to the door, and shut it. She turned and looked back at Philip, who was staring at the gun in his hand.

"They teach you that at Dalton?" Polly asked.

"I've been watching a lot of *Bonanza* lately," he shrugged. Then he smiled, just a little bit, and put the gun down on the table.

"That was in*cre*dible," Amelia said, as pleased and excited as I have ever seen her. She came out from the doorway to the bedroom, where she had been more or less stuck while all of this was going on, and she hugged Philip, and then she sort of hopped around the room, like a little bird. "It so *rocks* that you guys came to save me! What a jerk. I'm not kidding, I was in trouble, he was not kidding around," she informed us, as if we hadn't noticed. Polly went to the bed and pulled off the gorgeous pearl-gray quilt, and wrapped it around her, so that she didn't have to half hang out of her clothes anymore.

"Let me look at you," I said, pushing her hair out of her face so I could see how bad that black eye was.

"It's fine, I got him a lot worse than he got me," she grinned. Honestly, she has a lot of problematic traits, and a terrible temper, but she is simply not a whiner. And I started crying—I admit it, I was exhausted and frightened and it had been a long day—

and so then she put her arms around me and told me that it would all work out just fine, now that we were all there together. And it seemed so corny and true, that I cried some more, and hugged her, and hugged Polly, and I even hugged Philip, who was so much taller than I was now, that I had to look up at him, which made me cry even harder, so they all sat me down, and that is how the whole thing devolved, into me being the one they took care of, instead of Amelia. But they didn't seem to mind, and eventually I pulled myself together.

"I'm starving," said Philip. "What do you think would happen if we called up room service?"

And it may seem crazy—but we were all pretty hungry by that point. And since we were in Rex's room, and room service had no idea that the cops were about to descend, they happily got us our food lickety-split. That's the thing about movie stars: They get first-rate service.

"Listen, I did not know he was going to do that," Amelia informed us all. "No kidding, it was supposed to be a *script* meeting. He said there were going to be like six people here, he really did, they were all supposedly showing up for dinner and then nobody showed up. I feel so stupid, but how was I supposed to know no one would show up? There were seven thousand people around all day, who knew they were all going to disappear? Oh god I'm stupid. How did you *find* me?" she asked, cheerfully excited, almost a kid again. Honestly, her ability to be amused by the most serious of situations kept things pretty buoyant, like this really was a fantastic party, instead of a spectacular disaster.

"Edmund got Sam to tell us where Rex was staying," Polly

said. "I have no idea how Philip found you; he ran off before we even started looking."

"La Aura knows the person who does Rex's hair," he shrugged. I had no idea what this meant, but to Polly and Amelia, it made perfect sense. "Once I was here, I just bribed one of the maids to tell me what room he was in. She gave up her key card, too."

"How much did that even cost?" said Amelia, awestruck.

"Everything Mom had in her wallet," he said.

"And where'd you get the gun, again?" Polly asked, shoving french fries into her mouth. I admit that at that very moment I was wolfing down an enormous cheeseburger. Honestly, you're always so hungry when you're a model, that the instant you permit yourself to eat anything, you just end up stuffing yourself.

"Amelia had the gun," Philip told her.

"Of course she did," Polly said.

"That stupid photo shoot, they had them all lying around, I just took one," Amelia admitted. "I know it was kind of stupid? But you know, they were being so smug and shitty I thought it would freak them out if one of those dumb guns just disappeared, like I bet that dumb Denver got into a shitload of trouble for losing a gun. After he was so shitty to me, because I didn't want to go waving them around that day."

"Did you follow that?" Polly asked me.

"In a very elusive way, I think I did," I admitted.

"Yeah, right? That guy was such a jerk, so what if I got him in trouble? I mean, I didn't ever think about using it, but now I'm glad that I at least told Philip about it. Can you imagine how horrible this whole thing would have been if we didn't have a gun?" She giggled, happy, and started rooting through the minibar.

"You're in a good mood," said Philip.

"Well, this is fun, don't you think this is fun?" she asked, emerging with cans of soda pop. "So where'd you get the *bullets*?"

"La Aura lives in the East Village," he shrugged. "There are guys like selling bullets on *street* corners down there."

"Who is this person again?" I asked. Well, I didn't need to, because she actually showed up several minutes later. There was a very quiet rapping at the door, which was startling; we were all waiting for the cops to break the thing down, and then what came was a sort of quick knock. We all froze, and went silent. Then this strange voice came through the door. "Hey, Philip, you in there?" someone called. "There's like chaos all over this hotel, let me in, dude!"

"Oh," said Philip. "It's La Aura."

He opened the door quickly and let in this very unusual person who had actually done our hair for the *New Yorker* and then a second time when we made our memorable appearance on *Regis and Kelly*. Everyone except for me seemed not a bit surprised to see her, and in fact she knew a good deal more about what had been going on in the past few months than I did. She also knew more about what was going on in the hotel.

"What a riot!" she announced, laughing. "Rex was running all over the lobby for like ten minutes in his underwear, yelling about how you shot him! I was like, all right! Philip shot the dude! So security is there and they're all going to come charging up here and call the cops, then this huge woman in a green muumuu showed up, his manager or something, and she actually stops the action and takes that shithead Rex aside and starts telling him how bad this is all going to look, and eventually it was all going to catch up. She said all sorts of things, I got to tell you, I was like sitting behind this potted plant, right? Listening to every word! That guy's a terrible person, you guys. He's got a thing for little kids." This part made her sober up. "So she's telling him to walk away, and he's like no fucking way and they're arguing and he says some truly shitty things to her and she sort of laughs and says you know you're right you're right! Let's call the cops! Which if you ask me was what she was going for all along. Anyway, that's when I ducked into the service elevator and came up to let you know. The cops are on their way. Man these fries are fantastic!"

There seemed to be no question that we were just going to sit tight. It's not like they wouldn't know where to find us, even if we did try to run. So we just sat there and ate, and traded stories about what had happened all day, including the GQ shoot, and the fantasy bra and thong—which both Amelia and La Aura were sorry to have missed—and going through her meeting with Rex, and his promises to make her a movie star, and Philip's flip-out when he heard that she was missing, and our search through the city for her, and my annihilation of the clerk at the front desk, and the way we squeezed the information about where Amelia was out of that Maureen Piven, who had some relationship to Kafka that they all kept laughing about, and how Philip and La Aura had bought the bullets, and then how he got that maid to give up both the room number and the key card. Finally the police did arrive and arrested us, including the hairdresser, even though her involvement was marginal, if you ask me, and we all were taken down to the station house, amid great fuss, and Rex was in the lobby screaming at everyone about how long we were going to go to jail, but some of the photographers, who were of course *swarming*, laughed and gave us the thumbs up while they hauled us off. And down at the police precinct, things seemed a bit less hysterical, and not terrifying, honestly, because the police were quite sober when they wanted to know about Amelia's bruises, and in the telling of the story we honestly didn't sound quite as bad, for a minute, although we also didn't sound like complete innocents. I wouldn't say that anyone would call us that. But some of the things Rex let slip, while he was prancing naked around the halls of that hotel, frankly didn't help his story much.

I have to admit, while I was sitting in that hotel room, crying my heart out, the one thing I was thinking was: At least it will end now. Because bullets are endings, aren't they? Shooting a movie star? If that's not an ending, what is? But it hasn't stopped. Even shooting a movie star is something that just moves into the airwaves and the internet and the satellites and the atmosphere itself; and the story, even when you think it's over, it just keeps going. I thought being famous was what I wanted; it was always what I wanted when I was little. But now it feels like a disease to me, and everyone is sick; the reporters and the photographers and the commentators and the people, everyone has this disease, and what the disease does is it makes them hungry all the time, just like Polly and me, we're hungry all the time. Only for everyone else in America, me and my life and my family's lives are the thing that they're hungry for, and they can never be satisfied, and so there is no ending. There isn't an ending after all; there's only a trial. And then there's something else.

Perversely, Philip has recently become quite optimistic. He's actually looking forward to this trial. This is what he thinks is going to happen: We'll get up on the stand and tell this crazy story and everybody will believe us and not Rex, with his millions and his lawyers and his movies and his studios and his famous friends. Philip thinks that the media is going to turn on old Rex, and he's going to end up, not necessarily in prison, but in exile somewhere, playing golf with O.J. Simpson in Florida, or having cocktails with Roman Polanski in Paris, while the Hellers will be acquitted to great celebration. And then, he says, we'll all move to Ohio, where everything is different. And then, when he gets to that part of the story? He laughs.